ENOCH'S DEVICE

DRAGON-MYTH CYCLE BOOK ONE

JOSEPH FINLEY

TARASTONE PRESS

Published by TaraStone Press
First Kindle Edition: December 2012

Edited by Michael Carr
Cover Design by Jessica Bell
Map and Illustrations by Streetlight Graphics

ISBN: 978-0-9884108-2-4 (paperback)
ISBN: 978-0-9884108-4-8 (hardcover)
ISBN: 978-0-9884108-1-7 (ePub)

 Created with Vellum

A NOTE ON PRONUNCIATION

Much of this novel is set in tenth-century Ireland and France, so it contains a few Gaelic and old French names that can be a bit difficult to pronounce. The following is a rough pronunciation guide for some of the trickier words.

Adémar—A-deh-mar
Alais—AH-lay
Blois—Blwa
Cellach—KELL-ahk
Ciarán—KEER-in
Columcille—KULL-im-kill
Curach—KUR-ahk
Dónall—DOE-nall
Dub-dá-leithe—Doo-daw-le-he
Gauzlin—GO-slin
Évrard—eh-VRAAR
Maugis—MO-zhee
Poitiers—PWA-tee-ay
Tuatha dé Danann—Thoo-a-haw-day-dah-nawn

In Aquitaine a rain of blood fell upon the flesh of men, staining their clothes and even the stones, which could not be washed away.

—William, duke of Aquitaine, in a letter to Robert, king of France, c. A.D. 998

The first angel blew his trumpet, and there came hail and fire, mixed with blood, and they were hurled to the earth . . .

—Revelation 8:7

Europe
997 A.D.

Derry

North
Sea

Ireland   England

Atlantic Ocean

Reims

Paris

France

Poitiers

Spain

Al-Andalus

Cordoba

Mediterranean Sea

PART ONE

Who is there like Job . . . who goes in company with evildoers and walks with the wicked?

—Job 34:7-8

CHAPTER I
THE HERETIC

On the darkest day of November 997, a black-hulled ship arrived at Derry. It appeared at the holy hour of Sext, which marked Adam's sin and Christ's crucifixion. Storm clouds heralded the vessel's approach, as if God had seen fit to blot out the sun before the ship moored at the ramshackle pier on the river Foyle.

Nearly a hundred monks from the nearby monastery gathered on the riverbank. Among them, Brother Ciarán, a twenty-year-old scribe, craned his neck to get a glimpse of the black-robed bishop and three priests standing in the bow. The others who sailed with them were hard-looking men wearing round helmets and polished mail. Ciarán felt a lump of apprehension in the pit of his stomach. Armed men were rarely seen at Derry, and their presence never boded well.

"Why so many warriors?" Ciarán asked the senior monk standing beside him.

Brother Dónall mac Taidg drew his cowl over his balding head. His close-cropped gray beard framed a rugged face more befitting an Irish chieftain than a monastic scholar. "To intimidate us, I suspect," he muttered. "The bishop will be the one in charge."

"I've never seen a bishop in black robes."

"That's because God didn't love that man enough to make him Irish, lad. Back on the continent, they dye their robes black—think it's some grand symbol of piety or some such tripe."

Ciarán half smiled. "And I suppose you disagree?"

"Are you suggesting I'm disagreeable?" Dónall replied with only the hint of a grin. "I spent enough time over there, lad, to know something about the vanities of the Holy Roman Church."

"Where do you suppose they're from?"

"Do you not see the pennant?" Dónall pointed to a strip of blue cloth fluttering from the ship's masthead. Three golden lilies dotted the fabric. "That ship's from France."

"What are Franks doing here?"

Dónall leaned on his walking staff, looking as if he had aged overnight. "I wish I knew."

Ciarán looked back toward the ship, where a blunt-faced soldier with rope and tackle was lowering the end of a short, wide ramp to the pier. A broadsword hung at his side. The murmur of speculation from the throng of monks grew as two more soldiers emerged from the ship, each with the leash of a huge brown mastiff looped around his wrist. The great beasts, each the weight of an Irish wolfhound, padded down the ramp and sat obediently at their handlers' feet.

The bishop disembarked next. Taller than the soldiers, he regarded the monks with gleaming, almost feral eyes above a sharp nose and a mustache and beard flecked with gray. A silver crucifix hung from his neck, and a black skullcap topped a ruff of graying hair that only added to his wolflike visage. He strode down the pier as four more swordsmen, each with a mastiff on a lead, came off the ship. The murmuring on the riverbank stopped, and even the breeze died, as if on cue.

In a commanding voice, the bishop addressed them in Latin: "Who is abbot here?"

Dub-dá-leithe, the abba of Derry, stepped from the crowd, his hands clasped over the tip of a waist-length beard as white as limestone. In his eighty-second year, he could well be the oldest man in all Ireland. "*Ego sum abbas,*" he said. "And peace be with you. But who might you be?"

"I am Adémar, bishop of Blois. I have come here on behalf of the archbishops of Paris and Reims—and, through them, on the authority of our Holy Father, Pope Gregory, in Rome. I have twenty-three men and six dogs, who will need food and shelter. I pray the hospitality of your monastery is as good as rumored."

Abba nodded. "We can house your men. But, pray, why have you been sent here?"

The bishop surveyed the gathered monks as distant thunder growled in the charcoal sky. "I have come in the eleventh hour to warn you all," he said sternly. "For your lives—and your souls—are in danger. I have evidence that in this monastery, the devil works his mischief. For a sorcerer walks among you."

A gasp rose from the throng of monks. "Can you believe this?" Ciarán whispered over his shoulder.

But he spoke to no one. Dónall was gone.

Lightning flashed, followed by a violent thunder crack that drowned out the chorus of questions and speculations erupting in the wake of the bishop's pronouncement. The dark clouds flared and rumbled again, then unleashed a torrent of rain, scattering the crowd of monks.

Abba implored them to return to their work and gather again at Nones. "We'll discuss this then!" he cried over the pounding rain.

Before Ciarán could fumble for his cowl and draw it over his head, the downpour had soaked through his habit, and water streamed down his face. Scampering behind the others through the gateway of the monastery's earthen wall, he searched for Dónall. Surely there could be no connection between the bishop's dire words and Dónall's sudden departure. While it was true that Dónall knew things beyond most men's ken, such as Arabic medicine and the science of astronomy, these were things he had learned in France, at the Cathedral School of Reims, a gathering place for the greatest minds in Christendom—a place, Dónall said, where Virgil and Cicero lived again as if Rome had never fallen, and where Socrates still walked in the open spaces, posing questions to his disciples. Dónall had studied there years before Ciarán was born, and the fact the school had invited an Irish monk into its hallowed halls remained a source of pride at Derry. And while some of Ciarán's brethren found the ideas Dónall brought from Reims unorthodox and even a little crazy, no one at Derry had ever equated them with sorcery or the devil's work. Still, Dónall's sudden departure left Ciarán with a growing sense of unease.

The monks hurried up Derry's green hillside toward the monastery, a cluster of buildings with close-jointed dry stone walls and corbelled roofs. Rushing beneath the round tower built two hundred years ago as both lookout and sanctuary from Viking raids, they made for the workshops, granaries, and scores of beehive-shaped cells where the monks slept. A half dozen headed for the scriptorium—one of the larger buildings, with a high-peaked thatch roof. Ciarán followed them inside, out of the pounding rain, and they warmed themselves around the crackling fire in the hearth on the far wall. In the center of the room, the rough-hewn tables were strewn with scrolls and stacks of books, and along the rows of windows beneath the eaves sat the tilted desks of copyists, bearing sheets of parchment, inkhorns, and jars stuffed with brushes and quills. Ciarán removed his drenched cowl as his friend Niall walked up.

"So now the devil works among us?" Niall quipped. He shook the rain from his short-cropped hair, which was a shade of color somewhere between rust and autumn maple leaves. His eyes sparkled with a familiar mischief. "Guess I didn't notice when he moved his lodgings up here from the underworld. But seriously, who do you suppose that bishop is going on about?"

Ciarán shook his head. "These are our brothers. We've known them our whole lives." *And Dónall better than most.* Back when Ciarán's mother died of fever, so long ago he could no longer remember her face, it was Dónall who brought him here to the monastery and raised him as a son. That kindness had saved him from a less than promising life as the bastard of a nun from Kildare who had strayed from her vows, and for that Ciarán was grateful. He could not turn his back on Dónall now. "No one here's a sorcerer," he muttered.

"I didn't think so," Niall said. "But who do these bloody Franks think they are? We don't need any authority from archbishops in France or popes in Rome."

"Amen to that, brother."

Niall brushed the raindrops from his forehead. "And what's all this about coming to us in the eleventh hour?"

Ciarán smiled and shook his head. "Don't you ever *read* the books you copy? It's from scripture—a reference to the end times."

"Ah yes, the millennium," Niall groaned. "Only two years before the whole world gets swallowed up into hell. I've heard that's all those priests on the Continent think about. Do you believe it?"

"Saint Augustine didn't, and I think Dónall finds it all a bit nonsensical. Let's hope they're right—we're a bit young to be dying now."

"Can't say I disagree with you there."

Outside, thunder cracked again, followed by a cacophony of barking. Ciarán jerked his head toward the sound and rushed to the windows, along with Niall and a dozen others.

Ciarán gripped the windowsill and sucked in a breath. Downhill, past the earthen wall, six armed and mailed Franks unleashed their mastiffs, who bound toward the woods that framed the sprawling peat bog on Derry's west side. The Franks ran behind the dogs as fast as their heavy mail would allow.

"Whoever it was must have fled into the woods!" exclaimed Brother Fintan, one of the junior monks.

"I'll be damned," Niall said.

As the scribes around him broke into a flurry of questions and conjecture, Ciarán stood silent, struggling to comprehend everything that was happening. He prayed that Dónall was safe, but shuddered at the thought of those thick-jawed mastiffs and their sword-wielding masters. Ciarán went to his desk and sat down, ignoring the pages of Saint Augustine's *City of God*, which he had spent the past month illuminating. He was too worried about Dónall and the black-robed bishop's ominous pronouncement. No one else could work, either, and when the bells rang for the holy hour of Nones, he hastened with the others to the oratory, where Abba had promised they would learn more about this bishop and his troubling claims.

∽

CANDLES DIMLY LIT THE ORATORY, and the scent of burning tallow blended with the mustiness of the 112 woolen-cloaked monks huddled inside. On the altar sat Derry's treasured relics, all pertaining to its founder, Saint Columcille, and encased in vessels of silver and gold: the Psalter over which the saint fought the Battle of Cúl Dreimhne, a lock of the saint's hair, and a splinter from his cudgel.

A quartet of monks stood and sang, their voices rising and falling with the rhythm of the verses. At the end of each Psalm, the brethren bowed to the altar and then knelt for prayer. As junior monks, Ciarán and Niall prayed near the back of the oratory, along with several of their friends: Fintan, Murchad, and the twins, Áed and Ailil. Closer to the altar stood Abba and the senior monks, along with the bishop and his three black-robed priests.

At the end of the third Psalm, the brethren knelt and fell prostrate with their arms outstretched on the floor, for the final prayer. When it was done, they stood.

Abba looked reluctantly at Bishop Adémar. "Go on," he said, "say what you've come here to say. Then we must get back to the Lord's work."

Ciarán felt himself tense up the moment the bishop spoke. "Brothers of Derry," he began, "now is the time to fear for your souls. We stand here on the brink of the millennium—one thousand years since our Savior's birth. The time when, scripture tells us, the enemy of God shall be freed from his eternal prison. When the beasts of the apocalypse shall rise from sea and land to rule over men, while the armies of Gog and Magog gather to punish the wicked."

A hush settled over the brethren. *"See what I mean,"* Niall whispered to Ciarán, who gave a slight nod.

"The signs and portents of the end times abound," Bishop Adémar continued. "The Four Horsemen of the apocalypse—the Vikings from the north, the Bulgars and the Magyars from the east, and the Saracens from the south—besiege the kingdoms of Europe, raping, pillaging, and killing. Near Verdun, a convent of nuns saw fiery armies battling in the sky, and a dragon with great wings of flame! In England, a star shot across the heavens, burning so brightly it turned night into day. And near Rome, Mount Vesuvius erupted with brimstone and liquid fire, belching forth the stench of hell that lingered over the city for seven days."

The rows of gray-cowled monks shuffled uneasily, and a murmur spread throughout the oratory. The bishop regarded them with a cunning gleam in his eyes. "Despite these signs," he said, "there are heretics who deny these things, who serve the devil through their lies and threaten the souls of those around them. And as I warned you this morning, one of these heretics lives among you."

"Who?" asked Brother Cellach, a gaunt-faced senior monk.

The bishop let the question linger a moment before answering. "He is known to you as Dónall mac Taidg."

A gasp rose from the crowd. Even though Ciarán had expected the answer, it stung to hear Dónall's name. Throughout the oratory, heads turned.

"Where is he?" someone asked.

"As proof of his guilt," Bishop Adémar replied, "he fled the moment I arrived. But my mastiffs will find him."

"It cannot be," said brother Ewan, another of the senior monks. "Dónall, a sorcerer? *Think* about it!"

"Sorcery was his greatest crime," Bishop Adémar said. "But there is murder, too."

Ciarán felt the lump in the pit of his stomach harden.

"Impossible!" someone insisted as the murmuring subsided.

"Yet true," Bishop Adémar replied. "For when Dónall mac Taidg studied at the Cathedral School of Reims he became a servant of the devil. In a chamber beneath the school, he and eleven other monks practiced sorcery, using a forbidden book of spells—a dark and foul tome that is the very conduit to demons and all the denizens of hell! When Adalbero, the archbishop of Reims, suspected this heresy, he sent one of his canons to investigate, but they murdered this man of God to conceal their crimes."

Niall shot Ciarán a troubled look.

"This is mad," Ciarán whispered, clenching his fists.

"Seven of the devil's minions confessed," Bishop Adémar continued. "They were tried for heresy and convicted of their crimes. But Dónall mac Taidg fled and returned here. And now a heretic walks among you, ready to infect the brothers of Derry with his blasphemies, spreading his heresy—the greatest threat to our immortal souls as we prepare for the end of days." Bishop Adémar reached out his hands to implore the assembled monks. "We must be the sword of divine judgment in these end times. The book of Revelation instructs us that sorcerers and murderers are condemned to the lake of fire. So on this earth they must burn!"

Ciarán could resist no longer. "You're wrong!" he shouted above the murmur. "We know this man. He fears God and is our friend." A chorus of agreement swelled.

The bishop snapped back, "The devil's province is deception!"

"Listen to the bishop!" Brother Cellach cried, but the others shouted him down.

"Enough!" Abba yelled, his aged voice cracking from the strain. He turned to the bishop. "You've said what you've said. We respect the laws of the Church, but we will not rush to judgment. If Brother Dónall is found or comes forth, there must be a trial."

"As you wish," Bishop Adémar said coldly. "But remember this: to aid a heretic is to *become* a heretic." He stepped forward, standing nearly a head taller than most of the monks.

"That was a bit bold even for you," Niall said to Ciarán.

"I couldn't help myself."

Niall moved toward the door. "Let's get out of here." Ciarán turned to go with him, but hard fingers grasped his arm in a grip like a blacksmith's.

"You're the whelp mac Taidg brought here," Bishop Adémar said, his fingers digging into Ciarán's flesh. "A bastard of heretics."

Ciarán's eyes hardened. "My mother was a nun, not a heretic."

The bishop released Ciarán's arm. "Yes, I suppose that is what he would have told you."

"How do you know who I am?" Ciarán asked.

The bishop gave him a cold smile as he turned to walk away. "All you need know," he called back, "is that everything you have come to believe is a lie."

CHAPTER 2
HUNTED

A low baying cut through the hiss of the rain. Dónall grimaced at the sound. The Franks had unleashed their mastiffs. Down the oak-wooded swale behind him, twigs snapped and dead leaves crackled under the dogs' massive paws. And far behind them, he could hear the halloos of men rushing through the woods.

Dónall peered through the streaming rain. A dense labyrinth of oak, ash, and birch thickets surrounded him, but they would provide no concealment against the dogs' keen noses. He had hoped to work his way through the woods, around the peat bog, and across the hills to Aileach, his ancestral home, but that would have to wait.

His thoughts whirled and tumbled. Archbishop Adalbero of Reims was dead, his inquisition disbanded. So why had this new bishop from Blois traveled all the way to Ireland these twenty years later? Dónall struggled to remember whether he had seen the man before—working with Gerbert of Aurillac, perhaps, back at Reims.

The baying grew louder, punctuated with throaty snarls. Dónall hefted his staff. Sturdy and as tall as he, it had been cut from a lightning-struck alder and then painted with soot and flaxseed oil until it was as black as the tree that formed it. The staff was a formidable enough weapon against men, but Dónall knew it would be no match for the mastiffs. For these were the war dogs of Franks and Saxons, a terror to foot soldiers and strong enough to pull an armored man from his horse.

As the rain pattered against the bare branches and forest duff around him, Dónall saw the blur of a mastiff's tawny coat, bounding toward him through the trees. From a pocket in his rough woolen habit, he took out an opaque white crystal the size of a hazel nut. With an effort, he ignored the onrushing beast and cleared his mind of conscious thought.

The mastiff burst through the undergrowth, barking ferociously, its great teeth bared and snapping at the air. Eyes on its quarry, it leaped into the natural corridor formed by a broken line of birches. Not ten paces behind it streaked a second mastiff, spittle flying from its massive jaws.

Dónall held the crystal to his lips and, blowing softly, whispered a single word: *"Eoh."* Within the crystal, a tiny spark appeared. A verse rolled off Dónall's tongue, the words neither Irish nor Latin. He thrust his hand forward, and the crystal's spark flared into a soft yet brilliant white light. The two mastiffs skidded to a halt, just feet from Dónall. They ceased barking and cocked their heads, entranced by the light.

Dónall uttered another verse, and comprehension glimmered in the dark canine eyes. They sat submissively as the crystal's light faded to a warm glow.

"Good dogs," Dónall said, patting their heads. The lead mastiff let out a passive whimper. Then the pounding of boots and the faint *chink* of mail sounded from the woods. Dónall peered into the trees, looking for the Frank, but the man must still be well behind his dogs. Scratching the scruff of the lead mastiff's neck, Dónall spoke another strange word, then waved toward the trees to his left. Both dogs darted away.

Through the trees, Dónall spied the mail coat of a Frankish soldier. Heart pounding, he ducked behind the trunk of an ancient oak. The light within the crystal had died, and he stowed it in his habit.

The Frank, sword in hand, rushed down the corridor of birches, raindrops streaming off his helmet as his weathered face peered left and right, searching for the dogs. The mastiffs were gone, but their paws had punched deep into the wet forest duff. He stopped at the sight of the prints and put two fingers to his lips. A sharp whistle followed, cut to a mere chirp by the crack of Dónall's staff.

The heavy alder stave glanced off the Frank's helmet and crashed down on his shoulder, driving him backward. Dónall sprang from behind the oak and swung the staff again, catching the Frank behind the knees. Arms windmilling, the soldier went down hard on his back, the sword slipping from his grasp. He looked up at his attacker with a stunned gaze.

"Why are you here?" Dónall asked.

"Because the bishop wants you dead," the man growled.

Dónall drew back on the staff as if to strike again, and the man flinched. Rain pelted his face, thinning the blood till it looked like wine. "Why?" Dónall demanded.

The Frank grimaced. "Because of something you possess."

Dónall drove his heel hard into the Frank's rib cage. "*What,* damn you!"

"The book," the Frank gasped. "The one you stole from Reims."

Dónall's eyes grew wide. "No," he muttered under his breath. And bellowing with Irish rage, he slammed the staff downward, smashing it into the man's jaw.

Dónall breathed heavily as new and troubling questions arose in his mind. He knew what he must do.

For now, he would hide. Then he must go back to Derry.

CHAPTER 3

REVELATIONS

That night, the bishop's soldiers rousted the monks from their sleep, searching for Dónall among the cells. The soldiers were in a surly mood. Ciarán, who shared a cell with Niall, had to hold back his friend, and they watched in silence while a broad-shouldered Frank, with the monks' beer on his breath, invaded their home.

Though the cell was round like a beehive outside, inside the mortarless stone walls it was a single small, rectangular room with nowhere for anything bigger than a rat to hide. And yet, the Frank lingered, scanning every inch of the candlelit cell, and making the two junior monks lift their straw pallets just to prove nothing was hidden underneath. The whole time, the Frank fingered the pommel of his sheathed broadsword, while outside, the mastiffs filled all of Derry with their barking and baying.

"Go back to bloody France, you piss-drinking bastard!" Niall yelled after the Frank stepped back outside. The soldier whirled about, hand on his sword hilt, but Ciarán breathed a relieved sigh when it became clear that the Frank did not understand the Irish words. The Frank shot Niall a wicked grin before turning away and striding to the next cell.

"Are you looking to get us killed!" Ciarán hissed.

"Bloody Franks," Niall said. "There's a hundred of us and only twenty of them. We should make 'em leave!"

"I think Abba hopes to avoid a fight with the Roman Church. And besides, we can't fight mailed swordsmen. We're monks, not warriors."

Niall scowled and shook his head. "This is wrong. We should take a stand. Saint Columcille would've fought 'em."

Ciarán clapped Niall on the shoulder. "Well, it's our bad luck he's not here. Now, get some sleep."

Niall grumbled a reply, and Ciarán had to listen to him complain until the bell rang for Nocturns, when the monks gathered in the oratory for the next holy office of prayer.

The bishop and his priests did not attend the vigil, but rumors quickly spread that one of the Franks was found in the woods, half conscious with a broken jaw. Ciarán could not help but wonder whether Dónall was the cause, for though he was no warrior, he was big and strong, with a temper that could flare like a birch-bark torch. Ciarán prayed that his friend was safe for the night. With luck, he had fled to Aileach, where his cousin ruled as king.

When the monks returned to their cells, Ciarán could not sleep. The bishop's parting words still haunted him. Ciarán knew that his mother had sinned in the eyes of the church by abandoning her vow of chastity and having a child out of wedlock, but that was a far cry from the bishop's claim of heresy. And Ciarán's father was just a commoner, some charming Breton she had met during a pilgrimage through Brittany and France, who had left her before either knew that she was with child. Yet more troubling was that this bishop from Blois should even know who Ciarán was. Certainly, the bishop had lied, just as he had lied in accusing Dónall. But why? These questions heaved and churned in Ciarán's mind like an angry sea, causing him to toss on his straw pallet until the bells chimed again for Matins, the holy office observed between midnight and dawn to mark the moment Saint Peter denied Christ for the third time.

He slept no better after Matins, but by Terce the sun had risen, and while Ciarán suffered through fitful dreams the rain had gone, and now the sun shone bright on the green hills of Ireland. After observing the holy office, Ciarán and Niall, along with a score of their brethren, returned to their work in the scriptorium—until an hour before Sext, when another ship arrived at Derry.

A BELL SIGNALED the ship's arrival, all but emptying the scriptorium. Ciarán and Niall joined their fellow scribes heading down the clover green hill toward the riverbank. Passing the oratory's moss-speckled roof in the shape of an overturned boat, they met another score of monks streaming out of various workshops. They passed the round tower and arrived at the banks of the river, where sunlight shimmered like quicksilver on the water.

The newly arrived vessel moored next to the bishop's ship was an Irish curach, with a narrow wood-framed hull covered in black ox hide, and a single mast with one weather-stained sail. No fancy pennants adorned the curach's masthead, and rather than a crew of soldiers, six rugged Irishmen were busy unloading chests and barrels with the help of their burly, black-bearded captain, whom all the monks knew as Merchant mac Fadden.

Ciarán smiled when he saw mac Fadden's ruddy face, burned by the wind and sun from his constant journeying across the Celtic Sea. The captain had long served the monastery by transporting books between Derry and abbeys in France, continuing a practice started centuries ago in the days of Saint Columcille, when Irish monks and their quill pens saved countless written works from the Continent that otherwise would have perished at the hands of the Visigoths and Vandals. Ciarán always loved the arrival of new books, and this morning it was the only thing to brighten his day.

"What do you have for us today, Merchant?" asked Brother Áengus, a lanky senior monk who served as the scriptorium's provisioner.

"Some fine books from Saint-Germain-des-Prés," Merchant mac Fadden replied. "Several nice Psalters, a few epistles, a copy of the *Lives of the Saints* and one of that history book by Herodotus, and the cream of the crop: a complete Bible in Latin, just like Saint Jerome would've copied it. It fills a whole chest, though, and may take two stout lads to move it."

"Splendid!" Brother Áengus said, clasping his hands together like an eager child.

"Oh," Merchant mac Fadden added, "and a book for Brother Dónall." The old captain scanned the collection of monks who had gathered at the pier. "Now, where is he?"

Several of the brethren looked away, and Brother Áengus ran his fingers nervously across his chin.

"He's gone away for a while," Ciarán said, stepping up.

"That's too bad." Merchant mac Fadden reached into the nearest chest and took out a rather ordinary-looking book, bound in dark leather. "It's from a Brother Remi. Real odd bird, that one, and very anxious for Dónall to have it. Said it was urgent."

"I can hold it for him," Ciarán offered.

"That'd be good, lad." Merchant mac Fadden gave Ciarán the book, then squinted past him. "Now, who in the world might that be?"

Ciarán turned around. Striding toward the riverbank was the bishop with a half-dozen of his soldiers, followed by one of the black-robed priests.

"That'd be His *Holiness* from France," Niall answered. "Bishop Adémar of Blois, who thinks he can just sail over to Ireland and take over."

"He's part of some archbishop's inquisition," Ciarán said more evenly.

The bishop's long strides forced his soldiers and the priest to jog to keep up. "Inspect that cargo," Bishop Adémar snapped before turning to mac Fadden. "And who are *you?*"

"A poor merchant, Your Excellency. I transport books and wine between here and the continent." Merchant mac Fadden stood no taller than the point of the bishop's gray-flecked beard. "I've got charters from the abbots of Saint-Ouen, Saint-Denis, and Saint-Germain-des-Prés, among others."

The bishop's eyes narrowed. "I'd like to see those charters."

Merchant mac Fadden's cheeks flushed red, and a hint of anger furrowed his brow. But two of the bishop's mailed guardsmen stood beside him now, so he nodded and said, "I've got 'em back there." He turned to walk back to his curach, grumbling under his breath.

"Inspect all the books!" Bishop Adémar barked to his men. And before Ciarán could back away, the bishop snatched the book intended for Dónall. Ciarán froze. The priest standing beside the bishop seemed to gloat in silence. He was a thin-faced man with oily hair, whom the monks had quickly come to know and despise as Father Gauzlin.

Bishop Adémar flipped opened the book's leather cover. A title, penned in letters illuminated with interlacing patterns of purple and red, dominated the first page: *THE APOCALYPSE OF JOHN*.

A thin smile spread across the bishop's lips. "The book of Revelation," he said. "How appropriate."

To Ciarán's surprise, he handed back the book. Ciarán took it, exhaled a grateful sigh, and shrank back into the little throng lest the bishop change his mind.

"I want four men at this pier at all times," Bishop Adémar ordered his men. "No one leaves on this boat except the merchant and his crew."

Merchant mac Fadden came walking back from the curach with several rolled parchments in hand. Passing Ciarán and Niall, he whispered in Irish, "I'll be in Magh Bhile all week if you need me, lads." Niall gave a subtle nod as Merchant mac Fadden turned to the bishop and held out the charters.

"Let's go," Ciarán told Niall under his breath. He glanced at Father Gauzlin, who was watching them the way a hawk might eye a crippled hare. Ciarán lowered his head, looking away, and then followed a group of monks back to the scriptorium.

Once back at his desk and warmed by the crackling fire, Ciarán fiddled with his quills, sharpening and cleaning them and paying scant attention to the manuscript before him as he waited for the bell to toll Sext.

When it did, he whispered to Niall, "Linger here."

Niall looked at him, perplexed. "We're not going to the oratory?"

"No one will notice we're gone," he said, reaching for the leather-bound book that Merchant mac Fadden had given him. "The monk who sent this to Dónall said it was urgent that he get it. We need to know why."

Niall shrugged. "But it's just the Apocalypse of John. We must have five of them already."

"So, then, what makes *this* copy so important?" Ciarán asked.

"Ah," Niall said. "I see what you mean."

Ciarán waited until the scriptorium cleared out before opening the cover. The pages smelled of fresh-scraped vellum. "This is new," he observed. He began leafing through the pages. The script was well penned in the Carolingian style, but it was the illuminations that caught his eye. Vines of red, green, and yellow crawled up the margin of one page while, along the bottom, interlaced ribbons formed the image of a four-winged bird wreathed in flame. Green, blue, crimson, and gold filled the spaces between the lines of script. "Whoever illuminated this was a master," Ciarán said.

"It has pretty pictures—so what?" Niall remarked.

Ciarán thumbed through several more pages. "I'd call them *disturbing*." The page bore a large illumination of an angel with sprawling wings, surrounded by billowing clouds. The angel blew a long golden trumpet that spewed blood on a crowd of people, who writhed in apparent agony. Beneath the picture was a verse:

The first angel blew his trumpet, and there came hail and fire, mixed with blood, and they were hurled to the earth.

Niall stared at the image. "I should say so."

Another page depicted three trumpet-blaring angels, and a flaming star falling from the sky toward a walled town. A page later, another verse preceded another illumination:

And in those days people will seek death but will not find it; they will long to die, but death will flee from them.

20

Beneath those words, the illumination portrayed a horde of winged demons erupting from a smoking pit whose fumes blotted the sky. The demonic horde assailed a host of monks who prayed and wept atop a turf of flamelike grass, where another word was painted: *"Abaddon."* Two pages later, a cavalry of armored men charged across the land on fire-breathing lions with tails that were writhing snakes, and on the next page, a great city's majestic columns and domes collapsed to dust.

Ciarán flipped through two more pages, skimming the text, then turned another page, which was tagged with a bookmark of burgundy ribbon attached to the binding. "Someone marked this page," he said.

"This Brother Remi is not the cheeriest sort," Niall quipped, looking down to a verse that preceded a stunning illumination:

And war broke out in Heaven. Michael and his archangels fought against the dragon. The dragon and his angels fought back, but they were defeated, and there was no longer any place for them in Heaven.

The painting that followed, consuming nearly two full pages, portrayed a serpentine dragon in the sky, twisted in battle against the hosts of heaven. Angels thrust spears into the beast, except for Saint Michael, who held a blazing sword. Teardrop flames spilled from the dragon's mouth onto the earth below. In the bottom left corner, a great white horse with a flowing mane stood rampant, kicking out with its forelegs. And at the bottom of the second page, more angels threw cadaverous-looking demons into a fiery pit. From the pit, smoke rose, gathering near the dragon's tail, which swept stars from the heavens to the earth.

"Is this supposed to mean something to Brother Dónall?" Niall asked.

Ciarán shook his head, "I have no idea." He felt drawn to the painting's elaborate detail. Each of the stars had six white points outlined in black. The demons each bore red marks—the wounds wrought by the angels' spears—and each angel wore elaborate robes embroidered with lines of gold and blue, in between which the artist had painted small dots of color representing jewels. But none of these details could match the dragon's. Its white eye had a glaring red pupil within a jet black iris. And there was something about the scales. Each was painted in a distinctive pattern, alternating between red and gold over a black surface. Close up, the pattern appeared random, but from even a slight distance, the scales rippled over the dragon's snaking torso like tendrils of red smoke rising from a burning candle. At points, the pattern inexplicably shifted direction. Lost in this detail, Ciarán traced the patterns with his finger.

"What?" Niall asked.

Ciarán ignored him. In the middle of the torso, the scales devolved to an even stranger pattern. "My God," Ciarán said, "I think there's a letter concealed here." He pointed to the image. Against the black background, the scales formed a "D." "There's more, too." Amid an array of red and gold scales, an "Ó" emerged, followed by "N" and three other characters. The letters made a word, and down the dragon's tail, more hidden letters formed a second word.

Ciarán's blood ran cold. For together, the words made a phrase:

DÓNALL BEWARE!

Niall stared wide-eyed at the page. "I'll be damned," he murmured. "You were right."

CHAPTER 4

THE PALE HORSE

Niall looked to Ciarán for an answer. "Do you think this Brother Remi knew the bishop was coming?"

Ciarán glanced around the scriptorium to confirm that they were still alone. "Why else would someone go to such lengths to hide a warning?" He pondered his own question. "But this can't be all there is to it." He searched for more hidden words in the illumination's every tiny detail—the feathers of the angels' wings, the patterns in their garments, the flames surrounding Saint Michael's sword, the stars the dragon swept from the sky—but found nothing.

"There are a lot of pictures left in this book," Niall pointed out.

"True . . ." Ciarán leafed through the pages until he found the illumination of the demons crawling out from the pit. The ghastly creatures, the billowing smoke, and the terrified monks were every bit as intricately wrought as the war in heaven, but he saw only the strokes of the artist's brush. "There's nothing in this one."

"Go forward a bit," Niall said.

Ciarán turned the pages. In one illumination, a seven-headed beast emerged from a boiling sea. Each of the beast's heads resembled the dragon's, and its body was like a leopard's, yellow with clumped black spots. On the adjacent page, another illumination portrayed a horned priest with black venom dripping from his mouth. Still Ciarán found nothing hidden in the pictures. He thumbed through more pages. Even those without pictures had illuminated margins positively acrawl with vines or ribbons, tiny cherubs, animals of all kinds, and beasts from myth and legend: a unicorn, a cockatrice, and every manner of imp and devil. Ciarán sighed. "Whoever wrote the warning couldn't have expected Dónall to pore over the entire book."

"Do you have another solution?"

"The bookmark was a clue to the first words. What about the rest?" Quickly he paged back to the war in heaven, this time focusing on the verse that accompanied the painting: *Michael and the angels fought against the dragon . . .*

The illumination depicted it aptly: Saint Michael defying the dragon, the angels stabbing it with spears.

The great dragon was thrown down to the earth, and his angels were thrown down with him.

"All the images fit the verse," Ciarán said. Except for one, in the bottom right corner: the white horse with the flowing mane. "Everything but this horse."

Niall cocked his head. "What has a horse to do with the apocalypse?"

"Of course!" Ciarán said. He flipped toward the front of the book, searching through lines of Carolingian script for the verse. He found it in the chapter on the seven seals and read it aloud:

Then I saw the Lamb open one of the seven seals, and I heard one of the four living creatures call out, as with a voice of thunder, 'Come!' I looked, and there was a white horse! Its rider had a bow; a crown given to him, and he came to conquer.

"One of the Four Horsemen of the apocalypse," Ciarán said. Unlike so many others, this page did not bear the image of horses or riders—only a thorny vine that snaked across the margins. "The Four Horsemen are one of the most notorious images of the end times, yet the artist omitted it here, instead putting it out of place in the illumination of the war in heaven." Anticipation mounted as Ciarán read the next verse.

> *When he opened the second seal, I heard the second living creature call out, "Come!" And out came another horse, bright red; its rider was permitted to take peace from the earth, so that people would slaughter one another, and he was given a great sword.*

"We have to find the red horse!" Hurriedly Ciarán skimmed through the pages.

"Stop," Niall said. "Look." A charging red stallion decorated the left-hand corner of a page otherwise covered with script. The adjacent page, however, displayed another illumination of the dragon. Thick chains were coiled about the dragon's red-scaled torso, and angels tugged at the chains, pulling it toward a bronze tower with a massive door, which one of the angels unlocked with a golden key. Intricate details filled the rest of the painting: a curtain of stars above a hill blanketed with green grass and violet flowers, all of which swirled into flowing patterns that washed against the landscape like a tumbling sea. And that was where Ciarán looked.

"More letters," he said, pointing to a "P" hidden within the color-flecked grass, followed by seven more letters, then two more hidden words. Together they completed another phrase:

PROPHECY HAS BEGUN

"What's that supposed to mean?" Niall asked.

"Who knows. We have to find the next horse." Ciarán returned to the passage on the Four Horsemen and read the remaining verses. They spoke of two more broken seals and two more horses, one black and one pale green. They needed a black horse.

Ciarán found it near the back of the book, as part of another sprawling illumination. Like the painting of the war in heaven, this one consumed two entire pages and depicted the seven bowls of wrath, poured by seven winged angels. From the first bowl flowed a black liquid, which fell onto a small island with two penitent monks whose faces were disfigured by pox. The next two angels poured blood into a churning sea around the island, where the lines of the waves cascaded into chaotic designs. From the fourth bowl rained fire, from the fifth billowing smoke, and from the sixth spilled a swarm of green frogs. From the last angel's bowl, lightning arced into the blood sea. And there in the bottom right corner, a black horse galloped down the margin of the page.

Ciarán started with the blood sea, whose lines of churning waves reminded him of the grass on the meadowed hillside. Sure enough, he found seven hidden letters forming the first word. He spelled it aloud:

N-I-C-O-L-A-S

"Who's Nicolas?" Niall wondered.

Ciarán shook his head. There was no Nicolas at Derry. As he let his eyes drift out of focus, more letters, and then a question mark, stood out from their camouflage of billowing smoke swirls. Added to the first word, it formed a troubling question. He detected the third word in the chaotic sea, right where the lightning struck from the seventh bowl. The word made the phrase more ominous yet:

NICOLAS CAPTURED? KILLED?

Niall scratched the stubble of his chin. "Do you think the author believes this will happen to Dónall?"

"I don't know," Ciarán said. He ran his fingers through the hair that ringed his tonsured pate. "Let's find that green horse."

A few pages past the bowls of wrath, there it was: a gaunt horse painted in pale green, bucking in the margin of a frightening illumination that covered half a page. The scene depicted a monstrous beast covered in olive and brown scales, its mouth agape. The beast bore a single gigantic eye, its iris wreathed in flame. Yellowed fangs jutted from the beast's maw, into which a mass of humanity spilled from the wreckage of a burning city. And yet, as terrifying as the image was, the details were exquisite. Among the victims were kings and bishops and women, some clothed in rich robes, others naked and screaming. Scattered among them were red-hued devils and bestial horned and furred men wielding whips. A beard of flowing hair adorned the chin of the gigantic beast, each hair a serpent with its own terrible eye and fearsome fangs.

Ciarán combed through the painting. "There's a word hidden in the beast's mane. *F-E-A-R*." The furry hide of one of the beast-men concealed a second word. "*F-O-R*," Ciarán breathed. He searched for more letters, first in the red and yellow flames that engulfed the city, then in the shapes that decorated the robes of the beast's well-born victims, and finally in the scales of the beast. He found nothing more. He ran his fingers over his face. "Fear for *what?*" he muttered aloud. He scoured the image again, and then looked up at Niall. "What's left?"

Niall's face had gone pale. "You missed it." He pointed to the first letter, formed by the dark spaces between the victims falling into the beast's mouth. The gaps between the dying people shaped each succeeding letter. Ciarán stared in disbelief at the completed phrase:

FEAR FOR CIARÁN

"How is this possible?" Niall asked. But Ciarán barely heard him. For next to the warning, the image of the pale horse stood like an exclamation mark. A shiver crawled over his skin as he remembered the Horsemen's final verse:

When he opened the fourth seal, I looked and there was a pale green horse! Its rider's name was Death, and Hades followed with him.

CHAPTER 5

KEPT SECRETS

Ciarán left the scriptorium in a daze. "What has any of this to do with me?"

Niall shook his head. "I don't get it. A prophecy? Someone named Nicolas? Did Dónall ever mention a Nicolas or a Nick?"

"No," Ciarán said. "But the warning suggests *I'm* in danger. And now here is this bishop, who somehow knows who I am."

At the sound of honking, Niall glanced up as a chevron of geese glided above them. "You know, there were always those old rumors that Dónall was your father. Maybe they figure they can get to him by threatening his son."

"But Dónall's not my father," Ciarán insisted.

"*They* don't know that," Niall said. "But I'll tell you what: if we chase these bastards from our shore, then no one's gonna be in any danger."

As they walked up the green hillside, past the cluster of cells belonging to the senior monks, Ciarán began to wonder if his friend might be right. All the cells were round, hive-shaped huts of corbelled stone flecked with moss and lichens, and many had been patched with so much peat and mud, they looked like little hillocks.

28

"Aw, hell," Niall said when the door to one particularly moss-laden cell flung open and Father Gauzlin emerged, yelling at a Frank who followed him.

"Have you looked everywhere?" the priest snapped in Latin.

"Yes," the Frank insisted. "And we've searched this one twice now. It's not here."

"It must be! The Irishman couldn't have had it when he fled." The priest gritted his teeth. "Shall you be the one to tell the bishop it's gone?"

The Frank didn't respond but nodded in the direction of Niall and Ciarán, standing some twenty paces away. Father Gauzlin glared at them. "Move on, you!" he cried.

Niall balled his fist. "How I'd love to beat the sneer off that sneaking stoat's face!"

Ciarán grabbed Niall's arm and nodded toward the mailed Frank with the broadsword hanging at his side. "Not now," he said, nudging him toward their own cell across the monastery. When they were out of earshot, Ciarán turned to Niall. "That was Dónall's cell."

Niall glanced back to make sure they weren't being followed. "What do you think they were looking for?"

"I've no idea," Ciarán replied. "But I think tonight we should try to find out."

Ciarán and Niall waited a full hour after Vespers, certain that all would be quiet in Derry until the midnight bell signaled the holy office of Nocturn. The monks prayed at these offices seven times each day—four times before dusk and three times before dawn—which made for a fairly regimented life. And a predictable one, too, for now everyone in the monastery should be asleep.

Ciarán lit one of the tallow candles that the monks used upon waking each night to go to the oratory for Nocturns and Matins. "Do you think that's a good idea?" Niall asked, drawing his cowl over his head. "You could see that candlelight from the riverbank."

Ciarán pulled on his own cowl. "How else are we supposed to see what's inside Dónall's cell?"

"You're the one always wanting to be so cautious," Niall said with a shrug, and stepped outside. Ciarán followed him into the night air, where a half-moon pierced the haze of fading clouds. A biting wind soughed through Derry, so that Ciarán had to cup a hand to windward of the candle's flame to keep it lit. Around them, the monks' cells stood quiet.

They padded across the dew-damp grass toward the senior monks' cells, until Niall stopped abruptly at the first one. "Look," he whispered.

Outside Dónall's cell sat an armored Frank, half-asleep, slouched against the cell's stone wall, while near the door stood another, arms crossed, watching alertly.

"They're afraid Dónall might come back for whatever they're searching for," Ciarán said. "So what do we do now?"

A familiar look of mischief sparkled in Niall's eyes, and a devilish grin spread across his face. He reached down for some palm-size stones. "You'll hide for a moment, and then you'll find out what's inside that cell."

Ciarán stared wide-eyed at the stones in Niall's hand. "Where are you going?"

"Don't worry about me," Niall said with a wink. "I'll meet you back home."

Stepping out from behind the cell, Niall hurled the first stone. It struck the standing Frank's helmet with an audible clang. The Frank jumped, fumbling for his blade, as a second stone pegged the half-asleep Frank in the cheek. With a yowl of pain and outrage, the second Frank put his hand to his face and scrambled to his feet.

"Columcille!" Niall yelled defiantly, darting from behind the cell and sprinting toward the oratory. The enraged Franks lumbered after him as fast as they could in their heavy mail.

The beauty of the diversion was not lost on Ciarán. Niall could run like a hare, and he knew every stone and footpath of the monastery by heart. To these Franks, though, it must seem a maddening maze of hovels and sheds, thrown together without any semblance of a plan.

Ciarán waited until the clanking and muttered oaths of Niall's pursuers grew faint, and then scurried to Dónall's cell and ducked inside, where the pungent bouquet of dried herbs filled his nostrils. Dónall's wooden cupboard, which held his collection of medicines, had been torn from the wall and smashed. Ciarán closed the door. His heart sank at the sight of the devastation. The shards of earthenware flasks and mortars were strewn across the floor, amid the bundles of dried laurel, mint, mugwort, juniper berries, hops, and chamomile, all crushed to useless debris under the searchers' boots. A leather book satchel, ripped open at the seams, sat crumpled against a wall, and the two books Dónall kept in his cell—Pliny's *Natural History* and a tome on Arabic medicine—had been flung to the floor. Even Dónall's straw pallet had been torn apart, its remnants scattered across the room. Amid the tatters, a goose quill pen lay crumpled on the hand-spun wool rug, now ruined by a smashed pot of ink and ground-in herbs.

What were they looking for? At first, it occurred to Ciarán that these ignorant Franks might have viewed Dónall's medical texts and cache of herbs as evidence of witchcraft, but if so, why destroy them instead of confiscating them as evidence for a trial? No, they were searching for something else. So if Dónall needed to hide something, where would he put it?

The candlelight reflected off the only artwork in the cell: a cross with a ring surrounding its intersection, made of tiles cemented into the corbelled stone wall above where Dónall's pallet once lay. Most would recognize the symbol as a Celtic cross, introduced by Saint Patrick when he brought the Christian faith to Ireland. But Ciarán also knew of its second meaning, one that Dónall was particularly fond of. For it was an emblem of Ireland's pagan past—the symbol of the Tuatha Dé Danann, who ruled Ireland and built the ringforts of Aileach and Brú na Bóinne long before the coming of the Gaelic Celts. They were the mythical Fae folk of Ireland, and as Dónall often said, *"There's truth behind those old myths."*

"Of course!" Ciarán whispered. The answer was right before his eyes. To see it, one had to know Dónall and his love for Irish legends. Maybe that was why the Franks had found nothing: they lacked that knowledge of the Irish and their corbelled stones.

Ciarán began feeling around the wheel cross—for that was the symbol's original name—searching for a loose stone. Sure enough, there beneath the foot of the cross, he found one that wiggled slightly. Corbelled stones, fitted together without mortar, were like a puzzle. And if one found the keystone, the puzzle could come apart and the stones be removed. Ciarán knew that his tinkering would not threaten the structural integrity of the cell, for the walls were as thick as a man's arm was long. But under these finely jointed stones, one could hide things, just as the Tuatha Dé Danann had—which was precisely how Ciarán knew where to look. For when the Gaelic Celts defeated them, the Tuatha Dé Danann became known as the Sidhe, and according to legend, they hid beneath their hill forts and stashed their treasure under the stones.

Using his fingertips, Ciarán winkled out the first stone beneath the cross . . . and stared into blackness. The space beyond was hollow! He found the next loose stone beside the first and carefully slid it from the wall. Then, stone by stone, he lifted out the interlocking pieces to reveal an opening the size of a bread basket. He lowered the candle, and its flickering light caught a glint of metal. Reaching in, he felt leather and the weight of steel. He pulled it from the hollow cavity, and his eyes grew wide, for he found himself gripping the hilt of a short sword. The candlelight gleamed down the length of the blade, which was shaped like a leaf: wide in the center and narrowing toward the tip and the hilt.

Why would a monk need a sword? he wondered.

He set down the sword and peered back into the hollow space. Something else was down there—wide and thick and made of leather. It looked like the book satchel that the Franks had destroyed. Setting the candle on the stone shelf where Dónall's cupboard once stood, he drew the satchel from its hiding space and was surprised at its weight.

Carefully, he unlatched the satchel and removed its contents. It was a wedge-shaped book, thicker at the spine and closed at the narrow edge by a leather strap and metal clasp.

The dark leather cover had featherlike patterns pressed into its surface, but it was the image dominating the cover's center that captured Ciarán's attention. Cross-shaped with a looped head, the symbol was a *crux ansata*—a cross with a handle. But he had seen the symbol elsewhere, too, in the margins of Greek texts, where it had a very different meaning. Egyptian in origin, it was called an ankh, a symbol of life—or was it death?

He studied the closed tome. The vellum looked old and weathered. He ran his thumb across its edges. The pages were dry and cracked, leaving a hint of dust on his thumb. This book was at least a century old.

An unexpected anxiety welled up in him as he unfixed the clasp and opened the tome. The cover page was unilluminated and bore no title—only a sentence that had been scrawled by hand rather than penned in Carolingian or Irish script:

I, Maugis d'Aygremont, write of the Mysteries that were revealed to me, which cannot die.

Who was this Maugis d'Aygremont? Ciarán wondered. Below the sentence was a verse from scripture, also handwritten:

For when people began to multiply on the face of the ground, and daughters were born to them, the sons of God saw that they were fair. And they took wives for themselves of all that they chose. The Nephilim were on the earth in those days – and also afterwards – when the sons of God went into the daughters of men, who bore children to them. These were the heroes of old, the warriors of renown.

—Genesis, Chapter VI

"That's odd," he said as he began skimming through pages, concerned the Franks might return at any time.

The book appeared to be some sort of journal. The Latin was

not in any form of ordered script, and Ciarán struggled to make out some of the characters. It was not the sort of painstaking work done by monks. Like the cover page, the margins were curiously unilluminated, and the text was dense, with words scrawled in the margins, many of them dangling with no apparent meaning or referent, as if the author had been struck by madness.

The pages that followed contained less text, and a number of drawings. They were not the work of an artist of any merit, but more in the nature of diagrams. There was a picture of a key, and another of a tree with a blackened trunk. A third appeared to be a ring. Scattered among these were other characters—letters perhaps, though not Latin or Greek. These characters appeared to be the only artfully drawn things in the entire book. They were flowing in style, with broad arches and wispy strokes. Some had curling tails; others jutted with crosslike appendages or strange dots that floated like little moons above the body of the character. He wondered if the characters were Egyptian Coptic, or maybe a form of runes like those carved by the Northmen. The characters, or symbols perhaps, were arranged in rows and sometimes divided by strange lines as if grouped into tiny boxes. They filled whole pages, while other pages were entirely blank and others yet were dominated by pictures. A staff, a human skull, and then a sword—one with a leaf-shaped blade. Ciarán glanced at the sword lying on the ground. Its blade looked identical to the one in the picture. A feeling of unease knotted in the pit of his stomach.

With growing trepidation, he turned the page. The curls on the symbols now appeared as tiny horns, and the appendages jutting from many of the characters looked like daggers or hooked claws. As he ventured deeper into the tome, the symbols and images grew more ominous. He turned another page . . . and gasped.

An alarming image dominated the vellum: a circle surrounding a seven-pointed star filled with heptagrams and symbols. They filled the outer circle and the spaces within the star. And there was something threatening in their arrangement. Were they glyphs or sigils— or some form of sorcerers' script adorning a witch's circle?

The bishop's accusation flooded Ciarán's mind. According to him, Dónall and eleven other monks had practiced sorcery with a forbidden book of spells!

Ciarán gazed in horror at the sword. *And they had murdered a canon to conceal their heresy!*

He shoved the book and satchel back into their hiding place and dropped the sword in after it. Fumbling with the stones, he replaced them as quickly as he could and then staggered to his feet. Glancing once more to make sure the wall was sealed, he snatched up the candle and fled from Dónall's cell.

A sickening feeling seized Ciarán. He ran to his cell and pulled the door shut. A moment later, it opened again. Niall's face beamed with exhilaration.

"So what did you find?"

Ciarán shook his head, struggling for words. "Nothing really."

"Well, you missed a fine time. Those Franks are probably lost in the woods by now."

Ciarán slumped onto his pallet, waiting for Niall to finish his account of the chase. Then Ciarán pulled his blankets tightly around him. He didn't know if he could ever tell his friend the truth. Shuddering at the thought of what he had uncovered, he recalled the bishop's parting words. Indeed, what if everything he had come to believe actually was a lie?

CHAPTER 6

THE GATHERING

F ather Gauzlin paced through the scriptorium the next morning, eyeing the monks like a fox circling a henhouse. The bookbinders in the center of the room did not whistle their lilting Irish lays, and the scribes along the rows of windows worked with head down, hoping to avoid the priest's gaze. The scratching of pens and the fall of Gauzlin's boots on the rush-strewn floor were the only sounds save for an occasional whisper between monks.

Outside the windows, a cold mist lingered beneath a cloud-darkened sky, providing only feeble light for the scribes at their desks. Ciarán stirred a blue dye made from woad leaves, and dabbed it with a horsehair brush, adding the color to interwoven vines that meandered down a page of Saint Augustine's *City of God*. He cared little whether it was his best work, for images from the sorcerer's tome tormented his thoughts, and the presence of the priest with his condescending gaze only added to Ciarán's unease. A drop of dye spilled onto a verse of beautifully penned Irish script. Swearing under his breath, Ciarán tried to remove the dye with his thumb but only further marred the blessed saint's words.

"Leave it—it'll scrape off," Niall said under his breath.

37

Ciarán shook his head in frustration.

"What's wrong with you?" Niall whispered. "You've looked out of sorts all morning."

"I'm fine," Ciarán said tersely as the sound of footfalls stopped beside his desk. He looked up at the black cassock of Father Gauzlin, who stood leering down at the two monks.

"Out and about last night, were we?" the priest asked.

Ciarán tensed, but Niall looked amused. "Haven't the foggiest notion what you're talking about," he replied.

The priest's eyes flashed with anger. "You two are pushing your luck."

"In case it's news," Niall said, "we Irish have a lot of luck."

Father Gauzlin drew a hissing breath. "All things pass away." Then he continued his excursion down the aisle, peering over the shoulders of the other scribes.

Once the priest was across the room, Ciarán nudged Niall's sleeve. "What if he saw us last night?"

"No chance," Niall said. "If he had, the bishop would have tried to arrest us by now." He leaned closer to Ciarán. "Besides, I and some of the brothers have had quite enough of these Franks. We're going to organize against them. We're gathering before Vespers, at the grove. You need to be there."

"You're mad!" Ciarán hissed. "These are trained soldiers —killers."

Niall shrugged. "And we're Irish. Sounds as though we've got the upper hand. You coming?"

Ciarán looked away, despondent. All this because of Dónall— and, worse, the accusations were true.

Niall clapped Ciarán on the shoulder. "I'll come get you before we go."

An hour before Vespers, Niall and Ciarán made their way through the ground-hugging mist to the grove. The monks had gone there one or two at a time, to avoid alerting anyone that a dozen men were heading uphill for a gathering. Beyond the earthen walls, pairs of soldiers and their mastiffs patrolled the edge of the woods, but Niall was careful to make sure none were near the grove before the brethren headed there. Ciarán glanced around for any sign of Father Gauzlin, but in the thick mist and fading light, the monks' cells looked like shadowy hills, and a gray habit looked much like a black one.

When it was their turn, Niall and Ciarán walked uphill to the edge of the grove. They passed through the ring of ancient trees, treading across a carpet of damp leaves and acorns that were rich with the scents of autumn. To the druids of old, the grove was a sacred temple born of the Earth Mother. Yet Ciarán found it strangely like the oratory, though three times its size and a hundred times as beautiful—a cathedral crafted by God. Its walls were tree trunks, and its ceiling was a canopy of arching branches ablaze with leaves of russet and red. Normally, the grove was a sanctum where monks came to think and pray. But today they came to plot an uprising.

Ciarán was surprised to see so many of his friends, and more surprised to find them armed. Murchad, one of the young black-smiths, gripped his iron hammer, and Fintan, a thickset bookbinder, held a cudgel of ash wood. Senach, a wiry young shepherd, had a shearing knife in his rope belt, and the twin scribes, Áed and Ailil, held long-handled hay forks. A half-dozen older monks joined them, including Bran, Derry's hulking butcher, cleaver in hand, and other scribes and fieldworkers with hatchets, sickles, and staves.

"Ciarán!" Murchad said with a broad grin. "Knew you'd come!"

Ciarán forced back a smile, but his stomach tensed at the sight of these would-be warriors. Bran handed Niall a curved-bladed knife with a hooked spine, used for gutting pigs. It looked as though it could do much the same to a man.

"Glad you're all here," Niall addressed the group. "Because it's time we took back Derry!"

Nods and amens resounded from the monks.

"Last night it hit me," Niall continued, "when I lured two of them into the woods. That's when I realized how we should take them. We'll come at 'em like they did in the days of Cú Chulainn, harassing them at night, stealing their armor and weapons. We'll lure 'em into the woods for the others to find bound and battered, just as they found that Frank two nights ago. We'll move like shadows and make 'em think the spirits of this very grove have come from the Otherworld to haunt them. Me and Murchad will make the first sortie tonight, between Vespers and Nocturns. Then we'll take turns each night after that until these Franks hie off and sail from our shore!"

The monks nodded and clapped, while Bran uttered another amen. But Ciarán shook his head. "And what if they come at us en masse?"

"Then we take a stand!" Niall insisted. Muffled cheers followed his words.

"That's mad!" Ciarán said. "We're monks, not warriors. And yet, you'd risk your lives. But for what? Brother Dónall?"

The monks quieted. "Wouldn't you risk yours for him?" Niall asked.

Ciarán glanced at the leaf-laden ground. "We don't know what happened in France," he said. "What if these charges are true and these men have just cause?"

"Haw!" Bran scoffed.

"Then why did he run?" Ciarán asked.

"Because he's not daft, lad," Bran said. "These black-robed priests are liars, as everyone knows."

Ciarán sighed. "He was standing right beside me when their ship arrived, and then he was gone before the bishop even leveled his first accusation. Dónall knew they'd come for him."

"Listen to yourself!" Niall snapped. "You've known Dónall mac Taidg your whole life."

"How well can we know what *anyone* did twenty years before we were born? And if he's guilty, are we all to fight and die for his sins?"

Niall's face darkened. "We fight because we're brave and we're

Irish, because these Franks have no business coming here and lording it over us, regardless of what Dónall may have done!"

Ciarán stared at his closest friend, unable to summon another retort.

"We're all in," Niall said, "and it starts tonight. You're either with us or you stay out of our way."

Niall stormed from the grove, and the others followed by ones and twos. Ciarán glanced away from his friends. He could feel their disapproving looks prick him like daggers. He waited until they were gone. They didn't know what they were about to do. He should have told them about the tome.

As Ciarán fought back the growing surge of guilt, he heard the shuffle of leaves. His heart jumped, and he spun about, fearful that Father Gauzlin or one of the soldiers had overheard everything the monks had said.

From the shadows between two great oaks, a figure emerged, but it seemed to be robed in gray, not black—the imposing figure of Dónall mac Taidg.

"So, a heretic, am I?" Dónall mac Taidg leaned on his blackened staff. The mist shrouded him like a veil.

For a moment, Ciarán was too stunned to speak. But then his anger flared. "I found the tome hidden in your cell," he said bitterly.

"I figured that was you," Dónall replied. "Didn't think you'd find it, but then, you always were a clever lad."

Ciarán recognized the leather book satchel slung over Dónall's shoulder, the one containing the sorcerer's tome. A chill crawled up his spine. "It's a spell book, isn't it. The one from Reims. Did you kill for it?"

"I'm no murderer, lad. And you have no idea what that book is."

"I've seen the symbols!"

"What you saw," Dónall said, "is an ancient language, older than Noah and the Great Flood, preserved by Maugis d'Aygremont two hundred years ago."

"Was he a sorcerer, too?"

Dónall chuckled. "Hardly. He was one of the twelve paladins of Charlemagne, who recorded the secrets of the Fae."

Ciarán shook his head in disbelief. "The Fae? Then it *is* magic, and you practiced it. That's condemned by the Church."

Dónall growled, "This is not the sorcery spoken of in scripture! It is not the magic of the angels condemned to the abyss, nor the work of demons. This is the stuff of our Celtic heritage—the mysteries of the Tuatha Dé Danann, and Merlin of Britain, and the paladins of Charlemagne. Do you take *those* men to be evil? And what of the three magi who honored our Savior in Bethlehem? Were they sorcerers, too? The symbols you saw may be the language of creation—words that harness a power that, I'm convinced, exists within our immortal souls and can reach out to affect the elements of nature. Whether that power is used for good or for evil is the choice of the man who wields it."

"Yet you've kept this secret all this time."

"How could I expect you or anyone else to understand? It took me years to comprehend it myself."

Ciarán ran a nervous hand through his mist-dampened hair. "What has any of this to do with me? I found some warnings, hidden in another book that came from Saint-Germain-de-Prés. Whoever wrote them suggested *my* life was in danger, too."

"I know," Dónall said. "I went to Áengus this morning, before cockcrow. He told me of the book sent by Brother Remi, an old friend from Reims. I found it on your desk and discovered the messages. But despite what Remi thinks, this has nothing to do with you."

"Then why did he write it?" Ciarán pressed.

"Because Remi suffers from what the Greeks call *paranoia*—he often perceives threats where none exist."

"Aren't these Franks a threat? He could have been warning us about them."

Dónall shook his head. "Perhaps, but I doubt it. Remi mentioned the prophecy, and something that may have happened to our friend Nicolas."

"What prophecy?" Ciarán demanded. "What does it mean?"

"It means, among other things, that I have to go to France to see Remi. To find out what is happening and whether it has anything to do with this black-robed carrion bird of a bishop. But for now, all I want you to do is stay here and keep safe. And restrain your friends, too. Áengus told me that Dub-dá-leithe sent a secret message to the King of Aileach. So by tomorrow, there'll be a host of Irish warriors at Derry's gate. These Franks won't challenge them."

Ciarán drew in a long breath. The thought of the king's men brought a wave of relief, but the need for more answers clamored within him. "Did any of this have to do with my mother?" he finally asked. "The bishop called her a heretic."

Dónall winced at the question.

"It does, doesn't it!"

"Your mother was innocent."

Ciarán reeled. "You lied to me about her?"

"Almost everything you've learned about her is true," Dónall insisted. "She was a nun of Kildare and met your father on a pilgrimage in France. And she loved you more than anything in all the world. She died tragically, but not from a fever. I lied to spare you from that awful truth. Perhaps I was wrong."

Tears stung behind Ciarán's eyes. "How did she die?"

"She was accused of a crime she didn't commit, but I assure you, the truth was of no moment to the black-robed priests who condemned her. She was a victim of an archbishop's inquisition," Dónall said softly, "and was burned at the stake. Just as this Bishop Adémar would do to me now."

Ciarán felt as if the air had been stolen from his lungs. *Heretics* burned at the stake.

For an instant, Ciarán felt guilty about his anger toward the man who had raised him. And yet, Dónall *had* lied—about his mother's death at least, and perhaps about other things. Ciarán wondered if he had it within him to forgive such a betrayal. But then he noticed movement amid the trees, and the soft rustle of paws padding over leaves. Dónall turned and saw it, too. Ten yards away, a mastiff stood watching them. It gave a low, guttural growl.

At the sight of the massive animal, Dónall said, "Stand still. It'll follow me. And remember, do as I've asked." Raising a hand toward the mastiff, Dónall slowly backed away between the two oaks, heading in the direction of the peat bog. The great war dog, suddenly docile, trotted after him.

Ciarán stood dumbfounded as the mastiff disappeared into the mist and shadows. He waited a moment to see if Dónall might return, but as the grove grew darker, Dónall didn't come. Ciarán knew he had to get back, to tell Niall and the others about Abba's message to the king.

Nearing the edge of the grove, he heard the chink of mail. Moments later, six Franks stormed out of the mist-shrouded oaks. Two of the soldiers held blazing birch-bark torches, while the others had drawn swords. Father Gauzlin emerged from their ranks. And behind him strode the towering figure of Bishop Adémar of Blois. Torchlight reflected off the silver crucifix around his neck and cast his face in a sinister glow. His eyes held predatory gleam, while those of Father Gauzlin burned with sanctimonious triumph.

"As I said, my lord," the priest announced, "we counted thirteen of them going to the grove, but only twelve returned. And this one who lingered is chief among the troublemakers. I swear to you, he's up to something."

Ciarán shivered. Between the bishop's thin lips flashed the ghost of a smile. "Ah, yes, the whelp." In the torchlight, the bishop's eyes narrowed as if he were studying every pore on Ciarán's face. Ciarán stood too alarmed to speak.

"I can see the trouble in your eyes," the bishop said. "You know where Dónall mac Taidg is, don't you? Tell me where to find him."

Ciarán clenched his jaw.

"Tell me now!" the bishop growled. He grabbed Ciarán's right arm. Ciarán tried to pull away, but the man's long fingers felt like blacksmith's tongs clamping onto his flesh. Ciarán started to cry out under the bruising grasp, when another thought overwhelmed the pain. *If I confess, Dónall dies.*

"It's time you rejected his lies and saved your own soul," the bishop said.

"I don't know where he is," Ciarán replied. "And I haven't seen him."

The bishop's gaze seemed to bore into Ciarán's thoughts, but he stared back, praying his eyes did not reveal the truth. From the woods, in the direction of the peat bog, came the shouting of men, joined by the barking of dogs.

"We have him!" a Frank yelled from the woods beyond the grove.

Bishop Adémar cocked one brow. "Sadly, you must still believe him. But no matter, it appears we have what we came for."

Ciarán grimaced, praying the bishop was wrong.

The bishop turned to follow his men, who rushed across the grove toward the call. Then he glanced back at Ciarán. "Before Nocturns, your mentor will burn."

Ciarán tasted bile in his throat as the bishop strode away, leaving him with Father Gauzlin. The priest flicked his wrist, and the two remaining soldiers seized Ciarán by his arms. "Let me go!" he cried, struggling, but the mailed gloves held him tight.

"Unfortunately, there's no more need for you," the priest said, taking a long dagger from one of the soldiers. Ciarán shrank back, but they had him.

Father Gauzlin pressed the dagger against Ciarán's neck. "Where's your Irish luck now?"

CHAPTER 7

FIRE AND FURY

The moment he saw the mastiff, Dónall knew that the soldiers could not be far behind. He had run down the trail that led to the peat bog, a winding pathway through dense woods, crisscrossed by fallen limbs green with moss. From the near darkness ahead came the sounds of men moving through the woods, confirming his fears.

Spotting a briar thicket at the foot of a gnarled old oak, he tucked the book satchel deep beneath the briars, in a hollow formed between two great roots of the ancient tree, and then plunged his staff into the thicket. Next, he drew the short sword from its leather scabbard hidden beneath his habit, and tossed it into the briars.

Down the path to his left, leaves rustled. Dónall darted to the right, with the dog following obediently behind him. It was the same mastiff who had heard the Fae word of power Dónall uttered two days ago. He had no idea how animals understood that primal, elemental language older than man or why they respected those who could speak it—only that they did. The dog posed no threat to Dónall, but not so his human pursuers. Ahead of him, two Franks emerged from the mist with drawn swords.

"We have him!" one of the Franks cried in Latin.

Dónall spun around to bolt in the opposite direction, but a third soldier burst from the mist and barreled into Dónall, sending him crashing into a slick of leaves and mud. He landed hard on his left shoulder. The Frank peered down, holding his torch high, showing a grin of rotten teeth amid an untrimmed beard. Shoulder throbbing, Dónall heard the noise of more men approaching. In moments, three more Franks came down the trail, followed by four more and then a taller man with a more stately stride, clad in a bishop's robes: Adémar of Blois.

Under his breath, Dónall whispered a prayer for deliverance, and wondered for an instant whether he should have kept his weapons. But against so many men, they would have done little but hasten his own death.

The bearded soldier grabbed Dónall by his habit and yanked him to his feet. Clutching his aching shoulder, Dónall eyed the bishop. "I don't remember you from Reims."

Adémar of Blois made a faint smile. "I was not there," he replied. "But I have spoken to those who were. I know of your crimes."

"It's been twenty years since I was in France," Dónall said. "What brings you now?"

Adémar's expression darkened. "I want the Book of Maugis d'Aygremont."

"Why has the Church taken such an interest in a paladin of Charlemagne?"

"You know what that book contains," Adémar snapped. "Tell me where it is!" He punctuated his words with a stinging backhand across Dónall's face. The blow snapped Dónall's head to the side.

"I know you have it!" Adémar said through gritted teeth.

The coppery taste of blood filled Dónall's mouth, and he spat it at the bishop's feet.

Adémar stepped back as the bearded Frank bashed a mailed fist into Dónall's ribs. A rib cracked, and Dónall felt as if the breath had been sucked from his lungs.

"Tell me now!" Adémar roared. "Else, you'll burn before Nocturns."

"In . . . my cell," Dónall wheezed.

"You lie," Adémar replied. "We've searched it thoroughly."

"It's hidden in the walls," Dónall said, gasping for a second breath. "In a space between the corbelled stones."

Adémar glanced at one of his men, who just shrugged. "Show me," Adémar demanded. "And the book had better be there."

The bishop turned back toward the monastery as the bearded Frank pushed Dónall forward. His left side shrieked with pain. The Frank brought his face near and said, his breath reeking of ale and rotting teeth, "You'll burn regardless."

Dónall gave a weary sigh. For unless a miracle happened in short order, the Frank was right.

WITHIN THE OAK-CIRCLED GROVE, the priest's dagger bit into the flesh of Ciarán's neck. Father Gauzlin's grin widened, while the two soldiers held his victim tight. With another flick of the blade, it would all be over. A scream gathered in Ciarán's throat, but before it could erupt, another cry overtook it. A Gaelic cry.

Father Gauzlin spun toward the sound as the burled head of a cudgel smashed into his jaw. Blood and teeth arced across Ciarán's feet and onto the ground, followed by the flailing priest. Over Ciarán's shoulder, a blacksmith's hammer clanged against the helmet of one of his captors, whose arms fell instantly limp, releasing Ciarán from his grasp. The second Frank made a mewling noise as the pole of a pitchfork cracked into his groin from behind, practically lifting him off his feet. Niall's fist finished the job, sending the Frank sprawling onto the carpet of acorns and leaves.

Around Ciarán, twelve Irish monks grinned with the thrill of battle. Fintan the bookbinder stood triumphantly over Father Gauzlin, who moaned but did not try to rise. Murchad gripped the hammer that had felled the first Frank, while Áed held the tines of his pitchfork above the second Frank's throat.

"We saw 'em skulking their way up to the grove," Niall said. "Figured you were still up here."

Ciarán didn't know what to say. Then a desperate thought overwhelmed him. "They have Dónall!"

"He's *here*?" Niall asked.

"He came to me in the grove," Ciarán said urgently. "They caught him downhill, near the bog. They're going to burn him. We have to save him."

Niall glanced at the others. "You're damn right, we do," Bran replied.

"That's what I like to hear," Niall said, exchanging his knife for one of the Franks' sword. Bran grabbed the other Frank's blade and led them in a silent, loping charge toward the bog.

They could hear the Franks rustling through the woods, speaking in their native tongue and making more noise than a drove of cattle. From the direction of the sound, it was clear they were heading back toward the fields just outside the monastery's earthen wall. Night had fallen over Derry, and Ciarán feared they might lose their way through the trees in the darkness, wasting precious time. He was following behind Murchad, who vaulted easily over a fallen tree on the narrow path, when something glimmered weakly in the moonlight. He stopped and peered at the roots of a twisted oak.

"What're you doing?" said Fintan beside him. "Let's go."

Ciarán reached down and picked up a short sword with a leaf-shaped blade—the very one from Dónall's cell. And from the briar thicket poked the tip of a blackened staff, and tucked away beside it was a leather bundle.

"Wait!" Ciarán hissed.

Fintan stopped, and Niall doubled back. "What is it?"

"Dónall must have tossed these away before they found him."

"That's *Dónall's*?" Niall asked, marveling at the weapon, which was more finely wrought than the Frankish blades.

Ciarán slung the leather book satchel over his shoulder, still feeling uneasy about what it held inside, and picked up the staff with his free hand. "He didn't want the Franks to find these."

Ahead, Murchad called out softly, "I see 'em!" Ciarán and Niall rushed downhill to where the monks had gathered in a small

49

clearing amid a copse of birches. "They're heading along the edge of the woods," Murchad said, "back toward the monastery."

Ciarán peered through the trees. Farther downhill, the glow of the Franks' torches illuminated a band of ten soldiers and the bishop, along with three of the huge mastiffs and their gray-robed prisoner. They moved through one of the fields, beside a half-dozen haystacks that rose like hills in the darkness. The Franks were nearly as many as his twelve brethren and himself, yet the thought of attacking a band of trained fighters put a knot in his stomach. He had never used a weapon like the one he now held, nor had the thought ever occurred to him, for Church law forbade any monk or priest to shed blood.

"What do we do now?" he asked Niall.

Niall knelt on one knee, watching the Franks intently. "Like I said, we take a stand. Just like Saint Columcille would've done." He glanced at his friends, making eye contact with each of them. "We'll move through the woods, along the edge of the fields, quiet as we can until we get close. And once we're a stone's throw away, we'll charge 'em."

"We're going to stay and fight?" Fintan asked, his pudgy face etched with concern.

"Only as long as we have to," Niall replied. "You and Ciarán try to get Dónall. Once you do, head for the woods; we'll follow you. We can lose 'em in there."

"Those dogs will be trouble," Bran said.

"It's no different than protecting the sheep from wolves." Niall nodded toward the twins. "That's what those hay forks are for." He rose to his feet with a resolute look in his eye. "Now, let's go."

Gripping Dónall's staff in one hand and clutching the short sword in the other, he hesitated in his first step as Niall took off, scurrying deftly over the fallen branches, his sandals landing softly with each footfall. Murchad and Bran were less adroit, rustling dead leaves with every stride and snapping a twig now and then. Ciarán felt the blood rush to his cheeks as he charged after his friends, darting around trees and over deadfalls. Rushing through the darkening woods, the band of monks sounded like deer running from a wolfhound.

They were still forty yards from the Franks when the first soldier spun toward the noise. The soldiers with torches held them high as an alarmed chatter broke out among the Franks.

They can hear us, Ciarán realized as he strode to keep up with Niall, *but they can't see us in these shadows.* Ahead, Niall slowed to a halt and waited for the others to gather around him, while a chill breeze soughed through the trees.

"Let's show 'em what happens when you cross the Irish," Niall told them. "On the count of three."

Around him, the monks drew nervous breaths. "One," Niall said, as some made the sign of the cross. Bran recited a psalm: *"Vindicate us, O God, and defend our cause."*

"Two," Niall counted. Ciarán's heart drummed in his chest.

"Three!"

Another Gaelic cry rose from the woods, and Niall raised his sword. "Columcille!" he yelled.

Murchad led them, joined by Bran and Niall, while Ciarán stayed close to Fintan, searching for the quickest path to Dónall. They bounded down the grassy hillside, past two of the haystacks, but the Franks stood ready with swords drawn, forming an arc around the bishop and the burly Frank who held Dónall. The thrill of danger surged through Ciarán's veins as the monks closed on the mailed soldiers. Then the Franks unleashed their mastiffs. The first beast barreled into Senach and sent the young monk flailing backward, his screams blending with the dog's vicious snarls. Áed set his pitchfork, and the second mastiff pounced. Skewered on the tines, it howled in pain but took down Áed under its weight while, beside him, his brother fell to the third dog. The remaining monks collided with the wall of Franks, and around Ciarán everything became a flash of chaos and blood.

One of the Franks collapsed under a blow from Murchad's hammer, but then a sword blade ran the brawny monk through, and his eyes froze in shock. Bran cleaved through the arm of another Frank as, beside him, Niall ducked the blade of his nearest attacker and swung his sword upward between the Frank's legs. Then he lunged toward another soldier on the left, who had cut down Brother Ewan, one of older monks. Niall's blade sliced across the back of the Frank's neck, and as the soldier fell, Ciarán saw a clear path to Dónall, who gazed wide-eyed at the scene before him. Fintan, too, charged through the gap, smashing his cudgel into the face of Dónall's captor. Dónall, still weaponless, drove his elbow into the base of the same Frank's jaw, sending him crumpling to the ground.

"Well done, lads!" Dónall shouted as he grabbed his black staff from Ciarán's outstretched hand.

Beside Ciarán, Fintan spun to face another soldier, then doubled over as the Frank's sword caught him with a broad, arcing sweep. Ciarán watched in horror as viscera spilled from the opening onto the ground. Then a battle cry sounded behind them, snapping Ciarán back into the moment. He whirled to see a dozen more Franks charging up the hillside.

"Look out, lad!" Dónall shouted.

To Ciarán's right, a soldier lunged at him. Ciarán pivoted away, and the blade swept wide, its tip landing in Ciarán's side. The force of the blow sent him tumbling hard onto the damp grass. He groped for the wound, fearing what he would find. But his palm felt leather instead of bleeding flesh. The blade had caught the book satchel, and while it had scored the leather from top to bottom, it had pierced no further than the flap.

The Frank hit the ground next, his nose smashed by a whack from Dónall's staff. As Ciarán picked himself up off the grass, he saw Niall ten yards away, still holding his ground, with two Franks lying wounded at his feet. He fought a tall Frank, and Ciarán gasped when he realized it was the bishop. Adémar of Blois had grabbed one of the fallen Franks' sword and now parried Niall's blows as deftly as any skilled warrior.

The bishop's face burned with rage. "The days of Gog and Magog are upon us!" he shouted above the clamor of battle. "When death and damnation shall be the price of heresy! And the time of prophecy is nigh!"

Ciarán gasped at the bishop's words, so similar to Brother Remi's warning. Then the bishop's blade arced out with a cleaving strike. "No!" Ciarán yelled.

Niall's body staggered backward, a yawning red wound opening from his shoulder to his waist. Bran stepped into Niall's place, but the bishop swung hard, and the hulking monk fell with a feeble cry. More Franks filled the gap between the bishop and the remaining monks, who fought and screamed, falling fast to the soldiers' blades and their mastiffs. *This cannot be happening!* Ciarán thought. It seemed more nightmare than waking reality, and in a heartbeat, he wondered whether he had passed into the realm of dreams. For around him the air sizzled, and the blades of grass stood on end as if being drawn upward, where, in the twilight, ghostly blue flames wreathed the tops of the haystacks, like the fire of Saint Elmo before a storm.

"Get behind me, lad," Dónall commanded.

Ciarán turned to find Dónall holding a torch in one hand and his black staff in the other. Dónall uttered a string of words that were neither Irish nor Latin, and, as if in response, the torch's flame leaped to the tip of his staff, which flared with a plume of fire. Ciarán retreated behind Dónall, hardly believing his eyes. A half-dozen Franks stood before them, swords drawn, looking in awe at the fiery weapon. Dónall stepped forward, his face a mask of fury. "Stand back!" he yelled.

A bearded Frank lunged at Dónall, who bellowed another string of strange foreign words like a haunting song. The staff's tip flared again as it met the bearded Frank's chest.

"Now who burns?" Dónall growled.

The Frank's eyes opened wide as the flame raced up his beard as if on dry straw, spread to his hair, and ignited the jerkin beneath his mail coat. A ghastly wailing cry rose from his lips, and his flesh blackened, and in a heartbeat his writhing body erupted into a human bonfire.

Dónall tossed aside the burned-out torch. "My sword, lad!" he called to Ciarán.

As the remaining Franks backed away in terror, Ciarán handed

Dónall the leaf-shaped blade. Dónall pointed the sword at the burning man and uttered another foreign verse. At once, the gentle evening breeze howled into a violent wind that fanned the flames, blowing jets of fire toward the remaining Franks. It was as if Dónall were directing the wind with the wave of his leaf-shaped blade. The hair of one Frank caught fire. Another struggled to shed his brown cloak, now covered with licking, hungry flames.

Ciarán watched in dread and awe. The burning Frank had crumpled to the ground and now resembled a Beltane fire on May Day.

The soldiers began to retreat, but the bishop cried out, pointing a long finger at Ciarán. "He has the book!"

Ciarán's heart skipped a beat, but then he noticed Dónall, who had thrust his burning staff into one of the haystacks—through the wet outer layer and into the dry stuff—murmuring more of the haunting words in a steady stream. The haystack exploded into flames. Five of the Franks charged, spurred on by the bishop. But then Dónall swept his blade before him, and a screaming wind followed, blasting the conflagration onto the other stacks. Flames rose high in the air, and the first haystack collapsed to form a raging wall of fire at the feet of the charging Franks. A shower of embers erupted into the sky, and Ciarán had to back away from the searing heat as the inferno's roar drowned out even the panicked cries of the soldiers.

"What about our brothers?" Ciarán asked desperately.

"There's nothing we can do for them now," Dónall said. "In a few moments, every monk in Derry will run to put out this blaze. They'll outnumber these Franks ten to one, but we can't stay. My display here has given that bishop all the evidence he needs to convict me. And for helping me, you'll be just as guilty in the eyes of the Church." He yanked Ciarán toward the woods.

"What happens now?" Ciarán asked.

"I had Áengus send word to Rián mac Fadden. He and his curach will be waiting for us a half league down the river."

They hurried through the woods while the fire roared behind them. Ciarán stopped to catch his breath. "But where will we go?"

"I must go to Paris," Dónall said. "And I suppose you're coming with me now."

Ciarán stood speechless.

"We have to move, lad!" Dónall barked. "That bishop is hell-bent on getting his hands on the book you're holding, and he'll find a way to get his men around those flames."

Dónall pulled him deeper into the woods, and Ciarán lacked the strength to resist. A tremendous emptiness washed over him as he watched more smoke billow up in the distance, where his friends lay dead. Murchad and Fintan and the twins. And Niall, his dearest friend of all. *Killed for what? A book and the perhaps heretical secrets it contained?*

By the time Ciarán and Dónall reached the edge of the bog, his eyes stung with tears. He struggled to catch his breath and prayed that Paris held some answer. For if not, all his friends had just died in vain.

PART TWO

The Nephilim were on the earth in those days—and also afterward—when the sons of God went into the daughters of men . . .

—Genesis 6:4

CHAPTER 8
THE WOMAN IN WHITE

In the heart of the land the Romans once called Gaul, Alais of Selles gazed across the river Cher. A bleak winter was coming. She could feel it.

Even though she was not a year past twenty-one, she no longer felt young, for these past days had worn on her so much that she felt as thin and ragged as a threadbare cloak. She tied back her raven hair to keep it from whipping in the bitter wind, and sighed as she looked back on the small collection of cottages, hovels, and barns. Her husband was lord of this land, and lay abbot of the limestone abbey that stood atop the squat hill across the fields from their manor. But for how long would he continue? She gazed up at the sky, as gray as her own eyes and thick with the coming storm, and felt the constant ache in her chest. When it first began, she had prayed to Saint Radegonde until her eyes were red and swollen from the tears. But her pleas for the saint's intercession had gone unanswered, leaving her to wonder why the heavenly father let such things happen.

Prior Ragno insisted that Geoffrey's condition was a sign of pestilence, proof that the Four Horsemen now rode these lands and that the end of days was near. If this was true, Alais feared the day that the pale rider would come to Selles. And at times, she could hear the pounding of his pale steed's hooves in the borderlands of her dreams.

Even worse terrors would follow as the millennium approached, Prior Ragno had warned. Darkness would cloak the sun, the moon would disappear, and the stars would fall from the heavens. The Antichrist would reign over the earth, and the land would burn with fire until at last Christ himself returned from the clouds, riding his white horse, with an army of angels in his wake. Only then would the living and the dead be judged and the righteous be carried to paradise. Prior Ragno had spoken of this day with trills of ecstasy in his voice, pining for the time when the wicked would finally be punished. But Alais could not fathom such things—or, indeed, muster such hope. The trial she now endured was harder than anything she had ever faced. And as she looked out over the fields of Selles, the horizon held no savior on a white horse, charging to her aid—only a solitary black-robed monk, crossing the field from the abbey.

And she feared the news he brought as she feared the pale rider himself.

The abbey's infirmarer, Brother Thadeus, climbed the hill to the edge of Alais' garden. Nearing his fiftieth winter, he was a frail man, whose beaklike nose protruding beneath overgrown brows gave him the aspect of a merlin or a kestrel, though he was perhaps the gentlest man she had ever known. Thadeus regarded her with sympathetic eyes.

"He wants to see you," he said.

Alais' heart skipped a beat. "Is he improved?"

Thadeus shook his head. "All we can do is bandage the sores."

She touched her fingertips to her lips. "What of the salve you made from goat weed?"

"Perhaps it eases the pain, but . . ."

"Brother Thadeus, *please.*" She grabbed his habit. "I feared worse news when I saw you, but now, if he is lucid, if he still has strength?" Her eyes grew wide. "It means he's fighting it. Geoffrey is a strong man. If anyone could . . ."

60

Thadeus took her hands from his habit and embraced her. "Alais, he burns with this disease. I promise you, I will use all the medicinal skills I possess, but there is only so much we can do." He let her go but looked into her eyes, which welled with tears. "Our prayers to Saint Eustace may be the best medicine now. You've been praying, child, have you not?"

"I'm all out of prayers," she sobbed.

"Then you should try to summon a few more, my dear. Sometimes, prayer is all we have."

She followed Thadeus down the path toward the abbey. Across the nearby fields, smoke wisped from the chimneys of thatch-roofed cottages. Behind the village stood trees with spidery branches, their leaves long since stripped by the autumn winds. Alais noticed the quiet. A dog bayed in the distance, but that was all. Few villagers were about. The fields had been harvested, and the wheat, rye, barley, and beets had been stored for the winter, while the pigs and cattle deemed too weak or too old to survive the coming snows had been slaughtered and their meat packed in barrels of salt.

Not counting the sixty monks who lived at the abbey, there were nearly a hundred families in Selles, with wives and children and elderly folk who needed care. These were the lives Geoffrey had protected against raiders and famine, which had touched these lands twice in the six years she had lived here. Alais could not understand this great burden slipping onto her narrow shoulders, let alone grapple with the terrible loss that would accompany it.

It was never supposed to be like this.

She had been born a child of Aquitaine, the richest province in Gaul. Her grandfather was the third William, called Towhead for the pale flaxen color of his hair. He was both count of Poitiers and duke of Aquitaine, and her grandmother was the daughter of Rollo, then duke of Normandy. Her father, Odo, was cousin to the fourth William, called Iron Arm, who had ruled Aquitaine for nearly thirty years. William Iron Arm had strengthened his alliances by marrying his sister to Hugh Capet, the late king of France and father of the current king, Robert, and by arranging his own marriage to Emma, daughter of the count of Blois, who was lord of neighboring

Touraine. Alais' mother, Adelais, too, had been bound in a political marriage—a gift from her father, the count of Toulouse, who was currying favor with the house of Poitiers. Marriage, Alais had learned at a young age, was the way rich and powerful men enhanced their wealth and power. So it was predestined that she would someday be given in marriage to a man she had barely met, for reasons that had nothing to do with love. And that was the problem she always had with the situation.

Being of noble birth, Alais had lived a carefree life. She spent much of her youth in the palace of Poitiers, her family's ancestral home. There she would play in the gardens with their tiled Roman fountains and stroll with her family down the streets of the ancient city, in the shadow of its towering Roman walls. Outside the city, Alais and her sister, Adeline, would play hide-and-seek in the vine-yards lining the hillsides that sloped down to the river Clain, or amid the ruins of the old Roman baths or the ancient amphitheater just south of the city. The amphitheater, with its archways, tunnels, and broken pillars, provided many of the best hiding places. These gave Adeline, who was often the seeker, fits while Alais giggled under her breath or dreamed of ancient times when poets and actors once graced the theater's stage, performing for highborn Roman ladies who laughed and clapped and sipped wine from silver cups.

It was during one such game of hide-and-seek, one May after-noon when she was eight, that Alais learned the legend of Saint Radegonde. After wandering far from the amphitheater, Alais sneaked back through the city gate and ducked into the convent of Sainte-Croix. It was the perfect hiding place, she thought—too perfect, perhaps, and she wondered if Adeline would ever find her. But there was also the problem of the black-robed nuns, who walked the convent's halls in silent contemplation. Alais must hide from them, too, which, in the moment, meant descending a dimly lit stairwell that ended in a dark, narrow chamber. She was not scared of the dark, and this seemed as good a hiding place as any. A large stone slab of some type lay in the center of the chamber, and running her hands over it, she found that it was carved and polished. It was a bas-relief of a woman, slender and beautiful—a woman fit to be a queen.

She jumped when bony fingers grabbed her shoulder from behind.

"What do you think you're doing here, child?"

In the dim light penetrating from the stairwell, Alais could make out the withered features of a nun as old as her grandmother. But despite all the deep creases and wrinkles, the face looked peaceful, not angry.

"I didn't mean anything," Alais said, shaking. She tried to pull away, but the old nun held her firmly.

"You're one of the children from the palace, aren't you? Have you come to pay respect to Saint Radegonde?"

Alais looked at her sheepishly.

"That's unfortunate. A girl like you could learn a lot from her. Do you *want* to know?"

Still fearful about having been caught where she ought not to be, Alais simply nodded.

"Well, child, she was a princess of Thuringia, a kingdom near Saxony, some four hundred years ago," the old nun said. "But being a princess is not all wonder and magic as you young girls suppose. No, a princess's life is never her own, and when Radegonde's father was killed by her own uncle, it was men's lust for power, not love or romance, that came to rule her life. To kill the king, her uncle had allied with Clothaire, the Merovingian king of the Franks—a monster if ever there was one. Her uncle and Clothaire betrayed each other, but it was Clothaire who won, and as a prize he took Radegonde as his queen.

"Now, one day, Queen Radegonde summoned the courage to flee her husband. He pursued her, of course, his rage burning like an inferno. He stormed across the land on his black steed, but she hid in a field of oats, where she prayed for God's mercy. And do you know what happened then?"

Alais shook her head.

"A *miracle*," the old nun said. "The oats, which were already tall and broad, sprang up around her and grew taller yet. They covered her completely, and even the women who sowed the oats could swear they never saw Radegonde in the field. Clothaire rode on. Radegonde was free. And she came here to Poitiers and founded this convent, where she kept a shard of our Savior's holy cross and protected the city for the rest of her days. But none of this would have happened if not for her courage—her courage and her faith in God."

That was how Alais came to know the abbess of Sainte-Croix and Radegonde, the "queen saint," the patroness of Poitiers.

Ever since that day, the abbess had invited Alais to visit the tomb and light candles for the queen saint. There Alais would pray and wish that she might live a happy and carefree life, for it was the only life she knew. And that she would marry a man for love—a romantic love, like that the poets wrote of—and live free of the sort of tribulations that Saint Radegonde had endured.

Alais looked up at the gray sky and sighed, for those had been the wishes of a young girl. And with the passing years, she realized how foolish they were.

~

CAREFULLY STEPPING over a pat of ox dung as she followed Thadeus up the path to the abbey, Alais thought back to the time, six years ago, when her father arranged Adeline's marriage to Renaud, a Burgundian lord nearly twice her age. Alais would never forget the man's arrival at the palace. He was fat and brutish, with oily hair as long as a woman's, and a stubbly beard that collected the grease and crumbs from his hoggish eating. Alais blanched at his ill manners, for he wolfed his food as indecorously as the kitchen dogs. She shuddered when she imagined Adeline on their wedding night, spread-eagled beneath him for the first time, pinned by his rolls of fat as he ravaged her, grunting like a boar. It was as if Clothaire himself had come to Poitiers in all his monstrous barbarity.

In the days leading up to the wedding, Alais had prayed that her sister would summon the courage of Saint Radegonde and flee. But Adeline never did. She married Renaud at the palace in Poitiers and left with him the next morning for Burgundy. Adeline had written letters since then (for their father had insisted early on that his daughters learn to read and write), but Alais found no joy in those letters, and each one troubled her more than the last. For as the years passed, Alais knew that her own time to wed was coming.

Her time came three years later. The man's name was Geoffrey, the lord of Selles-sur-Cher, and even though he was not rich, he was a cousin of Emma of Blois, and a supporter of the king. This made him suitable enough in her father's eyes for the hand of his second daughter in marriage. The Lord of Selles was said to be thirty-four, more than twice her age. In Alais' mind's eye, he had already become an ogre—a Clothaire—before he ever arrived in Poitiers. Just the thought of him terrified her. Some days she prayed that when the time came, Saint Radegonde would give her the courage to flee and the miracle she would need to escape. On other days, her hope would fail. She would be better off drowning in the Clain than submitting to a man like Adeline's Renaud. At times, anger overrode her sadness. Her father and mother had made this decision. They had robbed her of her chance for love, the love of her daydreams at Saint Radegonde's tomb. *True* love.

Alais would never forget the time she first saw Geoffrey. It was a cold day in late September, when the leaves had begun to turn. Geoffrey and three of his men had ridden to the palace gates. He wore a wool riding cloak over his mail vest, a broadsword at his waist, and heavy leather boots—hardly the pretentious clothing of a man like Renaud. And to her surprise, he sat his horse well and did not seem an onerous burden to the spirited roan charger. In fact, Lord Geoffrey looked rather trim, even slight, atop his mount.

This was not at all what Alais had expected. Nor were his eyes. When he turned to look at her, she saw them: blue like the river beneath a bright sky. But he was old, and his nose was wide and crooked, as if it had been broken more than once. His cheeks were sunken, and his short-cropped beard was heavily flecked with gray. He looked her over, from her face to the toes of her sandaled feet, before opening his mouth to speak. But Alais had nothing to say to him. She *wanted* nothing to say. And before a word could escape his lips, she turned away and hurried down the narrow streets, back to Saint Radegonde's tomb, for one last chance to summon the courage to make her own destiny.

Hours later, the abbess found her, clinging to the relief of Saint Radegonde, her eyes red from sobbing. "You must go now, child," the abbess had said. "You can pray for the saint's protection, but you cannot defy your father's will. He is outside with his men. You must go back." Alais shook her head vehemently, but she felt worn. Broken. The abbess lifted her off the sarcophagus, and Alais' dreams of courage evaporated.

They were married the next day. In the dim and crowded cathedral, the somber rite seemed more funeral than wedding. That night, in one of the palace bedchambers, when he took her as his wife, she trembled and winced at the pain. She fought back the tears when she touched where he had entered her, and her fingers glistened with blood. But through it all, Geoffrey had been gentle, and the experience had been far from the violent ravishment she feared. Still, she felt nothing for this man who was her husband—only contempt for her father. And her mother. And, above all, for herself, for she was not the strong young woman she had hoped to become. She was no better than Adeline.

Until one day when her courage returned on a muddy road near the Anglin River. The day her miracle happened.

It was the fourth day after Geoffrey's party had left Poitiers following the wedding. Geoffrey and his men had stopped to water and rest their horses. The men were fretting about the dark storm clouds filling the sky and turning the bright fall day almost to night. Thunder rumbled in the distance, and the next village was still a full league away, perhaps more. For her part, Alais did not care if it poured all day and night, even if it should flood the land, as in Noah's time, and drown these men whom she hardly knew.

She had barely spoken to her husband, who seemed content to give her room. Maybe he was being kind, or maybe it was because he didn't care for her at all—at least, until the sun set and he desired to have his way with her again. She knew she had not been a good wife. But why would she be, when she was not in love?

The wind whipped up, rustling through the wheat fields bordering the road. Alais had no idea who farmed these lands, for there was no cottage or barn in sight. Just her and four foolish men worried about the rain. One of the horses' shoe had come loose, and the four men gathered around it like young boys fixated on a new toy. She half hoped the horse might kick one of them in the face. But soon she found her gaze and her thoughts drifting over the wheat field, which rippled like waves on the sea. And then Alais saw her: the woman in white.

Deep within the field, she seemed to float above the wheat like Christ himself on the Sea of Galilee.

Alais' first reaction was horror, as if she beheld some terrible apparition. But she stifled the cry that threatened to rip from her throat, and stared in awe at the ethereal figure in the distance. There was something about the figure—not ghostly, but regal. The folds of her white dress billowed, and her hair floated like spun silver on the breeze. She was slender yet tall and strong, like the statues the Romans had built of Diana or Venus. Like a queen.

Like Radegonde.

Alais trembled, and her heart began to race. She glanced back at the men. Not one of them noticed her. She felt the breeze calling her. She searched for the courage that until now had eluded her, but this time it was different. The woman in white beckoned her. *Radegonde . . .* This time, the courage was there, and summoning every ounce of it, Alais stepped off the road. She entered the field, brushing back the wheat stalks, each as high as her waist, and started toward the woman, who held Alais firmly in her gaze. Trepid steps hastened to a trot, then to a run. The wheat parted. Whether it was the wind or something else, she did not know. The woman stood just a few paces ahead. There was something about her—not only an unearthly beauty, but an *agelessness*.

"Saint Radegonde?" Alais stammered.

The woman said nothing but gazed at Alais as if she were measuring the worth of this scrawny girl who stood before her.

"Have you answered my prayers?" Alais asked breathlessly.

But the woman looked past her. Hooves pounded over the field.

Alais glanced over her shoulder to see Geoffrey's roan charger galloping through the wheat. Gripping its reins, he leaned forward in the saddle, like Clothaire himself.

"Cover me with the wheat!" Alais shrieked. "Take me from here!"

"Not now," the woman said in a voice like the wind.

"Please!" Alais sobbed, burying her face in her hands.

The woman responded with a single word. *"Choose."*

Bewildered, Alais looked up, but the woman was gone as if, with her last word, she had vanished in the wind.

Alais gasped. Geoffrey was nearly upon her. Her only instinct was to run. She bolted deeper into the field, yet the wheat stalks in her path no longer parted. Rather, their bristly beards caught at her clothing so that she must fight her way through.

Behind her, hoofbeats thumped louder.

She stumbled to the ground, certain that he would strike her or ride her down beneath his mount.

The charger burst through a wall of wheat and was almost on her when Geoffrey reined it back. He dismounted, his face as stormy as the sky behind it.

"Am I so terrifying to you that you would run off in the middle of nowhere?"

Alais could not find the words to answer. Had he not seen the woman in white?

"I am your husband!" he growled. "Your father gave me your hand in marriage. It is what he decided."

Sobbing, Alais shook her head. "It is not what *I* decided."

"Perhaps, but in time . . . who knows? I will be faithful to my vows, Alais, and will always protect you."

"Should not marriage be for love?"

"You may grow to love me." Geoffrey reached out his hand to help her off the ground, but Alais recoiled.

"I cannot love you."

"How do you know, when you have not tried?"

The sky rumbled, and the rain came—a few wet drops at first, growing quickly into a seething torrent. It drenched Alais' hair and dress and streamed down her face.

"Come," he said, forcing a smile, "before we both drown."

"I might prefer that," she spat.

Geoffrey sighed. "Alais, I will not take a wife by force. So if you cannot stand me, then so be it. I can take you back to your father. We could have our marriage annulled. I will swear the union was never consummated."

She looked at him in sheer bafflement. She could see in his eyes that he meant his words. But would the next time be any different? Indeed, might her father's next prospect be a brute like Renaud, who would have beaten her in this field, rather than the man who offered her this humane choice? For that was what it was, she realized: a choice.

Choose. The word echoed in her mind.

She found herself struggling with this newfound freedom. Had Geoffrey been anything but kind to her? She looked into his eyes and saw the blue of a summer sky, not the darkness of the storm. Cautiously she took his hand and let him help her to her feet.

Geoffrey lifted her into the saddle and began leading the horse back to the road. "When we reach the road," he said, "just tell me which direction to turn."

One last time, Alais searched the wheat field for any sign of the woman in white, yet she saw nothing but sheets of rain. She rode in silence, deep in thought, until they reached the road, where Geoffrey's three men-at-arms waited.

She turned to her husband, whose face looked pained with anticipation.

"Turn east," she said. "Take me to Selles."

~

69

As Alais followed Brother Thadeus up the broken path to the abbey, she realized how far things had come. Yet it still seemed like only yesterday when she awoke one April morning and found herself in a state she had never been: in love. Not the love of her girlish dreams, but a mature love—a realization that Geoffrey of Selles had become the most precious thing in her life. A man who adored her, honored her, who had lived up to the promise he made in that wheat field by the Anglin River—the place where she made the choice that changed her life. At the time, she had not known what brought her to that decision. A feeling, perhaps? Yet it was a decision she would never regret, even though her love for him now brought such sorrow.

They passed through the open gateway in the abbey's earthen wall and headed to the infirmary, a small stone structure set off from the cloister and surrounding buildings. When Geoffrey first became ill, he insisted the monks move him here. Alais had begged him to stay at their manor, where she could care for him, but Geoffrey refused to contaminate their marital bed, even though Alais had shown no symptoms of the terrible disease. Thadeus had suspected the disease was Saint Anthony's fire, but he didn't know for certain. Alais did not care about its name, only that it was killing the man she loved.

Thadeus opened the infirmary's narrow wooden door and led her inside. Gagging at the stench, she brought her hands to her mouth, fighting the urge to vomit. "It's getting worse, I know," Thadeus whispered to her. "But it will pass in a moment."

She stepped into the cramped room. Prior Ragno was there, standing beside the bed. In it lay her husband, covered to his chest in blankets. Stained bandages wrapped his arms and hands, and the sores had spotted more of his face, around his cheeks and neck. Alais choked back a sob. It was spreading. Her eyes caught his, those beautiful blue eyes that were the windows to her husband's soul.

A tear ran down Alais' cheek. He was wrapped in so many bandages that she could no longer see the tips of his fingers, but she took his hand nonetheless. Weakly he squeezed back.

"My day is already brighter," he said. His voice was thin and strained.

"As is mine." She smiled as warmly as she could bear.

Geoffrey hesitated for a moment, as if choking on his next words. Finally, he said, "I may not be here much longer."

"Geoffrey," she insisted, "don't. The salves could work. You could get well."

He shook his head. "But if I don't . . ." He coughed. "If I don't, you must stay here, in Selles. I've sent word to King Robert. He knows of my condition. He will send men to protect you until you can take a new husband."

"*Never,*" she said. "I want no one else."

"But you deserve someone else. I was never able to give you a child. And you will need one, a son who can inherit these lands. They have belonged to my family since the days of Charlemagne. They are my legacy. I want them for you."

Alais felt the tears welling in her eyes. She nodded, then leaned forward to kiss the corner of his lips.

Geoffrey closed his eyes for a moment. "There is one more thing," he finally said, glancing at the two monks in the room. "Let us be alone."

"Of course, milord," Thadeus said. Prior Ragno nodded reluctantly.

When they were gone, Geoffrey reached for Alais with his other hand. To her surprise, he placed something in her palm: a chain with a pendant—one she had seen before.

"I need you to keep this," he said. "Like every lay abbot before me, I have protected it."

She let the pendant dangle from the chain. It was of dark metal but outlined with gold and strangely shaped, like a cross with a handle. And she knew that it was more than a mere bauble, for it was hollow at the bottom, with metal teeth.

"This is your key," she said.

"You remember what it unlocks? It is the secret that I was sworn to protect since I came to rule these lands—part of a sacred oath taken from my father, and he from his, back to the early days of the Carolingian kings. Do you recall where it is hidden?"

She nodded.

"Then keep it safe, and let no one know about it unless you see this symbol again."

"I'll keep it next to my heart," she said, though she did not fully understand what he had meant. She placed the necklace around her neck and tucked the strange symbol beneath the neckline of her dress.

Geoffrey lay there, his eyes smiling up at her from his ravaged face. "I will always love you."

"And I you, my love. And I you." She embraced her husband and let the tears loose. As he wrapped his arms around her, she found herself uttering words under her breath. A prayer to Saint Radegonde, for Geoffrey.

Because Thadeus was right: prayers were all she had left.

CHAPTER 9

THE MYSTERIES OF MAUGIS D'AYGREMONT

From the stern of the Irish curach, Ciarán peered west, searching for any sign of the bishop and his ship. To the south, waves crashed against the cliffs of Antrim, which rose from the sea like the green-encrusted fortress of some ancient giant. For more than a day since fleeing Derry, Ciarán had seen no sign of the Frankish vessel, but fear of pursuit kept him on edge.

"They likely sailed west, lad," Merchant mac Fadden said, chewing on a rind of salt-cured pork. "Once the Foyle meets the sea, you can go east or west to head back to the continent. We went east, but let's pray the Northmen don't give us any trouble around Dublin. And while we're at it, let's ask that we not bump into those Franks when we reach the channel between Britain and France."

"I'll feel better once we reach the Irish Sea," Ciarán said.

Merchant mac Fadden gave a slight nod. "Won't we all."

Beneath the ox-hide hull covering the curach's wooden frame, Ciarán could feel the undulation of the sea, and the knock of the oars in their locks. His habit seemed constantly damp and permeated with the smell of brine, though the morning sun provided a hint of warmth. Ever since mac Fadden and his crew met Ciarán and Dónall a half league north of Derry, the six rugged oarsmen had rowed hard, resting only when the wind filled the curach's sail and carried the light little craft like a leaf on a rushing river. Dónall sat alone in the curach's bow, as he often had since their flight from Derry, staring at the sea and the sky as if beseeching the Heavenly Father for guidance.

When not searching the horizon for the bishop's ship, Ciarán sank into spells of melancholy, filled with sadness and guilt over his friends' deaths. "It wasn't your fault, lad," Merchant mac Fadden had said. But Ciarán knew that it was. For none of this would have happened had he embraced his friends' cause instead of lingering in the grove—the act that alerted Father Gauzlin to his presence. That act of indecision had also led to Dónall's capture and the battle that ensued, all because Ciarán had defied his friends and doubted his mentor.

But even in these restless moments, he wondered whether he could trust Dónall. For hadn't his lies brought this about, too? Without that accursed tome, none of this would have happened. That book was the reason the bishop came to Derry, looking for whatever secrets it held—secrets that Dónall still kept to himself.

By their first night on the Irish Sea, Ciarán was determined to learn some answers. He waited until Merchant mac Fadden and all but two of his oarsmen were asleep, leaving Ciarán alone in the stern with Dónall, who stared out at the sliver of moon in the night sky. His face bore the look of a tortured man.

"Why does the bishop want the book?" Ciarán asked in Latin, hoping the oarsmen did not speak the language.

Dónall sighed. After a moment, he turned his gaze away from the moon. "I presume he thinks it's proof I'm a heretic."

"I don't believe that," Ciarán said. "He came to Derry with all the evidence he needed. He said your brothers at Reims confessed to practicing sorcery, and that you and your friends murdered a priest to cover it up. What more proof did he need?"

"And you believe him?"

"I don't know what to believe. I saw what you did to those Franks, with the fire and the wind."

"That was the power of the Fae, not sorcery."

Ciarán eyed his mentor skeptically. Outside the curach, the waves, with their longer fetch, rose higher, rhythmically lifting the vessel and then sliding it down the lee side.

"What if the bishop wants that power for himself?"

"Impossible," Dónall said. "The Roman Church and its bishops are deathly afraid of anything remotely pagan. At best, they'd seek to destroy the book, like so many other things that threaten their joyless view of the world."

"But *isn't* it pagan?" Ciarán asked.

Dónall scoffed. "What does the word even mean? The Fae have existed in legend throughout history. The works of Homer and Virgil abound with tales of immortals, just as our own Celtic heritage does. To the ancient Greeks, the Fae were the nymphs and satyrs, while to us they are the Tuatha Dé Danann, the sidhe of Ireland. The real questions are, where do these myths come from and why are they so similar?"

"What are you trying to say?"

"That there's a universal origin to these myths. My friend Thomas developed the theory while we were students at Reims. If the origin of these myths was in fact universal, he reasoned, where else would the proof be but in the Bible?"

Ciarán shook his head. "It's not in Scripture."

"Really? Do you remember that curious verse from Genesis?" Dónall's brow rose as it often did when he posed an especially thorny challenge. "The one Maugis inscribed on the first page of his book: '*When the sons of God went into the daughters of men, who bore them children, and these were the heroes of old, the warriors of renown.*'"

Ciarán nodded, recalling the verse inscribed on the first page of Dónall's tome.

"*That's* what I mean. It's a verse the Church deliberately ignores, yet it tells of a time when angels came to earth and mated with mortal women. And that's not the only reference in scripture. The epistle of Jude tells of angels who had left their habitat in heaven for earth. This event brought about the war in heaven spoken of in the book of Revelation. Some of the angels who lost that war were

imprisoned in the abyss—both Jude and Revelation make that clear
—but what if some were not? What if some of the angels were
granted clemency and allowed to stay on earth, yet banned forever
from heaven? They could be the Fae, the immortals of legend."

Ciarán listened intently, wondering if any of this could be true.
"Do you think they really exist?"

"That's what Thomas and I were determined to find out.
Thomas discovered evidence in a diary that had been hidden in the
library at Reims, stuck in the back of a shelf, covered up by other
tomes. The diary's author was none other than Archbishop Turpin
of Reims, one of the paladins of Charlemagne, and his words
offered proof that the mysteries of the Fae were real. He wrote of a
time when the druids were in retreat, though something of the old
magic still lingered in the world. Of the relics of Merlin of Britain,
the tales of Oliver and Roland, and journeys to the Otherworld, the
land of the Fae. According to the diary, one of the paladins, Maugis
d'Aygremont, had been tutored by a Fae named Orionde, in a tower
called Rosefleur, where he preserved all that he learned in a book
that bore his name. All we had to do to have further proof of the
Fae was find this Book of Maugis."

Ciarán pointed with his chin at the satchel by Dónall's side.
"And you did."

"It wasn't easy," Dónall admitted. "We thought, if any books
existed bearing Maugis' name, we might find reference to them in
the royal library of Charlemagne at Aachen—in its day, it was the
greatest archive in all Christendom. Unfortunately, after Charlemagne died and his grandsons proceeded to tear the empire to
pieces, the library was scattered piecemeal among monasteries all
over Europe. Soon, ten of our brothers at Reims had joined our
quest, including Remi, who, after years of searching, found an index
to Charlemagne's collection in the Cathedral of Saint-Denis. Buried
in that index was a reference to a Book of Maugis d'Aygremont,
and the index even told where the book had been sent: to Reims, no
less! It was right under our noses! We scoured the school's library
but found no sign of it. Then one night, Thomas discovered a

hidden passage along a corridor connecting the school to the cathedral. It led to a room that proved to be a treasure trove, filled with tomes by Plotinus, Porphyry, Iambilchus, and others, all banned by the Church. We called it the 'Secret Collection.' And there, in a book shrine carved of oak, was the Book of Maugis. For the twelve of us, our lives changed forever. Over a year, we gathered at night in the Secret Collection and taught ourselves the book's mysteries: the power of the Fae."

"The bishop knows this," Ciarán insisted. "He said you and your friends practiced sorcery in a chamber beneath the school. And he knew about Remi's warnings, too. He spoke of a prophecy, just as Remi did!"

A look of alarm flashed across Dónall's face. "Are you sure?"

"I heard it with my own ears."

Dónall scratched his chin with his thumbnail, as he often did when working through a problem. "How could he know?"

"Did Maugis mention a prophecy? Maybe that's why the bishop wants the book."

Dónall shook his head in disbelief. "The book contains but a few cryptic references to prophecy—so obscure, no one really knows what they mean. Thomas thought he had figured it out, though I question that. The references may be nothing more than the delusions of a madman, once the power had ravaged Maugis' mind. It's dangerous to have faith in cryptic words. That's how people get killed."

"Did Thomas die for it?" Ciarán pressed.

"Without a doubt," Dónall said solemnly.

"Did my mother?"

"Her faith in Thomas and what he believed put her life in danger, even if it was Adalbero's inquisition that finally took it."

Dónall's words stung like a blow to Ciarán's gut. His anger, which had faded in the passing days, flared anew. "Then I damned well deserve to know about it! Show me what Maugis said."

One of the oarsmen glanced back at them, and Ciarán looked away.

After the oarsman resumed his dour humming, Dónall shifted on the bench until his back was to the oarsmen. "Turn around," he said, and Ciarán shifted, too, until he faced astern and looked out at the faint wake glistening on the sea. Dónall removed the leather-bound tome from the book satchel. "Maugis hid the reference to it on one of the blank pages."

"A blank page?" Ciarán asked, wiping the brine from his face. "How?"

"See for yourself," his mentor replied, leafing through the pages until he found a stained old vellum with no writing.

"I don't see anything," Ciarán said.

"That's because you're not reading it in the proper light . . ." Dónall drew a small crystal from his robe. "Watch." Closing his eyes, he sat still for a moment, then put the crystal to his lips and blew on it. "*Eoh*," he said softly, continuing to blow until the crystal glowed with a soft, pearlescent light. Ciarán's eyes opened wide. His hands clenched the side of the boat as the light dimmed to a faint glow. There was something about the light that seemed to calm his startled nerves—something in its color, pure and white like newly fallen snow. The light illuminated Dónall's face, which, for once, appeared not angry or threatening but serene. "This light is inside us all," Dónall said. "It is the spirit element that abides within our mortal shells."

Ciarán sat speechless.

"Are you surprised that my soul's not black as coal?"

"No, I . . . How?"

"Through a Fae word born of the tongue of angels, which allowed me to reveal an energy that lives within us at all times and produces an effect that one could call magic—that's how. Through the light in this crystal, I can see things hidden from our mortal eyes —the truth of our surroundings. You'll be happy to know that here on this boat, everything is as it seems. But that's not always the case." Dónall lowered the crystal until it illuminated the blank page. As the light hit the vellum, words began to appear as if being written by the pen of some ghostly scribe.

Ciarán stared slack-jawed at the page. The words formed a heading that read, "*The Prophecy of Arcanus.*" Beneath it flowed a verse:

Dark cycle of a thousand years,
when the dragon is freed.
The prophecy is etched in the heavens.
The sphinx is the key.

Then came the word "*Salvation,*" followed by a second verse:

In Virgo's seed of Charlemagne's line,
and Enoch's device, where the answer lies,
in the whisper of breath, or all hope dies.

"Not exactly clear, don't you agree?" Dónall said. "Thomas had his theories—Remi, too. But unlike our work on the Fae, I've never seen proof that any of their theories are true."

"The prophecy of Arcanus," Ciarán said, still gazing in awe at the cryptic words that appeared as if by magic on the page. "Who is Arcanus?"

"Homer referred to him as Alkynous, king of an island called Phaeacia, which many believe was the lost isle of Atlantis. Plato wrote of it in *Kritias*. Arcanus was a prophet, yet all that Maugis chose to tell us of his prophecy is that it is etched in the heavens and that the sphinx is the key."

"The riddle of the sphinx, the creature in the story of Oedipus?"

"A beast with the head of a woman and the body of a lion," Dónall said. "That's all, until one gets to the theories those few words have spawned."

"My mother believed those theories, didn't she?"

"Sadly, yes."

"Then I want to know what they are."

Dónall let the crystal's light fade until it was gone. The words disappeared, leaving only the stained blank page in the dim moonlight. "Knowledge of any value has to be earned, lad. So if there's any value to those theories, you're going to have to sort it out yourself. I've already given you the same clues we started with."

Ciarán shook his head. "What am I supposed to do with them?"

Dónall looked at him sternly. "Solve the damned riddle."

CHAPTER 10

THE BEGINNING OF THE END

T hat night, Dónall slept fitfully. During the long hours he lay awake, he prayed the rhythm of the sea would quiet his thoughts, but nothing could overcome the haunting memories of that terrible night in Reims. So many years had passed since then, yet in his mind's eye the images remained as vivid as yesterday.

He stood outside the city on one of the surrounding tree-crowned hills thick with autumn leaves, as the sun began to set. He was young then, a man of just twenty-five. Thomas was with him, dressed in his Benedictine habit, his angelic face clean-shaven and his dark hair rustling in the breeze. The treetops shimmered with a faint flicker of blue light as Dónall and Thomas swung their leaf-shaped swords, playing with the wind.

The blustering breeze whirled a pile of yellow and orange leaves high into the air. Thomas had arranged the leaves into a birdlike shape, which he directed with his sword, causing it to soar and dive and then rise back up, borne aloft by the complicit wind. His creation moved with grace and beauty, for Thomas was an artist, and he smiled and laughed as it flew. "What should I name him?" Thomas asked.

Dónall glanced at the swan-shaped creation gliding in circles above the trees. He had summoned his own wind, swirling leaves into a serpentine ribbon. Following the flicks of his sword, the ribbon coiled and looped above the ground. "Call him Icarus," Dónall said.

"Icarus?"

"Yes, because as soon as another thought invades that brain of yours, he's going to plummet from the sky."

Thomas laughed. He banked his creation and pitched it into a dive. The leafy bird pulled back its wings, like a hawk stooping on a hare. It plunged through Dónall's swirling ribbon, scattering its leaves in every direction. Then Thomas's bird beat its wings, climbing skyward.

"Icarus got hungry," Thomas quipped.

Dónall smiled and shook his head. Concentrating on his sword, he whispered a Fae word and waited. Around him, the wind whistled. Icarus soared above the trees before Thomas pitched it into another graceful dive, but halfway through the dive, the avian shape collapsed. Its wings crumpled into its body, which spun wildly amid a swirling funnel that churned leaves and dust, blasting them across an acre of wooded hilltop.

Thomas looked dumbfounded.

"Icarus shouldn't have flown into my cyclone," Dónall said with a grin.

Thomas shrugged. "We're getting better at this, you know."

"That we are."

"Do you think we could ever harness the wind to make a man fly?"

"Like a bird?"

"Not exactly, but I think it could be possible."

"There you go again with that unfettered imagination."

"Do you want to try?" Thomas asked with a mischievous grin.

"It's past dusk," Dónall said. "We need to get back before they close the gates. Besides, I'm worn out."

"So far, fatigue is the only untoward effect. Maybe tomorrow we'll try to fly."

"You really do want to be like Icarus, don't you?"

Thomas just shrugged. They stowed their swords in the sheaths hidden beneath their habits. They had had the blades forged secretly, based on a diagram in Maugis' book. As far as they knew, these twelve blades were the only ones like them in all the world—one for each of their brethren, the keepers of the mysteries of Maugis d'Aygremont.

Dusk faded to night by the time they reached the Porte de Mars, the three-arched gateway flanked by the towering Roman walls that surrounded the city. The two monks entered as the guardsmen were closing the gates, and made their way toward the cathedral, passing through cramped neighborhoods of thatch-roofed hovels. Beneath the eaves of several houses, oil lanterns dimly lit the narrow streets littered with offal and waste. Dónall ignored the stench, but he and Thomas could not help noticing the prostitutes who called out to them. The women wore scant clothing and were quick to bare their breasts—some plump like golden melons, others slight with dark nipples. Dónall and Thomas passed them by, though Dónall felt certain that these women had serviced their fair share of priests.

The school was part of a cluster of buildings that surrounded the cathedral. Many of its ivy-covered walls had fallen into disrepair, which had been a constant gripe of Archbishop Adalbero, especially when the winter wind whipped through the chinks, sweeping parchments from desks and chilling fingers till they could no longer hold a quill.

When the two monks arrived, they found the gatehouse empty, so they entered the school through the unlocked gate.

The foyer was quiet. In sconces on the walls, rushlights flickered with the breeze that hissed through a crack in the old slate roof. A wiry monk ducked through an archway from the common room. It was Nicholas, and his eyes were as wide as if he had seen a ghost.

"Something horrible has happened!" he exclaimed.

"What is it?" Thomas asked.

"Canon Martinus," Nicolas said, his jaw quivering. "He's . . . *dead.*"

Dónall looked at him, stunned. "How?"

"He's there, just past the common room, in the hall."

Thomas bounded through the archway, with Dónall on his heels. In the common room, some thirty black-robed monks and priests had gathered at the entranceway of the corridor leading to the cathedral. Many bore looks of shock; others wept outright. Some clustered in small groups, whispering or praying.

Another of their brethren, Lucien, slumped against the archway from the foyer. His normally cherubic face was ashen, and tears welled in his eyes. "You didn't tell us it would come to this," he moaned.

Thomas looked at Lucien, puzzled, but Lucien stared through him as if he were an apparition.

Dónall touched Lucien's shoulder. He didn't flinch.

Thomas backed away and then started working his way through the crowd.

"He didn't tell us it would come to this," Lucien sobbed again under his breath.

Dónall shook his head and left Lucien there. And at the entrance to the wood-paneled corridor, he saw the body.

Canon Martinus lay sprawled on his back. A long red gash ran from one side of his throat to the other, and the crucifix around his neck lay submerged in a pool of blood that filled the hollow of his throat.

Brother Omer stood beside the dead priest. Dónall gripped Thomas's shoulder. For the heavyset monk was pleading with upturned, bloody palms before a forbidding man in crimson robes —Archbishop Adalbero of Reims.

"I found him like this, I swear," Omer stammered. "As God is my witness . . . !"

Adalbero glared accusingly at Omer, while another of their brothers, Gerbert of Aurillac, whispered in the archbishop's ear. Gerbert's thin face was fixed with a grim expression. He glanced briefly at Dónall and, for an instant, caught his eye. But the glance betrayed no thought or feeling, and his attention quickly returned to the archbishop.

"We must go," Thomas said. "Now." He ducked back into the

crowd, and Dónall trailed him, wending his way through the monks and priests, praying he did not draw attention to himself.

Free of the crowd, Thomas rushed back into the foyer. He held his head in his hands before drawing them nervously from his face. "Didn't you see it—the hidden door? Canon Martinus must have found the Secret Collection."

"He couldn't have."

"The door was cracked! All they need do is examine that panel, and they'll find it." The color drained from Thomas's face. "What if they know about the book? They'll have damning evidence against us . . ."

Dónall could taste bile in his throat. "There's a rather bigger problem."

Thomas gaped at him. "Bigger than *this*? Bigger than the revelation of our secrets?"

"Yes," Dónall said with a sigh. "Because one of us has murdered Canon Martinus."

CHAPTER II

THE SECRET OF SELLES-SUR-CHER

The sun set behind the low hills backing the tiny village of Selles-sur-Cher, painting the sky with a salmon glow behind the cross-shaped gravestone of the man Alais loved. The stone stood in the cemetery south of the abbey, where the lay abbots were buried beside their family members and where the few monks whose prominence warranted burial outside the underground crypts were also laid to rest. Alais knelt beside Geoffrey's grave on the damp patch of grass where she, too, hoped to lie when the time came to join her husband in the afterlife. Two weeks had passed since his death, and each time she came here she wept—for him and for herself. For not only was Alais burdened with the loss of the man she loved, but she found herself alone—terribly alone.

The year after she and Geoffrey wedded, her father fell victim to a hunting accident, bleeding to death after being gored in the thigh by a wild boar. Within the year, her mother remarried a wealthy lord in Lombardy. Alais had written her since Geoffrey's death, but Lombardy was halfway to Rome, and it could be weeks before she received a reply. Still, Alais prayed that her mother would write back or even journey north, for she had never come to visit Alais in

Selles. Nor had her sister, Adeline, who had stopped writing years ago.

Alais held the strangely shaped pendant at her throat, the cross with a handle, and whispered the last words of a prayer. Then she kissed the tips of her fingers and touched Geoffrey's gravestone. "Good night, my love," she said. She had risen to return to her manor house when she heard footsteps at the graveyard's edge. She gave a relieved sigh, realizing that it was Brother Thadeus.

"Remember, child," he said, walking toward her, "this was but the first death."

"Whatever do you mean, Thadeus?" she replied.

"The book of Revelation speaks of two deaths. The first is the death of the flesh, which we all suffer. But a second death falls to those souls who, on the day of judgment, are cast into the lake of fire. Yet the Lord spares the souls whose deeds warrant entry of their names in the book of life. They suffer only the first death. Geoffrey was a good man. His only death is behind him, I think. His soul is in heaven now."

Alais tried to smile, but she couldn't manage it. "What about those left behind?"

"Some say life is a gift, but I think of it more as a test. And tests were never meant to be easy." Thadeus placed a hand on Alais' arm. "May I walk you back home?"

"Certainly."

The two of them left the cemetery and started down a path through the fields. Puddles of mud from the morning's rain dimpled the path. The grass on the hills had begun to yellow as winter neared, and the farmers had retreated to their homes. The smoke wafting from their thatch-roofed cottages tinged the air with a familiar dark sharpness that was indelibly linked in Alais' mind with winter and cold and gray.

"Have you received any word from the king?" Thadeus asked when they had gone some distance down the path.

Alais shook her head. "Nothing."

Thadeus's brow wrinkled in the way it did when something

concerned him. "I know that Geoffrey sent him a message. What about your cousin?"

He referred to William, whom she had known well when she was a child, even though he was eight years her senior. She had not seen him since her wedding, two years before William succeeded his father as count of Poitiers and duke of Aquitaine. After Geoffrey died, she had sent one of his few remaining men-at-arms to Poitiers to tell William. Although Poitiers was only thirty leagues southwest of Selles-sur-Cher, the roads were in such abysmal condition that even on a good horse, the journey would take five days. Yet nearly twelve days had passed since her messenger departed. For a week now, she had hoped to see a unit of horsemen carrying her cousin's standard emblazoned with its crimson lion, or the king's blue banner with its golden fleur-de-lis, riding to the aid of Selles. But no one came.

"The last I heard," she told Thadeus, "he was on campaign with King Robert in the south."

"I heard the campaign did not go well. Your cousin has made a few military mistakes of late. I had hoped his focus might return to things closer to home."

Alais just nodded. She feared that William had forgotten her. The king, too.

"Keep the faith," Thadeus said. "Help will come."

As they climbed the hill to the manor house, Alais realized how lucky she was to have the old infirmarer. Since Geoffrey's death, Thadeus had always been there. He was not judgmental like Prior Ragno, or frightened of an attractive woman as many of the monks were, or overly deferential like the village women, who were uncomfortable with her noble station. He was simply supportive, one of the few people who did not want something from her. He was perhaps the only person in Selles she could trust completely.

"Will you be all right?" Thadeus asked when they reached the manor's door.

"Yes, thank you," she replied.

"Very well, then." He bowed slightly before turning to walk back to the abbey.

"Wait." She found herself fingering the pendant Geoffrey had given her. Something about it had been troubling her since his death. "Have you ever heard of a secret kept by the abbey—a treasure, perhaps?"

The old monk smiled and shook his head. "We are a poor abbey, child, with only a few relics of Saint Eustace, I'm afraid."

"Not a saint's relic," she said, "but something that would be locked in a small chest—a secret passed down by the lay abbots."

His eyes narrowed. "Would this chest be large enough to hold a book?"

"I think so."

Thadeus chuckled under his breath. "There were rumors of an old tome, a rare book of knowledge, but we have so few books, and it's been so long, I had stopped even thinking such rumors might be true."

"What if I told you I am certain it's true?"

"But . . . how so?"

"Come inside," Alais said. "I'll show you."

The manor house that she had shared with Geoffrey was a simple structure. At times, Geoffrey insisted on calling it a castle, and he always had grand designs for its expansion, yet to Alais, having grown up in the palace of Poitiers, it seemed rather small. Unlike the villagers' wattle-and-daub cottages, the house had buttressed limestone walls, which made it the sturdiest structure in Selles, aside from the abbey. The house consisted of three main rooms: the hall, by far the largest room, where Geoffrey had held court and they ate all their meals on the trestle table in its center; a tiny garderobe; and the bedchamber. A kitchen stood adjacent to the house, along with a wooden stable.

Alais led Thadeus through the hall to the bedchamber. It was a small room with a canopied bed, a clothes chest, and a table with a basin of fresh water under the single window.

"We need to move the bed," she told him.

"Why?"

"It's hidden underneath it."

Thadeus looked perplexed. "Why isn't it in the abbey?"

"I got the sense from Geoffrey that the lay abbots had hidden it here forever."

Thadeus shrugged but did as she asked, grunting as, together, they pushed the heavy bed aside along with a small pile of rushes that had been laid over the floor. He started at the sight of a long sheathed dagger that had been hidden under the bed.

"I've not felt safe since Geoffrey died," Alais explained, picking up the dagger and tucking it under a pillow. "It helps me sleep better." She cleared away some more rushes where the bed had been, to reveal an old wooden plate on the stone-tiled floor. She knocked on the plate.

"Hollow," Thadeus remarked.

She nodded and then knelt, using the tips of her fingers to pry the plate out.

Beneath was a small, dark cavity. Something glinted inside—the warm glint of gold.

"Help me lift it," she said.

Thadeus knelt before the space and helped her lift out a small oak chest. His eyes grew wide at the chest's lid, which was inlaid with gold in a pattern of a seven-pointed star, within a circle containing twelve odd-looking symbols.

"Do you know what it means?" she asked, pointing at the pattern.

The monk stared in awe—perhaps of the symbols, or of the prodigal amount of gold. "The symbols may be astrological," he murmured, "but I can't be sure. Can you open it?"

"Yes," she said, taking the pendant-key's chain from around her neck. The base of the cross fit perfectly inside the keyhole. She turned it until she heard a click, and then carefully opened the lid.

Inside was not a book, but a scroll wrapped around two carved wooden spindles. Its dark-stained surface looked unbelievably ancient to Alais, as it had the first time she saw it.

"It is not written in the Roman script," she told him. "I don't know it."

Thadeus lifted the scroll from the chest as delicately as if he were lifting a baby chick from its nest. He unfurled it slightly. "The words are Greek."

"Can you read it?"

But Thadeus was already tracing a gnarled finger under the text. Within moments, he seemed lost in the old scroll. She brought him a candle and waited at the edge of her bed as he read, slouched over the table. His face was intense, even troubled at times, but she could not tell whether he struggled with the language or with the writing's content. Afraid to disturb him, she said nothing.

He read for what seemed like an hour. When he finally looked up, his face was ashen. "This speaks of dire things, my dear. *Fascinating* things, to be sure, but terrible."

His hands trembled as he rolled up the scroll. "I cannot say more." He gently laid the scroll back in the chest and closed the lid, then hastily lowered it into its hiding place.

"Why not?" she asked.

"There was a reason this was kept from the monks. I'm certain of it now." He replaced the wooden plate over the hiding space and began covering it with rushes. When he was done, he sighed with relief.

"Tell me, please," she begged.

"It is heresy," he said. "Even blasphemy."

"Then why is it here?"

Thadeus looked at her helplessly. "I wish I knew."

CHAPTER 12

SAINT-GERMAIN-DES-PRÉS

Two days after they entered the channel between Britain and France, Ciarán spotted land. Sheer white cliffs stretched for leagues east and west, and the cries of gulls rang from the shore. His spirits soared at the sight, for they had reached the mainland with still no sign of the bishop's ship.

While Ciarán stood on the bow gazing at the towering cliffs, the oarsmen unfurled the sail to capture the light breeze hissing off the sea. "What is that land?" he asked.

"That there's Normandy, lad," Merchant Mac Fadden said, standing alongside the young scribe.

Beside them, Dónall watched a seagull dive for a fish. "Its name means 'the land of the Northmen.' The Normans were Vikings who settled these lands long ago."

Ciarán glanced warily at his mentor. Vikings were something every monk had been raised to fear, for their brutal raids on Irish monasteries were legendary.

"Don't worry lad," Dónall said, clapping Ciarán's shoulder. "The Normans are Christian now, and they've become more like the Franks than their Northmen kin."

Despite Dónall's assurances, Ciarán couldn't stop scanning every inlet for the sinister low outline of a Viking longship as they sailed along the Norman coast. To his relief, they had encountered none by the time they reached the mouth of the Seine, the river that would take them to Paris.

After their first day rowing up the Seine, they docked at a town called Rouen, the seat of the duke of Normandy. The townspeople seemed welcoming of the Irish strangers, which was more than Ciarán could say for the town itself. For Rouen was altogether unlike Derry. There were no oak groves here, no fields of clover, no corbelled huts. A looming wall of stone, not earth, encircled the town, whose buildings were wedged cheek by jowl along narrow, dung-strewn mud streets that emitted a fearsome stench. The monks of Rouen, clad in their black Benedictine habits, seemed perfectly content to walk these cramped, fetid streets and alleyways, and that struck Ciarán as unnatural. For if God was indeed the lord of the elements, as Saint Columcille had written, then how could these Benedictines pay him proper homage in a place made entirely by human hands?

They left Rouen the next morning beneath fair skies, before a steady westerly breeze that aided their voyage up the Seine, which meandered like a twisting serpent through lush valleys toward the great city of Paris. When they finally arrived just before dusk, Ciarán could hardly believe what he saw, for Paris seemed to float on the river. Fortified walls, glowing with the light from scores of flickering lanterns, surrounded the city like the hull of some gigantic ship. In place of a ship's masts, steeples and towers topped with slate roofs rose through a haze of smoke from a thousand cooking fires. As they rowed closer to shore, it became apparent that Paris did not float but, rather, was built on a narrow island splitting the Seine. Ferries rowed between the island and the mainland, and where they did not, plank bridges crossed the river. Coracles and other craft jammed the docks, and to Ciarán's relief, none resembled the bishop's black-hulled ship.

Merchant mac Fadden's oarsmen rowed the curach toward a harbor flanked by stout, square towers flying blue pennons dotted with gold lilies. As they pulled alongside an empty stretch of pier,

Ciarán marveled at the city's size, for more buildings stood along the riverbanks, and more lanterns hung from posts along the road that ran parallel to the city, creating a trail of tiny lights unlike anything he had ever seen. He wondered whether there was a grander city in all the world. Rome, perhaps, but it was hard to imagine such a place.

At the docks, Ciarán and Dónall bade Merchant mac Fadden and his oarsmen good-bye. "Be good, lad," mac Fadden said, wrapping Ciarán in a bearlike embrace. "And listen to Dónall. He's a good man, and I'd trust him with my life."

Ciarán was surprised to feel the sting of tears. Whether mac Fadden's devotion to Dónall had caught him off guard, or he was just suddenly struck by the sadness of their parting, Ciarán felt certain he would miss the stalwart captain and his crew.

Dónall embraced Merchant mac Fadden before making the sign of the cross and uttering a prayer:

> *God be with you on the sea;*
> *Christ be with you on the land.*
> *Spirit be with you in every breath.*
> *May your journey bring you home,*
> *and your travels be swift*
> *to the fair oaks of Derry.*

Merchant mac Fadden clapped Dónall on the shoulder and then turned away, his rugged seafarer's eyes gone suddenly misty.

Dónall led the way from the pier, with his black staff in hand and the book satchel slung over his shoulder. As they departed, he drew Ciarán near. "Stay close," he said, "though it's hard to get lost —all roads eventually lead to the river."

Beyond the docks, throngs of Parisians filled the streets. Lit by more of the flickering lanterns, the streets were narrow like those of Rouen, though cleaner. And the churches were certainly grander, but the air still held the acrid smells of unwashed humanity, smoke, and dung. Dónall and Ciarán headed for one of the bridges that would take them to the southern bank of the Seine. They passed churches devoted to saints named Geneviève, Denis, and Christophe, and everywhere, shuffling along amid the throng, were dozens of Benedictine monks and black-robed priests. The priests and monks shot looks at the Irishmen in their gray habits, but it was the worried expressions on these clerics' faces that caught Ciarán's attention.

"What do you think's bothering them?" he asked.

"Let's find out," Dónall replied. Stopping a priest outside a basilica dedicated to Saint Étienne, he inquired in Latin why the priest and his brethren should look so troubled.

The priest, a slight man with a puckered mouth, twitched nervously. "Haven't you heard?" he replied. "Pope Gregory has excommunicated King Robert for his marriage to Bertha of Blois. Soon all France may be under papal interdict, depriving us all of the blessed sacraments! And this when the end times draw near, when our souls are already in grave peril!" The priest made the sign of the cross. "It is why the king fares so poorly in his conflict with Fulk the Black. Because God is angry with the king, and soon he will unleash the devil Fulk to punish us—all because the king married his cousin, his own kin!"

The priest seemed to grow more agitated the more he spoke, so Dónall quickly bade him farewell. "A papal interdict?" Ciarán remarked as they walked away. "That's *outrageous*!"

Dónall cocked one brow. "Tensions between the Franks and our new German pope seem to be running a tad high—though I suspect this is just a political move."

"Who's this Fulk the Black?" Ciarán asked. "He seems to have everyone on edge."

"According to Rián, he's the count of Anjou, who's opposing the Frankish king. Unless things have changed since my last visit, the king of France enjoys only modest power. It's the local magnates who rule this land—a gaggle of robbers, petty lords, and ruffians if ever there were. They make our tribal chieftains look like the communion of saints."

Ciarán shot his mentor a concerned look, but Dónall clapped him on the shoulder.

"Lad," he said, "welcome to the Continent."

THEY ARRIVED at the abbey of Saint-Germain-des-Prés beneath a cloaked moon. The abbey stood on the outskirts of Paris, amid sprawling vineyards and fields of yellowing grass. Stone walls encircled it, making it a fortress compared to Derry's earthen enclosure and corbelled huts. A half-built bell tower rose above the other buildings. Although partially obscured by wooden scaffolding, the tower was roughly square in shape, with sturdy buttresses supporting walls adorned with tall arched windows.

"Amazing!" Ciarán breathed. Apparently, the artists of this land must work with stone instead of pens and brushes.

"Wait till you see the things the Romans built," Dónall replied.

The abbey's gate was closed for the evening. Dónall rapped on it with his staff, and a narrow peephole slid open, revealing a pair of flitting eyes beneath a bushy black brow.

The man behind the gate barked something in Frankish, to which Dónall replied in Latin, "We're here to see Brother Remi of Paris."

"And who might you be?" the gruff voice asked.

"Brother Dónall mac Taidg, of Ireland. I'm an old friend of his."

A moment later, the gate opened. Its keeper was a pug-faced Benedictine no older than thirty, with thick hands and a well-fed gut. "Ireland—the edge of the world, eh?" the gatekeeper said. "You say you're an old friend?"

Dónall nodded. "From his days back at Reims."

The gatekeeper's eyes narrowed. "Reims, eh? You sure you want to see him?"

"We've traveled a long way," Dónall said.

"Suit yourself," the gatekeeper muttered. "Though why the abbot even lets him stay here is a mystery."

He led them into the cloister, consisting of four covered arcades lit by rushlights and arranged in a square at the center of the abbey's primary structures: the church, refectory, chapter house, and dormitory. Ciarán marveled at the elaborate Romanesque capitals, each carved with the image of a saint, atop the columns along the cloister. In the cloister's center garden, near a fish pond rimmed by smooth stones, they caught the scent of rosemary from pruned shrubs. Gregorian chants echoed from the church, reminding Ciarán that they had arrived during Vespers.

The gatekeeper opened the heavy door to the dimly lit vestibule and tiptoed to a nearby alcove and another door.

"He's not with the choir?" Dónall whispered.

The gatekeeper shook his head. "No, this door leads down to the crypts of the old Merovingian kings. Brother Remi went down there a week ago; he's not come up since."

Dónall and Ciarán glanced at each other, alarmed. "Is he alive?" Dónall asked.

The gatekeeper shrugged. "We place his food on the top step every supper, and it's always gone by morning. Remi had been saying odd things before he went down there—not the way he usually does, but muttering that all his brothers were dead. So now it seems he wants to be with the dead."

He cracked open the door that led to the shrine. Ciarán glanced hesitantly at Dónall, who nudged him through the doorway in response.

The monks' sandals clapped against the descending stone steps, and the air grew cool and damp as they descended. Near the bottom, candlelight flickered from an archway. The stench of urine choked the stairwell.

Ciarán peered through the archway and gasped. Dozens of flickering candles lit the small shrine surrounding a statue of a saint, but the rest had become the tapestry of a madman. Symbols and pictures, scrawled in chalk, covered every inch of the shrine's dark stone walls. Some of the symbols seemed arranged in patterns, forming circles or crosses, but these provided the only discernible order amid the chaos of other drawings: seven-pointed stars; an ankh; and sketches of chimeras, griffins, and other mythical beasts. It was as if the ravings in Maugis' book had been ripped from their pages and plastered over the damp, niter-encrusted stone.

Ciarán's nerves tensed. In the shadows, a rodent scrabbled. From behind Ciarán, Dónall stepped into the shrine and called out, "Remi?"

A flash of movement caught Ciarán's eye; then came a loud crack.

Dónall's head whipped back, his knees buckled, and his staff clattered to the stone floor.

From the shadows, a bony hand grabbed Ciarán's habit and yanked him from the stairwell. Ciarán tumbled sideways, landing hard on his shoulder against the stone-tiled floor.

A hand pressed into Ciarán's chest, and he looked up at the black-robed man who straddled him. Eyes bulged from a gaunt face dark with dirt and stubble. From the tip of a blackened staff, a torchlike flame burned inches from Ciarán's chin.

"What have you done with Nicolas!" the man growled between rotting teeth.

Ciarán looked wide-eyed at the flame. "I don't know!"

"Liar!" The staff's tip flared, singeing the down on Ciarán's cheeks and making him wince.

Then a strong hand reached over the man's shoulder and jerked him backward, and the flame whipped back from Ciarán's face. Back on his feet, Dónall flung the assailant to the floor.

"Remi!" he cried. "It's me."

The man's mouth widened as if to scream, but then his lips quivered as the flame on the staff's tip died, leaving only a wisp of smoke. "Dónall?" A tear rolled down one dirt-caked cheek. "You are *alive?*"

"Yes, old friend."

"Then this?" Remi looked at Ciarán, and his eyes grew wide. "Has it been so long?"

"Nearly twenty years," Dónall said. A painful-looking red lump stood out on the side of his forehead.

"Then it's not too late," Remi said.

As Ciarán crabbed backward and away and got gingerly to his

feet, Dónall stepped between them. "What happened to Nicolas?" he asked.

Remi ran his fingers through his disheveled hair. "They are hunting us," he whispered. "They know we are getting close."

"Tell me who, Remi."

"The same forces that worked against us at Reims."

"But Gerbert left France."

Remi's expression darkened. "Not him. It has servants—men in dark robes, who hide in the shadows . . . And not just men." The jittery monk's nervous twitching seemed to be gradually abating under the force of his old friend's gaze.

"After all this time, why would anyone harm Nicolas?" Dónall asked.

"Because he found another piece of the puzzle. We're close, Dónall—oh, so close."

Dónall's eyes narrowed. "What do you mean?"

"Nicolas located the Book of Enoch."

Dónall sucked in a breath. Ciarán glanced between the two men and saw something he had never seen before.

For Dónall mac Taidg looked as pale as a ghost.

CHAPTER 13

THE BENEDICTINE

On the banks of the Loire, alongside a row of fishing boats with furled sails and gathered nets, a lone Benedictine monk stood on a wooden pier, awaiting the arrival of Bishop Adémar of Blois. The monk raised a lantern in the evening mist that settled over the river. He rocked on his heels, trying not to shiver, unsure whether the chill in his bones came from the damp air or his apprehension over the bishop's return.

At last, the ship's stem post jutted through the mist, and he grabbed the line tossed by a crewman and helped guide the ship to the pier. He counted only thirteen soldiers among the crew, along with Father Gauzlin, the bishop, and the other priest. A wave of unease coursed through him. Where were the other eight men? Something terrible must have happened.

Two of the soldiers secured the ship to the pier, while the Benedictine searched the bishop's face for some sign of what had happened. He met Adémar's gaze and sensed the fury simmering behind the cold stare. The Benedictine looked away. He glanced at Gauzlin, whose face was swollen with bruises and scabbed-over wounds. Gauzlin shook his head subtly, and the Benedictine's heart sank. Their mission had failed.

Bishop Adémar disembarked first, and the Benedictine bowed before kissing his ring. "My lord," he said, "I rejoice at your return."

The bishop glared down at the much shorter Benedictine and snarled, "There is nothing to rejoice about."

"What happened, my lord?"

"Dónall mac Taidg escaped, along with the whelp," Adémar said. "And they took the Book of Maugis." Adémar turned abruptly and strode toward a flight of stone steps that climbed from the river to the town, where a stone fortress loomed beside the cathedral dedicated to Saint Solenne.

The Benedictine scurried to keep up with the bishop's long strides. "Where did they go, my lord?"

"If I knew, I would not be here," Adémar hissed. He slapped a leather-bound book into the Benedictine's chest. "We did find this," he snapped. "Sent to mac Taidg from a Brother Remi of Paris."

The Benedictine fumbled with the book, trying to hold on to his lantern while climbing the steep stairwell. At the top of the stairs, they passed through an arched gateway in the town's stone wall and headed for the cathedral—a grim structure with slot windows and a spire where perching stone gargoyles peered balefully down. Two black-robed priests waited at the cathedral's open doors, where candlelight flickered from the vestibule beyond. The priests bowed as the bishop entered. Following him, the Benedictine gave the lantern to one of the priests, then opened the book. As the candle-light spilled over the illuminations decorating the fresh vellum, the Benedictine realized what had happened. "My lord," he said, "Dónall mac Taidg was warned."

Adémar flung his black overcloak to the other waiting priest. "How?"

"Once Adalbero's inquisition began, Remi started hiding messages in his illuminations. Books passed freely between the abbeys. He felt it was the safest way to communicate."

Adémar's eyes narrowed. "What do these warnings say?"

"It will take some time to find them," the Benedictine admitted. "But Remi was always clever about leaving clues."

"Then make haste," Adémar said. He looked around them. "Not here, but in my chambers."

The Benedictine followed Adémar to an upstairs chamber in the rectory attached to the cathedral. Shutters had been drawn over the chamber's two windows, and the sweetish scent of old parchment lingered in the air. In the shadows of the far wall stood a bookshelf crammed with codices and tomes. Adémar took a seat behind an ash desk and beckoned the Benedictine to a chair beside a trident-shaped candelabrum. While the Benedictine lit three candles, one of the priests brought the bishop a goblet of wine, then hurried from the chamber, closing the heavy oak door behind him. The Benedictine settled into the chair to study Remi's handiwork. After realizing that Remi had marked one of the pages, he discovered the first warning. It took time to decipher the code involving the Four Horsemen, but once he did, the remaining messages revealed themselves.

"Remi told mac Taidg about Brother Nicolas," the Benedictine said, looking up. "And warned him that the prophecy has begun. This is quite favorable, I think."

"How so?" Adémar asked, setting the goblet aside.

"Because Dónall will have gone to Remi, which means they've come to Paris. And I know where they'll go next. In time, they will bring the Book of Maugis right within our grasp."

Adémar's eyes gleamed in the candlelight. "How can you be so certain?"

"Last week," the Benedictine said proudly, "Brother Nicolas succumbed to our methods of persuasion. He admitted to discovering a rare document from the Capitulary of Quierzy, when Charlemagne's grandsons divided his empire along with the contents of his library. In that document, Nicolas found a reference to the Book of Enoch—and to the place where it may be hidden. He sent word of this discovery to Remi, who surely will take Dónall to find the book, for they believe they need it to locate Enoch's device."

Adémar steepled his fingers beneath his chin. "Are you sure of this?"

"I am positive, my lord."

"Where do they believe the Book of Enoch is hidden?"

"At the abbey of Selles-sur-Cher," the Benedictine replied.

"Lord Geoffrey's domain?"

"Lord Geoffrey died recently," the Benedictine said. "His young bride now rules in his stead. Shall I go there?"

Adémar took another sip of wine, wiping a drop from his lips as the hint of a smile formed. "No, leave that to me. I've been searching for a cause to bring the count of Anjou deeper into our fold. We need to keep him motivated, so I think it's time the good count Fulk helped me rid the Touraine of this heresy."

"And what about Dónall mac Taidg?"

"I want to be there when he arrives. He has the means to find Enoch's device, and we cannot let that happen!" Adémar slammed his fist onto the desk, his eyes aflame with sudden anger. Across the desk, the Benedictine cringed.

"Events must happen as they've been foretold!" Adémar raged. "We cannot let anyone stop it. Mankind must suffer for its sins as the race of Gog and Magog enacts its divine vengeance!"

The Benedictine swallowed hard. "What shall I do to serve you, my lord?"

"Is Brother Nicolas of any more use to us?"

"No, lord."

"Then return home," Adémar said coldly. "And sacrifice him."

The Benedictine shuddered. He had hoped it would not come to this, but he knew what must be done. He rose from his chair and gave a grim nod.

"As you wish."

CHAPTER 14

THE ARCANIAN PROPHECY

Standing before the wall of scrawled symbols in the crypt of Saint-Germain-des-Prés, Dónall looked stunned. "Say that again?" he asked Remi.

Remi smiled perversely. "We know where the Book of Enoch is hidden."

"What's the Book of Enoch?" Ciarán asked.

Dónall tried to explain. "Remember that curious verse in Genesis? The Book of Enoch supposedly tells the whole tale."

Ciarán blinked in astonishment. "But it's not part of scripture."

"That's because the Church does not want you to know about it," Remi insisted. "It is the subject of the greatest conspiracy ever perpetrated in the name of theology. Nearly every copy of this book, a book that had been well known to the apostles and the ancient Jews—a book as old as the book of Genesis, perhaps—was destroyed by our church fathers five hundred years ago, by men who perpetrated a fantastic lie conceived by none other than Saint Augustine!"

Remi's face reddened. "What *of* that verse in Genesis? '*When the Sons of God went into the daughters of men . . .*' Who are the sons of God?

Throughout the Old Testament, 'sons of God' refers to the angels. Nowhere does it refer to mortal men. The early Christians and the Jews accepted that the sons of God were divine beings. But did that deter Augustine? No! To hide the divine origins of the sons of God, he proclaimed they were the righteous—and mortal—sons of Seth. And that the 'daughters of men' were not just human women but, specifically, the sinful daughters of the line of Cain. Are we to believe that God's wrath was brought upon the earth because the Sethites and Cainites interbred? Was that the great sin that nearly destroyed all creation? And what of the Nephilim, the giants spoken of in that verse? How could two mortal lines produce such offspring? Augustine ignores all this, all in the name of rationalizing religion and suppressing the supernatural origins of everything the Church fears! And now even to suggest the true meaning of that verse is heresy!"

Remi's voice echoed through the crypt. The hulking shapes of the Merovingian sarcophagi loomed beyond the shrine, dimly visible in the flickering candlelight. Dónall still looked dazed. "How did you find it?" he asked.

"The truth can never be completely suppressed," Remi said vehemently. "A copy of the Book of Enoch remained in the Royal Library of Charlemagne—perhaps the only copy in Europe to survive. It was referenced by Maugis d'Aygremont and undoubtedly preserved by him, for Maugis understood the sanctity of the truth. But the book never showed up at Saint-Denis or Reims or anywhere the great library was supposedly scattered. For twenty-five years we searched for it. Then this summer, at the abbey of Saint-Martin, Nicolas found an obscure reference to it, and its possible location. He sent a letter from Tours saying he was going to the place where the book was hidden." Remi glanced at them hopelessly. "I never heard from him again."

The color was returning to Dónall's face. "That doesn't mean Nicolas is dead."

"You know what happened to our other brothers!" Remi snapped. "Do you think that was all just an archbishop's inquisition? Someone else was telling them where we were. Someone who was watching us, who wanted us dead, who needed to make sure we never found that book."

"But why?" Ciarán pressed. "The book is ancient. Why does it matter now?"

Remi gave him a curious look. "It is the final clue, the crux of the prophecy."

Dónall shook his head. "He doesn't know."

"My God, Dónall!" Remi cried. "The most important secret you hold—and one that affects him, and affects us all. You never *told* him?"

"There is no evidence," Dónall said.

"*Evidence!* Have you not gazed at the stars?"

Ciarán had a sudden thought. "Maugis said the prophecy was etched in the heavens."

Remi looked confused. "So you *do* know?"

"I've only shown him the verses in Maugis' book," Dónall sighed.

Remi grimaced. He grabbed Ciarán by the sleeve and pulled him to one of the drawings on the wall: a sphinx, lion-bodied with a woman's head and full, unseemly breasts. The image had been sketched in fearsome detail, from the claws on the feline paws to the high cheekbones and flowing hair of the womanly visage. "Do you know the meaning of the sphinx?" he asked fervently.

"Actually," Ciarán replied, "I think I do."

Ciarán studied the symbols. Amid a score of others, twelve of them formed a roughly circular pattern around a narrow seven-pointed star. "Etched," Ciarán said, "means written or drawn, as in a picture. So pictures in the heavens must refer to the constellations."

"Exactly," said Remi. "It has been written there since the beginning of time, and you don't need Maugis to tell you that. Remember the Psalm: '*The heavens declare the glory of God; day to day they pour forth speech, and night to night they declare knowledge; their voice goes out to all the earth, and their words to the end of the world.*' The stars declare the knowledge, don't you see? The knowledge of the prophecy!"

"The signs of the zodiac," Ciarán said.

"Precisely! The ancient Greeks, the Egyptians, the Babylonians —every people throughout history has recognized these signs. When read together, they tell a prophecy of things to come. The signs are arranged in a circle, so what they mean depends on where you start reading. If you begin at Aries and end with Pisces, the meaning is very different from beginning with Capricorn and ending with Sagittarius."

"It leaves a little room for interpretation, doesn't it?" Dónall added.

"Not if you read them in the right order. The first riddle refers to the sphinx as the key. There it is." Remi pointed a bony finger at the drawing of the mythical beast. "What does it mean?"

Ciarán had contemplated the answer since that night on the Irish Sea. He studied the picture, then glanced at the circular pattern of symbols.

Remi's mouth hung open in anticipation.

"The riddle of the sphinx," Ciarán began. "I thought about the riddle it posed to Oedipus: what creature goes on four legs in the morning, on two at midday, and on three in the evening? The answer, we know, is *man*. So maybe man is the key, but what does that have to do with the constellations?"

"Gemini is sometimes depicted as twin men," Dónall offered, "and Orion is also a man."

Remi flashed him a bitter look.

"But Orion is not part of the zodiac," Ciarán said. "So then I thought, what if the sphinx itself is the riddle? If the sphinx literally *is* the key? A key is used to unlock something—not just chests or doors, but codes. To interpret the symbols, you need a key, something that tells what letter each symbol corresponds to. If the sphinx is literally the key, it should tell us how to read the code—in this case, the constellations. The sphinx has the head of a woman and the body of a lion—a woman first, and lion last. So what if the first constellation is a woman, and the last is a lion?"

"Virgo and Leo!" Remi beamed. "The prophecy starts with Virgo and ends with Leo. That is the key!"

"So it tells you the order in which to read the constellations," Ciarán said. "But how do you know what they mean?"

"Ah," Dónall replied, half smiling. "Now you're traveling farther down the river of interpretation and into the misty seas of theory."

"But some theories prove true," Remi insisted. "Open your mind to the possibilities. Enlightened thinkers since ancient times have seen meaning in these constellations. But when the constellations tell the whole tale . . ." He shuddered. "Are you prepared for this?" he asked Ciarán. "It is a secret that forever changes the lives of any to whom it is revealed. A secret for which countless men over thousands of years have sacrificed their lives. One that has wrought great destruction in the past, yet offers a bare sliver of hope in the dark future to come. Once you have seen this, you will never look at the stars the same way again, knowing the dire warning they hold for us all."

Ciarán had to wonder, was this simply a product of Remi's madness, or something far graver? Yet he could not restrain his curiosity. "I want to know."

"Good." Remi's eyes brightened. "First, put your mind in the frame of the man who first discovered the prophecy: Arcanus of Atlantis. The Atlanteans were like the ancient Greeks, so you must interpret the story the way a Greek would: in three acts—a beginning, a middle, and an end—with each act composed of four signs. If you begin with Virgo, the first four signs are Virgo, Libra, Scorpio, and Sagittarius." He gestured to the four symbols that formed the top left third of the circle.

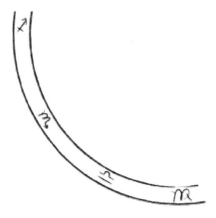

"Virgo, the first sign," he said, pointing to the bottom of the four symbols, "is depicted as a woman holding a sheaf of wheat—a universal symbol of a seed. The Egyptians saw her as the goddess Isis. To the Celts, she is the Earth Mother. Others see her as Eve. Yet it is her seed that matters, her offspring. Perhaps the seed represents mankind. But Maugis saw something more specific: a bloodline traced through history from Arcanus to Constantine, to the heirs of Charlemagne—the bloodline of a champion of men who must fulfill the prophecy or all will be lost.

"Next is Libra, the scales. They speak to something being weighed and measured—a test. Third comes Scorpio. In Hebrew, its name is *Akrab*, which means war or conflict. Yet in Coptic, the name is *Isidis*, meaning attack of the enemy. And last is Sagittarius. He is the archer who aims his weapon at the heart of Scorpio."

As Remi spoke, Ciarán recognized the meaning of another picture scrawled on the shrine's wall: a muscular centaur pulling a bowstring and targeting a monstrous scorpion, its deadly curved sting poised to strike.

"Together, these tell the first act of the prophecy," Remi continued. "A champion of men will be measured in a battle against the enemy. Only by wielding the weapon, Sagittarius, can the champion survive and defeat the enemy in this battle. Maugis called this the prime conflict."

Remi pointed to the next four symbols, which completed the next third of the circle.

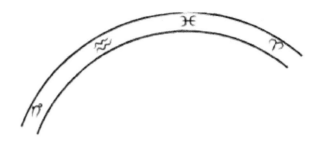

"Of the next act, we know much less. It begins with Capricorn, the goat, a universal symbol of sacrifice. Next is Aquarius, the flowing waters. It is believed this represents a journey. The waters flow into the constellations that surround Pisces, the next sign. Pisces is depicted as two fish bound by a chain. The chain also binds two other constellations: Andromeda, a woman, and Cetus, the Leviathan, a great monster of the sea."

Flanking the symbols in this half of the circle were sketches of a woman, shamelessly naked yet beautiful, and a creature that looked like a whale, but with the scales of a fish and the jaws of a shark. A chain linked the woman's wrists to the sea monster's tail.

"This is where the meaning of the second act becomes a mystery," Remi continued. "Maugis says nothing of it. Last of the four is Aries, the ram—again, a symbol of sacrifice. So the second act represents a journey of some type that begins and ends with sacrifice."

Ciarán nodded, his eyes still riveted on the image of Andromeda and the Leviathan.

"The meaning of the final act is clearer." Remi tapped a finger beside the last four symbols.

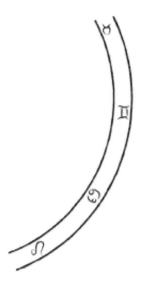

"First," he said, starting at the bottom, "we have Taurus, the raging bull. It represents a great conflict. Next is Gemini, the twins. In the old Coptic tongue, the word for Gemini is *Pi-Mahi,* meaning 'the united.' After Gemini is Cancer, whose name in the ancient languages is significant. In Arabic, its name is *Al Sartan,* meaning 'to hold or bind.' It has the same meaning in Hebrew. And in Greek, it is *Karkinos*—'to encircle.'

"Finally, there is Leo, the lion. This is the symbol of the champion of men. Beneath it, however, is another constellation: the Hydra, a symbol of the enemy. Both the lion and the Hydra head toward Cancer."

Beside this third of the circle, Remi had drawn a dragon, terrible and twisting, with snakelike scales. "This completes the act's meaning: that the champion and the enemy will be bound in a final, decisive conflict. Only one shall prevail. And there the prophecy shall be fulfilled."

Ciarán still found it an abstract mystery. "How can you tell when any of this will happen?" he asked.

"It already has," Remi said, his eyes growing wide. "And its time is coming again."

"I don't understand."

"This is more theory," Dónall said. "The zodiac is a wheel, and a wheel turns over and over. Maugis spoke of a cycle of darkness that turns every thousand years. So, the theory goes, the cycle of the prophecy repeats itself every thousand years or so."

"Three times man has survived," Remi said, "but the enemy has grown stronger—and wiser. And now the end of the millennium is nearly upon us."

Dónall shook his head. "We don't know, in fact, if it has ever happened before, but Thomas believed the first time may have been around the time of Arcanus, about three thousand years ago."

"And you want your proof?" Remi said. "Where is Atlantis? Sunk into the sea in the aftermath of the great conflict. That is what we are dealing with! Almost every civilization has a story of a battle between light and darkness, whether fought by gods or by mortal men. And as the cycle of the prophecy has been repeated, these myths have been reinforced until they became embedded in the legends of mankind. To you Irish, the story is reflected in the battle of Mag Tuired, where the Tuatha Dé Danann defeated the Formorian giants and their king, Balor of the Evil Eye. The Babylonians have their battle between the hero-god Marduk and the dragon Tiamat. The priests of Persia tell of a great war between Ahura Mazda, the god of good, and Ahriman, the god of evil, when darkness will cover the sky and the world will be devoured by fire. The Northmen believe in a final battle that will plunge the world into darkness, when the world serpent rises from the sea and armies of giants and demons do battle with the gods, while the earth burns. The Northmen call that battle *Ragnarok*.

"But we have long known it by a different name, the name by which the battle will be called when the cycle of the prophecy repeats again." Remi's expression had grown frighteningly serious.

"To us it is known as Armageddon."

CHAPTER 15

ENOCH'S DEVICE

"**N**ow do you understand the significance of the book I sent to Derry?" Remi said. "Of the images I chose?"

A lump of dread formed in the pit of Ciarán's stomach as Remi's illuminations flashed vividly through his mind: the rain of fire and blood, the figures writhing in pain, the demons with horned heads rising from a smoking pit. "The apocalypse," he murmured.

"*Yes.*" Remi's eyes narrowed, and his voice fell. "The book of Revelation tells of portents in the heavens, battles on earth, and a final conflict called Armageddon. And it tells of the enemy of prophecy."

"The Dragon," Ciarán almost whispered, unwilling to utter its true name. He recalled Remi's illumination of the serpentine beast battling the hosts of heaven.

The mad look returned to Remi's eyes. "Now do you see who we are dealing with? The Dragon is present in every myth. He is the snake of Eden, Balor of the Evil Eye, Tiamat of Babylon, Ophion to the Greeks, the world serpent of the Norse. The book of Revelation says that after a thousand years, the Dragon must be released from its prison, where it has been bound since its war against God.

Maugis says the prophecy is a cycle of a thousand years. Thus, with each millennium, the war that broke out in heaven continues on earth!"

"You're talking about the end of the world," Ciarán said.

"No!" Remi exclaimed. "Revelation tells of the world's end: the trumpets, the fire, the earthquakes, the stars falling from the sky. Those are the things that will happen if the final battle is lost. To prevent these horrors—*that* is what we are fighting for."

Ciarán glanced between Remi and Dónall. "How does God let this happen?"

"Why does God let *any* evil exist in this world?" Remi asked. "Because man did this to himself! In the garden, when Eve became Pandora. It was man who broke God's laws and listened to the serpent and ate of the forbidden fruit. Man who brought about the end of paradise and let evil into the world. And it was man who, after the war in heaven, sided for a time with the fallen angels, cavorting with them, bearing their offspring, corrupting the world to the point that God nearly drowned it all in the great flood. But still evil lingered, all as a consequence of man's doings. The prophecy is the ultimate trial, where man is forced to confront the evil he let into this world—a test to see if mankind deserves to live another thousand years."

Ciarán found himself at a loss for words.

"Thomas believed it was a consequence of free will," Dónall said. "Just as man can choose to do good or evil, so he can choose to defend himself in these times and preserve the world that God gave him, or stand complacently by and witness the end of all things. Yet the fact that men can read this meaning into the zodiac does not make it all true."

"Dónall, ever the skeptic!" Remi declared. "The signs of the apocalypse are everywhere. The Four Horsemen ride unchecked over our land. The king and his magnates are at war, and beyond our borders, the Vikings and the Saracens threaten all godly life. There is famine so bleak that men are rumored to eat other men just to survive. Disease and plague follow the famine, killing children, the old, and the weak. And everywhere walks death, stalking, killing, and reaping souls. Only those who choose blindness can fail to see these things."

"But war, famine, and disease have existed throughout history," Dónall argued.

"Never like this!" Remi insisted. "Why you remain in denial has always vexed me, especially since Thomas gave his life for this. And there is one fact you have always ignored, even though it compels a belief in these things: Maugis taught us the secrets of the Fae, which are real, and then he tells of prophecy and how to find the weapon."

"You mean Sagittarius," Ciarán said.

"Precisely!" Remi looked at Dónall. "Go on, show him."

Dónall sighed and unslung the leather satchel from his shoulder. "It's another cryptic clue," he said. "Another damnable riddle."

"In the book," Ciarán murmured.

"The book is full of riddles," Dónall replied, pulling the Book of Maugis d'Aygremont from the satchel. "I think even you have seen it." He set the thick book on the table, opened its cover, and flipped through the centuries-old vellum until he came to the image of a symbol-filled circle with two seven-pointed stars.

"The witch's circle," Ciarán said.

"It is no such thing," Remi insisted.

"No," Dónall said. "We have always believed it's some type of pictorial representation of the prophecy—a hieroglyph of sorts."

"Surely it is," Remi explained. "These symbols"—he pointed to twelve glyphs along the outer circle—"like those on the wall, are the symbols of the zodiac, arranged appropriately in a wheel. In the gaps between the points of the first seven-pointed star are more symbols, representing the planets, which are closer to the earth: Mars, Jupiter, Saturn, the Moon, Venus, Mercury, and the Sun. The large seven-pointed star symbolizes the seven days of creation, when the stars were set in the sky and the prophecy was written. The star is also a glyph to ward off evil. The smaller seven-pointed star in the center is called the fairy star, a symbol of the Fae, suggesting they have a role to play in the cycle of prophecy. Within it is the ankh, a symbol of life but also an Atlantean symbol of Arcanus. That is why Maugis chose it to adorn the cover of his book. Surrounding the fairy star and the ankh are words, written in the heptagrams within the larger star. And do not let your mind fool you given all the myriad symbols: the letters are *Greek.*"

Ciarán's eyes grew wide. It was true: the letters within the heptagrams were Greek—amid the unnerving symbols, he had failed to notice until now.

"When you read them," Remi said, "they tell a story."

Though Greek was not his strongest tongue, Ciarán slowly read the words aloud:

> *Enoch saw a great and glorious device*
> *at the ends of the whole Earth.*
> *There Arcanus found the Stone of Light.*

"Do you see what I meant about another riddle?" Dónall said.

"But it is a riddle that gives us the clues to solve it," Remi insisted. "'Enoch' is a clear reference to the author of the Book of Enoch. We know this book was kept in the library of Charlemagne, and I believe it was intended to be kept alongside the Book of Maugis, although somehow over time they became separated. The Book of Enoch must tell us how to locate the weapon, which Maugis calls the Stone of Light, though elsewhere he refers to it as

Enoch's device. This is why we need the Book of Enoch. To find the device, the weapon needed to survive the prime conflict." Remi gazed at them with fierce eyes. "And we are running out of time."

"What do you mean?" Ciarán asked warily.

"On the fifth of March, Mars, the Roman god of war and bloodshed, shall pass between Scorpio and Sagittarius. So don't you see, war and bloodshed between Scorpio and Sagittarius? The prime conflict is nearly upon us!"

"That's less than four months from now," Ciarán realized.

"One hundred and five days," said Remi. "And six hundred sixty-six days from the millennium." He looked to Dónall. "Don't you realize its significance?"

Dónall turned away.

"If I am wrong," Remi argued, "we lose nothing by finishing Nicolas's mission and finding the Book of Enoch. If there is nothing to the book, so be it. If all of this is nonsense, what harm will have been done? But if I am right and the prophecy has begun, then you *know* we must do this. Or all will be lost. The horrors of the apocalypse will rain down on all. Dónall, the price of being wrong is unimaginable. Surely your logical mind brings you to this conclusion."

"There is one thing," Dónall admitted. "We fled Derry after a bishop from Blois came to arrest me for heresy. He knew all about Reims. But he came for Maugis' book, and he spoke of the prophecy."

A look of alarm flashed across Remi's face. "He *knows*? What if he learned that from Nicolas? Perhaps this bishop was the one who seized him! Dónall, listen to me. The enemy works in many ways. Not even priests and monks can be trusted. You and Ciarán were in great danger, just as I had feared!"

Ciarán felt the blood rush to his cheeks. "What has any of this to do with me?"

"Because of your blood," Remi said. "Because your father's ancestry can be traced to Gisela, the wife of Maugis d'Aygremont and the daughter of Charlemagne, which makes you of the bloodline of the champion. *That* is why your life is in peril."

Ciarán's jaw fell slack.

"You shall not drag him into this!" Dónall yelled. He grabbed Ciarán by the shoulders. "Listen, lad. What Remi just told you is not true. Yes, it appears that Maugis fathered a child with one of Charlemagne's daughters, even though the king had pledged them to life in convents. And their bloodline did exist among the Carolingian court. But when the Carolingian heir, Louis, and his mother were forced to flee to England, the bloodline of Maugis and Gisela followed them, and there, on that island, it died. I've seen proof of it with my own eyes, in the annals of a church in Winchester: proof that the last of their line perished in the year 928. So whatever bloodline you descended from, it is not the line of the champion."

"Those annals in Winchester may have been forged or amended," Remi countered, "to cover up the very fact that the bloodline exists."

Dónall rounded on him. "That is your blindness talking!"

Ciarán's chest heaved. "Who was my father?"

"Thomas was your father," Remi said. "And everything I've told you, he believed too. So did your mother."

Ciarán reeled while, before him, the color drained from Dónall's face. "I never told you," Dónall said, "because I wanted to protect you. Thomas was wrong, though he never could have known what I later learned at Winchester."

"Yet he believed so strongly in it that it cost him his life," Ciarán said through clenched teeth, blinking back the tears. "And my mother's as well."

Dónall reached for him, but Ciarán pushed him away. "No," he said, backing away from the shrine. "You lied!"

He bolted up the stairs, where chants still echoed from the nave, and rushed from the church into the cloister's garden. He threw back his head and looked up at the night sky with its glimmering array of stars. Was this why his parents died? And his friends, too?

Ciarán prayed to the heavens for an answer but received no response from the starlit vault—only the whisper of a chill breeze through the garden of Saint-Germain-des-Prés.

CHAPTER 16

WHAT THEY DIED FOR

"Lord God, let him forgive me," Dónall prayed quietly. "And grant me the wisdom to understand what is happening."

He knelt before the altar of the abbey church, breathing in the rancid scent of tallow candles. Ciarán had not spoken to him since he found the lad in the cloister last night while the monks of Saint-Germain-des-Prés filed from the church after Vespers. The gatekeeper had met the two Irish monks and escorted them to a guesthouse not far from the house where the abbot lived. Dónall's apprehension over Remi's latest theories and the fate of dear Nicolas was enough to keep him awake, although it was his guilt over deceiving Ciarán that tortured his sleep. By Prime the next morning, the solemn-faced lad could barely look at the man who had raised him since childhood, and the dagger of guilt twisted deeper in Dónall's breast.

Hearing footsteps behind him, he turned his head to see a gray-robed figure in the left transept. Dónall rose, making eye contact with Ciarán, who stood before an alcove containing a casket-shaped reliquary of Saint Vincent the Martyr, the abbey's patron until the death of Saint Germain. A golden crucifix stood next to the reliquary, which itself was overlaid in gold leaf and flanked by sweet-scented beeswax candles in silver holders—a display perhaps surpassing all the wealth in Derry.

"Ironic," Dónall said, approaching the lad, "that Saint Germain was also known as the 'father of the poor.'"

Ciarán stared at the reliquary. "When do we leave?"

"To return to Ireland?"

"No. To find Enoch's book. I want to know what my parents died for."

"I feared you'd be of such a mind," Dónall said gently. "You must understand, you are not of Charlemagne's line. I believe what I saw in Winchester."

"But what about the rest? What about this prophecy? My parents believed in it and died for it. I deserve to know if even a shred of it is true."

"I remain skeptical," Dónall replied.

"Yet what of your friend Nicolas? What if Adémar of Blois did have him killed, all for this, just as Remi said?"

Dónall grimaced. "I swear, it was Adalbero's inquisition and Gerbert's treachery that led to the deaths of most of my brothers at Reims, including your father. But Gerbert has fled France, cast out of Reims as a usurper by the pope himself. And Adalbero is long dead. But if someone has taken up their cause, then I must know. This has to end."

"And if this is about more than accusations of heresy?" Ciarán asked.

"We'll know soon enough." Dónall was glad to see that Ciarán's anger had subsided, but the lad's question raised more troubling thoughts. "Let's pray this is nothing more than a bishop's inquest," Dónall said. "Because if what Remi believes should prove true, then God help us all."

AFTER NONES, they took supper in the abbey's refectory with Remi, who, much to the astonishment of his fellow monks at Saint-Germain-des-Prés, had left the crypts. The open hall, lit with rushlights, was filled with the scents of smoke and cooking fat. After washing at a small basin near the refectory door, the monks gathered at the long trestle tables arranged in a U. An elderly Benedictine called them to silence and spoke a prayer, and at his amen, the monks sat down on the benches as others brought food from the kitchen.

The monks of Saint-Germain-des-Prés ate like kings compared to Dónall and Ciarán's Irish brethren. Loaves of wheat bread, spits of roast crane, and bowls of dried apples and nuts were served, along with pepper and mustard and carafes of red wine. Dónall watched with amusement as Ciarán wolfed down his food the way only a growing young man could, and then licked the grease from his fingers to avoid wasting a single drop.

Later that night, after the holy office of Compline, Ciarán slept quietly, but Dónall tossed and turned despite the warm blankets and pallets amply stuffed with straw. His guilt at deceiving Ciarán all these years hung over him like a lead cloak, while the implications of Remi's theories stabbed at his mind like tiny knives. Dónall closed his eyes, recalling the first time Remi voiced his troubling concerns —the night Canon Martinus died.

Dónall remembered it vividly. In the hours after the murder, he and nine of his brethren had gathered in one of the classrooms. For light, they had only a few tallow candles, dancing in the cold gusts that invaded the chamber through coin-size chinks in the stone walls. Thomas, who had called the gathering, stood in the classroom's well, while the others sat in the nearest of the desks that rose in tiers on the chamber's stepped floor. They were whispering about the fate of Omer and Vicelin, whom Archbishop Adalbero had arrested for the murder of Canon Martinus.

"Here is what we know," Thomas said, shushing the whispers. "The door to the Secret Collection was cracked, which means Canon Martinus either discovered it or discovered his killer, who was heading for that door."

Orlando, a swarthy Genoese, shook his head. "None of the canons know of the Secret Collection."

"Unless someone told them about it," Lucien replied.

"Who would tell them?" Orlando demanded.

Lucien's gaze turned to Gerbert. "One who wished to curry favor with the archbishop."

"He was whispering in Adalbero's ear," snapped Burghard, a quick-tempered Frank with the build of an ox.

Already nervous and fidgety, Gerbert protested, "You think I would betray our oath?"

"Men have betrayed lesser promises for power," Lucien suggested.

"We've no proof the canon knew about the hidden door," Dónall said.

"But the man who killed him did." Again Thomas commanded the attention of the entire room. "Which leaves only the twelve of us."

"Omer couldn't have done it," Nicolas said, his eyes red with tears. "He wouldn't have hurt a mouse."

"What about Vicelin?" asked Sigbert, an awkward monk who was one of the keener scholars among them. His question lingered in the air.

"He was with me," said Theodulf, whose shaven head and pock-marked face were veiled in shadow behind an upper desk. "We were studying in this very room at the time of the murder. Vicelin was Omer's closest friend—that's why they arrested him."

"Which means all of us could be in danger," Sigbert fretted.

And one of us is a killer. Dónall could not rid himself of that horrifying thought.

"Especially if someone has betrayed us to the archbishop." Lucien again directed his remarks to Gerbert.

"You've no proof I was anywhere near that corridor when the murder took place," Gerbert argued. "I resent your implication!"

Burghard pointed to Gerbert from across the room. "Yet you did not deny it!"

"I was in the library," Gerbert snapped.

"Are there witnesses?" Sigbert's question came more as an accusation.

Gerbert scowled. "I do not need to defend myself to you!"

"Brothers," Thomas implored, "let us use logic, not accusations."

"Careful, Thomas," Burghard warned. "Logic is his weapon. He'll trick us all with his devil's tongue."

"Enough!" Dónall said as sharp words erupted around the room. In an instant, the brethren were out of their seats and face-to-face, shouting in anger and threatening with gestures, their venom focused on Gerbert of Aurillac.

"To hell with your lies!" Gerbert cried. Grimacing, he stormed for the door. Orlando reached for him, but Gerbert shoved him away and Orlando staggered back, nearly toppling a desk before Lucien grabbed his arm to keep him upright. The door slammed, and Gerbert was gone.

"His flight betrays his guilt!" said Burghard.

"Brothers!" Thomas said, fighting to maintain order. "We are not some angry mob. We are scholars!"

This quieted the room to a grumbling murmur. Remi, who had been silent until now, finally spoke. "There is one possibility that all of you have failed to mention. What if our enemy is not in this room? What if there are darker forces at work? Forces beyond these four walls—even beyond the world itself—that wish to divide and disperse us."

"What do you mean?" Sigbert asked as the chamber abruptly fell silent.

"Is it not obvious?" Remi said. "We have deciphered the prophecy, which means we have become dangerous to them. We are the only ones who can stop them, and they will not rest until every last one of us is dead."

Remi's words lingered in Dónall's mind as the image of the room faded. The events that followed seemed a blur.

Thomas had stolen the Book of Maugis d'Aygremont, and he came to Dónall the next evening, when the moon was dark and an early frost blanketed the ground. "I don't know whom we can trust," Thomas said, clutching the book in his arms. "But one among us has blood on his sword, and I fear he was going for the book, to steal it for himself."

Dónall didn't know if paranoia had sparked those words, but suspicions had been spreading like a plague among the group, ever since the rumors of heresy had begun to circulate. Many of them feared that the book might be lost. Could the Fae arts have proved too strong a temptation for one of them, with the book supplying the source? Could it have driven a man to *kill*?

That night, Dónall and Thomas hid in one of the city's brothels —a place Adalbero would never think to look. They had paid the prostitutes for their accommodation but not their services, and escaped Reims the next morning as soon as the gates were open. The initial plan was to contact their brethren one by one and determine who could be trusted. Yet Adalbero's inquisition proved relentless. Omer and Vicelin burned at the stake within the first week. Many of the others fled the school, but Adalbero's men pursued them. Burghard and Theodulf were arrested in Paris, trying to procure passage aboard a ship to England. They were tried, convicted, and burned at the stake in the square outside the cathedral of Saint-Étienne. Orlando made it as far south as Troyes before the inquisition found him. Sigurd, who had stayed at the school and professed his innocence, was caught a year later practicing the Fae arts. Adalbero himself presided over the execution.

For a time, Dónall and Thomas sojourned in England until Thomas's pursuit of the prophecy took them back to France, to Laon. The city was racked by war between King Lothair and Otto the Red, the Holy Roman Emperor, who had laid siege to the walled city. That was where they had met Martha. *Beautiful Martha.*

If only the conflict had not forced them to go back through Reims.

Dónall recalled their last night together, in a cramped, musty inn room, where Thomas was drunk on wine and his obsession with the prophecy. He was bearded by then, his hair grown long and wild, and the strain of five years as a fugitive lined his once angelic face. He wore layman's clothes, having cast off the last vestige of his monastic station. By then, they had broken so many vows, it was pointless to live as monks. Behind them, Martha tried to rock her and Thomas's infant child to sleep, but the child wailed incessantly.

"The Dragon hunts us," Thomas said, ignoring the infant. "All along, Remi was right."

"Adalbero thinks he's doing God's will," Dónall said, trying to prevent Thomas from slipping deeper into one of his dark melancholy moods.

"Adalbero is being deceived," Thomas said bitterly. "It's the Dragon's nature; it's what he does. But we know his secret, his weakness. And for this, he will not stop hunting us till we're dead."

"So today you see only doom?"

Thomas's eyes brightened. "No, I see hope. Don't you?" He gestured to the infant and Martha. "*There* is our hope. We're already fulfilling the prophecy. When the time comes, we'll be ready." Grinning like a madman, he drained his cup of wine. "When we lose hope, that's when we're doomed."

The image blurred once more, and Dónall could hear the crackling of flames and smell the burning pitch as if it were happening again. He hid among the hundreds of people who had gathered outside the cathedral of Reims at noon. The archbishop's guardsmen, hard-faced warriors wearing mail and bearing spears, kept the crowd at bay while Adalbero, surrounded by his personal troops, presided over the spectacle. Standing at his side, looking frail and wan in his Benedictine habit, was Gerbert. His hands touched his lips as if in prayer, and his eyes were closed, unable to gaze upon the friend he had betrayed. Bound to two stakes, above pyres of pitch-coated wood, Thomas and Martha gazed into each other's eyes. Their arms and legs were bound, though the fire had not reached their flesh. Tears ran down Martha's face, though Thomas's steely gaze told her to be brave. The end would come soon, but before it, the inferno.

Dónall, with the child swaddled in cloth and cradled protectively in his arms, watched in silent horror. Slung over his back, a leather book satchel concealed the Book of Maugis. But not even the Fae arts could save them—there were too many guardsmen. Adalbero or Gerbert would spot him, and he would accomplish nothing but to share his friends' fate. When the fire licked their feet, and his friend could not help but scream and cry out prayers to God, Dónall lowered his head. The crowd, whipped into a frenzy, shouted cries of "Heretic!" "Witch!" "Let them burn!"

The rabble surrounding him stank and screamed, and the infant started to wail. Dónall feared that one of the guardsmen had seen him—or soon would if the infant continued to cry. His heart raced.

"Kill the devils!"

"Curse them!"

"Damn their souls!"

The crowd had become a seething mass of hatred and bloodlust. Dónall tried to push his way free, past wild-eyed rabble with their rotting teeth and dirt-streaked faces twisted in rage. The crowd enveloped him, and he struggled for breath, wedged between bodies. The child had grown strangely silent and still in his arms.

Dónall shuddered as his thoughts returned to the present. Sitting in the guestroom of Saint-Germain-des-Prés, he uttered a promise to himself: *"never again."*

Beside him, Ciarán stirred awake. "What is it?"

"Just a bad memory." Dónall drew his blanket more tightly around himself. "Nothing more."

By morning, he, Remi, and Ciarán were ready to set off on the ten-day journey to the small village where they hoped to find the Book of Enoch. Remi seemed exuberant over their mission, and Ciarán, too, appeared eager to leave. Yet Dónall's mind was no more at ease.

For he had a bad feeling about the journey that lay ahead.

CHAPTER 17

THE SACRIFICE

Two days after departing from Blois, the Benedictine stood in a torch-lit chamber alongside twenty-two black-robed and cowled monks. Their chanting subsided to a mournful hum. Against the far wall, the prisoner rattled the chains shackling his wrists. Long scars from burnings and lashings crisscrossed what flesh still clung to his gaunt form.

"You can plead all you want," the Benedictine told the prisoner, "but the time for mercy is long past."

The prisoner's hair dangled before his dirt-stained face. "Why now?" he asked.

"Because you are no longer of use to us," the Benedictine replied. "The Book of Maugis d'Aygremont is within our grasp. And so is Dónall mac Taidg."

"You lie," the prisoner growled.

"Am I lying about what shall happen next? That you shall be sacrificed for our cause?"

"You are not a killer," the prisoner said.

"*Au contraire.* Murder has become less troubling after all these years." The Benedictine raised his arms and gestured toward the far wall, dominated by a massive carving of a dragon's head. "Look upon the face of the one your blood shall serve."

The dragon's stone jaws, bathed in the torchlight, opened in a silent roar framed by sharp teeth as long as a man's arm. Its eyes glowed red from the candles set within the sockets.

The prisoner's eyes narrowed, and his breathing quickened.

The monks' chanting rose again in haunting strains. The gate within the dragon's mouth ground open, and the stench of decay wafted forth, punctuated by a hissing growl.

As the chanting crescendoed, the Benedictine's heart beat faster.

The prisoner's eyes grew wide, and his jaw started to tremble.

From the dragon's mouth slithered an abomination. A reptilian snout emerged first, followed by a head covered in feathery scales. The eyes, black and merciless, shifted hungrily beneath three pale tubercles that rose from the top of its head like a rooster's crown. The leering head swayed back and forth on a serpentine neck attached to an avian torso the size of a mastiff's, while two eagle's legs with hooked claws clattered on the stone floor.

The prisoner flailed in his chains, trying to rip them from the wall.

A terrible hiss escaped the creature's mouth as it whipped its snakelike tail.

"Behold the basilisk," the Benedictine proclaimed. "It is rather more ferocious, I'm afraid, than Pliny described. It came to us as an egg from the Otherworld. You can see how much it has grown."

The basilisk fixed its gaze on the prisoner and flicked out its forked tongue.

"Merciful God," the prisoner stammered.

"It's a common misconception," the Benedictine continued, "that the basilisk's gaze causes death. As you will soon see, that is untrue. Its real threat is not magical at all but purely chemical."

A guttural sound issued from the creature's throat. It reared back its head and spat a stream of viscous liquid that splattered against the prisoner's naked chest, onto his face, and into his eyes.

The prisoner screamed and tried to claw at the spittle, but the chains held back his arms.

"The venom burns, I know," the Benedictine observed. "Soon it will paralyze your muscles, though, alas, that does not dull the pain."

The prisoner began to twitch, then made a heaving gasp as the basilisk eyed its prey, testing the air with its tongue.

"Fear not, Nicolas," the Benedictine said. "With luck, the venom might kill you before you are eaten."

The chanting became frenetic. Like a coiled serpent, the basilisk struck. Its teeth sank into the prisoner's neck, and its clenched jaws shook him savagely. The prisoner let out a final, sickening moan.

The Benedictine turned his gaze, unable to watch any further. "My lord," he said under his breath, "your will is done."

CHAPTER 18
OR THE KING'S MEN

December 13, 997, was as beautiful a day as Alais could remember. The sky was bright blue, touched by only a few wisps of fleecy white cloud. The air was warmer than normal for this time of year, and the village of Selles-sur-Cher was alive with sound.

Dogs barked, and chickens clucked in their coops. Overhead, a chevron of greylag geese honked as they glided over the village to the millpond at the edge of the river, where the waterwheel thumped and groaned. Near the road, a group of boys ran and wrestled and called challenges to one another. Alais smiled at two women as she passed, walking downhill from the manor house to the roadside, where Brother Thadeus waved to greet her.

"Brother Thadeus," she said warmly. "What brings you away from the abbey?"

"Believe it or not, my dear, no one is sick today. It seems a miracle of sorts, so I thought I'd take a stroll on this fine, balmy day."

"It is beautiful, isn't it?"

"Yes," he replied, taking a deep breath of fresh air. "And I wanted to see how you're doing, of course."

"Better," she said. She nearly choked up as the words left her mouth, but it was true, she did feel better. Her love for Geoffrey remained as strong as ever, but somewhere along the way, she had realized that she had a choice. She could either let her grief drag her into some dark abyss—one from which she might well never return—or just let her grief go. She chose the latter, difficult as it was. It was the courageous thing to do, and what Geoffrey would have wanted.

"I must say," the old monk remarked, "you do look more at peace."

"Perhaps it's the time of the year. I always loved Christmastime."

"There's much to do to get ready, you know. And the people—they'll look to you to make sure it happens."

She laughed. "Geoffrey always left that for me anyway. I like preparing for the festivals—gives me something to do."

"And I'm sure the village will be grateful for it." Thadeus opened his mouth to speak again but stopped short of a word, his eyes fixed on the road.

A cloud of dust stirred above the hilltop nearest the village. And through the cloud came horses—and not just any horses, but big destrier chargers. Riding them were perhaps three or four dozen men.

A spark of hope welled within Alais.

"Your cousin?" Thadeus asked.

She clasped her hands to her chest. "Or the king's men!"

Brimming with excitement, she squinted to see which banner the approaching riders carried: the crimson lion of Poitiers or the fleur-de-lis of the king of France. The horses thundered down the road. She spotted the lead rider, a large man clad in mail but holding no banner. She looked beyond him to the next rider, then the next. These men held something in their hands—batons, perhaps, but not banners—and their cloaks were dark, neither crimson nor blue.

"Alais . . ." Thadeus muttered, his voice now grave.

As the riders bore down on Selles, their batons seemed to glow and give off smoke.

"For the love of God," Thadeus said, "run!"

Alais felt rooted to the ground. She watched with horror as one of the horsemen tossed a burning torch into a cottage at the edge of the village. The dry thatch caught flame at once. The village women began to scream. Several scooped up children; others ducked into their cottages. In the fields, the farmers scattered, scurrying toward their homes. A second cottage burst into flames. The column of riders charged into Selles, nearly trampling a small girl who scrambled to save her dog, which stood defiantly in the road, barking at the horsemen.

Alais' heart pounded.

"Go!" cried Thadeus. "To the manor, and bar the door!"

Alais shook her head in disbelief. The air now reeked of burning thatch, and the line of cottages at Selles' west end had become a wall of fire.

The thunder of hoofbeats and the crackle of flames mixed with the alarmed screams of the villagers.

Alais glanced back at the women she had passed on her way to the road. Their eyes were wide with terror. They needed to move, to hide. But like her, they knelt, all but frozen with the shock of the riders' onslaught. Alais' first attempt to call to them brought nothing but a fear-choked whisper. But her second try was a yell. "Hide!" Her voice grew stronger. "Grab your children and hide!"

The women moved now, as if they had been slapped awake. They dropped their hand shovels and buckets and ran for their wee ones, who had already shown the good sense to run away from the road.

Thadeus was pushing her now. "You, too, Alais. Do as I say!"

She started up the hill, lifting her dress with both hands so as not to trip. She ran until she reached the garden outside the manor. The horses sounded now as if they were right behind her. Glancing over her shoulder, she was dismayed to see that Thadeus had not followed her. Rather, the black-robed monk stood defiantly in the road, his hands raised above his head, his face burning with rage.

"In the name of Saint Eustace and Christ our Savior," he cried, "I command thee to cease! Lest your souls burn in the lake of fire!"

But the lead rider, the large man in mail who held no torch, did not cease. For an instant, Alais saw his face: younger than Geoffrey's, framed by a thick black beard and a mane of oily black hair, and filled with wanton cruelty.

"Thadeus!" she screamed.

Behind the black-bearded leader, who was just a few lengths away from Thadeus, half the riders followed. The other half dispersed among the cottages, more of which were now in flames.

"In the name of the Father, the Son, and the Holy Spirit, I demand that you cease!" Thadeus shouted. "Your souls are at stake, man—your eternal souls!"

The lead rider lowered his head and kicked his spurs hard into his mount. The horse charged forward and never swerved.

Alais screamed. She had never experienced the horror of seeing a man run down. It happened horrifically fast. In one moment, her dear old Thadeus stood waving his arms, and in the next, he looked no more alive than a scarecrow that had been tossed to the ground.

The column of riders thundered down the road, heading for the abbey and leaving in their wake the lifeless form of Brother Thadeus, covered in dust and blood.

A new thunder of hoofbeats shocked Alais back into action. A small cohort of riders, five in all, had veered away from the column and started up the pathway to the manor.

Alais had just time to make it inside. Hearing the screams of women around her, she lunged toward the manor door. A terrible realization gripped her, for she knew what men like this did to women. After the pillaging would come the raping.

As soon as Alais was inside, she slammed the door shut. Outside, the galloping hoofbeats grew louder. She fumbled for the heavy wooden bar, but it slipped from her fingers and crashed onto her foot. A sharp pain shot up her foot and leg, and she began to panic, fearing she would not set the bar in time. She could hear the horses snorting and whinnying just beyond the door, and hooves stomping in her garden. *Focus!* she demanded of herself. Using all the strength her arms possessed, she raised the bar, struggling to set it in the iron brackets that would hold the door closed. *Just a moment more . . .*

Then the door exploded open.

The impact hurled her to the ground, and the bar flew from her hands, clattering over the stone-tiled floor.

A Frankish warrior loomed over her—a hard-looking man in a mail shirt and iron helm.

"No," she pleaded, crawling away from the man.

His hand reached for the pommel of his sheathed broadsword. But then another, taller man pushed the Frank aside. He whisked off his dusty riding cloak to reveal a black cassock, and a silver crucifix at his throat. He tossed the riding cloak to the Frank.

"I said she was not to be harmed."

The man addressed the Frank in a commanding tone befitting his presence, which seemed to fill the whole room. He looked at her with a piercing stare that unnerved her. Beneath those eyes was a strong, angular face framed by a narrow, close-cropped mustache and silver-flecked beard. She had seen this man before, she realized. His vestments sparked a memory—a bishop's vestments. Geoffrey had introduced her to him once: Adémar, the bishop of Blois.

"Lord Bishop," she stammered, "what is—?"

"What is, my child, is that you are in great danger." Bishop Adémar extended a hand to help her from the floor, but she crawled backward and stood unassisted.

"This attack . . . how *dare* you!"

"It was not my doing," he replied. "It is the count of Anjou who assaults your lands."

"Fulk the Black!" The very name struck a chord of terror that made Alais shudder.

"I see that comprehension has begun to dawn." As he spoke, Bishop Adémar stepped farther into the room, backing Alais up to the trestle table in the center of the narrow hall. Behind the bishop, two more Franks entered the room. "The question, my child," he continued, "is whether he has just cause."

"*Just cause?*" she gasped. "How? My husband was a loyal servant of the king. He never raised arms against the count of Anjou or his vassals."

"Fulk of Anjou no longer recognizes the authority of an excommunicated king. He acts on the authority of the Holy Church itself."

"The *Church*? My husband was lay abbot. We've done nothing to offend the Church."

"Is heresy not an offense to the Church?"

Her response was barely a whisper. "Heresy?"

"We have a confessor who swore that the monks of Selles-sur-Cher keep a heretical tome, a book so antithetical to the teachings of the Church that harboring it is an affront to God himself."

The scroll! Alais' pulse quickened. The thought flashed in her brain that if she gave Bishop Adémar the scroll, he would leave Selles alone. But what of her promise to Geoffrey? Her hand went to where Geoffrey's key hung between her breasts, beneath the collar of her shirt. "I know of no such thing."

"Of course you don't, my child. I did not expect you to." His tone was sympathetic and reassuring. "But that puts you in no less danger."

"But why?"

"You are a beautiful woman. Although I do not sanction their behavior, I can't very well control the passions of four dozen men, especially when they have been whipped into a frenzy."

"You would let them ravish the women of this village?"

"Men will be men. But they are the count of Anjou's burden."

"And the Church saw fit to trust its work to *him*? I've heard the stories of what he did to the priests at Chateauneuf."

The cleric shrugged. "The count of Anjou may be a black-hearted devil, but even a devil has his uses when pointed in the right direction."

"You men disgust me!" she hissed.

Adémar walked closer as he spoke, but Alais pushed him away.

"Your words wound me," he said. "I insisted on joining this mission to make sure innocents such as yourself were not caught up in the violence. I am but a shepherd. And you, my child, born of noble blood, are a member of my flock. It is my duty to protect you."

Alais found herself backing away. She was at the threshold to her bedchamber. Bishop Adémar sounded sincere. He smiled at her, baring perfect white teeth between his narrow lips.

He extended his hand. "If it is found that no heretical book exists, I'll make sure that none of the monks are harmed and that the count makes reparations to your village. You have my word."

Alais hesitated. They wouldn't find the scroll in the abbey. She looked into Bishop Adémar's eyes. His feral gaze from a moment ago was gone.

"You, of all people, have no reason to fear," the bishop said kindly. "I know you had nothing to do with this. Why, you hail from the finest family in Aquitaine, a good Christian family. In fact, the piety of your cousin William is grown legendary. I could never let you be harmed."

She let Bishop Adémar take her hand. His touch was gentle. "You promise?"

"Of course," he said, drawing her into an embrace.

For a moment, she let herself be held. The terror that filled her began to ebb away, displaced by grief over Thadeus's death. Alais started to sob. She could no longer hold back the tears.

"See, my child, all will be well," Adémar said, stroking her hair. "This time of trial will pass."

Then she felt the kiss of his lips on her cheek.

Her muscles tensed. She realized now that he had slowly backed her into the bedchamber.

With his foot, he shut the door behind them.

Panic seized her as one of his hands fell to the small of her back.

Alais let out a muffled scream. "No!" She pushed him away with unexpected force, and he slammed against the door. His eyes narrowed, and his lips broke into a feral grin.

His arm flashed toward her, and she felt the stinging slap against her face. The blow knocked her back onto the bed. The pain was so intense, she wondered if he had broken her jaw. She felt his warm breath on her ankles. This couldn't be happening! Alais fought back, kicking her legs as violently as she could. The seam of her dress ripped all the way to her waist. Hands clamped down on her arms. His grip was like iron, stronger than anything she had ever felt. His body fell on top of hers. He was twice Geoffrey's weight, and she cringed as he dragged his tongue up her neck and to the tip of her chin.

"No," she whimpered, tears spilling into her mouth. "For God's sake, *you're a priest!*"

"And you're a woman," he said contemptuously. "The vessel through which sin entered the world, by which Paradise was lost—the reason for which Christ had to suffer and die on the cross!" He had worked himself between her legs. She struggled beneath his grip, but her arms did not move. She closed her eyes. *Saint Radegonde!* she screamed inside her mind. *Take me from here!* She cringed at his first violent thrust.

"Through woman came sin," he grunted. "Through woman came temptation. Through woman came damnation!"

Alais felt numb, lifeless. Bishop Adémar relaxed his iron grip, though he continued thrusting and rutting on top of her. She realized that one of her arms was free. Her consciousness snapped violently back to reality. She opened her eyes and saw him huffing with lascivious pleasure. Hate filled her soul, and a single thought shot through her mind. Her hand fumbled under the pillow on the other side of the bed, and she felt the hilt of the dagger. She worked her fingers around the grip and raised it high.

Bishop Adémar grinned savagely—until Alais thrust the dagger downward with every ounce of her strength, sinking it between his shoulder blades.

The bishop roared. He sprang off her, ripping the hilt from her hand. But the dagger still protruded from his back. The hem of his tunic fell to his ankles as he grasped frantically for the dagger's hilt.

Alais rolled off the bed and darted for the door, opened it, and burst into the hall. The Franks, who were lounging on the benches to the trestle table, had no time to react.

"*Stop her!*" Bishop Adémar's voice bellowed from the bedchamber.

Alais fled from the hall and out the manor door—right into a burly chest covered in mail.

The Frank wrapped her in a bear hug. She recoiled at the stench of his breath, and her body went limp. Alais could no longer summon the strength to resist.

Bishop Adémar stormed into the hall. To her horror, he held the bloody dagger in his hand.

This can't be possible! she screamed within her mind. *It should have killed him!*

"Witch!" the bishop screamed. "She's a witch! She seduced me with a spell."

The Franks looked wide-eyed at him.

"Need I remind you, the devil works his way through the bodies of women!" he yelled. "Take her outside." He leveled his gaze at Alais. "She is a witch, I tell you. And a witch must burn."

Alais' lower lip began to tremble. *Saint Radegonde!* she cried out in a silent plea. *Holy Savior, please!*

Yet as they took her from the manor down the pathway to the abbey, past the burning cottages of Selles, Alais knew that this time she was truly alone. This time, there was no one to save her.

CHAPTER 19

SO CAME DEATH

O
n the outskirts of Remorantin, the village where they slept on the ninth day of their journey, Ciarán, Dónall, and Remi spied a man hanging from a tree.

Remi started toward the corpse, dangling from a limb of a great oak whose leaf-bare branches clawed at the sky. "Nicolas!" he cried as he ran. Chasing after him, Ciarán grimaced when he neared the hanged man. The face, gazing absently at the ground, was gray except where bleached bone showed through where the ravens had pecked the flesh clean. Ants crawled over the skull, down the neck, and beneath a tattered brown tunic. Ciarán gagged at the stench and tried not to retch.

Dónall strode up beside them. "It is not Nicolas," he said softly.

Remi pushed up the man's chin with the tip of his walking staff, carved of alder and stained black like Dónall's. The dead man's head tilted sideways, staring back through hollow eyes. "No," Remi agreed. "Just a thief. Lucky him—thieves hang; heretics burn."

"We don't know if Nicolas suffered that fate," Dónall said.

"For nine days we have been on these roads," Remi insisted. "I have inquired in every village along the way. No one has seen him."

Dónall nudged Remi away from the dead man. "There are other roads that lead to Selles-sur-Cher."

"The enemy is always searching," Remi said, his lower lip trembling. "I fear that the enemy has found him." With a desperate gasp, Remi gripped his face in his bony hands and staggered away.

Ciarán watched the Benedictine stray toward a copse of oaks bordering a pale meadow. "What if Nicolas had traveled through Blois?" he asked. "Right through the bishop's realm."

"I've had that concern, too," Dónall replied. "Which is why, after we're through with Selles, I want to check on my old friend Lucien. He evaded Gerbert's treachery and Adalbero's inquisition back at Reims, but he never had the stomach for Remi's quest. I'm told he retired to a small priory in the Touraine, near Saint-Aignan. If Adémar of Blois has threatened Lucien, too, then we are indeed all being hunted, just as Remi fears."

"There is no way the bishop could know where we are," Ciarán said. "He didn't pursue us to Paris, and we've seen no sign of his men along the way."

Dónall smiled faintly. "I trained you to think logically, didn't I?"

Ciarán shrugged. "I paid attention." He turned as Remi approached. The Benedictine had regained some of his composure, though the tears left streaks from his eyes to his unkempt beard.

"Let us not linger," Remi announced, "or forget why we have come. For before this day ends, we may hold the Book of Enoch in our hands."

They started down the road, a path of trampled grass and dirt that traversed the meadow. Though it was a meager road, Ciarán far preferred it to the old Roman roads they had traveled after Paris. Once paved with stone, they were now littered with massive potholes that became muddy troughs with each rain. Also, miles of road had become overgrown as the forests reclaimed land the Romans had cleared a millennium ago, leading Ciarán at times to fear that they would be lost in dense woodlands where only the wolves might find them. Fortunately, at Saint-Germain-des-Prés they had joined a party of a dozen Benedictines traveling under the abbot's charter to bring a shipment of illuminated tomes to the bishop in Orléans, an old Roman city on the Loire that rivaled even the grandeur of Paris. The Benedictines knew the roads, and their numbers were great enough to deter bandits and even the violent local lords who plagued travelers in France. South of Orléans, the roads proved better as they journeyed through four more villages, the last being Remorantin.

Although midwinter was just a week away, Ciarán found the last leg of their journey blessed by pleasant weather. Beside him, Dónall walked with his staff, his book satchel slung over his shoulder. A few paces ahead, Remi chattered with anticipation as they neared Selles-sur-Cher. After several hours, they crested a hill topped with winter-brown grass.

"There it is!" Remi announced, pointing toward a winding river below. On its southern bank were fields and cottages, but it was the limestone abbey perched on a squat hill that captured Remi's attention. To Ciarán, it looked about like half the other villages they had passed through on their way from Paris. He just hoped the lord of Selles was not a bandit.

"Do you see smoke?" Dónall asked.

Ciarán shielded his eyes from the sun and peered across the river. Sure enough, a few tendrils of smoke rose from the far west side of the village. "Chimneys, perhaps," Remi said. But as he spoke, those threads of smoke swelled into dark, billowing plumes. As they watched, the plumes began to spread, choking the air above the village in an angry black cloud. Ciarán could hardly believe his eyes. Selles-sur-Cher was *burning*.

Remi started down the hill. Dónall and Ciarán, still stunned, could not take their eyes off the burning village. "The enemy knows!" Remi raved, motioning with his staff for the other two monks to follow. "He is upon us! All is in peril!"

Ciarán glanced at Dónall and then darted after Remi, who continued gaining ground, though the river still looked a quarter league away. Downhill, the road ran through a brown meadow to the river, where a ferry dock stood on the bank. Across the river, a swarm of figures moved rapidly through the village. Ciarán realized they were horsemen. The black cloud above Selles swelled, fed by more plumes of smoke as more cottages were put to the torch. Panicked screams sounded across the river, mixed with the shouts of men and the cries of beasts.

Remi reached the dock first, with Ciarán on his heels and Dónall trailing them. In the river, a small ferry with three passengers was nearing the dock.

"Dónall, make haste!" Remi cried.

Gasping for breath, Dónall caught up just as the ferry reached the dock. Ciarán grabbed the mooring line and secured the craft, and three Benedictine monks stepped ashore. One of them was an abbot or a prior, judging from the gold-leaf crucifix around his neck. Fat as a penned hog, he carried an armful of treasure: a golden communion cup, two gold-plated candlestick holders, and a small reliquary that likely carried the tooth or knucklebone of some saint or other. The other two monks, who were much younger, each carried a wooden coffer.

"What is happening?" Remi demanded of the fat monk.

"Fulk the Black," he replied. "Our blessed abbey is under attack! Flee if you value your lives!" The fat man pushed past Ciarán but bumped square into Dónall, who stood to his full imposing height.

"Move!" one of the fat monk's companions demanded.

Dónall didn't budge. "Are you abbot or prior?"

"Prior," the fat man said. "Our lay abbot is dead." He tried again to push his way through, but Dónall stood fast. When the prior's companion tried to muscle his way past, Ciarán grabbed his arm. The man, who was as thin as his superior was fat, gave Ciarán a startled look.

"Why are you being attacked?" Dónall pressed.

"'Tis madness. They've arrested the lady under accusation of witchcraft, as a servant of the demon. And they ride with the bishop of Blois, hunting for heretics!"

Ciarán's heart jumped. *How could this be possible!*

Alarmed, Remi looked to Dónall, who nodded faintly, still staring down the prior. "Witchcraft, you say?" Dónall asked.

"Something about a devil's tome. They were driving the stake as we fled."

142

Dónall's face reddened. "They are to burn her?"

"Yes," the prior spat. "And if she's the one who brought this upon us, I say let her burn!"

"Enough!" Dónall grabbed the prior by his habit and hurled him off the dock. Arms flailing, the fat man splashed into the Cher. His golden relics, visible for an instant in the brown water, sunk beneath the river's depths.

"We're taking your ferry," Dónall told the prior's two stunned companions.

"We're going *there*?" Ciarán moaned, glancing at the burning village.

"You heard him," Dónall replied sternly. "Heresy? A devil's tome? And once more, Adémar of Blois is in the middle of it. I'll be dammed before I let another innocent die for his misbegotten cause."

Ciarán did not argue. Neither did Remi, who was already in the ferry, ready to go. A mad smile spread across his face.

"And so came Death!" he crowed. "And hell followed with him!"

The acrid smell of burning thatch wafted across the river, and Ciarán thought back on Derry. The clash with the bishop's men flashed vividly in his mind, as did the faces of his brothers as they died one by one: Senach and Áed, Murchad and Fintan, and Niall falling to the bishop's sword—all amid the smoke and fire raging from the haystacks. As Ciarán poled the ferry across the Cher, he could not help but feel that he was heading straight back to the horror that had befallen them back home. The odds once again would be vastly against them. They were but three, yet these attackers must number three score or more. *And monks are not warriors,* he reminded himself.

He glanced at his companions. The wild look had returned to Remi's eyes. Dónall sat deep in thought, just staring at the village ahead. Ciarán prayed that his old mentor was working on a plan, for if not, they were about to die for a cause that Ciarán was not even sure he believed in.

Nearing the dock on the river's southern bank, he could see the mail-clad riders gathering near the limestone abbey—twenty or thirty men in all. Ciarán began to whisper a Psalm. *"Deliver me from my enemies, O God . . ."* He stopped in mid verse, for Niall's battle cry rang out in his mind. *Columcille!* An Irish cry, a call for courage.

And Ciarán prayed that God would grant him a double measure of courage when they reached the riverbank.

OUTSIDE THE ABBEY, the bishop's men bound Alais to a wooden stake they had driven into the ground and surrounded with a bed of kindling. They tied her hands behind her back, around the stake, then bound her by her waist and neck and, finally the ankles.

Bishop Adémar watched with a thin smile. A score of horsemen had gathered around, many having dismounted and moved closer to watch the grisly spectacle. Behind them, a group of black-robed monks cowered, though they, too, looked on intently.

Between her pleas to the bishop's men, Alais thought of Saint Radegonde, but no saint was on hand to save her now. Her thoughts drifted to Geoffrey. *My love,* she prayed silently with what courage as she could muster, *soon—I will be there soon.*

If thoughts of Geoffrey brought her peace, it dissolved into panic when the Franks started slinging pitch from a bucket onto the kindling. The harsh-smelling tar stung her nose. A second Frank used a straw broom to brush more of it onto her dress.

"The more pitch," he said, "the faster the heretic burns."

Everywhere she looked, there were men: soldiers and the craven monks who had done nothing in her defense, but no villagers. With luck, they had fled, she thought briefly before her heart began to race again.

From the ranks of the Frankish horsemen strode the bearded man who had led the charge into Selles, a man whom Alais had grown to fear by reputation alone: Fulk the Black, count of Anjou. He stood half a head taller than most of his men, and broader chested. He looked her up and down with the clear blue eyes of a man not yet thirty years old. Those eyes were dangerous and lustful and arrogant. She had seen eyes like that before, in her late uncle,

William Iron-Arm. They were the eyes of a warrior. But Fulk's eyes also held another quality: a mercilessness that her uncle had never possessed. Looking her up and down, he gave a lecherous grin.

"Be careful, my lord," Bishop Adémar warned. "For she is a temptress."

Undeterred, Fulk brought his face so close to hers that she could smell the sweat on him. "You're a pretty thing, aren't you?" he whispered, fondling one of her breasts.

Turning her face from his, she felt his fingers at the base of her neck, followed by a violent jerk and the tearing of cloth. The front of her dress flapped free. Between her bare breasts dangled Geoffrey's key—the cross with a loop.

"See!" the bishop cried, pointing to the pendant. "A sign of the devil! She's an enchantress, a sorceress—a witch! She can cast her spell on men and make them do things against their will!"

Fulk backed away, his gaze fixed on the symbol hanging between her breasts, and for the briefest moment, she saw a hint of fear in his eyes. Fulk tore his gaze from the pendant and turned to the bishop.

"Then I swear by the souls of God, the devil's whore will burn."

"God will be most pleased," Bishop Adémar replied.

Fulk turned to his men. "Light the torches!"

Alais gasped when fire crackled from the first torch. The Frank waved his firebrand just inches from her face, and the searing heat bathed her cheek and singed her hair before he dropped the torch onto the kindling. Two more Franks followed suit, and flames sprang up from the pitch-soaked straw. A baking heat reached her toes, then her feet and ankles. Her body shook with ragged sobs as the flames crackled and flared.

Tears streaming from her eyes, Alais looked to the heavens for angels coming to take her from this world, but she saw something else. Ghostly blue flames wreathed the rooftops of the abbey and the tops of the trees, spreading from the direction of the river. All around her, the air sizzled.

And from the banks of the Cher, three odd-looking monks charged up the hill, screaming a battle cry at the top of their lungs.

CHAPTER 20

AND ḦELL FOLLOWED WITH ḦIM

A s the ferry neared Selles, Dónall focused his thoughts on Thomas. He waded through a sea of memories to a hilltop outside Reims. Thomas stood with him. Icarus, in all its autumn glory, soared like a bird above the trees. The wind whistled, and Thomas's leaf creation pitched and dived. Then, halfway through the dive, the birdlike shape imploded, its wings collapsing into its body, spinning wildly and scattering yellow and red leaves across the hilltop.

"*We're getting better at this, you know,*" Thomas had said.

By the time Dónall reached the riverbank, the answer seemed clear. "Thanks, old friend," he said aloud, drawing an odd look from his companions.

Ciarán poled the flat-bottomed ferry to the dock. Atop the nearest hill, amid the gathered men outside the abbey, a tendril of smoke curled skyward. A line of destriers with mailed and helmed riders obscured any view of what was happening. But Dónall knew what was happening, for he had watched it happen to Martha and Thomas. That day, he had been helpless, with an infant in his arms, surrounded by a mob of townsfolk and soldiers and self-righteous priests. There was nothing he could have done—at any rate, that was what he had told himself whenever doubt crept into his mind and kept him awake on all those sleepless nights. But this time, it would be different. He was wiser now, and stronger.

Unsheathing the leaf-shaped sword hidden beneath his habit, he said, "Remi, can you handle the fire?"

"Of course." And the mad look in Remi's eyes seemed to confirm his words.

Dónall leveled his sword toward the hilltop. "Ciarán, when we get there, you find the lady and take her from the pyre. Remi will control the flames."

Ciarán answered with a hesitant nod.

"This is not like Derry," Dónall reminded him. "They don't have a clue we're coming. Just follow my lead, but remember to stand back when you hear the noise."

"Noise . . . ?" Ciarán asked.

Dónall nodded. "You'll know it when you hear it. Like God's own wrath, it will be loud." Then he made the sign of the cross and uttered a verse from the Psalms: "*Let ruin fall upon them unawares,*" he said. "Now, go!"

～

To Ciarán, the charge seemed sheer madness. But he was not about to let Dónall down.

The air stank of ash and smoke, and when once again Niall invaded his thoughts, a cry of "Columcille!" leaped from Ciarán's lips. "Columcille!" he shouted a second time. With each battle cry, the word emboldened him, and the Irish in his veins seized control. *"Columcille!"*

"Eno-o-o-och!" Remi yelled, keeping pace with Ciarán as Dónall started to fall behind, waving his sword in wide arcs.

At the hilltop, several horsemen, alerted by the battle cries, turned toward Ciarán and Remi. To Ciarán, the Franks' powerfully built destriers appeared gigantic and fierce, to say nothing of the men astride them, decked in mail and bearing swords and lances. Indeed, the Franks were laughing at them. One of the bearded riders gestured with his lance, and several more Franks turned toward them, snickering to one another.

"Columcille!" Ciarán cried defiantly.

Remi shook his staff, shouting "Eno-o-o-och!"

Several of the riders set their lances, preparing to charge. *Dónall,* Ciarán prayed, *do whatever you're going to do.*

An instant later, a pale azure light shimmered over the treetops and the spire of the abbey church, and the gentle breeze whipped up into a howling gale. Bare branches bent. On the hillside, dirt and pebbles, blown up by the wind, began to form a swirling cloud of debris. The horsemen were no longer laughing. They held their ground, but now their mounts began to whinny and stamp their hooves. Ciarán had to shield his eyes from the dust in the rising wind.

Smoke from the burning fires was sucked into the wind, which swirled now in a conical pattern, growing louder and taller with each breath. Ciarán and Remi retreated a few steps down the hill as the cyclone—for this was what it had become—grew in size and force. The horsemen backed away, and a few riderless mounts bolted toward the fields. Ciarán could hardly believe his eyes. The whirling black tempest stood impossibly high, roaring like a thousand lions, devouring every wisp of smoke and debris in its path. And halfway down the hill stood Dónall mac Taidg, waving his sword in the air.

The horsemen closest to the whirlwind broke ranks, but before they could retreat, Dónall whipped his sword arm toward them, and the cyclone followed.

It sucked the three nearest riders and their horses into its churning mass and then barreled into the next group of men, both mounted and on foot. The thunderous din of swirling cloud drowned their screams, and when at last it released its prey, it dashed man and horse to the ground with such force that nothing could have survived. The cyclone chewed into the hillside, feeding earth and rock and fleeing soldiers into its hellish funnel.

"Holy Mother of God!" Ciarán uttered, unable to take his eyes off the carnage.

Remi tugged at his sleeve. "Have you forgotten why we are here?" Remi pointed to where the horsemen had stood just moments ago. A stake surrounded by rising flames jutted from the hilltop. And in the midst of that burning pyre stood a raven-haired girl more beautiful than anyone Ciarán had ever seen.

ALAIS WAS sure the end of days had arrived. As the flames engulfed the kindling beneath her feet, she knew that the rest of her life would be brief and horrible. No sooner had this thought occurred to her than the air began to sizzle, followed by the ghostly blue light and an impossibly loud and violent wind. And as that wind grew into a swirling, howling black funnel, she realized that it, not the fire, was to be her end. She watched in stark horror as it sucked up horses and men like so much thistledown. In a heartbeat, a half-dozen men-at-arms perished in the cyclone, along with two of the craven monks, while the rest scattered like rats. Even Fulk the Black, who seemed so fearless in his arrogance, bolted when the whirlwind whisked away his men. The bishop, looking equally terrified, fled with him.

Alais could not shield her ears from the deafening sound. The wind emanating from the swirling tempest whipped her hair and burned her face. *It comes now!* her mind screamed.

But it never did. What happened next seemed unreal, as if she were no longer in this terrifying moment but had somehow entered a dream. The cyclone turned, as if it had a will purpose—*as if it could think*—and followed the fleeing horsemen.

A panicked rider and his mount were its next victims, followed by two Franks who had fled on foot. Alais closed her eyes as one of the men was hurled against the abbey's limestone wall with a sickening crunch.

Hearing voices near at hand, she opened her eyes again. It was two of the suicidal trio who had charged the Franks: a skinny, wild-eyed Benedictine and a young monk in a gray habit unlike any she had ever seen. The Benedictine, who was speaking a language Alais had never heard, thrust his walking staff into the pyre, and to her astonishment, the flames, which were nearly licking her toes but a moment ago, began to diminish, as if the fire had lost its air. Alais no longer knew what world she was in. A dream? The afterlife? None of it seemed real. Beneath her feet, heat still emanated from the blackened kindling, but the flames were gone.

~

"CIARÁN—NOW!" Remi cried. "I cannot hold it at bay forever!"

Ciarán shook off his stunned disbelief at what Remi had done to the fire. The girl looked at him, shaking and sobbing, the tears making pale channels through the soot that caked her face.

He stepped onto the pyre and felt the heat beneath the kindling radiate through his sandals. Ignoring the pain, he tried to untie the ropes that bound the girl's hands.

"Hurry!" Remi cried.

Ciarán tugged at the ropes, trying not to imagine what would happen if Remi lost his tenuous control over the fire. "Wiggle your hands free," he told the girl in Latin, praying she understood.

And she must have, for she managed to free one hand. Then the other slipped easily out of the rope. "Can you help with the knots?" he asked. She nodded, though the dazed, disbelieving look remained. Ciarán went first to the rope that bound her ankles. Pulling on it, he found it hot to the touch. The girl screamed. Her feet had been singed, though not terribly, it appeared. Fortunately, the knot gave way.

"*Hurry!*" Remi groaned.

The girl had managed to untie the knot at her neck. All that remained now was the one at her waist. As they both worked feverishly at the knot, Ciarán could not help noticing that her dress had been ripped. Between the entrancing swells of her naked breasts hung a pendant with a strangely familiar shape.

"Ciarán!" Remi gasped.

The rope around the girl's waist came free, and Ciarán took her in his arms and leaped down from the pyre. Behind him came a loud *whoomp*, and searing heat as a column of flame billowed skyward. An instant later, it settled back to earth, engulfing the stake and what remained of the pitch-smeared kindling in a raging inferno.

A few feet away, Remi lay panting on the ground. Dónall rushed toward him, and he, too, looked pale and drained, like a man who had not slept in days. Only then did Ciarán notice that the thundering noise was gone. He looked to the road. The cyclone had dissipated, leaving an ashy gray haze in the air. Smoke still rose from the cottages, many of which had burned to the ground. Far down the road, a line of horsemen fled at a gallop from Selles-sur-Cher.

Ciarán helped the girl stand. "Are you hurt?" he asked. She nodded at first but then shook her head, and he could only imagine what must be going through her mind.

Dónall said something in the Frankish tongue and pointed at the pendant the girl wore, whereupon she blushed and crossed her arms to cover her breasts.

Carefully Dónall lifted the Book of Maugis d'Aygremont from its satchel and turned the book toward her. On the cover, the golden ankh glinted in the sunlight. The girl's eyes grew wide. And then she fainted dead away.

CHAPTER 21
ANKH AND STAR

"What happened?" the girl asked, looking up at her three unlikely rescuers. Dónall translated the Frankish words for Ciarán, who wondered how she could be involved in any of this.

Dónall had already removed his cowl and placed it over her bare shoulders and bosom, and for this she seemed grateful. Behind them, the last embers still crackled in the pyre, now reduced to ash and cinder and a few tendrils of smoke that still carried the acrid scent of pitch. As Dónall continued to speak in the girl's native tongue, she periodically shook her head in disbelief, her lower lip trembling.

"Her name is Alais," Dónall explained. "She is indeed the lady of Selles-sur-Cher, and her late husband was the lay abbot the prior spoke of. She asked about the cyclone. I told her it must have been a miracle, for what other explanation could there be? And let's not work too hard at coming up with one, shall we?"

"Tell Ciarán what she said about the pendant," Remi pressed.

"Her husband gave it to her before he died," Dónall said. "She claims it's a key that unlocks a secret, something she was not to reveal unless someone arrived with the same symbol. She never actually expected anyone to show up with an ankh, which is why she was so stunned when she saw it on our book."

Dónall asked the girl if she could speak Latin, for if so, they could all understand what she had to say. Ciarán had never met a woman who spoke the language of the Church, but as it turned out, this Alais of Selles-sur-Cher was the exception. When the first Latin words left her lips, Ciarán swore to himself that if he had to spend much more time in these lands, he would learn the Frankish tongue, or, as Dónall called it, *le langue d'oil.*

"Has a monk named Nicolas ever come to the village looking for this secret?" Remi asked her after finally picking himself up off the ground.

"No," she answered.

He shook his head grimly, and Ciarán could see the look of pain in his worn face.

"Can you show us this secret?" Dónall asked her. "It is the reason we came here—and, I fear, the cause of all the trouble you have been through."

She looked at him, her eyes still fearful. "Yes," she said softly.

She led them toward the manor, built of gray limestone blocks, down the road from the abbey. At the sight of burned-out cottages and trampled fields, tears spilled from her eyes. Villagers had begun to emerge from their hiding places. Some wept for their own dead and injured: men who had tried to protect their daughters or wives from the horsemen, women who had been raped, and elderly folk who had seen their life's work destroyed, stolen by the invaders from Anjou. Others were already picking through the charred wreckage of their homes. Mothers huddled with children, while several of the men and boys roamed the fields to herd in the sheep, cows, oxen, and hogs that had scattered during the fires and the cyclone. The crackle and pop of the dying fires punctuated the anguished moans and sobs of the people of Selles.

Ciarán looked away from the devastation. "All this suffering," he said to Dónall. "All at the hands of this bishop of Blois. He knew about the secret she protected, didn't he?"

"I see no other explanation," Dónall replied. "Adémar of Blois must have found Nicolas and wrested from him all the secrets he held, including the one about this place."

"As well as where to find the Book of Maugis," Ciarán added. "And where to find us."

Dónall nodded. "Nothing else makes sense." He glanced at the broken body of a horseman, its chain mail bloody from wounds wrought by the cyclone's debris. "Let God judge them now."

When they reached the pathway to the manor, Alais stopped abruptly, her eyes fixed on the lifeless form of an old Benedictine monk. "I cannot leave him like this," she sobbed. "You have to help me move him."

Ciarán nodded, touched by her sorrow. He tried not to look too closely at the man's injuries. Part of his skull had been mashed in, and the bloodied limbs protruding beneath his black habit were broken and twisted. Ciarán cradled the dead man's trunk in his arms while Dónall picked him up by the legs.

"Oh, Thadeus," Alais said, choking back tears. "Why did you just stand there? Why didn't you run?"

Ciarán searched the girl's beautiful face for some clue to what had happened. Clearly, this old monk had been dear to her.

As Dónall and Ciarán laid the body in a garden outside the entranceway to the manor, she said, "He defied them. Thadeus warned Fulk the Black that he would burn in hell. And now he's dead." She buried her face in Dónall's habit.

"Then he died a brave man," Dónall said softly. "We should all be so courageous when our time comes."

Remi knelt over the body. He closed the monk's eyes and traced a cross on his forehead. "Deliver him, O Lord, from eternal death, on the day when the heavens and earth shall be shaken and you shall come to judge the world by fire." Then he looked up at the others. "We bury him before we leave. He was a Benedictine; he deserves no less."

Dónall nodded his agreement, but he spoke with urgency. "Then we have even less time. At some point, those riders will regroup, and they may even return. If they do, we don't want to be here."

Alais grew paler as Dónall spoke.

"Can you show it to us now?" he asked.

"Yes," she answered. "But I warn you, Brother Thadeus said it speaks of terrible things."

Dónall glanced at Remi. "History is made of terrible things," Remi said. "We would expect nothing less."

FROM THE MOMENT they entered the manor's main hall, Ciarán sensed this was the scene of something terrible. A bloody dagger lay where it had fallen on the stone floor. The trestle table had been upended, its benches kicked aside, and the wooden bar to the door lay across the room from where it belonged.

The bedchamber where Alais took them was even worse. Blood spattered the floor and the blankets of a canopied bed. At the sight of the bed, the color drained from the girl's cheeks.

"We have to move the bed," she said, turning her head away.

Ciarán and Dónall did as she said. Beneath a thin layer of rushes, they found a wooden plate fitted between the stones in the floor.

"Underneath that," she said.

Using his fingertips, Ciarán winkled the plate loose, revealing a cavity below the floor.

"That is surely it!" Remi kneaded his hands in anticipation.

Dónall lifted out a small oak chest whose lid was richly inlaid with gold. The symbol carved into the lid was unmistakable: an interwoven seven-pointed star—the symbol in Maugis' diagram of the prophecy.

"The Book of Maugis was housed in a similar chest in Reims," Dónall explained. "But it bore an ankh on the lid."

"Maugis clearly intended to keep the two together," Remi said, the familiar manic lilt back in his voice. "Thomas was right. Each is the key to understanding the other—ankh and star. But through some cruel twist, they were separated." He stared, wide-eyed. "Open it."

Dónall turned to Alais. "We'll need the pendant now."

She nodded, her eyes still pained, and Ciarán realized that she only wanted to be gone from this scene of awful memory. Reaching under the cowl, she lifted the chain from around her neck and handed it to Dónall.

"It *is* a key," Dónall said, noticing the teeth at the ankh's base. Carefully, he fitted the pendant in the keyhole and turned it. The lock gave a loud click, and he opened the lid. And there it was.

"God, but it looks old," Remi breathed.

"It's not even a book," Ciarán noticed.

"No," Remi explained. "Books as you know them did not exist until the late Roman empire. It would have to be a scroll."

Remi carefully removed a scroll wound around two wooden spindles. It appeared to be papyrus, heavily stained by the ages.

"If it's what we think it is," Dónall said eagerly, "it should date from the time before Christ, during the reign of the Romans, or even the Greeks before them."

"Thadeus said the words were Greek," Alais said.

Remi nodded in wonder. "Of course," he said. "Maugis used Greek when he wrote of this document." Unfurling enough of the scroll to reveal a large block of handwritten text, he read aloud:

The words of the blessing of Enoch, who walked with God and shall witness the time of trouble, when the wicked and ungodly are taken from the world.

"I'll be damned," Dónall whispered.

Ciarán felt a chill. He did not want to contemplate the implications this might have for Remi's theory. Nor could he tell, given the scroll's thickness, how long it might take them to sort it out. "It'll take at least a day to read."

"Then let us start now," Remi said, plopping himself down on the bed.

"No," Dónall said. "Not here. We need to find a safe place first."

"My cousin is the duke of Aquitaine," Alais said. "You could go to Poitiers."

Dónall shook his head. "Poitiers lies days from here. I was thinking of somewhere closer, in case that bishop decides to return with more men." He turned to Remi. "How far from here did Lucien retire?"

"At a priory, south of Saint Aignan," Remi replied.

"I know of one there," Alais said. "The priory of Saint-Bastian —only a half day's ride from here."

Dónall almost smiled. "Then perhaps we're in luck. I saw a stable out back. Have you horses?"

Alais nodded. Even in her present state, smudged with soot and racked with grief, Ciarán found her captivatingly beautiful. "What about her?" he asked. "If those men come back . . ."

Dónall looked up from the scroll and said, "You won't be safe here. Those men will surely return—tomorrow, in a week, in a month. Even if they don't, you stand accused of being a witch, and if any of those spineless churchmen from the abbey were to cling to that accusation . . ." After pausing a moment to let the implication sink in, he said, "We could take you to Poitiers. If your cousin is duke, then surely you'll be safe there."

Alais stared at the floor, her arms crossed over her chest. She wiped a tear from her cheek. "There is nothing left for me here," she said. "Take me home."

CHAPTER 22

THE PRIORY OF SAINT-BASTIAN

P art of Alais wished she had died, so that she might join her beloved Geoffrey in heaven or wherever one went upon leaving this world. That she was still alive seemed unreal, as if she were still in that dreamlike world where the black tempest had arisen out of nowhere and routed the men who sought to kill her. The older Irish monk had called it a miracle. Could it be? Might Saint Radegonde finally have come to answer her prayers? If only she were in Poitiers, she could ask the abbess of Sainte-Croix. *She* would have an explanation. Alais vowed silently to see the abbess when they made it to Poitiers . . . *if* they made it there.

She tried to focus on the hope of returning home, but her mind kept drifting back to the tempest and the fire and poor Thadeus and, worst of all, what the bishop had done. She prayed that she could banish that memory to the darkest recesses of her mind. But where those memories had been, hate would linger—that much she knew. Many times since they left Selles, she had wished that the tempest had claimed one more life, obliterating the rapist who hid behind a priest's mantle, instead of the Franks who merely did his bidding. As she rode alongside the three strange monks, the hatred coursed through her veins like venom, and she knew she would never purge it from her heart.

Geoffrey's horses were all she had taken from Selles other than a few dresses, including the simple gray shift she now wore, and the pendant. Despite its peculiar shape, it had been her last gift from Geoffrey, and she had sworn that she would wear it close to her heart. She sat in the saddle of a dappled mare, riding as a man rode and as no lady ever did. It was the way she preferred, ever since she and Adeline had learned to run their ponies along the banks of the Clain. It also allowed her to ride faster, for they needed haste more than decorum. The older Irish monk had warned that Fulk the Black and the bishop would return sooner or later, and Alais could not bear the thought of that horror. She was relieved to be gone from Selles, though she felt a pang of regret at abandoning Geoffrey's lands. They had meant so much to him. But King Robert had never come, nor had her cousin. So what could she have done to protect the land and its people from the likes of the count of Anjou? Someday, perhaps, the king would finally arrive and restore her lands. Maybe then she would return. But that seemed so remote now. Too much had happened. For now the only hope she would allow herself was that they reach Saint-Bastian's safely tonight.

The road from Selles wound through a thick and tangled wood, filled with enough shadows and whispery noises to make even a seasoned traveler uneasy. Alais had heard more than a few stories of hapless wayfarers killed by wolves or wild boars, and even tales of aurochs still running wild, goring or trampling riders in their path. And three monks with wooden staffs were hardly the protection she was accustomed to after traveling with Geoffrey and his men-at-arms. The young Irish monk looked fit enough to put up a struggle, but he rode completely unarmed. The other two were probably too old to do much of anything, although the Irish one named Dónall was tall and imposing—the type of man who might hide a fierce temper. The Benedictine, shifty-eyed and thin as a distaff, just made her uncomfortable, as if something were not quite right about him. That these three men had become her saviors simply added to the strangeness and unreality of it all. The forest, though, with all its shadows and gnarled trees with their clawing branches, seemed all too real. Between the clip-clop of the horses' hooves, she listened for movement in the woods, any grunt or rustle that might represent a wolf or boar. But after hours of travel, even after sunset, when a big gibbous moon provided the only light on the shadowy road, they had encountered no sign of trouble.

After some time, they spotted lights flickering through a thick stand of trees just past a bend in the road. Soon enough, the moonlight revealed the faint outlines of a cluster of buildings. The road emerged from the woods. Ahead, one of the lights was moving, raised high by the hand of a black-robed monk.

"Who goes there!" a husky voice cried out in the *langue d'oïl*.

The Irish monk named Dónall reigned in his chestnut stallion and answered in Latin, "Peace, brother. We seek warmth in your cloister, and refuge in the name of our holy Savior."

"From whence do you hail?" barked the thickset Benedictine holding the lantern. He stood before an earthen wall with a half-open wooden gate.

"From Paris," the wiry Benedictine named Remi replied. "Has Brother Lucien of Saint-Denis taken vows here?"

"In truth?" the husky-voiced gatekeeper said. "Brother Lucien is the prior."

"Then Providence has found us twice today," Dónall said. "For we are old friends of his, from Reims."

The gatekeeper eyed them warily as the four riders came into the glow of his lantern light.

"So be it," he said. "Welcome to the priory of Saint-Bastian."

OF ALL THE abbeys and priories Ciarán had seen since arriving in France, the priory of Saint-Bastian was by far the coziest—or most cramped, depending on one's perspective. The buildings, all built of brown sandstone, were small and closely spaced, and the cloister's covered passageways were scarcely wide enough for two men to walk side by side. Rushlights lit the meager walkways, which were framed by humble arches with narrow pillars. The scents of rosemary and mint drifted through the cloister from a well-tended garden, and a splashing fountain provided the only sound besides the crickets' chirring.

They waited in the cloister while the gatekeeper went to fetch the prior. Before he left, the gatekeeper had been visibly discomfited upon realizing that a woman had entered the priory. Despite Dónall's assurances that all would be fine, the monk had looked at her as if the devil himself had set foot in Saint-Bastian's. Ciarán could sense Alais' discomfort. He would feel better once she was safely in a guesthouse—assuming that this humble priory even possessed one.

After some minutes, the gatekeeper returned, accompanied by a squat, graying Benedictine. From the way his eyes sparkled when he saw Dónall and Remi, he must surely be the man they sought.

"I can hardly believe my eyes," the prior said, and a warm smile spread to his ruddy cheeks.

"Lucien." Dónall wrapped the prior in a brotherly embrace, and Remi clapped him on the shoulder. The gatekeeper, apparently satisfied that the prior was not in imminent danger of perdition, returned to his post, casting a fearful glance at Alais as he departed.

"How many years has it been?" Lucien asked.

"A lifetime too long," Dónall replied.

"What brings you back to the Continent? I heard you had returned to that rainy gray island of yours."

"A great discovery brings us here," Remi said, cradling the gold-inlaid book shrine that contained the scroll from Selles-sur-Cher. "After so many years of searching, we have found the Book of Enoch."

The color drained from Lucien's face. "I have long since put that part of my life behind me," he said.

"I know," Remi replied, "but have you considered its significance? It is a lost book of scripture, a chronicle of the darkest secrets of mankind's past."

"Is this why you've come—to show me this?" Lucien asked.

"No," Dónall assured him. "We found it at Selles-sur-Cher. But we happened upon some trouble there with one of the local magnates. We come here seeking sanctuary."

Concern furrowed Lucien's brow. "My priory is yours, of course. But this trouble—it is related to Enoch's book?"

"I can't tell," Dónall said.

"We need a place to study it," Remi added.

"*Tonight?*" Lucien said.

"I've waited a lifetime to read these words," said Remi.

"We do have a library, which also serves as our scriptorium. It's not much . . ." Lucien pointed to a nondescript door off the adjacent walkway. "I could get some candles."

"Would you?" Remi's eyes grew wide. "And you'll join us, right? After all, it was you who first saw a connection between the verse in Genesis and the existence of the Fae. This discovery could affirm that link. After all these years, all the speculating and conjecture, surely you are still curious."

Lucien wrung his hands. "What about *her?*" he asked, nodding toward Alais.

"She is the lady of Selles-sur-Cher," Dónall said, "and in need of sanctuary, too, I'm afraid. Have you a guesthouse?"

"Certainly," Lucien replied, though still seeming a little mystified by her presence. "It's out back—and vacant, fortunately. Consider it yours for as long as you need it."

"Our debt to you is great, old friend," Dónall said, taking Lucien's hand. "Ciarán, can you escort Alais to the guesthouse and then meet us in the library?"

"Of course," Ciarán said with a nod. He was relieved to learn that the priory had such accommodations. Alais looked relieved, too.

Prior Lucien showed them the pathway from the cloister to the guesthouse, and as they left, Ciarán glanced over his shoulder. Down the narrow walkway, the three old brethren from Reims headed for the library, carrying a book shrine between them—and within it the scroll whose contents might change all their lives forever.

A gravel pathway led to the guesthouse, which proved to be

nothing more than a square stone building with a thatch roof. A cold breeze had blown up, and Alais shivered as they walked down the path. There was something delicate about her, something fragile, and Ciarán found himself wanting to put an arm around her and keep her warm, to protect her. *Or just to touch her again?* He tried to suppress these disturbing thoughts as he opened the unlocked door to the guesthouse.

It appeared to be a single room, barely lit by the moonlight that spilled in through the open door. Six straw pallets, three on each side, were the only accommodations except for a wooden bench with a washbasin, and a candle in a wrought-iron holder. A flint and steel and a ball of tinder, to light the candle, lay beside it on the bench.

"This won't be what you're accustomed to, I'm afraid," Ciarán said.

"It will be fine," she replied.

Ciarán lit the candle. "It's not much light."

"I'll not need it. I've never felt so tired."

"Can I get you anything?"

"No, I'll be well."

He turned to leave.

"There is one question," she said. "It's silly, I know." She lay down on the pallet nearest the candle. "Why do you and Dónall leave your robes the color of fleece?"

"We Irish are not so vain as to need to dye our clothes."

"So the Benedictines are vain?"

"Those I've seen, yes. But we are the foreigners here, and it is not ours to judge." He smiled. "And anyway, not everyone can be so blessed as to be born Irish."

"Are all Irishmen so proud?"

Ciarán flashed her a smile. "God could make only one place so beautiful on all the earth, so at least we come by it honestly."

She looked at him skeptically, and then a hint of a smile bent her lips. "You Irish are a curious lot."

Ciarán merely shrugged. He waited there until Alais closed her eyes and he was sure she was asleep. Then he set off for the library.

Dónall found the library no less cramped than the rest of the priory. The place was rich with the smells of parchment and dust. The far wall had three good-size windows, through which streamed enough moonlight to illuminate the desks of the scribes. A small reading table with four chairs occupied the center of the room, and a modest hearth took up much of one wall, the rest of which held narrow shelves sparsely populated with books. Four more shelves, mostly empty, occupied the library's two remaining walls.

"We don't have many books, I'm afraid," Lucien explained. "This is but a poor priory."

"It is no matter," Remi said, setting the book shrine on the reading table and pulling up a chair. Dónall laid his book satchel and blackened staff down beside Remi's staff.

"You still carry those?" Lucien said, taking three candles from one of the lower shelves.

"One never knows when a stout knot of alder might come in handy," Dónall replied.

As Lucien lit the candles one by one, the flames glinted off the gold of the book shrine. "It's just like the one that held the Book of Maugis," he said. "My God, but that seems so long ago!"

Remi was practically shaking with anticipation, and for good reason. For Dónall knew, in the pit of his stomach, that what they might find could shatter the walls of skepticism that his scholarly mind had erected around Thomas's and Remi's theories.

Remi opened the book shrine and reached inside, when Lucien suddenly grabbed his hands.

"Do you realize what we're about to do?" Lucien asked. "Do we really want to know what truth lies behind Arcanus's prophecy? Have you thought about what that could mean? Understanding *that* could change everything."

"Yes, brother," Remi said. "It is all I have ever searched for. I would give up everything for this knowledge."

"And you, Dónall?" Lucien asked.

Dónall thought for a moment. Since first learning of the book's discovery, he had wrestled long and hard with the question. "The truth is all I have ever longed for."

"Then our fate, whatever it may be, is sealed," Lucien said. Again Dónall caught the boyish sparkle in the man's eyes. "I'll admit I was hoping you'd say that. I'd forgotten how it feels to stand at the precipice of discovery with one's toes dangling off the edge."

"Then we begin," said Remi. Lifting the centuries-old scroll from its box, he carefully unrolled the left spindle on the tabletop. As he read the lines of Greek, Dónall listened with a growing sense of awe.

For word by word, that cryptic verse from the book of Genesis was coming to life.

CHAPTER 23

THE SONS OF GOD

"*And it came to pass that the sons of men had multiplied, and fair and beautiful daughters were born to them. And the Watchers, the Sons of God, saw them and lusted after them, and said to one another, let us choose wives from the daughters of men.*'"

Ciarán entered the library as Remi read the verse aloud.

"Can there be any question now?" Remi asked. "The sons of God are the watchers, the angels who looked down from the heavens with lust in their hearts. This is the truth the church fathers tried to bury."

Dónall and Lucien barely looked up as Ciarán took the empty chair at the table. Remi continued reading: "'*Under their leader, Semyaza, they bound themselves by mutual curses to do this deed. In all, they were two hundred who descended to earth in the days of Jared on the summit of Mount Armon. They took wives of the daughters of men and defiled them. And the women conceived and gave birth to the Nephilim.*'"

"My God," Lucien whispered, "it's all here."

Dónall rose from his chair. "Angels on the earth, defying the will of God."

"It speaks of sorcery, too," Remi said. "'*The Watchers taught men the casting of spells, and divinations, and the eternal secrets that were made to be*
166

kept in heaven. And men drifted away from God, and they were led astray and corrupted.'"

"What of the offspring?" Lucien asked. "The Nephilim?"

"Here," Remi said. *"The children of the Watchers, the Nephilim, consumed all the labor of men, and when mankind could no longer sustain them, they turned on men and devoured them. And as men perished, they cried out and their voices reached to the heavens."*

"It all goes back to Genesis," Dónall said in amazement. "The wickedness on earth became so great that God regrets the very act of his own creation."

"It is even more than that," Remi insisted. "It confirms the truth of other myths. Did not the Egyptians speak of a time when the *neteru*—literally translated as 'watchers'—lived on earth and guided men? This reign of the gods was followed by another era, the reign of the demigods—the offspring of men and divine beings. The Nephilim, without a doubt. They, not mortal men, were the ones who built the great pyramids. And what of the Greeks? Their mythology is rife with stories of gods procreating with mortal women, many of whom bore children described as giants. Tityos and Hercules, and the Babylonian Gilgamesh."

"The heroes of old," said Dónall. "The warriors of renown."

"Precisely," Remi said. "And look at the Greek Titans and giants, creatures born literally of Uranus—of the heavens—and of Gaia, the earth. The offspring of heaven and earth, of angels and their mortal concubines! The stories of the Gigantomachy and Titanomachy, the wars of the giants and the Titans—does this not describe a time when the Nephilim wreaked havoc on earth?"

"The common origin of all those myths," Lucien remarked. "Thomas was right."

As Ciarán listened, he found himself, curiously, accepting all of it. With his own eyes he had seen the tremendous standing stones such as the Giant's Ring near Béal Feirste—creations that could not have been built by human hands. And the Giant's Causeway in Antrim—thousands of basalt pillars that traversed the sea from Ireland toward Scotland, supposedly laid by the mythical Finn mac Cumhail, a giant hero born of a mortal woman and a Celtic god.

Legend held that the same was true of the great Cú Chulainn. And then there were the many tales of the Formorians, the giants who fought the Tuatha Dé Danann. "But then, what became of all those giants?" Ciarán asked. "The Great Flood?"

Remi wore a wicked smile. "No, not yet. *War broke out in Heaven.* The archangels—Michael and Raphael, Uriel and Gabriel—heard the cries of men and saw the evil being done on earth, and made accusations against the rebellious angels before God Himself. That is when God decided to destroy the earth by water and told Noah to build his ark. But first, he ordered the archangels to round up the fallen: '*Go, bind Semyaza and his followers and split open the desert and cast them into the darkness of Dudael, and seal them in the hills of the earth until the Day of Judgment, when they shall be hurled into the Fire.*' So," Remi continued, "the archangels waged war on the watchers and imprisoned them within the earth."

"Jude wrote of this," Dónall observed. "And Saint Peter, too. '*God did not spare the angels that sinned, but cast them down to Tartarus, putting them into gloomy dungeons to be held for judgment.*'"

"It's also in Revelation," Lucien added. "Remember the passage? From the abyss shall rise smoke, like the smoke of a great furnace, that darkens the sky, and from the earth shall come locusts—armed devils with human faces and iron breastplates. The fallen angels, freed to wreak their vengeance on the world."

His words recalled the chilling image of Remi's illumination in the Apocalypse of John: the winged demons rising from the pit and attacking the monks and priests who cowered in the margins of the page.

"It speaks again of the giants," Remi said, continuing to read. "Enoch tried to petition for God's mercy on behalf of the fallen angels, but God rebuffed him and stood firm in his condemnation. Then he tells Enoch of the giants' fate, though whether they were slain by the archangels or drowned in the flood, the text doesn't say. '*Now the Nephilim, who were born of spirits and of flesh, shall remain on earth and shall be evil spirits. Their spirits shall be like clouds. And they shall rise up against man and woman and oppress and destroy and cause trouble on the earth until they perish on the Day of Judgment.*'"

"The origin of demons?" Dónall mused.

"There is more," Remi added hastily. "It speaks of female angels who were led astray. Uriel tells Enoch they shall be *'sirens'* on the earth. It says nothing of binding them in chains. Don't you see? Sirens, creatures of myth, like the nymphs—*the Fae*—are one and the same!"

"But why would these angels receive leniency?" Lucian asked.

"Perhaps they did not sin against man," Remi offered.

"Or maybe," Ciarán said, "someone more persuasive than Enoch pled their case."

"The first link between scripture and the Fae." Dónall walked over to the hearth to warm himself. "If only Thomas could have lived to hear this . . ."

Lucien rose from his chair. "He would have liked to be here. The prophecy was his Golden Fleece, his Grail, and for a time we were his Argonauts, his fellow knights." He put a comforting hand on Dónall's shoulder. "I know I'm not the worthiest to speak of it, for I was among the first to abandon his voyage for this cloistered life. And when I learned what you had brought to the priory, I admit I was hesitant. But with this discovery, if Thomas was right about all he believed . . . ?"

Remi stopped reading to watch Lucien and Dónall.

"There is still time to finish Thomas's quest," Lucien said. "But that raises a question, if I recall correctly. What of Enoch's device? We've found no reference to it in the book."

"There is much left to learn." Remi gestured at the scroll, still thickly wound around its second spindle.

"Do you remember the verse from Maugis' map?" Lucien asked.

"Of course," Remi said.

"Do you still have it?" Lucien stepped back toward the table. "Maybe there was something we missed before we had the benefit of Enoch's words."

"It's right here." Dónall took the Book of Maugis from its satchel on the floor. On its cover, the ankh glittered in the candlelight.

Lucien let out a little sigh. "I had forgotten how beautiful it is."

Dónall opened the book on the table, carefully turning the pages of scrawled characters and strange symbols, until he found the map. The larger of the two seven-pointed stars was indeed the same image as that on the book shrine containing Enoch's scroll. The ankh in the center of the small star was the same as Alais' pendant. Around the septagrams that comprised the larger star were the words in Greek. Leaning over the book, Ciarán read those words again:

Enoch saw a great and glorious device
at the end of the whole earth.
There Arcanus found the Stone of Light.

"Look for a reference to the ends of the earth," he said.

Remi nodded as if he had already thought of this, while Lucien studied every facet of the old diagram. Dónall stood by the hearth, looking deep in thought. In silence, Remi read the scroll, tracing each word with his finger.

Ciarán could feel fatigue weighing on him. The day's events had left him far more exhausted than he knew. But he snapped alert when Remi looked up from the scroll.

"Interesting," Remi said. "Uriel takes Enoch to the top of a mountain that reaches all the way to heaven, and there shows him wondrous things: a river of fire, great mountains, the mouths of all the rivers, and the storehouse of all the winds—the four elements of God's creation. Then he takes him to the abyss, the prison of Tartarus, where the defiant angels are confined. Raphael joins them and, with his brother archangel, shows Enoch the place where the spirits of the dead reside. Then they take him to the desert where Eden once was, and show him the tree of knowledge. And here it says that Uriel showed Enoch the stars and their names and positions, and he wrote them down."

Lucien looked up from the diagram he had been studying, and blinked in astonishment. "The angels showed Enoch the prophecy etched in the heavens."

"Of course!" Remi said. He continued reading, then nearly

jumped up from his chair. "Eureka!" he cried. *"From there I went north to the ends of the earth. And there I saw a great and glorious device."*

He turned to Dónall. "Ye of little faith, here is your evidence! If the device exists, then how can you deny the prophecy?"

Dónall shook his head in amazement.

Lucien glanced about at his old friends, then clapped his hands. "This deserves a celebration," he announced. "To think that after all these years, we finally found it—or at least a reference to it. We shall remember this breakthrough for the rest of our lives." He headed for the door. "We keep a few bottles from Bordeaux in our cellar. One of the benefits of a small priory is that everything's within easy reach."

As Lucien left the library, Ciarán wondered what Dónall must be thinking. His eyes still held a misty, disbelieving look as he came back to the table and closed the Book of Maugis, then carefully returned it to its satchel. "If the prophecy *is* real . . ." His voice trailed off.

"But where *is* Enoch's device, then?" Ciarán asked. "It's not much help knowing it exists, if we haven't a clue how to find it."

Remi wrinkled his brow. "Do not be naive. Why would Maugis simply leave us with proof of Enoch's device, but no way to find it? He was the last protector of the prophecy. He would have given us the means to discover its location."

Dónall buckled the satchel and said, "What if there are no more clues in the scroll?"

Ciarán grew uneasy. He had seen Dónall play the role of contrarian and had seen how it sometimes angered those debating him. "Maybe the scroll's only purpose," Dónall continued, "is to confirm the truth about the fallen angels, the Nephilim, and the origins of the Fae."

"No!" Remi insisted. "There must be more."

"Let's reason from what we know," Dónall said. "Assuming this writing confirms the existence of this Stone of Light, then Arcanus found it, presumably at the ends of the earth, wherever that might be. But in any event, Arcanus would have taken it to Atlantis."

"Do we even know what it looked like?" Ciarán asked.

"We might," said Dónall. "Another of Maugis' drawings may have shown the device: a staff topped with an ankh, and in the center of the ankh's loop was a stone. In the Secret Collection, we also found references to an Atlantean crystal called the *tuaoi* stone, or fire stone. Perhaps there's a connection."

Ciarán tried to imagine this thing. For some reason, he thought of the staff that Moses carried in the desert, depicting a bronze snake entwined around a cross. "So if this staff was in Atlantis, then what? Atlantis sank into the sea."

Remi ran his hand over his face and rubbed his eyes. "An old tale from the Hebrew mystics says that Abraham had received a so-called testament of a lost civilization—a stone small enough to hold in the palm of his hand. Nicolas and I once spent a week musing about it, but we never found any more reference to it in the texts. I suppose it is possible . . ."

The door to the library swung open, and Lucien entered with a bottle of wine and four wooden cups. "The best our cellar has to offer," he said, filling the cups. He raised his cup. "Other than our former friend Gerbert, we are, sadly, all that remains of our brother-hood of twelve. To the survivors."

Remi lifted his cup and drained it in a single draft. Ciarán inhaled the pleasant bouquet of blackcurrant, then raised the cup to his mouth. But Dónall's hand shot out and grabbed his wrist with a grip like a vise. The wine sloshed over the rim and onto the rush-covered floor.

"What about Nicolas?" Dónall demanded

A look of alarm flashed across Lucien's face.

Dónall, who had not touched the wine, slammed his cup on the table. "I've heard nothing of Nicolas's death."

Beside them, a gurgle rose in Remi's throat. His eyes bulged, and his cheeks flushed a violet red.

Abruptly, Lucien barged Ciarán in the chest with his shoulder, knocking him aside. Ciarán barely managed to keep his feet, but the cup slipped from his hand as Lucien bolted for the door.

Remi staggered backward, nearly collapsing on the table.

Dónall's eyes were dark with fury as he stared after the receding patter of running sandaled feet.

Both Dónall and Ciarán turned toward Remi. Foaming spittle dribbled down his chin, but his face was a mask of rage. Dónall and Ciarán reached for him, but Remi pushed them away.

Then he lurched forward and darted after Lucien, flailing his arms like a man possessed.

CHAPTER 24

BETRAYAL

As Dónall darted after Remi through the library door, Ciarán stood stunned for an instant before grabbing the book satchel and scampering after them.

Dónall pivoted and dashed down one of the cloister's covered walkways. Ahead, a black-robed figure ducked into a doorway. The staccato of sandaled feet echoed through the cloister. Ciarán was only steps behind.

The doorway opened into the nave of the priory church. Enough moonlight streamed through the windows to reveal rows of benches. Raving screams emanated from the left transept. Dónall dashed down the nave and into the transept, where he disappeared in a narrow alcove.

Ciarán slid to a halt. A stairwell in the alcove descended into darkness, and he could hear footfalls pattering down stone steps.

Ciarán had no time to ponder where the stairwell might lead. He could hear Dónall ahead of him, but the howling had stopped. Steadying himself against the stairwell's damp stone wall, he slowed his pace to avoid tripping. The stairs descended to a disturbing depth, in absolute darkness. Ahead, a voice cried out. It was Dónall's voice.

Ciarán's heart raced. At the bottom of the stairs, a reddish glow revealed a stone floor. He rushed down the steps toward the light, when a sudden force hurled him forward.

He felt himself falling. His shoulder slammed into stone, and he tumbled and went sprawling. A stomach-turning stench filled the air around him.

Looking up from where he lay, Ciarán gasped. Against the far wall of the dimly lit chamber glowed the red eyes of some great beast. A dragon, with skin like stone and teeth as long as swords!

Ciarán started to scream, but a hand on his shoulder cut him short.

"It's only a statue," Dónall whispered. He knelt beside Ciarán. Next to them, Remi rocked on his hands and knees, shaking and dripping vomit from his mouth and chin.

Metal screeched against stone, followed by a loud crash, and he turned to find an iron portcullis barring the archway to the stairwell. Behind the iron bars stood the man who had pushed Ciarán down the steps and who would have poisoned them all: Lucien of Saint-Denis, the prior of Saint-Bastian's.

Clutching his own throat, Remi glared at Lucien. "What did you do to Nicolas?" he rasped.

"He died not far from where you sit," Lucien replied.

"But why, brother?" Dónall asked.

"Because a war is coming, and Nicolas served the wrong side."

"And Canon Martinus?"

"He died to protect the Secret Collection—the secrets we held most dear."

Dónall stared at Lucien in disbelief. "The Fae arts were never worth murder."

Lucien shrugged. "You and I followed those same arts down different paths, I'm afraid. From other tomes in the Secret Collection, I learned the ways of contacting the dead from the gloom of Sheol. I thought I had found a beloved friend, who took his own life when faced with the hypocritical judgment of the Church. I spoke with him each night while you and the others slept. He told me fascinating things about the world and the black void beyond. But after many conversations, I discovered I was wrong in my assumptions. For it was not my friend whom I spoke with all those nights, but *he*." Lucien gestured toward the statue, whose glimmering red eyes washed his face in a hellish glow.

"This is madness," Dónall said, rising to his feet.

"Is it!" Lucien fairly screamed. "You have no concept of his power—or his greatness! *He* who led the rebellion against the greatest tyrant the world has ever known."

"Blasphemer!"

"When did it become blasphemy to speak the truth? Your God was the most prolific slayer of innocents in all history: all life in the flood, the children of Sodom and Gomorrah, all Egypt's firstborn. Did they deserve to die? Are those the acts of a merciful god? No, Dónall—*that* way lies madness. Yet it is precisely this tyranny that the Dragon defies. Do not believe Enoch's lies. The world of the Dragon was the world we dreamed of in Reims: the world of Apollo and Daphne, of Jason and his Argonauts, of glorious Olympus! This is the past to which he seeks to return, like the Ouroboros, coming full circle to a greater time that once was."

"You have forfeited your soul," Dónall said grimly.

Lucien looked away. "I have chosen my side in this war."

"You murdered Nicolas!" Remi cried, grimacing with pain.

"He was but a sacrifice for a higher cause," Lucien replied coldly.

Behind Ciarán, a guttural sound began to emanate from the dragon statue, as if the thing were coming to life. Ciarán grabbed the hem of Dónall's cowl and bent his ear toward the statue. The sound ended in a long hiss.

Remi turned his bloodshot eyes toward the statue.

"Ah, yes," Lucien said. "Soon you will find the evidence of the Otherworld that you have sought for so long."

The hissing grew louder, and a shadowy form seethed within the dragon's mouth. Something clicked against the tiled floor.

"Behold," Lucien said, "the basilisk, a creature of myth!"

In the flickering candlelight, a shape emerged, reptilian and as large as a wolfhound. A pale ridge like a cock's comb topped its head, which bobbed and waved on a serpentine neck above a huge, scaled birdlike body.

Ciarán froze. The creature was but six paces away, cocking its head from side to side and watching them with gleaming, round obsidian eyes.

"Legend has it that the basilisk's gaze can turn a man to stone," Lucien said from the stairwell, "yet I think you'll find it has far deadlier aspects than its eyes. *Au revoir,* old friends."

The basilisk hissed, revealing a mouthful of sharp, evenly spaced teeth. Its breath stank of carrion. As Remi rose to his feet, the fear surging through Ciarán's veins brought a strange clarity, as if time had somehow slowed. From his left, Dónall barked an order, then held out the leaf-shaped sword. Ciarán grasped it by the hilt. Using the sword against this creature seemed as improbable as taking on a wild boar with only a fruit knife. Ciarán had never even hunted game with a spear, let alone attacked something as large as the abomination that stood leering and swaying before him now.

Then Dónall spoke another word: *"Eoh."*

Blinding light exploded from the small crystal held between his thumb and index finger, and the basilisk's head whipped to one side. The light quickly faded to a white glow, illuminating the immediate area of the cavernous chamber.

The basilisk recovered with a hissing vengeance, inching toward them, its great, curved talons clattering on the stone floor.

"Look!" Dónall grabbed Ciarán by the back of his hair, jerking his head to the side. The crystal's glow revealed a small alcove at the end of the chamber, off to the side of the dragon's-head statue. "A way out."

But the basilisk blocked their path.

Ciarán brandished the sword, and the grotesque head reared back. A cry of terror rose to Ciarán's lips, but another voice filled the chamber.

Remi was screaming at the basilisk. Then, with arms raised and fingers clutching the air, he lunged toward it. From the basilisk's mouth streamed a jet of viscous liquid, spattering Remi just before he collided with the beast. The snakelike neck whipped about, and teeth sank into flesh. The basilisk held Remi's chest in its great jaws, crushing the life from him.

With strangely lucid eyes, Remi looked at Ciarán and Dónall and gurgled, "*Run!*"

~

DÓNALL PLUNGED INTO THE ALCOVE, with Ciarán a step behind. The choking smell of dust lay thick in what the illuminating crystal revealed to be a narrow passageway cut through the bedrock. Behind them, Remi's dying screams, mixed with the basilisk's guttural growls, filled the chamber.

The passageway widened, and the dust smell grew thicker, as did the stench of decaying flesh. The crystal's pearlescent light glinted off a human skull. Ciarán gasped. On shelves carved in the earthen walls were rows of skulls, stacked several deep—a gallery of the dead, grimacing at all who came this way. The shelves climbed to a ceiling cloaked in shadow, perhaps twelve feet from the floor.

Feeling something crunch under his sandals, Ciarán looked down to find small bones—fingers and toes—littering the stony floor. Along the walls, more shelved recesses held entire skeletons and a miscellany of loose bones: thighs and shins, rib cages, arms with hands and clawlike fingers still attached. Dirt or grime, or perhaps the mummified remnants of human flesh, still clung to the grisly relics.

"We are in an ossuary," Dónall said, "beneath their cemetery." He pressed forward, the crystal's light spilling from his palm. The passage went on as far as Ciarán could see, into the shadows beyond the crystal's white glow. A horrifying thought came to him: what if the passage dead-ended? The basilisk would not be satiated, and they would be trapped with the hellish creature.

The scrape of metal echoed from the chamber behind them, followed by a somber chanting.

"Faster!" Dónall cried. Ciarán glanced behind them but saw only darkness and the faint outline of bones.

The chanting from the chamber behind them grew louder. It

was the voice of more than one man, singing in the manner of a monastic choir. Although Ciarán did not recognize the words—for they were not in Latin or any other tongue familiar to his ears—he recognized the haunting sound of a requiem.

Something sharp bit into Ciarán's ankle, and he cried out in pain and alarm. To his horror, a skeletal hand with dirt-stained nails protruding from fingers of bone reached out from the shelves, groping for Dónall's neck.

"Holy Patrick!" Dónall cried as the skeletal hand tore his cowl. From the opposite side of the passageway, another hand clawed at Ciarán. A second bony hand wrapped around his ankle, and this time, he could not contain his fear.

"Necromancy!" Dónall growled.

From the piles of bones, skeletons emerged like moths bursting from cocoons. They clawed at the air. One tore the sleeve of Dónall's habit as another tried to climb onto his back. The chanting grew louder, and the air around them seemed to pop and sizzle.

Ciarán swung the sword at one of the skeletons, cleaving off its arm and knocking it aside, but another body of bones took its place. The very walls had come alive. Ciarán and Dónall stood back-to-back as the skeletons pressed in on them like great, clattering marionettes, their mouths hung open in silent screams, vacant orbits staring balefully.

Ciarán bled from a dozen stinging scrapes and cuts. He clung tightly to the book satchel's leather strap as a column of whispering dead five or six deep mobbed toward him. "Dónall!" he cried.

"In the name of God and Saint Patrick!" Dónall bellowed, pulling skeletons off him and kicking them asunder.

And still the dead surged forward in what looked like a final charge. Then, from the back of the column, the bones started to fly apart. Rib cages exploded, and skulls caromed off the walls and floor as arms and ribs scattered. A terrible hiss filled the passageway, and through the thinning throng stared the eyes of the basilisk.

Ciarán reached back and grabbed Dónall. "Look!" The basilisk thrashed and snapped at the skeletal forms, clearing a swath through those still blocking its path.

"Merciful God," Dónall muttered.

Ciarán pushed Dónall forward, and using their combined strength, they punched through the pile of skeletons. More of the dead filled in behind them, clutching and clawing at their habits, but against this rearguard of bones the basilisk plowed forward with vengeful fury. Its whiplike tail twitched off skeletal arms and skulls and flung them against the walls. It knocked still others aside with its head, and a few it crushed to powder in its jaws. Its screech drowned out the chanting. "The necromancy is fading," Dónall panted.

Ciarán pushed through the next wave of skeletons with ease, knocking them to the ground as if they were scarecrows. It was true, he realized: whatever sorcery had given the dead life had begun to wane. But behind him, too, the dead began to collapse en masse.

"They won't slow it down!" he yelped.

"There!" Dónall pointed to one of the shelves ahead of them. Above the shelf was an opening of some sort, adorned with a row of grinning skulls. From the crystal's glow, it appeared to lead to another passage. "Climb for your life!"

Standing by the shelf, Ciarán cupped his hands under Dónall's foot, helping him up. Dónall swept aside the skulls and called back, "The alcove is narrow, but there's a way out!"

Ciarán glanced over his shoulder to see the basilisk tearing through the remnant of the skeletal army that had filled the passageway. It tossed skulls and bones aside like leaves in the wind.

"Now!" Dónall reached for Ciarán's hand as he jumped up.

The basilisk gave a fierce hiss, and a blob of its spittle soaked Ciarán's shoulder. Droplets spattered against his face, and his cheek went numb. An icy cold invaded his veins, and the muscles in his left shoulder and arm began to cramp.

Dónall pulled Ciarán onto the stone shelf, which was barely wide enough to hold a man. A small passageway less than half a man's height led away at right angles. Dónall ducked under first as, below them, the basilisk waded through the last of the bone barricade and scuttled toward them with terrible speed.

Ciarán's left arm had gone limp, but his legs and right arm still had strength. Willing his body to move, he tumbled through the opening and found himself crawling on the floor of a narrow tunnel. Behind him, a snarling reptilian head burst through the hole. The basilisk hissed, thrashing and snapping its jaws as it struggled to squeeze through. Bits of stone crumbled from the opening.

"Ciarán, run!" Dónall said, tugging at his sleeve. "It'll get through!"

"No."

Ciarán shook his head and let the book satchel fall to the floor. Sweat beaded on his brow. He could feel a fever coming, but he fought to ignore it and forced himself to sidle along the wall, staying clear of the snapping jaws. Raising the sword, he brought it down on one of the shining black eyes. The blade sank in, and the eyeball exploded into something the consistency of blackcurrant jam.

The basilisk howled and yanked its head back from the hole. Ciarán heard the huge, writhing body slide off the shelf as its howls reverberated through the passageway of the dead.

The beast was gone.

"Well done!" Dónall exclaimed. "Are you all right?"

Ciarán just grimaced. Half his face was numb. His left eye had frozen open, and his left arm, screaming from the icy venom, was useless.

"It isn't the basilisk's gaze," he said. "It spits some sort of poison." Ciarán sensed the venom spreading to his chest and lungs, and found himself straining to breathe.

Dónall looked at him grimly. "Perhaps I can drain it out." And pressing the crystal into Ciarán's shoulder, he uttered a string of alien words. The white light flared anew, and Ciarán could feel its calming warmth, dissipating the icy cold. Liquid began to bead on the shoulder of his woolen habit. Then the droplets started to sizzle and steam away, like water on a hot skillet.

Ciarán clenched the fingers on his left hand and felt the muscles slowly returning to life. "Like a miracle," he said, amazed.

"Not precisely," Dónall said. "The power simply forced a chemical reaction, breaking down the venom."

Ciarán thought about that, feeling grateful for this mysterious power of the Fae, until another question entered his mind. "How will we get out of here?"

Dónall looked around. "This cavern's natural," he observed, "and the walls are cool. I suspect there is water not far from here."

Ciarán picked up the book satchel from the rocky floor, where the basilisk's eye was but a smudge of dark ooze. Then a new and terrible thought struck him. "What about Alais?"

Dónall's expression grew dark, and he placed a hand on Ciarán's good shoulder. At his next words, Ciarán's heart sank.

"I fear there is nothing we can do for her now."

THEY TRUDGED through the tunnels for what seemed like hours. At times they stopped to rest, and Dónall closed his eyes and extinguished the light summoned to his crystal. The *soul light*, as he called it. Ciarán sensed that it took a fair amount of energy to keep the crystal lit, and Dónall could not go too long before needing to rest. During those dark intermissions, Ciarán could not help but feel as he had when they left Derry, when he had to leave behind his dead and dying friends. This time, it was Alais whom they left behind, and Remi who had given his life—trying to save them, for that could be the only explanation his charging the basilisk. Maybe the poison he had drunk would have killed him anyway. Still, if not for Remi, they would all be dead.

When Dónall had rested again, he spoke the simple Fae word and blew on the crystal again, conjuring its cool light, which always faded to a soft, white glow. Continuing through the tunnels, they found water dribbling down the walls, disappearing into small fissures in the rock. The air grew damp.

"A stream of some sort can't be too far away," Dónall said.

They walked farther. At times, the tunnel walls grew dry again, and Ciarán feared they may have taken a wrong turn. Other tunnels intersected the one they traveled down, and though he had little choice but to trust Dónall's sense of direction, he worried that they would lose their way.

Eventually, Dónall's crystal went dark, and the tunnel went as black as a tomb. "What happened?" Ciarán asked.

Dónall let out a long sigh. "I've never had to sustain it so long. I must have hit a limit of sorts. We'll have to continue by feeling along the rock—or else we sleep here."

The thought of actually sleeping in the featureless blackness was unnerving, especially not knowing for certain that the basilisk was deterred. That horror was the last thing they needed creeping up on them as they slept. No, Ciarán decided. He would rather chance stepping off a precipice or making a wrong turn.

"Let's go," he said.

They searched for the source of the water. And when the walls grew wet, Ciarán began to sense a dampness in the air—and a freshness. There was a difference, he realized, between the air wafting in from tunnels near the source of the water, and the dry smell that rose from the side tunnels that must continue deeper into the hill. In time, he began to hear the faint sound of rushing water. A waterfall, perhaps?

As the tunnel rounded a bend, a blinding sliver glinted through the darkness. Ciarán blinked, and it took him a moment to realize that he was gazing at daylight.

Exuberance surged through him as he stepped out into the morning sun. At first, he had to shield his eyes, but gradually, the outside world came into focus. Through the mist of falling water bouncing off stone, his eyes made out the green of trees on a hill-side. A rock ledge flanked a cataract that spilled into a pool below them. He could see moving motes of brown, chestnut, and gray. Large shapes, some moving ever so slightly—a score of them at least. The scent of horses mixed with the freshness of the falls.

Ciarán squinted, struggling to sort out the brownish shapes and, above them, the glint of metal and the brown of cloaks. Horses, he realized, bearing riders.

Amid the roaring falls, he heard the *thrum* of a bowstring. Then the first arrow zipped past his ear and splintered against the rock wall behind him.

CHAPTER 25

ABDUCTION

The guesthouse door crashed open, jolting Alais awake. Wide-eyed, she strained to see in the thin moonlight. As shadowy figures charged into the room, a surge of panic seized her, and she sprang to her feet, only to collide with sinewy arms. A rough jute sack, reeking of stale oats, went over her head and was cinched tight at her neck. She feared she would suffocate, but through panicked breaths she tasted air through the fabric.

She let out a muffled cry: "What is happening?"

"Silence!" growled a hard voice inches from her ear. She struggled to break free, but her captors bound her wrists with rope that bit into her flesh until she could feel the slickness of blood on her palms. Yanking her to her feet, they pushed her out of the guesthouse and into the bitter air. Her bare feet ached on the icy ground.

"What have you done with the Irish monks and the Parisian?" she demanded.

"They defied the rebel lord and have been punished."

His voice was husky and cruel, and despite the hood, Alais felt certain it was the voice of the surly gatekeeper who had greeted them at Saint-Bastian's. "*What* rebel lord?" she asked.

184

Her captor just grunted and pushed her down a path, keeping a firm grip on her left arm.

They were near a stable, for she could smell the horses and hear their faint snorts and whinnies. Keeping her panic at bay was like damming the waters of a raging river. Yet after everything that had happened during the day, she knew she must try to stay calm. The men had not hurt her yet, but they surely would. Until then, there was still time for clear thinking. She feared for the Irish monks and even the lanky, half-crazed Benedictine, but she knew that if she dwelled on their fate, she would lose the battle with her fear. Under her breath, she whispered to Saint Radegonde a prayer for deliverance.

The men helped her onto a saddled horse. They spoke in whispers. Others had joined them, though how many there were, she could not tell. Someone started leading her horse by the reins. The other horses followed, their hooves clomping against the hard ground both ahead of her and behind. They were leaving the priory.

To fight the dread clawing at her insides, she concentrated on the things she could notice: the chirring of crickets, the scent of beech trees. Her horse was picking its way down a rocky path. Pebbles crunched under hooves. The path was winding, for she felt her horse turn at each bend.

"Where are you taking me?" she asked, choking back a sob.

"Shut it!" one of her captors hissed.

As the horses plodded along, the men began chanting. It sounded monastic, haunting yet strangely beautiful. One voice began; then a chorus of six or seven more joined in. Alais tried to follow the words, but if they were Latin, it was of an age or dialect she did not understand. The chanting rose and fell as their horses maneuvered down the tortuous path. In the pauses of the chant, as the faint gray of dawn began to filter through the weave of the hood, she caught the sound of rushing water. They were nearing a waterfall.

After a time, the chanting stopped and so did the horses. Two men lifted her from her saddle and stood her upright on the cold, damp ground. One of the men removed her hood. The morning sun was blinding, even in the shade of the tall pine trees that surrounded them. As her eyes adjusted to the glare, she counted seven black-robed monks, two of whom had dismounted. In a clearing ahead were more than a dozen horsemen, clad in familiar dark cloaks. Her heart began to race. One of the monks beside her was the prior of Saint-Bastian's. He acknowledged one of the riders in the clearing. A cloak covered all but the hem of the rider's black robe, but it could not disguise the sharp cheekbones and silver-flecked beard, or those feral eyes that even now were undressing her.

"I heard the bishop of Blois was looking for a witch," the prior said.

"No," she stammered. "Please!"

The twang of a bowstring split the air, and Bishop Adémar's eyes shot up toward the falls, to what looked like the mouth of a cave. Two men in gray habits now stood in the opening, shielding their eyes from the glare.

WHEN A SECOND ARROW clattered against the cave's rocky walls, Dónall grabbed Ciarán and hauled him backward. Above the roar of the falls, he could hear men yelling. Another arrow zipped past his shoulder and splintered against the rocks. "Down on your belly, lad!" Dónall growled.

Ciarán dropped to the cave's rocky floor. "What in the hell . . . ?"

Two more arrows struck the rock, one of them glancing and clattering to a stop just before Ciarán's nose. He glanced warily at the sharp iron arrowhead. "Didn't you see those men?" Dónall said. "They're led by the count of Anjou and the bishop of Blois."

Ciarán's eyes grew wide. "They were waiting for us, but how?" He crawled to the edge of the cave and peered downward, then sprang back as another arrow splintered against the cave's roof.

From the clearing, Adémar of Blois bellowed, "Kill the one with the sword! He is the sorcerer who slew your brothers in arms at Selles!"

Ciarán glanced at the leaf-bladed sword, which he had kept since their encounter with the basilisk, and offered it to Dónall. "Can you use it again?"

Dónall shook his head. "I've not enough strength—keeping the light going in the tunnels took too much."

Another arrow clattered against the cave's wall, but no more followed. Ciarán looked questioningly at Dónall. "They don't want to shoot their own men," Dónall said. "They're climbing up."

"Then we go back," Ciarán said hastily. "There are other tunnels. We can hide."

Dónall shook his head wearily. "We'll never find our way in the darkness. If only I'd saved some strength . . ."

Ciarán looked at the sword, then at the mouth of the cave. It was so narrow that not more than a man or perhaps two could enter at a time. He could try to hold the breach. But these were seasoned warriors—men trained to fight, who, moreover, would like nothing better than to get their hands on the monks who had rescued the witch and killed their comrades. For an instant, he wondered whether Niall had entertained such thoughts when he stood against the Franks at Derry. And had Saint Columcille considered his own mortality when defying King Diarmait's army? "*We fight because we're brave,*" Niall had said, "*and because we're Irish!*"

Ciarán lay there for a moment, listening to the sound of his own breath. Then he rose to his feet.

"Don't be daft, lad!" Dónall yelled. But Ciarán started toward the cave's mouth, gripping the sword's hilt. Any moment, he expected the first of the warriors to charge into the cave.

From outside, a great din erupted, as if all the warriors were joining in a battle cry. Screams followed, horses whinnied, and branches snapped.

Peering out of the cave, Ciarán could hardly believe his eyes. The archers were under attack.

~

ALAIS FELT the ground tremble beneath her feet, and as she watched, the prior's expression went from concern to outright panic. The pounding hooves of so many horses, accompanied by the cries of men, raised a frightful din before she even saw the first cavalrymen through the woods ahead, setting upon the bishop's soldiers. At least a dozen more men than her captors, in chain mail and iron helms and charging with leveled lances, caught Fulk of Anjou's men flat-footed. Spears smashed through the Angevins' painted shields, splitting wood and plunging into the bodies of men. Alais saw one warrior pierced through the neck. Another toppled from his mount, felled by the bloody arc of a cavalryman's sword. The cavalrymen were beardless, and one carried a banner of a crimson lion: the arms of her cousin, William of Aquitaine.

Alais felt a sudden surge of hope. *Thadeus,* she thought, *finally they came!*

The prior cast a fearful glance to his monks, who were scattering into the woods like rats from a burning barn. Alais stood there alone, watching wide-eyed as the fierce riders of Aquitaine hacked away at the Angevins, who were so stunned by the sudden attack that they could not form a defensive column or dismount to establish a shield wall. The Angevin archers, who moments ago had nearly killed Dónall and Ciarán, died on the points of Aquitaine lances. Other Angevins, who were scaling the hillside toward the cave, now returned to defend their frantic comrades, who were fighting back as best they could. An Aquitanian mount toppled onto the churned earth, a spear protruding from its belly. Its rider fell clear, only to be crushed under the hooves of a panicked Angevin destrier, whose rider died an instant later when an Aquitainian sword cleaved through the side of his neck.

Alais' awe at the initial attack quickly turned to vengeful glee. With each Angevin sent to his death, she felt a sense of justice. She scanned the chaotic scene for Bishop Adémar. He had fallen behind a cluster of Angevins. Seeing a blade flash before the bishop's face, she drew a sharp breath, praying the sword would strike true. But then, seeing the blade sink into the neck of one of William's men, she realized that it was in the bishop's hand.

She watched in horror as the bishop struck down another, wielding his blade like a trained swordsman, fighting his way toward the center of the Angevin force, where the black-bearded count of Anjou battled the cavalrymen with the fury of a wild beast. Fulk the Black plunged his sword into an Aquitainian horseman, then withdrew it in a backhanded swipe that cleaved through a second horseman's jaw. Alais could hear Fulk's voice above the din of battle. "Kill!" he roared. "By the souls of God, kill them all!" William's men pressed forward, battering through the Angevin shields, but reaching Fulk, the attack broke like a wave against a sheer cliff. He split the head of one of the Aquitainian mounts, which bucked in death, spilling its rider into a sea of stamping hooves. Fulk's rage inspired his Angevin forces, who held fast as their leader continued his bloody onslaught. In a heartbeat, Fulk cut past another rider to challenge the one holding the banner of the crimson lion. The standard-bearer raised his shield, which Fulk split with a hard downward blow. Then the count recovered and thrust his sword, and the crimson banner fell beneath the cavalry's hooves.

Alais' hopes faltered as the Angevins let out a cheer. But the Aquitainian cavalry surged, spurred on by their leader, who was cutting his own path toward the count. The left flank of the Angevin wall began to buckle, and for the first time, Alais saw Fulk and the bishop backing their mounts toward the woods. William's men outnumbered the Angevins and had already taken more than half of them to their deaths. A battle cry rose among the Aquitainian ranks as one of the lead Angevins fell, a broken lance protruding from his mailed chest. Alais held her breath, teetering between fear and elation, until Fulk's pocket of resistance began to collapse. The riders of Aquitaine swelled into the gaps, and the Angevin horsemen broke and fled into the woods.

The Aquitainian leader rode forward. He had a proud face with a sharp nose and prominent jaw. Grateful tears tinged Alais' eyes, for she recognized Lord Raymond, one of William's dearest friends, whom she had known since childhood.

"No mercy!" Raymond cried. "Chase them down for William, for Aquitaine, and for God!"

"No!" cried a voice from above them on the hillside. It was the older Irish monk, Dónall, who had climbed down the rocky incline near the falls. The younger one, Ciarán, was just behind him.

Raymond glanced toward the monks as his cavalrymen gathered in a semicircle around him.

"My lord," Dónall said between huffing breaths, "call back your men, that they might live to fight another day."

"But we have them!" Raymond shouted.

"You've won through surprise," Dónall replied, "but there are evil forces in those woods."

"Then all the better to strike them down!"

Dónall shook his head. "No, my lord. There be sorcerers, minions of the devil. Not even the pope himself could stand against them."

"But God stands with us this morning! Back off, old man, or be trampled!" Raymond reared his destrier, and its forelegs kicked the air.

"Raymond, no!" Alais ran into the clearing. "He speaks true."

Raymond pulled off his helmet. His black hair was cut short in the Roman fashion. "Alais?" he gasped.

"These men freed me from Fulk's soldiers at Selles," she said, standing between Dónall and the Aquitaine lord. "But I sense it, too. There's something wicked about this place and about those men." Alais believed every word she told him, yet in her mind the wickedness of which she spoke had an all-too-human shape in the form of Adémar of Blois. But there was something about the prior and her captors from Saint-Bastian's, something about their haunting chant, that told her Dónall was right.

Raymond dismounted. "Were you hurt?"

She winced but shook her head. She didn't want to tell him—or anyone. She began choking on her tears but fought them back. "I am fine."

Raymond embraced her. "They bound your hands," he said, anger flashing again in his eyes. He unsheathed a dagger and carefully cut the cords around her wrists. This time she embraced him and kissed the corner of his mouth. "We received word of Geoffrey's passing," Raymond said softly. "William sent me to secure your lands at Selles. We arrived there yesterday at dusk. I know what happened. Fulk of Anjou will pay for what he did, as will that vile bishop."

She gave a thankful sigh. "These monks were trying to escort me to Poitiers. They are in need of sanctuary."

"Yet they would have me forego our chance to run the enemy down?"

"If you are meant to destroy him," Dónall interjected, "then at the right time, God shall make it so. But for now, take the story of this victory to your duke and make him proud."

Raymond's eyes narrowed. He thought for a moment and then spoke. "For the sake of the lady, I will desist. But do not think that it means an Irish monk can tell a lord of Aquitaine when to fight." Raymond called to his men. "This is Alais, the lady of Selles-sur-Cher and cousin of our beloved Duke William. Treat her accordingly."

As the cavalry gathered, Ciarán turned to Alais. "Are you truly all right?"

"Yes," she nodded. "I feared you had been killed."

"They tried," he said. "But they killed Remi."

Alais felt a sudden sadness for the Benedictine. "Why would they do this?" she asked, noticing the pain in Dónall's eyes.

"Lucien betrayed us," Dónall said grimly.

"But why?" she asked.

He looked down and shook his head. "Because I've been a fool for far too long."

PART THREE

And now, the giants, who are produced from the spirit and flesh, shall be called evil spirits upon the earth, and on the earth shall be their dwelling.

—Enoch 15:8

CHAPTER 26
THE LION OF POITIERS

O n the second morning of their journey, the first snowfall of winter came—a scattering of white flakes on a breeze thick with the scent of pine.

Ciarán drew his cowl over his head. He rode beside Dónall on a horse abandoned by one of the dead Angevins, whom Lord Raymond had left for the crows in a clearing not far from Saint-Bastian's. The first drifting flakes soon turned into a steady snowfall that blanketed the surrounding pines and obscured the road from view. Fortunately, Lord Raymond and his men knew these lands well, and despite the snow, they never strayed into the tangled forests or down some other path that might lead them to danger.

Riding with a column of cavalrymen was far different from the rest of their journey since Paris. Ciarán and Dónall rode in the middle of the column, with cloaked riders bearing painted shields before and behind them, following a cavalier who carried the standard of Poitiers: a crimson lion over gray, with claws of gold. When the column passed through villages, the local lords either welcomed Raymond with gifts or gave his men a wide berth, and if there were bandits afoot, they were not inclined to waylay twenty-four armed and mounted soldiers.

Ciarán had barely seen Alais. She rode near the column's head alongside Lord Raymond, whom she clearly knew well from some earlier time. Perhaps they had been more than friends, for the few times Ciarán had glimpsed Alais, she clung to Raymond's side. When he first saw this, Ciarán turned away, realizing right then how little he liked the Aquitainian lord. Maybe it was the way Raymond ignored the Irishmen, as if they were beneath his station, or how he rode so proudly through his ranks, who, with their short hair and clean-shaven faces, seemed to fancy themselves the last of the Roman legions. Or maybe it was because of Alais. That could be what troubled Ciarán the most—besides Dónall.

Ciarán's mentor had sunk into melancholy since the battle with Bishop Adémar and Fulk the Black. He had barely spoken of the events at Saint-Bastian's. Ciarán had never seen Dónall so grim, and he could only imagine the troubled thoughts churning in his mind as he grappled with the deaths of Nicolas and Remi, and the betrayal by Prior Lucien of Saint-Bastian's, who would have killed them all. Today Dónall rode weary-eyed, in silence, as flecks of snow collected on his beard.

When the column slowed to cross a bridge over one of the land's many rivers, Dónall turned to Ciarán and finally spoke. "I never saw it," he said softly.

The comment out of the blue surprised Ciarán. "You mean Lucien."

"I was so confident that our brothers' deaths were the result of Gerbert's ruthless ambition and Adalbero's blindness. Yet could Lucien have been manipulating them all along? And now he's in league with Adémar of Blois. But does this bishop truly hunt heretics, or does he side with Lucien's dark master in this so-called war?"

"Both bishop and prior pursue the prophecy," Ciarán said. "That's why Adémar wants the Book of Maugis. And both of them have killed for it."

Dónall shook his head. "I had become too complacent in my belief that it was all just a figment of Remi's madness and your father's obsession. When I saw others drawn to that obsession like moths to a flame—innocents like your mother, who paid the highest price for believing in it—I came to view the prophecy as destructive, a mad riddle penned by Maugis after the Fae arts had addled his mind."

"Lucien believes in the prophecy. I think he fears it."

Dónall looked at Ciarán grimly. "I've had the same thought. And if Remi was right about the timing . . ."

"Then we have barely two months," Ciarán said. "But to do what—find Enoch's device? Where do we even start to look?"

Dónall tilted his chin toward the falling snow. "I wish I knew," he said. "By God, I wish I knew."

THEY ARRIVED at Poitiers on the fifth day of their journey. The city was breathtaking, grander even than Paris—and, for that matter, than any other city Ciarán had ever seen. Perched on a promontory, the city overlooked the snow-lined banks of the river Clain. Halfway up the promontory loomed gigantic walls with half-round turrets and battlements, their warlike aspect softened by mantles of snow. Above the walls, the spires of at least a dozen churches and abbeys rose amid a sea of slanted rooftops, with smoke from hundreds of chimneys drifting into the December sky. At the city's pinnacle stood a fortress, an imposing structure with crimson banners fluttering from the highest towers—the banners of William, duke of Aquitaine.

"You look impressed," Dónall said, pulling his horse abreast of Ciarán's.

"Just look at the walls!" said the awestruck Ciarán.

"They're Roman, and never since Rome fell have men built such things. I still remember the first time I saw them."

"You've been here?"

"Twice actually, with your father. As students, we took a pilgrimage to Aquitaine, to the tombs of Turpin, Roland, and Oliver, and returned again years later when searching for Rosefleur."

"Rosefleur?"

"According to Maugis' book, it's the tower of Orionde, the Fae who taught him the secrets he recorded. Maugis wrote that the gateway to Rosefleur lies in the heart of Aquitaine."

"Did you ever find it?"

"God, no! At some point, I fear, the Fae retreated from these lands and closed the gateways to their Otherworld."

The column of horsemen crossed a wooden bridge over the River Clain. The bridge was built of logs and planks so sturdy that they barely creaked under the weight of so many destriers and armored men. At the head of the column, Lord Raymond, followed by Alais, started up the winding road toward one of the city's massive gates. Great stone blocks, framed by wild bushes white with snow, jutted from the hillside along the road. As they neared the wall, the stone blocks became more massive, the many crenellations more awe inspiring. Every twenty paces or so stood a half-round tower, and from its battlements, thirty feet above the wall's foundation, soldiers witnessed the cavalry's return. The city's massive gates stood open, and soon the head of the column disappeared under the arched gateway. The air inside the gateway was dank, and the tunnellike entrance spanned nearly twenty feet, which made Poitiers' defenses more forbidding than any except the walls of Troy—the only suitable comparison Ciarán could imagine.

Emerging from the tunnel, Ciarán caught his first glimpse of the townsfolk, who clapped and cheered the warriors' return. The men, women, and even children reminded him of the Parisians, though they bundled themselves in cloaks, many of which were brightly colored, and gathered along the narrow streets in rows six deep. Others watched from the balconies above their shops. Towering over the buildings was one of the bell towers Ciarán had seen from outside the walls. It belonged to a church of yellow-hued stone, which, judging from the black robed nuns who stood watching the procession, must be part of a convent. The sight of the nuns, many of them elderly and with stern faces hardened by years of rigorous discipline, made Ciarán think of his mother. Briefly he wondered how her convent would have reacted had she returned from France heavy with child.

Past the convent, the column of horsemen turned up another narrow street and then quickly down another, seemingly in the opposite direction, though still ascending the steep hillside. After a few more turns, Ciarán sensed that a madman must have designed the streets of Poitiers, for they seemed to form an anarchistic maze pinched between cramped buildings and towering church spires. An icy sludge had built up along the sides of the roads, and the crisp air was tinged with the whiff of refuse, reminding Ciarán once again why he preferred the humble, earthy environs of Derry to these crowded cities of the Continent. He had long ago lost sight of the head of the procession, and could see only a half-dozen riders ahead of him before the column snaked up some other crooked causeway. After climbing what must have been hundreds of feet of urban hillside, he finally spied the fortress.

The horsemen slowed to a near stop. Ahead, the fortress towers loomed over the pitched roofs of the surrounding buildings. The fortress, which Dónall referred to as the palace, was built of the same pale gray stone, though many of the blocks had the now familiar yellowish hue. Arched windows and arrowslits climbed up the tower walls, while small statues of Aquitainian warriors perched like gargoyles on brackets jutting near the battlements, where gray banners bearing crimson lions fluttered in the wintry breeze. Riders at the forefront began dismounting, and stable boys in drab brown tunics scurried to take their mounts while the men disappeared through a tall open gateway. Lord Raymond and Alais must have already gone in, for Ciarán caught not a glimpse of them.

"What happens to us now?" he asked Dónall.

"I suppose we'll discover how hospitable this duke is."

Once all the cavalrymen had dismounted, two stable boys met Ciarán and Dónall and waited impatiently until both had dismounted. As soon as they were on the ground, and without so much as a word, the stable boys grabbed the reins and led their horses away, leaving them alone on the snow-covered pavement outside the palace gates.

"So much for hospitality," Ciarán muttered. "Where do you suppose we go?"

Dónall surveyed the area. A block away, a church steeple peered over the pitched roofs.

"With luck, it will be an abbey," he said. "If not, maybe the priests will welcome us in."

They had started toward the church when a voice at their backs hailed them in Latin.

"Brother monks!" cried a man who had emerged from the palace gates. He wore the baggiest trousers Ciarán had ever seen, with one leg red and the other green. A crimson tunic, bulky cloak clasped with a broach, and foppish hat completed the man's ensemble. "Don't leave!" He hurried up to the two monks and took a moment to catch his breath. "His grace, Duke William of Aquitaine, invites you to sup with him this afternoon, to reward you for aiding his cousin, the lady of Selles-sur-Cher."

Dónall winked at Ciarán and then smiled at the man, who introduced himself as Duke William's steward. "We would be honored," he replied.

"Excellent!" The steward eyed both monks up and down and crinkled his nose. "Of course, *that* won't do."

"What?" Ciarán asked.

"Your clothes, or whatever you call that undyed sackcloth. You'll have to change. You both reek of horsehair and—if you don't mind my saying—look as if you haven't washed in ages. I'll try to round up some suitable habits from the Benedictines."

Ciarán's jaw clenched. "We'll never wear—"

"That would do nicely, thank you," Dónall interjected, placing a calming hand on Ciarán's forearm.

"Good, then," the steward said. "Follow me."

"Relax, lad," Dónall said in answer to Ciarán's annoyed glance. The sparkle had returned to his eyes. "There's an old saying for times like these: 'When in Rome . . .'"

≈

THE STEWARD LED them across the palace courtyard, through a rabbit warren of passageways beneath the main structure, eventually stopping at a small chamber that contained a privy and washbasin. Judging by the room's simplicity, it probably belonged to the palace servants. When the steward left, Ciarán and Dónall washed themselves. Ciarán found the cold water refreshing on his windbitten face. The steward soon returned to drop off a pair of clean habits and cowls, all dyed Benedictine black. After he left, Ciarán held up the smaller of the habits. "I can't believe we've sunk so low."

"Actually," Dónall said, "these will do quite well. If Adémar or Lucien should have men trying to find us, we'd stand out like a cow's bum in our Irish clothes. I doubt there's another gray-robed monk in the whole city. But between the Benedictines and the Cluniacs, there's hundreds in black."

"Cluniacs?"

"From the Abbey of Cluny. It was founded by one of the first dukes of Aquitaine. They're like the Benedictines, but far more serious in their devotion and even narrower-minded, if you can picture that."

"Can't wait to meet them," Ciarán said. He pulled the Benedictine habit over his head, followed by the cowl, and tied the cord around his waist.

"Smile, lad," Dónall said. "Black suits you."

Ciarán scowled, though he welcomed the old familiar sparkle in place of the melancholy that had lingered in Dónall's eyes since they left Saint-Bastian's. When the steward came to fetch them after what seemed like an hour, they had transformed into black-robed Benedictines.

"Much, much better," the steward said. "Those woolen sacks you rode in with were simply dreadful." Ciarán wanted to hit the man, but a stern glance from Dónall made him think better of it.

As the steward led them up a stairwell to the palace's main floor, a bell rang announcing supper. They entered a small foyer that opened into a hall of breathtaking size. The palace hall must be fifty feet wide and nearly three times as long, with a lofty ceiling supported by thick wooden trusses.

"Our whole oratory would fit in here," Ciarán whispered. Dónall simply nodded, enthralled by the chamber's grandeur. Arcades and pillars ran along the walls, broken only by narrow windows covered in vellum thin enough to let sunlight spill through. Three massive hearths, each with a crackling fire, dominated the center of the far wall, and a carpet of fresh green rushes scented with basil and cowslip covered the floor. In the center of the hall, a long trestle table was covered with a white cloth and set with silver flagons, pewter cups, and fine wood mazers. Along the table were chairs instead of benches, and an ornately carved high-backed chair stood at the table's head. Many of the guests were already seated.

"I suspect you're not used to this," the steward whispered, "but today you dine with lords and ladies, so act like you've been here before." Ciarán glowered, but Dónall calmed him with a friendly nudge.

The steward nodded toward a matronly woman seated to the left of the high-backed chair. A broad, pleated wimple covered her head, and a jeweled cross hung from her neck, over a damask dress. "The lady at the head of the table is Emma of Blois, duchess of Aquitaine and mother to our fair duke. Next to her"—the steward indicated a man with a thick mustache and a head of curly black hair—"is Lord Ramiro, ambassador of His Majesty, King Alfonso of León."

"Who are the Cluniacs?" Dónall nodded toward two black-robed monks seated to the right of the high-backed chair. One was a haughty-looking fellow whose girth suggested he rarely missed a meal, and the other was an old, sallow-faced priest in a canon's black robe.

"Prior Bernard of the abbey of Saint-Hilaire-le-Grand," the steward replied, "and the older priest is Canon Frézoul of the Cathedral of Saint-Etienne." The two clerics eyed Ciarán and Dónall critically, but Ciarán's eyes were on the figure two seats to the Cluniacs' right. For there she was, sitting beside Lord Raymond, and Ciarán had never seen her so magnificently attired. Instead of the simple dress she had worn since they left Selles, she wore a wine-red gown with a white mantle. A wimple covered her head, and while she certainly looked noble, Ciarán realized he much preferred seeing her long raven hair to the severe cloth wimple. She smiled demurely at them but quickly looked away as Raymond leaned over and whispered something in her ear. Ciarán felt his cheeks turn warm.

"Remember your vows, lad," Dónall whispered.

The steward looked annoyed at their comments. "You obviously know Lord Raymond and the Lady of Selles-sur-Cher. The other three gentlemen," he said of the cavaliers sitting at both sides of the table, "are lords of His Grace: Lord Dalmas, Lord Guy, and Lord Trencaval."

The steward urged Ciarán and Dónall toward two empty chairs beside Lord Trencaval. Dónall glanced again at the two black-robed clerics. "Where's the abbot?" he whispered to the steward.

"Duke William is lay abbot," the steward replied, "and here he comes." The steward bounded toward the far end of the table and announced in a formal voice, "All rise for William, Count of Poitou and Duke of all Aquitaine!"

Everyone at the table stood and turned as a slender man of average height approached through an archway. He had an angular face and a head of wavy, short-cropped hair that made him look like the illuminations of Caesar Augustus that Ciarán had seen in books from Rome. A pleated white cape draped one shoulder and hung to the heel of his calfskin shoe, and a golden medallion hung from his neck against a crimson tunic. He motioned for his guests to be seated as the steward pulled out his chair. Then William of Aquitaine surveyed his guests, stopping with Alais, to whom he cast a warm smile. "How blessed am I to have my dear cousin returned to me safely!" he said in a voice that seemed less commanding and more feminine than Ciarán had expected.

"I am grateful, and thankful to be home," Alais said, smiling.

"Fulk's defeat was a sign, Your Grace," Raymond interjected. "We were in the right; they were in the wrong."

Prior Bernard nodded his approval. "God favors the righteous."

"Oh, how right you are, Bernard," William said. "Without just cause, Fulk invaded the lands of a daughter of Aquitaine and a vassal of the king. God has condemned Fulk for the devil he is. The tide of this conflict is turning." He raised his cup of wine. "To deliverance!"

Ciarán drank. The wine tasted dark and rich. He followed it with a second, heartier gulp.

"I am told that two men of God helped rescue our fair Alais from the villain," William said to Ciarán and Dónall. "Remind me of your names, brother monks."

"I am Dónall mac Taidg of Derry," Dónall answered, "and this is—"

"Ciarán mac Tomás, my lord," Ciarán interjected, earning a raised brow from Dónall.

William stroked his chin. "Your names sound Irish, yet you appear before me as refined Benedictines."

Dónall nodded politely. "We are indeed Irish, but we have your steward to thank for these fine robes. And we are most grateful for your hospitality."

"Tell us how you came to save our fair Alais," William said.

"We had nothing to do with it, really, "Dónall replied. Alais watched him carefully as he spoke. "It was the wind. It stirred into a tempest, and the count and his men fled like rabbits before the hounds."

"A tempest, you say?" asked Emma of Blois.

"A cyclone, actually," Ciarán said.

Lord Ramiro clapped his hands. "How remarkable!"

"It's another sign," William said breathlessly. "God stands with us now."

"Is it true the bishop of Blois was present?" Prior Bernard asked. Alais turned pale, and Ciarán noticed the fear in her eyes.

"The bishop was there," Raymond replied, "with Fulk the Black."

"I heard that the bishop was hunting heretics," Canon Frézoul added in a raspy voice.

Prior Bernard eyed Alais warily. "There have been many rumors of heresy in the Touraine of late. But in coming to Selles-sur-Cher, the bishop must have been mistaken."

"Of course," William said. "Adémar of Blois has always been a faithful man. Surely he tried to temper Fulk's actions, but I suspect that not even a man of God could reach that black soul."

Leaning toward Dónall, Ciarán whispered, "*Some man of God.*"

"Amen to that," Dónall said under his breath.

When the conversation grew quiet, the duke clapped his hands. "Shall we eat?" he said. "Prior, lead us in the grace."

Prior Bernard obliged, and when he finished, servants emerged from the archways carrying bowls and platters. The aroma of roast pork and steaming onion stew spilled into the hall. A whole roast pig with an apple in its mouth was set in the center of the table, flanked by platters of pheasant and bowls of peas and nuts. Several of the servers drew long knives and began carving the meat, while others served bowls of stew and refilled the cups with wine. Ciarán heaped several helpings of pheasant on his mazer and topped it with spoonfuls of peas, ignoring the steward's disapproving gaze.

"Alais informs me that Brother Dónall studied at Reims," Raymond said with a wry smile once the meal began.

"Is that true?" William asked. "Many great scholars come from Reims."

"And many controversial ones," Prior Bernard added. "The rumors of heresy at Reims are legendary. Did you witness any such things while you were there, Brother Dónall?"

Dónall cocked his brow. "If by 'heresy' you mean the study of Virgil and Aristotle, then yes, it was rampant."

Prior Bernard sniffed in disapproval. "Authors of lies, all of them. Rome should have acted more sternly against that den of heresy. I've even heard of monks at Reims studying *Saracen* texts. What will be next: the heretical mysticism of the Jews? Those who sided with the devil in the persecution of our Lord and Savior? You know, Brother Dónall, Saint Peter knew none of these works—only God's word. And we would all do well to remember the words of our great Pope Gregory: '*The same mouth shall sing not the praises of Jove and the praises of Christ.*' Don't you agree, Brother Dónall?"

Ciarán had stopped eating, and the tension around the table had grown palpable. Dónall stroked his beard for a moment, then said, "I actually prefer the words of our Irish saint Columcille: *'Don't banish the bards,'* he said. *'Just make them teach others what they know.'"*

Prior Bernard's lower lip began to tremble, and his eyes narrowed to reproachful slits. Before he could respond, William interjected, "I've always found the Irish to be a curious people. Charlemagne always kept the council of an Irish monk. Perhaps it's because he, too, found them so curious."

Ciarán whispered to Dónall, "Glad we amuse him."

Canon Frézoul turned toward them and pointed a crooked finger from his shaking hand. "You know, the time fast approaches, Brother Dónall, when men will be judged by what they believe. The Antichrist stirs. The day of judgment draws nigh!"

Ciarán spoke without thinking. "And you know this for certain?"

"You presume to *challenge* me?" Canon Frézoul gasped.

Dónall tugged at Ciarán's sleeve, but Ciarán shook him off. "If there's one thing I've learned, it's that there are a hundred questions we don't know the answers to, so it seems a bit presumptuous to think *you* know when this will happen, or how people will be judged."

"It is the ignorance and hubris of youth that breeds presumptuousness!" Canon Frézoul growled.

"Who says the world has to end so soon?" Ciarán pressed. "What if mankind can prevent this?"

Canon Frézoul pounded a fist on the table. "Nonsense! You Irish have ruined your minds with pagan tales!"

Ciarán leaned over the table. "And what if there's truth in those tales?"

Canon Frézoul's face turned a purplish red, but before he could speak again, William interrupted. "Enough debate. Raymond, why don't you regale us with the tale of your victory against our ungodly foe?"

Raymond responded eagerly to William's request with a much-embellished account of the battle by the falls. Despite the exaggerations, Ciarán felt relieved, for at least it took the focus away from him and Dónall, leaving only the hateful stares of Prior Bernard and Canon Frézoul.

When the meal ended, servants cleared the table, and a troupe of musicians filed into the hall. Dónall seized the moment to thank the duke for his hospitality and politely requested his leave. "I fear we've been away from a church for far too long," Dónall said, "and we are starved for the humility of prayer."

"Naturally," William responded.

Dónall asked the duke for directions to a nearby abbey, but William insisted they stay at Saint-Hilaire-le-Grand, even though it was outside the city walls. Ciarán wished the duke had offered some other accommodations, for the last thing they wanted was to be under the roof of an abbey controlled by Prior Bernard, but Dónall graciously accepted the duke's invitation. As the steward escorted them away, Ciarán glanced back at Alais. To his surprise, she was gazing back at him. Lost within those storm-gray eyes, he found himself unable to turn away, hoping their gaze would hold. But then she quickly looked away and laughed at something Raymond had said.

"Let's go," Dónall told Ciarán.

"I can't wait to leave," Ciarán said bitterly.

They followed the steward from the hall, through another foyer and outside into the biting air. The sun had set, and a light snowfall wafted down, gathering on the rooftops of Poitiers. At the palace gates, the steward told them how to find the abbey of Saint-Hilaire-le-Grand. They would have to leave through the south gate and travel down the old Roman road alongside the Boivre, the second of two rivers bordering Poitiers.

They bade the steward farewell, gathered the belongings they had left behind in the servants' quarters, and left the palace for the city's narrow maze of streets. Dónall drew his cowl over his head before turning to Ciarán. "So when did you decide that we hadn't enough enemies and needed two more?"

"They didn't like us anyway," Ciarán said. "And I fear we've more enemies than those two, including the supposedly faithful bishop."

"And let's not forget Lucien," Dónall said with contempt. "But we may owe something to Prior Bernard. His comment about the Jewish mystics reminded me what Remi said just before Lucien tried to kill us: the notion about Abraham and a stone, a testament from a lost civilization."

"I don't remember that part in Genesis," Ciarán replied.

"It's not there. But that doesn't mean anything—there are many other Hebrew sources."

"And how do you suppose we find those?"

"I can think of only one way," Dónall said with a sparkle in his eyes. "We'll find ourselves a Jew."

CHAPTER 27

THE BLACK GROVE

Twenty-three black-robed monks filed through the woods not far from Saint-Bastian's, humming a somber chant. Flecks of snow drifted through the bare trees and settled on their black cowls. Many of the monks clasped glowing candles, while two bore a large iron brazier from which tendrils of smoke snaked skyward through the spidery branches. A third man held a caged white dove, and a fourth carried a lamb, bound at the hocks and bleating faintly.

Lucien led the procession, his face hidden beneath the broad black cowl that he wore on his missions to Blois, in the guise of the shadowy Benedictine who would visit the bishop in the dark of night. The crucifix that Lucien wore as prior of Saint-Bastian's had no purpose here, for he had long ago forsaken any hope of Christ's salvation.

Next to Lucien strode the priest Gauzlin, and beside him, the man they called simply "my lord." Taller than the others and wearing only a monk's habit, Adémar walked barefoot to this ritual on the midnight of midwinter—a sabbat of great power.

"Tonight," Adémar told Lucien and Gauzlin as they

approached the grove, "we shall ensure that these Irishmen do not live to find Enoch's device."

Ahead, twisted oaks stretched toward the night sky, their branches clawing like greedy skeletal hands at the stars. Steam rose from between the trees, creating an opaque veil around the sanctum of the grove. The ground within was unnaturally warm, devouring the snowflakes as they landed. At one time, Lucien knew, the grove had belonged to a sect of druids who sacrificed humans to their horned god. And over time, the horror of so many deaths had changed this place, for it held a power unlike anywhere else in the Touraine, as if the roots of the trees here burrowed deep enough to touch the underworld.

Adémar drank in the steamy air before speaking to the assembled monks. "Behold this ancient place and secrets long forgotten by men, since before the days of Rome."

He led them through the curtain of steam. Beneath a canopy of bare branches, dead leaves carpeted the ground, mixed with the boney remains of small animals and birds that had lingered too long. In the center of the grove stood an ancient stone, an altar carved with druidic symbols and stained dark with ancient blood. The two monks holding the brazier set it on the altar and removed its lid. The coals within emitted a ghastly red glow. A third monk set the caged dove at the altar's base as Gauzlin and the others encircled the altar, leaving Adémar alone in the center. The monks stopped their chanting, and in the silence, Adémar removed his habit and stood naked. Lucien stared breathlessly at his master's perfectly endowed physique, like that of a statuesque Greek god. Runes painted on Adémar's bare flesh ran up his back and chest, down his arms, and up his neck, forming ancient words in an ancient tongue.

"Make the circle," he commanded.

Gauzlin drew his knife and slit the lamb's throat. Then he handed Adémar the knife.

Carrying the dying lamb, Gauzlin encircled Adémar and the altar. Blood spilled from the lamb's neck and hissed as it struck the warm ground. Then Adémar sprinkled a handful of wormwood onto the brazier's coals. The poisonous herb crackled and flashed, and a tendril of smoke curled skyward as Adémar began a guttural chant. Reaching for the cage at the altar's base, he removed the squirming dove. With a flick of the knife, he slit the bird's breast, carved out its heart, and threw it on the coals. The brazier sizzled, and the air became electric. Glowing blue flames danced over the treetops, and the circle of lamb's blood erupted into a wreath of fire. With each word of Adémar's chant, Lucien could sense the power drawing toward the altar.

Still clutching the knife, Adémar stretched his hands broadly above his head, and his chant became an incantation:

> *I call you, spirits of the ancient world,*
> *Souls of gods and men,*
> *Queens of wrath and vengeance.*
> *Serve me now as sisters,*
> *For murder must be had!*

Then Adémar slit the palm of his hand and squeezed his blood into the brazier. With a sudden jolt, the ground trembled. Lucien felt it in the pit of his stomach. Several of the monks backed away as, from the brazier, a column of red smoke hissed up toward the stars. The oaks creaked, as if the tips of their branches were grasping at the smoke.

"With my royal blood I summon thee!" Adémar commanded.

> *Come, Alecto!*
> *Come, Megaera!*
> *Come, Tisiphone!*
> *Our king, the Dragon, needs your aid!*

The earth growled and rumbled beneath their feet. Above the grove, a red tempest swirled, churning with the brazier's smoke as the circle of flames grew to an inferno. Some monks shielded their eyes; others stared in awe. Lucien's heart pounded as he watched Adémar calling toward the night sky.

Then a collective voice answered—a ghastly shriek that echoed on the edge of the wind: *"We come!"*

CHAPTER 28

THE QUEEN SAINT

Alais strolled through the gardens of her ancestral home for the first time since leaving with Geoffrey for Selles-sur-Cher. Snow dusted the hedges and fruit trees, all the pomegranates, pears, and apples long since picked and stored in the root cellars. Herb bushes lined the gravelly paths, and the rich smell of coriander still lingered on the air. On the curtain wall that framed the garden's western half, soldiers stood atop battlements, sunlight gleaming off their helms. Alais pulled her ermine-lined cloak tight about her as she spied the stems of a rosebush that she and Adeline had once cherished. Although the stems were winter bare, she well recalled the color of its blossoms: not red but a purplish pink, like the sweet wines of Beaujolais. Each spring, after the roses had bloomed, they would pick a flower and dream of marrying a prince, plucking each petal in games of he-loves-me, he-loves-me-not.

Oh, but how differently from their dreams things had turned out.

A door to the palace opened, and William emerged, attired in a lavish fur-lined cloak and overlong tunic. He gently embraced her and kissed her cheek. "How blessed am I to have such a beautiful flower returned to my garden!" he murmured.

She smiled. "Wherever did you learn such flattery?"

"I'd been hoping to find you," he said as the cheeriness vanished from his face. "I want to know what really happened in Selles."

Alais turned away. "I'd rather not talk of it."

"You can be candid with me. And as duke of these lands and protector of the Touraine, I must know. Is it true you were to be burned as a witch?" He fixed on her eyes. "Alais, why would they think you guilty of such things?"

She felt a tear threatening. She could not bring herself to tell him what the bishop had done to her. Deep inside, that pain still felt like the cut of a jagged knife. William placed a comforting hand on her shoulder. She thought quickly.

"They were hunting for heretics and suspected the monks of the abbey. They needed someone as an example." Finally, she met his gaze. "Who better than the lady of Selles?"

William frowned. "Do you know if there was heresy at Selles? Monks can delve into many wicked things, you know. Was Geoffrey not vigilant in guarding against this evil?"

"Geoffrey was a good man," she snapped. "How can you suggest that?"

"He was not the strongest of lords. He never marshaled a suitable force of men—always averse to the demands of nobility and content just to live on his little farm. A man lax toward his duties is often lax toward his subjects."

"He was strong enough, and fair."

"There is no room for fairness when it comes to punishing the enemies of God. But no matter. You shall be back there in no time, and then you can clean up the mess and root out this heresy."

"What do you mean?" she asked. "I'm staying in Poitiers."

"Alais, I need to maintain my strength in the Touraine. And so does our cousin the king. I shall marry you to a more able husband."

Alais felt as if her legs would buckle. "Who . . . ?"

"Not Raymond, although he would be most eager to receive that honor. But I can't have him traipsing off to a farming village; I need him at my side. I'll find someone else: a strong man, God-fearing—with money, of course."

Her heartbeat quickened. A vision of Renaud exploded in her mind: his lecherous stare and his hoggish jowls dripping with grease.

"I have to go." She brushed past William, feeling suddenly short of breath.

"Alais?" William called after her. "Surely you expected this!"

She didn't answer. Her world was spinning, tilting, sliding away from her. *How could this be happening again!* She felt as if she were once again sixteen, confronted with her first arranged marriage.

"Alais!" William shouted. But she barely heard him as she bolted from the palace. Down the winding streets of Poitiers she fled, to the place that had been her sanctuary: to Saint Radegonde's tomb.

A CLUSTER of flickering candles in red glass jars lit the sanctuary, illuminating the graceful carving of Saint Radegonde on the stone lid of the sarcophagus. There, under the domed roof of the shrine, Alais thought and wept and prayed. She could not subject herself to another arranged marriage, yet William would force upon her a new Renaud, a new Clothaire. After the horrors at Selles—and the bishop's vile assault—she had dreamed of peace and safety in Poitiers. Not this.

She rested her head against the saint's face, her tears wetting Radegonde's stone cheek. When the patter of sandals echoed down the stairwell, Alais looked up as a figure emerged. At first, she feared it was a ghost aglow in the flickering candlelight, hooded and draped in long, wispy robes. But as it came into the light, Alais saw that it was a woman, very old and almost preternaturally frail. The cowled figure spoke with a familiar voice.

"Alais? Is it you, dear?" The figure groped along the walls, with halting movements.

"Abbess?" Alais asked breathlessly.

"Yes, it is I, dear. Can you help an old woman down the stairs? My eyes went some years ago, and my body's a bit more fragile, but our Savior yet waits to call me from this world—I often wonder why."

Tears of joy poured from Alais' eyes. She rose to help the frail woman, who clung to her until her sandaled feet were firmly on the cold stone floor. The abbess patted Alais, feeling for her face and then caressing it as if she were seeing with her hands. "You've come back," she said with a warm, toothless grin.

"To where I saw you last," Alais replied. She embraced the old woman, and her story spilled along with her tears. She told of Geoffrey's death and the murder of poor Thadeus, who had been so kind to her, and of the ravaging of Selles, omitting only her rape at the bishop's hands. Perhaps not speaking of it made it seem less real. Alais described the miracle that saved her from the stake, to which the abbess replied that the Lord worked in mysterious ways. Alais mentioned her abduction by the monks of Saint-Bastian and her rescue at the hands of Lord Raymond and his men. Then she spoke of William and their confrontation, and wept some more in the abbess's arms.

"Dear, dear," the abbess said, stroking Alais' hair. "You overcame this once. You can do so again."

"But last time, I was given a choice," Alais sobbed.

The abbess cocked her head. "Your father gave you no more choice than Duke William gives you now, yet you persevered."

"No," Alais said. "After the wedding, I fled from Geoffrey. In a field of wheat. That's when I saw her: a woman in white, like an angel. Her feet floated above the ground! I begged her to shield me in the wheat, to hide me like the queen saint. But she wouldn't. Instead, she told me to choose. Then, like the wind, she was gone. Yet when Geoffrey found me, he offered me a choice. He was willing to annul the marriage and return me here. I saw the goodness in him then, but the choice was mine. William offers no such thing."

The abbess sat silent for a moment. "You speak of miracles. Where did this happen?"

"About four days east of here, in the Val d'Anglin."

The abbess placed a frail hand on the saint's visage. "Some

believe that Radegonde's miracle happened in the Val d'Anglin. Are you sure of what you saw?"

"Yes, Abbess. Do you think it was she?"

"That doesn't seem possible. But then, nothing about miracles ever does. And now you tell of another miracle: this cyclone that saved you from the count of Anjou." The old woman's eyes were foggy and pale, yet the rest of her seemed invigorated. "When Saint Radegonde was saved from Clothaire, she found her calling and did great things for this convent and for Poitiers. She fought injustice and, at times, stood against the minions of the devil himself!"

Alais shook her head. "What are you saying?"

"That your purpose in this life may be greater than you believe," the abbess replied. "You have already fled and been saved more than once. This time, you may have to stand against injustice and, like our queen saint, fight for what you believe is true."

Alais breathed a long sigh and clung to the old woman. *I don't know if I can fight this battle,* she thought in silence.

"Yes, you can, dear," the abbess replied as if she could read Alais' mind. "Yes, you can."

CHAPTER 29

THE STREET OF THE JEWS

After the last Gregorian chant for the holy office of Nones, Prior Bernard eyed the two Irishmen shrewdly as the monks of Saint-Hilaire-le-Grand filed from the dimly lit choir into the pale sunlight of the cloister. The rotund prior had positioned himself like a sentry at the door to the cloister, patting backs and whispering niggling reminders or petty criticisms to each monk who passed. Ciarán and Dónall were among the last to leave. Ciarán kept his head down, hoping to avoid the prior's meddling, but concluded that it was futile. He had known a few monks like this at Derry, forever lusting to know everyone's business, and the prior was no different. As the two Irishmen approached the doorway that stood open to the wintry air, a sneering smile spread between the prior's fat, pink cheeks.

"Brother Dónall," the prior said with more than a hint of disdain, "I've heard you plan to visit the Jewry."

Dónall gave the prior a curious look. "Apparently, the monk we asked for directions saw fit to report this epic event."

"The monks of Saint-Hilaire think ill of secrets, Brother Dónall. May I inquire why two Irish monks seek to cavort with Jews?"

Ciarán expected Dónall to lie, and he did. "Young Ciarán here has never seen a Jew," Dónall explained. "We have none in Ireland, so I thought I'd contribute to his education while we're in town."

The prior grunted. "A paltry lesson it will be. You know, Brother Dónall, Canon Frézoul and I have often wondered whether we should rid Poitiers of the Jews."

Ciarán blanched. Dónall glanced at him, and then a wry smile formed on his lips. "Christ was a Jew," he pointed out, "and so were his twelve apostles."

"The Jews murdered Christ," the prior spat. "How can you think of them kindly? You're aware, are you not, that the Antichrist will be born of the Jews. Adso of Montier proved as much in his letter to our late queen Gerberga."

"Isn't it curious," Dónall said, "that the term 'Antichrist' appears nowhere in the book of Revelation. In fact, John of Patmos wrote only of the Beasts of the Apocalypse and the Whore of Babylon, but no Antichrist born of the Jews. And certainly you know that the early church fathers, who lived much closer in time to Christ than our good Adso of Montier, viewed the symbolism of Revelation as pertaining to the persecutions of the first century. Babylon was a symbol for Rome. The first beast was the Roman Empire, led by seven emperors, the likes of Caligula, Nero, and Domitian. And the second beast represented apostate Christians, who sought to turn true Christians to the heathen ways of Caesar. In other words, there was not a Jew among them."

The prior's lips pinched and his eyes narrowed, as if his brain was struggling mightily for a retort. After a moment, he growled, "Your views of scripture are very troubling."

Dónall smiled. "We Irish have always had an irreverent point of view. Now, Prior, if you'll excuse us, we have business in town."

Prior Bernard fumed. And as Ciarán and Dónall started down the cloister, he called out behind them, "Young Ciarán, remember to look for the little horns atop the Jews' heads."

Ciarán barely glanced back. "They have *horns*?" he asked Dónall.

Dónall rolled his eyes. "Thomas and I knew a rather pretty

Jewess back in Reims. Trust me: they don't bite, and they don't have horns."

They found the exit to the cloister and walked briskly through the courtyard toward the abbey's gatehouse. Now only a scattering of snowflakes drifted through the air, carried from tree limbs by the scarce breeze. Around them, monks attended to the inhabitants of the nearby animal pens, rousing a cacophony of squealing and bleating from the hogs and sheep. The courtyard stank of dung. "Was it true what you said about the early church fathers?" Ciarán asked hopefully as they neared the open gate. "If they were right, then maybe there is nothing to the prophecy."

Dónall's expression turned grim. "I fear that in less than twelve weeks, we'll have the chance to test that theory ourselves."

THEY CLIMBED THE HILLY STREETS, looking every bit as ordinary as the other black-robed monks moving through the city of Poitiers. The streets' labyrinthine arrangement reminded Ciarán of yesterday, but this time without horses to do all the work. The sludge-lined streets still gave off their stench of dung and refuse, which Ciarán had begun to see as the one common trait of every town in France. Traveling on foot did provide a slightly different perspective, however. For one thing, he noticed a mix of architecture, including some newer structures with slate roofs and wooden trim, and a few with jutting posts from which colorfully painted signs hung. Other structures were decidedly older, such as the block-shaped Baptistry of Saint-Jean, with its narthex surmounted by a triangular Roman roof and supported by thick rectangular columns built of hundreds of stacked stones. Along many streets stood churches with lofty bell towers and high-arched vestibules. The hum of Gregorian chants echoed at times from the religious buildings, only to blend with the cluck of an occasional chicken pecking in the grimy sludge, the bark of stray dogs, and the music of daily life provided by hollering merchants, creaking wagon wheels, and clopping horses.

A myriad of Christmas wreaths hung from the doors of shops,

houses, and churches—a reminder that the holiday honoring Christ's birth was but four days away. It would be the first Christmas Ciarán had ever spent away from Derry, and the thought naturally resurrected memories of Niall and Murchad, and Fintan and his other friends. But Ciarán tried to force them from his mind and shut away the sorrow that followed those thoughts. Instead, he thought of Irish Christmas feasts: tables crammed with platters of steaming capon, bowls of rich Irish stew, baskets of honey-topped bannocks, plates of apples and nuts tossed with cinnamon, and cups of spiced Christmas mead. His stomach was almost growling for that feast by the time Dónall announced their arrival at the Jewry of Poitiers, which, as best Ciarán could tell, was no larger than a single narrow street crossed by a few even narrower alleyways.

The first thing he noticed about the Jewry was the absence of Christmas wreaths. But second was the sludge. It was more the color of snow than of refuse, and instead of the whiff of excrement in the air, he detected the aroma of chicken stew. The buildings were no different from most of the newer structures along the way. Many had wooden frames and thatched roofs, although a few had roofs of slate.

A scrawny boy no older than ten was the first to notice the two monks. He darted toward one of the houses, but Dónall said something in the Aquitainian tongue that made him lose his fear and stop and chat for a moment. The boy, who wore a tiny brown skullcap atop his thick mop of hair, pointed to one of the larger houses along the main street. Dónall patted him on the head, and the boy headed toward the large house, waving them along.

"What did you say to him?" Ciarán asked.

"I wished him a happy Hanukkah. I don't think he expected to hear that from a Benedictine monk. In any event, I asked him to point us to the rabbi here because that's the man we need to see."

They followed the boy, who scampered up a short flight of brick steps to a sturdy wooden door, where a hand-size six-pointed Star of David had been neatly carved. The boy waved for them one last time and ducked inside. Dónall and Ciarán climbed the brick steps. A moment later, the door opened again.

"I want nothing to do with Benedictine monks!" a man's voice shouted in heavily accented Latin. The man who poked his head around the door stood no taller than Ciarán's shoulder. He had a bushy gray beard, and a skullcap on his head. "Go away! Get out!"

Dónall took a step back. "We're not Benedictines," he replied calmly, "despite these robes."

"I don't care what—"

"We're Irish."

The old Jew scratched the curly hair beneath his skullcap. "Irish, eh? From the edge of the world?"

"Where not a single Benedictine is to be found," Dónall said.

"Hm-m-m," the Jew mused. "Then you're obviously lost. Go south to Bordeaux, find a boat, and sail north. Have a good trip home, and do try to avoid the Vikings along the way." The door slammed shut.

Dónall sighed. "After meeting Prior Bernard, can you blame him?"

"Not really," Ciarán said.

Dónall rapped on the door. "We need to speak with a rabbi," he yelled.

"I've no interest in religious debates!" the Jew cried from behind the door.

"No debates," Dónall said. "We have a historical question of sorts."

"Then find yourself a historian!"

"It's a question of Jewish history."

"Read the first half of your Christian Bible. It's all there. Good day!"

Dónall, smiled, shaking his head. "It's not in the Torah. Perhaps the Talmud, or more obscure sources."

The door opened again. The Jew poked his head out. "Are all Irish so persistent?"

"We're a very stubborn people," Dónall said.

A hint of a smile cracked the Jew's lips, revealing less than a full set of teeth. "*How* obscure?"

"We're particularly interested in the history of sacred stones that may have been passed down from Abraham."

The rabbi's eyes narrowed.

"We're looking for a stone of light," Ciarán added.

The Jew began to chuckle. "My dear monks," he said, "you seek something that has eluded Jewish mystics for more than fifteen centuries. Please, do not waste your time."

"Then you know what it is?" Ciarán asked.

"Of course. It's a gemstone etched with a single word."

"What word?" Dónall asked.

The Jew's expression grew suddenly serious. "One that no man can utter: the one true name of God."

CHAPTER 30

THE STONE OF LIGHT

"How do you know?" Dónall asked the question before Ciarán could formulate the words. The thought that Remi and Thomas had been chasing a real historical relic, and not some chimera born of Maugis' mind, emboldened Ciarán, but he had never imagined the relic being what the rabbi just described.

"First," the rabbi said, "I want to know how you have come to search for it. But please, come inside before you catch cold."

The old man welcomed them into a warm, sparsely furnished room. It was a cozy space, although the boy was gone, so the house must have other rooms as well. A generous layer of soot covered the angled ceiling, and a comfortable hearth crackled with a burning birch log. The air was flush with a sweet aroma. "Roasted chestnuts," the rabbi said. "My niece makes them for me every winter." He picked a bowl of the nuts off a round table that displayed a small, curious-looking candelabrum shaped like a bowed arc, with nine candles, only six of which were lit. "Have one?" he said to Ciarán.

Ciarán took a chestnut, peeled away the hull, and savored its sweetish flavor. As he chewed, he noticed a large desk strewn with scrolls and parchments and several inkhorns. A colorful rug lay across the wooden floor.

"I am Rabbi Isaac ben Ezra," the rabbi said, making a slight bow.

"Dónall mac Taidg," Dónall replied, "and the lad here is named Ciarán."

"Please, sit." The rabbi gestured to two empty chairs. Once Dónall and Ciarán sat, the rabbi pressed them again. "So, Dónall mac Taidg, will you answer my question?"

"We came across a reference to it in a rare Frankish text. The author was a mystic of sorts. He wrote of a 'Stone of Light' and made reference to the lost Book of Enoch."

"That is all?"

"Not really," Ciarán added. "But we found the Book of Enoch."

The rabbi blinked in astonishment. "Say that again?"

"We found it," Ciarán said. "It spoke of a great and glorious device at the ends of the earth—what Maugis, the author, called the Stone of Light."

"Do you *have* the Book of Enoch?" the rabbi asked, still incredulous.

"Unfortunately," Dónall said, "we are not the only ones looking for it. Our rival ended up with the book."

"That is unfortunate," the rabbi frowned. "I would have liked to see it." He eyed them shrewdly. "Why do you and this *rival* seek the stone?"

"It is an intellectual curiosity," Dónall lied.

"Hm-m-m," the rabbi said, "I wonder. But I suppose it doesn't matter, because you will never find this thing. You are obviously an educated man, Dónall mac Taidg. Are you aware of any works by Jewish mystics?"

"Vaguely," Dónall replied.

"There is a text, the *Sefer Yetzirah*—the Book of Creation—that tells how Abraham received a divine testimony of mystic lore. He lived long before Moses received the Torah, so he must have received something different. Abraham was the father of Jewish mysticism, much of which focuses on the origins of the many names of God, and the various combinations of sacred letters that make up those names, all in the quest to realize the one great name of God. *That* is the knowledge that many believe Abraham received. If this knowledge was embodied in a physical object, one theory is that it was a gemstone."

"*That's what Remi said*," Ciarán whispered in Irish to Dónall, who nodded back.

The rabbi shot them a curious look but then continued. "You realize," he explained, "that much of this is speculation. But my teacher was a sage from Al-Andalus, the land of my birth, where they are more educated in these things. Regardless, from here we must move to the Book of Exodus, for that is where we first read of the great stones. It describes the breastplate of Aaron, the first high priest. On the breastplate were many gemstones, but only two of them—the Urim and Thummim—bore unique names. They were to be worn over Aaron's heart when he spoke with God. The Thummim was called the Stone of Perfection, or Stone of Truth. That is not the one you are interested in. You seek the other stone, the Urim, translated literally as 'Stone of Light.'"

A wave of astonishment crashed over Ciarán: the stone was mentioned in the Bible.

Dónall gaped at the rabbi. "You believe the Urim is the same as Abraham's stone?"

"The light is a focus of Jewish mysticism," the rabbi explained. "Creating Light was the first act of God. It is the very essence of creation. If the father of mysticism had a sacred stone, it would have been the Urim, passed down through a long line of mystics, through Aaron to the kings of Israel, most notably King Solomon. And that is where we find the likes of the Urim again. The story comes from the Talmud and tells of a stone called the Schamir, or 'lightning stone'—a gem that radiated light. Is this the Urim? I think the similarities suggest they must be. Solomon set the Schamir into a ring."

"The Seal of Solomon," Dónall breathed.

"Quite observant," the rabbi replied. "According to legend, it was a ring etched with the name of God."

Dónall rubbed his forehead. "There are stories that Solomon used that ring to subdue demons."

"A ring holding the Urim would have bestowed such power."

Ciarán listened intently to the two scholars, riveted by their dialogue. It was the same fascination he had felt hearing Remi and Lucien unravel the secrets of Enoch.

"What happened to the stone after Solomon?" Ciarán asked.

The rabbi held up his palms. "I sense that this is more than a mere intellectual curiosity. You have not been frank with me. Before I tell you any more, I want to know why you seek the Urim."

Ciarán looked to Dónall, who was already unfastening the straps to his book satchel. He lifted out the Book of Maugis and set it on the table before the candelabrum. A glow from the flickering candles danced across the golden ankh etched into the cover. The rabbi's eyes grew wide at the sight of the tome. He reached for it, then pulled back his hand as if afraid to touch it.

"Its author," Dónall explained, "was Maugis d'Aygremont, one of the twelve paladins of Charlemagne—an expert, you could say, in the more arcane lore. It was written near the end of the eighth century."

"May I?" the rabbi said, touching the cover. His hand trembled.

"Of course."

The rabbi opened the book and began leafing carefully through the timeworn pages. He scanned paragraphs of scrawled Latin, squinting to read the poorly penned words, eventually abandoning the effort and delving deeper into the book. He stopped when he reached a page decorated with Fae symbols. He seemed captivated by the flowing beauty of the Fae script. With a crooked finger, he traced one of the letters from its stem to the arch, to its brilliant hooked serif.

"What is this script?" he asked reverently.

"According to the author, it is derived from the tongue of the angels."

The rabbi looked up. "You believe this?"

"The author claimed to have known one, of a sort," Dónall said. "Hidden among those symbols is an obscure reference to an event that occurs every thousand years—an apocalyptic event reminiscent of that described in the book of Revelation. The first time it occurred would have been three thousand years ago, with the fall of legendary Atlantis. The second would have been around the reign of King David or his son Solomon. The third would have been around the time of Christ's birth."

"And the fourth," Ciarán added, "would be around now."

The rabbi shook his head as if he had bitten a sour grape. "So this is some Christian prophecy you have fixated on."

"Not exactly," Ciarán said. "The prophecy is supposedly written among the stars, embedded in the signs of the zodiac—a good while before there were Christians."

"Ah," the rabbi said. "Astrological foolishness."

"For years, I was skeptical, too," Dónall said. "And I still am, to a degree. But of late, everyone who has chased this mystery has been murdered by people who believe very seriously in the truth of these things: the rivals I spoke of—men who seemingly will stop at nothing to ensure that the Stone of Light is never found."

"And still you pursue it?"

"It is supposedly a key to this prophecy," Dónall explained. "A linchpin, if you will—a thing needed to survive the prime event of this conflict."

"And the author does not tell you how to find such an important thing?"

"There may well be more answers hidden in this book," Dónall said, "but we don't even know where to start looking—which brought us to you."

The rabbi rested his chin on his hands and stared into the flickering candelabrum. Then he closed his eyes as if deep in thought. After a moment, he opened them again and sighed. "What you have just told me seems very dubious. But even if it were true, I am afraid I can be of little more use. For the Urim is gone, lost in the sands of history, just like the vessel that contained it."

"What vessel?" Ciarán pressed.

"The holiest of all vessels. Built by Moses, overlaid with gold, and topped with cherubim, to carry the testimony of God's covenant."

Ciarán could hardly believe his ears. "The Ark of the Covenant —the chest that contained the Ten Commandments?"

"We know that the Ark held more than just the tablets of the Ten Commandments," the rabbi explained, "but also the most sacred objects of the Levite priests: a golden urn of manna from heaven, Aaron's rod, and, undoubtedly, the Urim. But when the Babylonians destroyed Jerusalem and plundered the temple, the Ark, along with the Urim, disappeared into legend. So, you see, to seek the Urim is to seek the lost Ark—as futile a quest, I assure you."

Ciarán looked to Dónall, hoping for a response, but Dónall shook his head, looking dejected.

"Well," the rabbi said, rising from his chair, "that is all the time I have. I am sorry I could not be of more help." Dónall returned the book to its satchel, and the old man ushered his two visitors from their chairs to the front door. "Remember what I told you about the voyage from Bordeaux," the rabbi said, clapping Dónall's back. "Watch for Vikings. Good day." The door closed.

Standing outside the rabbi's house, they felt the wintry air gnaw at their bones. Snowflakes fell like frozen tears.

"Why would Maugis intend such a wild-goose chase?" Ciarán asked.

Dónall shook his head. "Maybe he *was* mad."

"If so, then Remi died in vain—and my parents, too."

"Perhaps they did," Dónall said, dispirited.

"I don't want to believe that."

Dónall looked at him fondly. "Now you're starting to sound like your father."

"Maybe he was onto something. I've got an idea."

"Speak."

Ciarán looked Dónall in the eyes. "Only after you show me all the secrets in that book."

CHAPTER 31
FAE DEALINGS

In their austere, drafty guest room at Saint-Hilaire-le-Grand, Ciarán and Dónall huddled over the Book of Maugis d'Aygremont, which lay open between them. Beside the book burned two tallow candles, their flames flickering in the draft of a narrow window that sucked in the night's chill like a long-drawn breath.

"Go back to where Maugis talks about the prophecy," Ciarán said.

"If you insist." Dónall leafed through the ancient vellum until he found a stained blank page. Then, taking the small milky-hued crystal from a pocket in his robes, he closed his eyes and blew on it, whispering the Fae word that Ciarán had heard twice before: *"Eoh."*

The crystal flashed brightly before dimming to a warm glow.

Ciarán looked on with familiar awe as lines of verse appeared on the empty page. He read the first verse aloud, below the words "The Prophecy of Arcanus":

> *Dark cycle of a thousand years,*
> *when the Dragon is freed.*
> *The Prophecy is etched in the heavens.*
> *The Sphinx is the key.*

This time, the meaning of the first two lines struck Ciarán like a thunderbolt. "Remi said that according to scripture, the Dragon must be freed from his prison after a thousand years."

"He did," Dónall replied. "And so did John of Patmos. He wrote in the book of Revelation that *'When the thousand years are ended, Satan will be released from his prison and will come to deceive the nations at the four corners of the earth, Gog and Magog, in order to gather them for battle.'* Coupled with the cycle of a thousand years and our now familiar riddle about the zodiac and the sphinx, Thomas and Remi developed their theory of the prophecy."

Ciarán nodded, staring now at the second verse, beneath the word "Salvation":

> *In Virgo's seed of Charlemagne's line,*
> *and Enoch's device, where the answer lies,*
> *in the whisper of breath, or all hope dies.*

"The last two lines concern Enoch's device," Ciarán observed.

"But where does that leave us?" Dónall asked. "All that remains is the hieroglyph and its reference to the Stone of Light at the ends of the earth. And even if the stone is the Urim, as our good rabbi believes, the trail ends in ancient Babylon, and from there only God knows."

"But we know one thing," Ciarán said, revealing the idea that had struck him outside the rabbi's house. "If this prophecy *is* real, then a thousand years ago, someone found Enoch's device. After all, the world's still here, right? Don't we just need to figure out who found it and where they went?"

Dónall blew on the crystal again. The light winked out, and the words on the page disappeared into the stained vellum. "And how do you propose we do that?"

"What about the other blank pages in the book?"

"They contain either Fae words or instructions on how to use them. Maugis hid his most precious knowledge on the blank pages, almost as a rite of passage, forcing the seeker to learn how to summon the soul light before being able to uncover the greater secrets of the Fae."

Ciarán gazed at Dónall in the flickering candlelight. "Then don't you think it means something that Maugis hid his reference to the prophecy in the same way?"

Dónall looked away, frustration knitting his brow.

"I need to learn how to read them," Ciarán said, tapping on the blank page.

"Nonsense," Dónall snapped.

"And what if something happens to you? The secrets of this book will be lost. *Everything* could be lost!"

"I never wanted this for you," Dónall said solemnly.

"Did my father?"

"Do you realize how dangerous the power can be?"

"How dangerous will it be if what Remi believed is actually true?"

Dónall grimaced. "Blast it to hell! It's against my better judgment, but so be it. In the morning," he said curtly.

Ciarán breathed a deep breath. His astonishment at Dónall's acquiescence was followed by a sudden wave of apprehension. For by tomorrow, his life as a dutiful, ordinary Christian monk would end.

THE NEXT MORNING, storm clouds gathered in the east, slowly advancing on Poitiers like a dark, threatening army.

Ciarán glanced up from one of the stone benches that bordered the floor of the ruined Roman amphitheater. Rows of steps encircled the bowl-shaped theater, which was littered with fragments of stone columns and broken benches. Tufts of yellow grass sprouted from the jagged fissures, and splotches of gray-green moss speckled the ancient stone steps that climbed to the amphitheater's crumbling back wall. The ruins stood by the road between the abbey and the city's southwestern gate—a vestige from a long-gone era when the city bore its Roman name, Lemonum. Ciarán and Dónall had entered through a half-collapsed arched gateway, squeezing past the remains of an iron portcullis and through a tunnel into the theater, although judging from the gaping breaches in the outer walls, this was not the only way inside. Snow dusted the rows of steps and formed a patchy white veil over the floor where Roman actors once performed. But for the two monks, the amphitheater was deserted.

"Perfect," Dónall said.

He crouched next to the bench, using a stick to trace a diagram in the snow. Drawing a line, he crossed it with another and then described a circle around the cross. Ciarán recognized the symbol at once.

"A wheel cross, like the one in your cell."

"Very good, lad," Dónall replied. At the bottom of the cross, he made a small circle. At the end of the left arm, he drew another symbol: a straight vertical line. Moving to the top of the cross, he sketched a shape that looked like a sage leaf with a cross at its base, and at the end of the right arm, he drew a downward-pointing triangle.

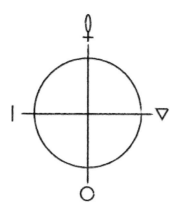

"The circle represents our world," Dónall said, "comprised of the four elements." Starting at the base of the cross and working clockwise, he named them: "Earth, fire, air, and water. The Fae words allow us to manipulate these elements—at times, to bend them to our will. Each element has an associated object that one must use, while speaking the words, to focus the power. Thomas thought the objects might be a sort of crutch to help us focus our minds, but without them we were never able to make the power work. Perhaps the Fae don't need them, but who knows?"

"What are they?" Ciarán asked, still trying to decipher the symbols Dónall had placed around the circle.

Dónall pointed to the small circle at the bottom of the cross. "For earth, the object is a crystal or a gemstone. You've seen the one I use." He took the crystal from in his habit pocket and rolled it between his fingers and thumb. "Thomas used a ruby that he mounted on a ring."

"You used the crystal to neutralize the basilisk's venom."

"True," Dónall said. "We are but creatures of earth, so the power can accelerate the body's natural healing." Next, he pointed to the vertical line beside the left arm. "The object for fire is a staff baptized by flame. You saw mine before I lost it at Saint-Bastian's."

"Can you make a new one?"

"Yes, but it would take some time. First, we would have to find a suitable piece of wood—an alder tree struck by lightning, for instance. And then it must be enchanted by the recitation of Fae words and an infusion of light."

"That's the purpose of the pictures in the book, isn't it?" Ciarán asked him. "Maugis told you how to create these."

"Good deduction." Dónall pointed to the oval with a crosslike handle. "For air, the object is a sword—the one you're now familiar with." Finally, he moved to the upside-down triangle.

"A cauldron," Ciarán interjected. "The object for water."

Dónall gave a wry smile. "We call it the cup, or the chalice, but it's the same thing. How did you know?"

"The Four Hallows of Ireland—the treasures of the Tuatha Dé Danann: the cauldron of Dagda, the sword of Núada, the spear or staff of Lugh, and the stone of Fál. It's another pattern."

"Clever, lad. Thomas and I saw the connection, too. It affirmed for us that this magic—if that's what you want to call it—was indeed the art of the Fae."

In the distance, the sky growled. The angry black clouds had begun to encroach on the pale gray sky overhead. Ciarán wondered how much time they had before the storm hit. Dónall glanced quickly at the clouds and continued the lesson. "In the center of the cross, where the lines intersect, is the fifth and most critical element: the spirit—the light I revealed to you, empowered by our everlasting souls. Maugis had an apothegm for it: *'Stone cuts earth, staff kindles fire. Sword parts air, cup binds water. Spirit incites the power.'* Only by tapping into the spirit—the light, which exists within each of us—can you give effect to the Fae words and channel the power."

Ciarán had no idea how to tap into his inner spirit. Indeed, the more Dónall spoke of it, the more he doubted he would ever be able to do it. "I assume it's a little harder than just saying a magic word and blowing on a crystal."

Dónall shrugged as he sat down on the ancient stone bench. "Just a bit. But it won't be nearly as hard for you as it was for us. You see, the conscious mind erects a barrier around the spirit, such that normal people never know what power lies within them. We don't know why this barrier exists—perhaps to protect us, for this power can be quite dangerous. Or maybe, over time, mankind forgot how to use the spirit, and it gradually became sealed off from the generations that followed. But the spirit exists in us all, beyond our conscious mind. To tap into it, we must shatter the barrier that surrounds it."

"But *how?*" Ciarán asked.

"Maugis called it self-initiation. Thomas and I, along with many of our brothers, did it this way, inducing a state of delirium, fasting for days, locked in the darkness of our cells, deep in meditation, to break through the barrier of the conscious mind. The hunger tears at your insides until it seems you're going mad, wishing that the horrors conjured by your delirious mind would go ahead and devour you and free you from the torment. But then, in the darkest moment, you break through and finally see it: the light in all its brilliance."

Ciarán looked hesitantly at Dónall. "And that's what we're going to do today?"

"Are you afraid?"

"No," Ciarán said, drawing a deep breath. "Well . . ."

"Using this power is not for the faint of heart or weak of mind. Remi, for one, felt that self-initiation was a necessary test to prove whether one was worthy to learn the secrets of the Fae. Fortunately, though, Thomas and I discovered a more expeditious and humane way to help others shatter the barrier. My one reservation is that this method avoids the suffering—when the power is earned in that fashion, it creates a profound respect. But I suppose we can't lock you in a cell in Saint-Hilaire's, raving like a madman, without attracting the attention of Prior Bernard and his pack of sour-faced Cluniacs."

Dónall held the crystal to his lips, then hesitated. "I warned you many times how dangerous this is. It is not too late to change your mind, but soon it will be."

Ciarán glanced at the wheel cross. He thought of his parents, hiding in some dimly lit stable of a village inn to practice the Fae arts in secret, all for the cause they believed in. Two fugitives chasing the prophecy—a quest that Ciarán now continued. He knew what had to be done.

He looked up and met Dónall's gaze.

"I'm ready."

DÓNALL PUT the crystal to his lips and whispered the now familiar Fae word. Within the crystal, a faint spark erupted into a bright flash before settling into a soft white glow. Dónall held the crystal before Ciarán's eyes. "I'm told this won't hurt too much," he said. "Close your eyes."

Ciarán closed his eyes and took a deep breath. He felt the crystal's warmth bathe his forehead just above his nose. Silently he asked Saint Columcille for strength, an instant before he felt the crystal's heat pressing against his head, lancing into his skull. A sudden rush of energy followed, and Ciarán felt himself falling. In a panic, he opened his eyes but saw only blackness. He was plummeting into a dark abyss. He cried out for Dónall but could not hear the words that left his tongue—if he even still had a tongue, for he could no longer feel his body or his limbs, as if he were nothing more than a consciousness suspended in darkness. The rushing slowed, and Ciarán felt himself floating in a starless sky, drifting toward the source of the darkness: a black obsidian wall, shimmering and impenetrable. Another sudden rush bore down on him like a violent wave, forcing him into the wall. What remained of his consciousness threatened to be pulverized between wall and wave. A scream roared up through the blackness. In the obsidian, a glowing crack formed and spread like a spider's web—jagged lines of light crawling across the wall.

Then the blackness exploded into a billion sparkling shards.

Searing heat followed blinding light, and he stood in the core of a blazing white sun. It felt powerful, energizing. He breathed it in through his lungs, stretched the muscles of his chest, felt every bone and sinew of his arms and legs, and the heat on the tips of his fingers and toes. Around him, all was a glorious incandescent white.

Slowly, it faded to gray—the gray of a gathering thunderstorm.

CIARÁN AWOKE spread-eagled on the amphitheater floor, with Dónall standing over him. "Did you see it?"

"I stood inside the sun," Ciarán answered, still struggling for breath.

"You've looked into the light of your soul. If you're to use the power, you'll need to recall that light and harness it." He helped Ciarán to his feet. "Do you feel like going on?"

Ciarán tried to shake the wooziness from his limbs. "Yes."

"Very well." Dónall held out the little opaque crystal. The light within it was gone. "Use this for now. The first thing you must learn is to summon your soul light. The Fae word for this is '*eoh*.'"

Ciarán took the crystal and held it between his thumb and fore-finger, as he had seen Dónall do many times. He tried to speak the word, but it came out wrong.

"Let the sound come from inside, through your breath, not your tongue."

He tried again but to no avail. The crystal seemed to have darkened with the sky above them. Wind whipped through the amphitheater, and bright flakes of snow, blown off the steps, glittered in the air. With a growing sense of despair, Ciarán doubted whether he could ever do this.

"You have to *imagine* what you want to happen," Dónall said quietly as his apprentice grew more and more frustrated in his efforts to utter what seemed a simple word. "Recall the light you saw in your mind, and envision it within the crystal."

Ciarán nodded, but no matter how many times he tried, the tone was never right. He growled in frustration.

"You have to relax, lad. At this rate, you'll soon have us sitting in the eye of a storm."

Ciarán tried to calm down. The sky was nearly as dark as night. Storm clouds rumbled overhead and around them, and the wind whistled and howled.

"The light is within you," Dónall explained. "You just have to draw it into the crystal."

Holding the stone once more to his lips, Ciarán closed his eyes and tried to picture the blazing light as if it burned within his chest. He filled his lungs, imagining the heat, and then exhaled. The word formed with his breath, pure and perfect.

"*Eoh.*"

White light flashed. The crystal glowed, and in its light, everything around him looked strangely different: clearer and more real. He saw Dónall, almost shimmering with a faint blue aura. Behind him, snowflakes wafted through the air like glowing motes of light, carried aloft in graceful arcs by the wind. All around them, misty tendrils from the storm clouds crept into the amphitheater, floating and twisting, as if nature herself had come alive. The smoky clouds billowed closer, drawn toward the light.

Then ice filled Ciarán's veins. For within the encroaching black tendrils, burning red eyes stared back at him—three pairs in all.

"Holy Mother," Ciarán cried, though his voice was deathly faint. "We're not alone!"

CHAPTER 32
DEMON STORM

For an instant, Ciarán feared that the attempt to break through his psychic barrier had cost him his sanity. It felt as if shattering that obsidian wall had severed the cord anchoring his rational mind, loosing a torrent of madness that manifested in the hellish apparitions he now beheld. For what he witnessed seemed conjured from a madman's nightmare: three horrible phantasms, female in form, born of the smoky clouds snaking their way into the amphitheater.

Their bodies, if they could even be called that, were twice the size of mortal women—grasping, with elongated fingers and claw-like nails. Withered breasts hung over gaunt ribs, and hips and legs were lost in the wispy folds of tattered robes that disappeared into the billowing clouds. More horrifying yet were their faces, with fanged mouths agape in ghastly screams. Their hateful eyes dripped tears of blood, and their wild hair writhed like hissing vipers, and Ciarán recalled the three Gorgons of myth, whose very gaze would turn one to stone.

He struggled for breath, trying to muster sound from a suddenly mute voice. His feet felt nailed to the earth, every muscle frozen.

From the phantasms' mouths came a horrid, keening wail that felt like daggers scraping over his bones.

Dónall wrenched the crystal from Ciarán's hand. The light died, and the ghoulish images vanished. Dónall summoned his own light and held the crystal to his eye, and his face went ashen. "Merciful God," he murmured.

Ciarán knew. They were still here.

Within the bowl-shaped amphitheater, the wind whipped violently, stirring snow up into the air and howling in a ghostly echo of the creatures' wails.

"Ciarán!" Dónall cried. "Flee for the abbey, and pray it's hallowed ground!"

Jolted by Dónall's words, Ciarán willed himself to move. He ran toward the entrance gate, thirty yards away, and a sudden pain stung his shoulder. Glancing at the torn black robes, he saw blood seep through the wool. Another stinging pain strafed his cheek, something hit him hard in the ribs. He looked up in horror. Stones, torn from the ruins by the howling winds, hurtled toward them like a swarm of hornets.

Dónall cried out. His forehead was bleeding. Shielding his face with the book satchel, he pressed toward the gateway.

A fist-size rock streaked past Ciarán's nose. His heart pounded as more debris pelted his back and limbs, and he realized that his only chance was to charge ahead, ignoring the pain of each new blow. Around them, the wind shrieked like a banshee.

Ciarán tasted blood on his lips as the tunnel to the gateway loomed ahead, offering shelter from the storm. With debris exploding just above him against the ancient archway, he bounded through the tunnel's entrance.

The rusted portcullis lay ahead, but as he approached, it slammed shut with a deafening crash.

"Ciarán, get out of there!" Dónall yelled.

At the tunnel's entrance, a vaguely human shape stood silhouetted against the streaking snow. It was in here with them.

Ciarán backed into the portcullis. He could feel the entity's foul breath against his neck and hear the hissing of its writhing mane.

The air in the tunnel froze. Ciarán tried to scream, but something was forcing its way into his mouth, gagging him, as a presence bored into his mind.

The invader was calling to him, *commanding him.*

As Dónall stumbled toward him, images of unspeakable perversion and cruelty flooded Ciarán's thoughts. The thoughts, once so alien, filled him with wanting, with an insatiable lust for pain and suffering. And murder.

DÓNALL PEERED through the light of the crystal, gripping it tightly against the battering wind-borne debris. His body ached from a dozen blows and wounds. Beneath a night-dark sky, one of the demons had entered the tunnel.

"Ciarán!" Dónall cried.

A choked scream answered back, and a few moments later, a single figure emerged from the crumbling archway. By outward appearances, it was Ciarán, but in the crystal's light, a shadowy form surrounded him. The silhouette of the Gorgon's mane wreathed his head.

A sickening fear washed over Dónall. He had read of such things, and his clerically trained mind told him they were possible, but he had never expected to witness them with his own eyes.

For Ciarán was no longer a being of free will.

The other two demons streaked about the amphitheater, stirring the wind and ripping small stones from their brittle foundations. They squealed perversely as their sister emerged in Ciarán's form. Dónall watched in terror mixed with a rising anger. Then Ciarán charged toward him.

Dónall leaped back through a stinging rain of sleet and debris. He struggled to think. There was no time to consult the book. His sandals slid on loose gravel as Ciarán's full weight drove him to the ground. The crystal flew from his fingers and skittered across the amphitheater floor.

Ciarán's fists hammered Dónall's head, and pain spread through him like ripples through a pond. The lad's eyes bulged, and spittle flew from his lips. Raising the book satchel to parry Ciarán's fists, Dónall knew he could not withstand another blow.

"In Patrick's name, release him!" Dónall cried.

Ciarán grabbed the satchel with both hands. Though Dónall was strong, the lad was stronger, and he ripped away the satchel. But this gave Dónall an opening, and he rammed a knee into Ciarán's exposed midsection, just below the breastbone.

"In the name of Columcille and Brigid and Kilian!" Dónall roared. "By Brendan and Brogan and Aengus and Finnian!" He slammed an elbow into the youth's jaw.

Gasping, Ciarán staggered back as Dónall struggled to his feet.

The rage in Ciarán's face burned like an inferno. He lunged, and Dónall collapsed again under his weight. Now Ciarán straddled him, and his fingers closed around Dónall's throat. Dónall grabbed Ciarán's wrists, but it was a bad trade, for the lad still had him by the throat.

"Too late for you, Irishman!" The voice that came from the lad's mouth sounded hoarse and ancient. Ciarán squeezed harder.

Dónall gagged. But with asphyxiation came a strange clarity. He could see the blackness swimming in Ciarán's eyes. All the light that Dónall had seen inside the lad when the barrier was broken had vanished. *When the barrier was broken* . . . when he had been inside Ciarán's mind! If only he could get in there again . . .

Around the two combatants, the demons wailed like a raging tempest. From the corner of his eye, Dónall saw the crystal. He reached, slapping the ground, but hot breath washed over his face, and Ciarán's hate-filled eyes bored into him. Dónall's fingertips touched the smooth surface of the crystal, and he drew it into his palm and brought it between his face and the lad's. Summoning a last faint bit of breath, he formed a sound: *"Eoh!"*

A blinding flash erupted, and at once Dónall thrust the crystal against the lad's forehead. With all the power of his mind, he projected himself inside.

⁓

Dónall mac Taidg found himself in a sea of inky smoke swirling around two eyelike motes that burned with a hellish glow. He sensed the intruder's name: Magaera. This was her realm now. Her eyes flared like molten stone.

"Too late!" she hissed.

Dónall felt the last vestige of life slipping from his mortal shell, as if the silver chord that bound body and soul had stretched to the snapping point. He knew he had but one chance. Drawing upon his raging anger, he answered her.

"In the name of all the angels and all the saints and Christ the Lord Almighty, *let there be light!*"

Blazing white heat exploded, and the demon loosed an enraged scream. Dónall fed the light, pouring his soul into the space. *There's only room for one of us!*

He willed a second thrust of light, and the demon screamed again, this time in agony. The light flared like a brilliant star, consuming the darkness until only specks remained before they, too, flashed into nothingness. Within Ciarán's mind, Dónall found himself alone.

Ciarán slumped over Dónall's chest, unconscious and barely breathing. Dónall wriggled free, praying he had not killed the lad. Through the crystal's blazing light, he could see the three enraged demons circling the amphitheater. Magaera had somehow survived.

The demons ripped up stones from the steps and benches, hurling them into the screaming wind. Dónall extinguished the crystal and stowed it in his habit, then slung the book satchel over his shoulder and hoisted Ciarán onto his back. They were but twenty paces from one of the gaping breaches in the outer wall, but a tempest of debris and three incorporeal demons raged in their path. With his free hand, he fumbled for the sword sheathed beneath his habit. He felt its pommel and wrapped his fingers around its comforting hilt.

Then Dónall cried out to the invisible spirits: "So, you want to play with the wind!"

He unsheathed his sword and uttered Fae words to manipulate the air, feeling the surge of power that came with each precisely spoken syllable. Envisioning a tunnel of swirling winds between himself and the breach, he gathered the air around him with the arcing movements of his blade, turning the wind in circles, faster and faster. He focused his will on the strength of the tunnel's walls. Around him, the wind roared, sweeping the air into a broad cylinder. The whipping clouds of sleet and debris buffeted against the deafening force of Dónall's wind. The din of swirling air smothered the demons' wails. Dónall projected his conjuration to the breached wall, blasting away fragments of bench and steps in his path.

Then he dragged Ciarán down the wind tunnel, praying that it was enough to shield them both from the storm of debris. To his great relief, the wall of wind held, and he reached the end unscathed. He pulled the lad through the man-size breach in the outer wall, carrying him over the remains of the great stone blocks mortared in place long ages ago by Roman masons.

At the bottom of the hill stood the abbey of Saint-Hilaire-le-Grand. Dónall hoped it would serve as a sanctuary. Otherwise, all this would be for naught.

He started down the hill, moving as fast as he could under Ciarán's dead weight. Glancing back over his shoulder, he saw the black cloud over the amphitheater begin to billow and slither. Like a giant serpent, it glided toward the abbey, and through the howl of the storm winds, Dónall could hear the demonic squealing.

A wall of black clouds gathered, with three columnar heads protruding, chasing the monks like a rolling avalanche. Dónall's heart raced. Seconds later, a violent wave of clouds crashed over them. Dónall cried back at the demons' piercing screams. Alongside the road, shrubs flew into the sky, wrenched from their roots by invisible hands, and the whipping winds picked up pebbles and cobbles from the ground. From the abbey, human voices cried out in alarm.

Dónall raised his sword and began to reconstruct the protective wall, and soon piercing cries rose from the battering winds that slammed into the wall of air he had summoned. Amid this black chaos, he trudged toward the abbey.

Ahead stood the walls of Saint-Hilaire-le-Grand. From the slate-roofed gatehouse, monks cried out in terror while others screamed prayers at the bizarre storm barreling toward the abbey.

"Open the gates!" Dónall yelled.

A panicked monk disappeared from the gatehouse window, and a moment later, the gate creaked open. Summoning the last of his strength, Dónall grabbed hold of Ciarán and ran. Crossing the threshold, he collapsed.

A terrible wail rose from the encroaching blackness. The storm cloud, unable to invade the air over the abbey, boiled and billowed and then climbed back up the hill as if it had been sucked skyward. The angry black mass collected over the amphitheater. Overhead, thunder pealed furiously before the cloud slowly dissipated into a gray sky.

Dónall grasped a handful of earth and brought it to his lips. Under his breath, he muttered a prayer: "Thank you, Lord, for hallowed ground."

CHAPTER 33

DELIVER US FROM EVIL

Dónall lay on the snow-dusted ground, every inch of him hurting beneath his tattered, bloodstained robes. He glanced at Ciarán beside him, unconscious and breathing weakly. Then he looked up into the faces of a dozen black-robed monks.

The gatekeeper was trying to explain. "They were caught in the storm."

"It was an evil wind," another monk said.

"A sign of the apocalypse!" cried a thickset monk.

Chanted Ave Marias rose from the most frightened of the brethren. *"Blessed art thou among women, and blessed is the fruit of thy womb, Jesus . . ."*

"It was the devil's own tempest!" one insisted.

"Holy Mary, Mother of God, pray for us sinners, now and at the hour of our death . . ."

Prior Bernard waddled into the crowd. His face was ashen. "What in God's name was that?"

"A terrible omen," moaned the doomsaying thickset monk. "A sign of the end times!"

Grimacing from a hundred aches and scrapes, Dónall picked

himself up off the ground. His right hand clung to the strap of the book satchel.

Prior Bernard blanched. "Brother Dónall? Look at you! I demand to know what happened!"

Dónall did not answer but glared at the gatekeeper and pointed at Ciarán. "Take him to the infirmary," he said. "Let him rest, but make sure he's breathing."

As the burly gatekeeper stooped to lift Ciarán, Dónall pushed past Prior Bernard, who grasped him by a torn sleeve. "Brother Dónall, I must insist . . ." The prior suddenly recoiled, his plump fingers stained with Dónall's blood.

Dónall looked the dumbfounded prior in the eye. "It was just a freak storm—hell of a nasty wind."

Ahead, one of the novices had picked up Dónall's sword, holding it by the pommel as if it were a live snake.

Prior Bernard winced. "What is *that*?"

"Open your eyes, man," Dónall snapped. "It's a Roman blade we found in the ruins. I'll donate it to the duke next time I see him." He snatched the sword from the novice, who looked relieved to be rid of it. Dónall tipped the blade toward Prior Bernard. "Now, if you'll excuse me . . ."

Prior Bernard stared wide-eyed at the blade, backing away and nearly tripping in his haste. The little knot of startled monks parted quickly, and Dónall strode through them and headed for the guest-house. He had to consult Maugis' book. Someone or some*thing* had sent those demons against him and Ciarán. And they were still out there, which meant that as soon as he and Ciarán left this abbey, the demons would be waiting.

When he reached the guesthouse, Dónall closed the door and pulled the Book of Maugis from its satchel. Setting the water basin carefully aside, he opened the book on the night table and flipped through pages toward the back. There Maugis had written of demons, which were just as the Book of Enoch had described. *The slain Nephilim shall remain on earth as evil spirits, and they shall be like storms, rising against man and wreaking destruction.* According to Maugis, demons could not be killed, for they were already dead. But they could be warded off.

For an instant, he thought back to Reims, to the time when Brother Orlando longed to test the demon wards in Maugis' Book. Orlando had searched the Secret Collection for tomes that told how to summon the evil spirits. Luckily, his first attempts had failed before Dónall and Thomas could convince him to stop. Dónall believed that such an act would be unholy—a dark turn down the path to forbidden magic. Thomas had shared that view, but it was clear now that Lucien had not. Had he become so powerful that he could bind demons to his will?

The question was so troubling, Dónall tried to banish it from his mind. Shuttering the window, he removed the opaque crystal from his habit. With the whisper of the Fae word, light flared and then settled to a soft white glow. He scanned the room to make sure all was as it seemed. Then he turned the weathered pages until he found one that was blank except for the heading, scrawled in brown ink: *"The Warding and Binding of Demons."* As the soul light settled onto the vellum, diagrams and flowing script cascaded down the page.

Maugis had warded demons with a talisman, pictured as a disk etched with a heptagram—the same design Maugis had used in the prophecy's hieroglyph. Instructions for constructing the talisman followed, accompanied by a litany of Fae words.

Dónall took four silver coins from Remi's purse—all that remained of a gift from the abbot of Saint-Germain-des-Prés. He stacked them in twos and then brought the stacks within the crystal's light. Fae words for metalworking flowed from Dónall's tongue, and as he spoke, the coins grew hot and unstable, melting into molten pools whose shape changed with a wave of his finger. Over the next hour—perhaps more, for in the heat of the ritual, with his mind focused on speaking the language of the Fae, he lost all track of time—Dónall molded the stacks into two smooth disks. Next, he traced the heptagrams, carefully drawing the seven points of each star, with each point touching the edge of the disk. The heptagram was an ancient shape honored by the Jewish mystics and Oriental magi, but early Christians also used it to symbolize the seven days of creation and to protect against evil. As Dónall finished the symbols, his Christian nature demanded something more, so he traced a high cross into the heart of each heptagram and whispered a prayer to the Father, Son, and Holy Spirit. He ended with a singular request: *"Deliver us, O Lord, from evil."* Then he drew a long breath and uttered a series of poetic incantations to seal the power within the talismans.

When he was done, Dónall's hands trembled and his brow dripped with sweat. What energy had remained after their skirmish with the demons was now spent, and with a deep yawn, he collapsed on the nearest pallet and slept.

DÓNALL WOKE SUDDENLY at the cock's crow. He rubbed his weary face and opened the shuttered window to let the sunlight spill through. Moments later, church bells rang the canonical hour of Prime.

Still wearing his tattered Benedictine habit, he exchanged it for his Irish habit and then glanced at the empty pallet beside him. "Ciarán?" he called out before realizing what had happened. *Dear God, I've left him in the care of an infirmarer!*

He bolted from the room. Down the steps from the guesthouse, he darted into the courtyard, past curious monks filing toward the church, nearly trampling the chickens in his path.

Dónall threw open the door to the infirmary, and the two monks inside jumped in alarm. The windows were still shuttered, and a log burned in the hearth. Four candelabras provided the only meager light surrounding the bed where Ciarán slept. He was half naked, and here and there, black, thumb-size lumps clung to the skin of his chest, stomach, and arms, glistening in the candlelight.

"Get those bloodsucking things off him!" Dónall growled.

The infirmarer, a wiry monk with a pinched nose, and his apprentice, a novice no older than fifteen, looked confounded.

"Why?" the infirmarer asked. "He surely has a disease of the blood. We have applied the leeches."

"Leechcraft is not medicine!"

The infirmarer puckered his mouth. "What do you know of the four humors? When the blood is poisoned, it must be leeched."

Dónall poked a finger at the infirmarer's chest. "I studied at Reims with Gerbert of Aurillac, who had knowledge of Arabic medicine, which is a damned sight more sophisticated than yours. Have you ever thought of trying to diagnose the disease rather than just jumping to reckless conclusions? Most likely, the lad's just exhausted. You'd be better off putting wine from Cognac under his nose and into his mouth. Then see how he reacts before you start letting his blood."

"We have that wine," the trembling apprentice offered.

"Then for the love of God, lad, go get some!"

THE COGNAC WORKED BETTER than Dónall had expected. Ciarán woke, groggy as if from a deep sleep. He seemed to have no recollection of his possession by the demon, which Dónall supposed was a good thing, although he would have liked to know what master the demon served.

Dónall sat with Ciarán all that day while he rested. By the next morning, Ciarán was sitting upright in bed, slurping down bowls of broth brought by the infirmarer's apprentice, and grateful to be back in his familiar Irish habit. Dónall had slipped one of the talismans around Ciarán's neck, hanging it from a leather thong obtained from the abbey's tanner. "Always wear this under your habit," he said.

"What is it?" Ciarán asked.

"Something to protect you from the demons."

"Is that what they were?" The color had yet to return to his face.

"If Maugis is right, with us wearing the talismans they shouldn't be able to come near us."

Before Dónall could say more, the infirmarer returned, accompanied by the gatekeeper.

"Brother Dónall," the gatekeeper said, "there's a man here to see you."

"Oh?"

"It's the rabbi ben Ezra."

Dónall glanced at Ciarán. "Curious. I'll see what he needs."

"I'm coming with you," Ciarán said.

"You need rest."

"I've had rest aplenty." Ciarán threw off his blanket and bounded out of bed. His knees buckled, and he sprawled on the infirmary floor.

The infirmarer handed him a walking stick, and he rose gingerly to his feet. "No worries," he said.

"Hobble along, then, if you insist," Dónall said.

As they stepped into the crisp morning air, Dónall searched for any sign of the storms that had preceded the demons, but only a canopy of gray-white clouds blanketed the sky.

At the abbey gate stood the rabbi, wrapped in a heavy blue cloak and leaning on a walking stick of his own. Rabbi Isaac ben Ezra smiled as Dónall and Ciarán approached.

"To what do we owe this honor?" Dónall asked.

"I am glad that you have not embarked on your journey home," the rabbi said. "There is something you should know."

"Not another warning about Vikings, I hope," Dónall said.

"This is more timely than that," the rabbi replied. A cunning smile spread across his face. "For I know how we can find your Stone of Light."

CHAPTER 34

THE NEXT JOURNEY

C iarán moved stiffly after Dónall and the rabbi to the abbey's church. Still dazed at learning of his brief demonic possession, Ciarán prayed there were no lasting effects, and he was much relieved to see the morning sky without any sign of the demons' storm clouds. Still, he found the church a welcome sanctuary. Dónall had picked it because the brothers of Saint-Hilaire-le-Grand were now between holy offices, so the place would be deserted.

Window slits covered in vellum palely lit the cramped church, and the resinous scent of incense lingered in the air. The rabbi looked around him, as if studying a foreign place. Dónall offered him a seat on a stone bench in the well of the nave and sat down beside him, while Ciarán leaned on his walking stick.

"Tell us, Rabbi," Dónall said. "I am eager to hear."

"You will forgive me if what I tell you sounds strange," the rabbi began, "but I would not be here if I did not think there is some truth in it. Since we met, my sleep has been plagued by dreams. In many, I have been haunted by a great beast as large as ten horses, long-necked and red-scaled like the dragon of Babylon, with broad wings like an eagle's. I could smell the stench of its evil. It scoured the earth, searching for something. By the depth of my fear, I knew that it was looking for the Urim. Then this dream faded, and I was in another. I saw the Ark of the Covenant—beautiful beyond imagination, its sides gleaming with gold. Its lid, thick and adorned with Bezalel's designs, bore the two cherubim kneeling atop the Ark, with outstretched wings that met in the Ark's center, their tips touching at the very place where Moses would commune with God. My body trembled, although I could not see my hands or arms. It was as if I were a spirit floating in the darkened chamber that held the Ark. Voices were chanting in the darkness, but the language was one I could not comprehend. Then, as if guided by the invisible hand of God, the lid opened and rose above the Ark. The cherubim glowed as if wreathed by blue fire. A pair of hands emerged into my line of sight, and I wondered for a moment whether they were my own. They reached into the Ark, disappearing with the smoky mists that swirled within, like steam rising from a lake. When they emerged from the mists, they held the Urim."

The rabbi spoke with closed eyes, recounting the dream as if he were experiencing it again. Ciarán hung on his every word.

"I could hardly imagine such a thing," the rabbi said, his voice filled with awe. "It was like a diamond, slightly smaller than the palm of one's hand, cut with hundreds of facets—thousands maybe—reflecting a light more brilliant than any I have ever seen. It was blinding in its brightness, like the sun itself, but with the purity of Sirius burning in the night. I felt as if I might die, so enrapt was I by its light. But then, fearing that my spectral form might cease to exist, I awoke, grateful that it was only a dream."

"Could you tell where the Ark was?" Dónall asked.

"That is not the point," the rabbi said. "The dream made me realize that when we last met, I had made a bad assumption: that the Urim remained in the Ark. Yet what if it was removed?"

Ciarán nodded. "We've thought of that, too."

"But where does that lead us?" Dónall asked.

"That is where we must focus on history," the rabbi said. "According to scripture, the Ark remained in the Temple of Jerusalem long after the time of Solomon, up until the time when the Babylonians came. When Nebuchadnezzar invaded Jerusalem and ravaged the temple six hundred years before the birth of your Jesus, the picture becomes less clear. The Second book of Maccabees states that the prophet Jeremiah hid the Ark in a cave, in the mountain that Moses had climbed to see the Promised Land. Yet some question the accuracy of that story, believing that it was written to raise the people's spirits during the revolt against the Greeks. Also, there are far earlier writings that contradict the Maccabean account. The Second book of Chronicles, for one, states that when the Babylonians destroyed the temple and stole the sacred pillars of Boaz and Jachin, Nebuchadnezzar's forces took *all* the temple's vessels and treasures to Babylon. And the Fourth book of Ezra is even clearer, speaking to the destruction of the temple and the plundering of the Ark of the Covenant by the Babylonians. A half century later, Babylon was conquered by the Persians, led by Cyrus the Great. Cyrus allowed the Israelites to return to Jerusalem, but he took possession of the treasures that the Babylonians stole. If the Ark was among them, then it fell into the hands of the Persians."

"What would have happened after that?" Ciarán asked.

"There is a place in the city of my birth," the rabbi said, "where the answer may lie: in Córdoba, the greatest city in all Europe. A center of learning like nothing in all Christendom. Unlike your Christian towns, where the local abbey might have an armful of books, throughout Córdoba are libraries with hundreds of books. And there is one library grander than them all, grander than any other in Europe: the library of Al-Hakkam the Second, the wisest caliph ever to rule Córdoba. This library holds not hundreds of books, but *hundreds of thousands.*"

Ciarán could hardly conceive of such a place. He doubted there were that many books in all the world.

"Al-Hakkam had hundreds of scribes," the rabbi continued, "both Ishmaelite and Christian, translating works from Latin and Greek into Arabic. He acquired works throughout Christendom, from Rome and Aachen and Constantinople. And from Africa and the Arab lands. Baghdad and Damascus, and Alexandria and Jerusalem. And if you know anything about libraries . . ."

Dónall's eyes lit up. "There's a secret collection."

"Of course," the rabbi said with a mischievous smile. "All collectors have a special place for their rarest things. And Al-Hakkam was an extraordinary collector. We Jews often heard rumors that the library held texts from Solomon's temple, taken by the Babylonians and, later, the Persians and now in the hands of the Muslim caliphs. There are other works rumored as well, acquired from Baghdad but originating from the ruins of Babylon, undoubtedly dating from the time of Cyrus the Great. If an account of the Urim's fate exists, the only place in all of Europe you may find it is Córdoba."

"So . . . you want us go to the Saracen lands?" Ciarán asked.

"There is no other way," the rabbi replied. "Getting access to the secret collection will be very difficult. But my cousin in Córdoba is well connected. He will know people who can help us when we get there."

"When *we* get there?" Dónall said. "You're coming with us?"

"I am not a young man, Brother Dónall, and I have not seen the beauty of that city since long before my Sarah passed. And I dearly wish to see Córdoba once more before I die. I have stayed here only because the people needed their rabbi. But my nephew has finished his studies now and will do a fine job in my stead. It is time he came into his own." The rabbi paused, a troubled look in his eyes.

"There's more," Dónall said, "isn't there?"

"There was something about the script in your book that I have not been able to purge from my mind," the rabbi said. "Those letters and their shapes—I could swear that each character, at its root, is Hebrew. Our mystics believe that God made the universe through the letters of the Hebrew alphabet, hewing them, weighing them, and combining them into creation. And now you show me what purports to be written in the tongue of angels, and they look like Hebrew letters. I would like very much to study them. And if this book speaks of the Urim . . ."

The rabbi closed his eyes for an instant and shuddered. "But there is something else: I fear from my dreams that some terrible evil seeks the Urim." His eyes sprang open, as if compelled by the fierce determination burning within them. "We cannot let him have it!"

For a moment, Ciarán thought he caught something of Remi's fervor in the rabbi's eyes. "There's something I still don't understand," Ciarán said. "The mystics have been searching for the Urim for centuries. If it's as simple as digging through a library, why hasn't anyone found it?"

"I do not know why," the rabbi said. "But we have an advantage that they did not, no? A book written in the tongue of the angels! Perhaps it is the only advantage we will need."

A smile crept across Dónall's face. "Well, lad," he said, rising from the bench, "grab your things. We're going to Córdoba."

THEY WALKED BACK to the city with Isaac, as the rabbi insisted on being called. Although Dónall advised against it, Ciarán made the short journey, still leaning on his stick but eager to regain the strength in his legs. Their first steps beyond the abbey's gate were trepid, but once they had set foot on the road, and still the storm clouds did not manifest, Ciarán felt a degree of relief, though the whole time he kept a cautious hand on the talisman around his neck. Dónall, too, seemed wary at first, ever vigilant of the air around them, but gradually he relaxed, confident perhaps that the Fae magic had worked. If the demons were about, they dare not approach.

By the time they reached the street of the Jews, Ciarán had learned much about the good-natured rabbi. Isaac hailed from a family of Córdoban merchants, Jews who prospered under the reign of the Moorish caliphs and eventually expanded the family's business to Bordeaux, importing Spanish olive oil and African spices. Isaac had neither love nor aptitude for the merchant's trade, so his younger brother succeeded their father in Bordeaux while Isaac studied under the Córdoban rabbi who had traveled with the family to Aquitaine. Years later, when the rabbi of Poitiers died and the Jews of the city needed another, Isaac settled here with his late wife, of whom he spoke so fondly even though she never bore him a child. With the exception of Benjamin, Isaac's youngest nephew, his other nephews continued their mercantile trade in Bordeaux, prospering as well as any Jew in a Christian land could hope. To transport their goods, they owned a ship, and now that ship would take them to Córdoba.

After a brief rest at the rabbi's home, refreshed with roasted chestnuts and cups of spiced wine, Dónall and Ciarán bade farewell to Isaac. By design, they would leave just after the Christian New Year, to give Isaac time to alert his nephews in Bordeaux and to prepare Benjamin to serve as rabbi to the Jews of Poitiers. Both Dónall and Ciarán were grateful. For without Isaac's family wealth and his offer of assistance, they would be nothing but two stonebroke Irishmen wandering this foreign land. Ciarán could not shake the feeling that they had been touched by the hand of fate.

CHRISTMAS CAME THE NEXT MORNING. Ciarán and Dónall joined the procession of monks that traveled from Saint-Hilaire-le-Grand to the Church of Saint-Etienne in Poitiers, where the duke of Aquitaine would celebrate Christmas mass. The procession entered the city under a platinum sky—seventy-nine monks walking two-by-two and chanting Christmas hymns.

A chorus of church bells rang through the streets, and on nearly every door hung wreaths of holly, ivy, and bay, while from the bell towers and church steeples fluttered banners of crimson and gold. The citizens, dressed in their finest clothes, made their way to mass, stopping at times to watch the monks.

If the monks of Saint-Hilaire's felt any Christmas spirit, it had been dampened by the manner in which Prior Bernard had commenced their procession. For he had gathered the brethren a full half hour early in the abbey's freezing courtyard and forced them to listen to an overlong sermon about God's anger at all the wickedness in the world some 997 years since the birth of Christ. And yet, among the citizens of Poitiers, Ciarán sensed genuine happiness, for Christmas was a day when they were excused from work and when some were even invited to feasts of wine and roasted beef, hosted by their lords, while those less fortunate received gifts of bread and soup from the local abbeys and churches. Thus, the people throughout Poitiers showed good cheer toward the monks and their blessings.

The brothers of Saint-Hilaire-le-Grand entered the Church of Saint-Etienne, where the rich smell of incense wafted through the narrow nave. On pillars along the arcade burned candles set in sconces and surrounded by wreaths of pine boughs. The procession split to walk down the right and left aisles that flanked the vestibule, beneath the rounded archways while intoning their rhythmic Gregorian chants. Worshipers filled the nave. There were nobles, ladies, and men of warrior stock, though no common folk that Ciarán could see. He followed Dónall down the left aisle as the monks filled the transept of the cross-shaped church. In the chancel, beyond the altar, where priests in white vestments gathered around the aged bishop of Poitiers, stood rows of black-robed monks from another monastery, who joined the chant as the monks of Saint-Hilaire took their places in the far transept.

The monks nearly overflowed the cramped transept, and Ciarán found himself on the edge of the nave, just feet from the first row of worshipers. At their head, Duke William prostrated on the stone-tiled floor, his crimson cape gathering in folds around him. Behind the duke stood members of his entourage—the same people Ciarán and Dónall had supped with just days ago: Emma of Blois and Lord Ramiro of León, Lord Dalmas and Lord Guy, and, of course, Lord Raymond. And beside Raymond, looking like a winter angel, stood Alais.

Although Ciarán had hoped to catch a glimpse of her before they left Poitiers, he was unprepared for what he saw. Her lithe form was wrapped in a green damask dress cinched tightly around her slender waist, with a mantle of silver and white above her breasts. Ciarán glimpsed her eyes, gray like the storm, but they made no search among the monks to find him.

His gaze left her as two columns of nuns filed into the aisles alongside the nave. They walked silently amid the joyous processional, for women were not allowed to raise their voices in the church. Canons closed the towering church doors behind the nuns, and then the mass began. The monks sang canticles, and the bishop read from the Gospel of Saint Matthew. The congregation prostrated for the great litany, and the choir sang during the communion, and all the while, Ciarán found himself drawn to Alais.

The chanting swelled before the benediction. The bishop stepped to the threshold of the nave and raised his arms above the prostrate duke. Before the bishop could speak, the vestibule doors swung open. A rush of wintry air blew through the nave, and a hush fell as the congregants near the vestibule began to part. The bishop looked up, startled, and the duke, too, stood and turned toward the open doors.

Down the newly formed passageway strode a column of Benedictine monks, their hands steepled in prayer. A miter crowned the head of the monks' leader, who wore white episcopal vestments trimmed with silver.

From the first row of worshipers, Alais gasped.

The intruder tilted his bearded chin toward the ceiling before leveling a wolflike gaze on the chancel. Ciarán's blood froze.

For Adémar of Blois had come to Poitiers.

CHAPTER 35
GOD'S WRATH

"What is the meaning of this?" the bishop of Poitiers stammered.

"Heresy, Lord Bishop, is what brings me here." Adémar let his accusation linger in the air. William's eyes flew wide, and behind him, Poitiers' elderly bishop had grown suddenly pale.

"Heresy," Adémar proclaimed, "which darkens my joy on the day of Christ's birth. Heresy, which has spread through the Touraine like a disease, from Selles-sur-Cher and across the rivers to threaten all Aquitaine."

Dónall tugged at Ciarán's sleeve. "Stay sharp," he whispered, "Lucien may be among them." Ciarán nodded subtly, but he could not be any more alert. His muscles tensed as he eyed the monks in the bishop's entourage, searching for the prior of Saint-Bastian's.

In the candle-lit nave, flustered nobles looked to William, who stood just paces from the bishop, separated by a thin haze of incense smoke. William pursed his lips before speaking. "Bishop Adémar, I beg your pardon. I have heard accounts of the atrocities that Fulk the Black inflicted on Selles-sur-Cher—atrocities which you yourself witnessed and did not abate."

"Fulk of Anjou is a devil indeed," Adémar said, "whose passions I could not abate. But know well, Lord Duke, sometimes God uses the devil as his sword. Especially when God has grown angry at how his subjects behave."

"Explain yourself!" William demanded.

Adémar implored the congregation with outstretched arms. "Is it any wonder why God has not favored your forces in battle? Why the Almighty allows the devil Fulk to build castle upon castle, such that you are becoming a prisoner in your own lands? My dear duke, God favors the victor. So why is Fulk so often the victor?"

William looked stricken, and a palpable tension filled the church as Ciarán saw Dónall's hand move to the hilt of his hidden blade. Ciarán searched for a way out but found only the vestibule doors, still open to the wind. And the aisle to those doors remained clogged by nuns engrossed in the unfolding drama.

"The answer," Adémar announced, his eyes burning with passion, "is because God's wrath burns like fire!"

William moved back a step. Among the nobles gathered beside him, Alais ducked toward the aisle. Just feet from Ciarán, a skeletally frail woman in an abbess's robes pulled her behind the column of nuns.

"God's wrath burns," Adémar continued, "when the king whom you hold so dear has unholy relations with his first cousin, warranting excommunication by Pope Gregory in Rome; when heresy runs rampant in your own lands; when your own cousin adorns her neck with a devil's sign, practicing witchcraft against the servants of Christ and cavorting with sorcerers from a pagan isle!"

Ciarán's pulse quickened. He reached for Alais, brushing her arm with his hand. She glanced back, terrified, until her gaze met his. She held his hand tight, and he could feel her body tremble.

Beside Ciarán, Dónall nodded toward the vestibule doors, his expression grave.

"So," Adémar exclaimed, "should it surprise anyone that as we stand here today, Fulk's ally, the viscount of Limoges, gathers an army to his new castle at Brosse on the banks of the river Anglin, seizing your eastern flank for his own?"

The color drained from William's face. "Brosse?"

"Yes," Adémar replied. "It is time, Duke William, that you lived up to your pious reputation. That you regained God's favor through courage. As the winter snows thaw, summon your cavalry. Gather your army. Raise the crimson banner of Poitiers and strike against the allies of Fulk the Black. Earn God's blessing of victory!"

Adémar's call hung in the air. Behind the curtain of complicit nuns, Ciarán and Alais shuffled along the wall toward the doors, with Dónall hurrying behind them.

"But first," Adémar said coldly, his finger raised high, "cast away the heretics and let them burn!"

Just paces from the open doors, Alais screamed as a black-robed priest lunged into the aisle, pushing past the startled nuns. With long-fingered hands, he grabbed Alais' arm. Ciarán's heart jumped. A wicked smile stretched across Father Gauzlin's pale, thin face. "Too late," he sneered.

Ciarán cocked his fist and swung from the hip, smashing into Gauzlin's jaw and knocking him back into the crowd.

From the transept, a voice bellowed, "Brother Dónall, stop!" Prior Bernard waved a plump finger at Dónall and Alais. "Your Excellency, *he* is your sorcerer, and *she* is your witch!"

Dónall nudged Ciarán. "Go!"

The church erupted in shouts as, hand in hand, Ciarán and Alais rushed through the vestibule doors and down the steps into a snow-dusted square. A flock of startled pigeons burst skyward, while a dozen black-robed monks in the square gazed toward the clamor emanating from the church. They stared in surprise as Alais and the two Irishmen bolted past. "Trust no one in a black robe!" Dónall huffed.

A mob of monks and priests poured out of the vestibule, with cries of "Stop!" and "Heretic!"

"To the Street of the Jews!" Dónall said. "It's our only chance."

"Do you know where it is?" Ciarán asked Alais.

She nodded and, gripping his hand, ran toward a narrow alley. Behind them came the mob.

The alley intersected another. At the crossway, Alais and Ciarán glanced back to find Dónall standing defiantly before the oncoming mob. At its head was Father Gauzlin, his face infused with rage. Beside him screamed Prior Bernard and Canon Frézoul, followed by a crowd of priests and monks in black. Dónall raised his right arm. A crystal burned brightly in his hand.

"What is he doing?" Alais gasped.

"Saving our lives," Ciarán replied. "Come!"

Dónall uttered a verse in the Fae tongue, a melodic sound that filled the alleyway. At once, a beating sound followed, not from Dónall's lips but from the rooftops.

The beating of wings.

Like a fierce gray cloud, hundreds of pigeons dived into the space between Dónall and the oncoming mob, heading straight toward the pursuers. Gauzlin gasped, and Prior Bernard blanched as a cry erupted from the startled monks and priests. The flock collided with the men, pecking and clawing and tearing at black robes. Then came a piercing caw as dozens of huge black crows swooped into the alley, followed by yet another horde of pigeons.

Dónall rushed to Ciarán and Alais, who looked awestruck at the swelling, twisting cloud of birds. "Just get us to Jewry," Ciarán whispered to her, "and I'll explain."

As the wingbeats and raucous cawing behind them competed with the screams of men, Alais led them down the alley to the left, only to turn immediately down another in the maze of streets. They ducked under clotheslines with hanging linens and hurried down the narrow stairways that descended the city's steep hills. The cries of the birds and the mob receded to a dull clamor, and soon Ciarán found himself on a familiar street of simple thatch-roofed homes. Searching for the one with the Star of David carved on its door, he prayed that Isaac was home.

Alais stopped Dónall before they went any farther. "What just happened?" she demanded.

"I asked Mother Nature for a favor," Dónall said, wiping the sweat from his brow.

"You *spoke* to the birds?" she asked, fear tingeing her voice. "And the tempest back in Selles? Are you what the bishop called you?"

"No more than you," Dónall replied.

She ran her fingers down her face. "Why is this happening?" Her eyes grew moist. "It has to do with the scroll Geoffrey kept, doesn't it?"

"Yes," Dónall said.

Ciarán placed a hand on her back. "The bishop won't let this go. You can't stay in Poitiers."

"I would leave anyway," she sighed. "William plans to arrange another marriage, and I won't do that again. But where can I go?"

"Come with us to Spain," Ciarán said.

Dónall gave Ciarán a look that said he'd gone mad. "Absolutely not!"

"Why not?" Ciarán insisted. "We're looking for Enoch's device, and she held a key piece to finding it. What if it's fate that brought us to her?"

"*Fate?*" Dónall groaned. "You sound like your father again."

"Has he turned out to be wrong lately?"

"He was wrong about *you*," Dónall snapped. "You never came from Charlemagne's line."

Alais stepped between them. "What does that have to do with anything?"

"The thing we're searching for," Ciarán said, "which was mentioned in your husband's scroll, can be used only by a descendant of Charlemagne's bloodline."

For a heartbeat, Alais stared at them, spellbound by what she had just heard. "So . . . you mean someone like *me?*"

Ciarán's eyes widened. "You . . ."

"I'm from the House of Poitiers. My family is descended from Ranulf of Aquitaine, the great-grandson of Charlemagne."

Ciarán could scarcely believe his ears. He turned to Dónall. "Now, *that* sounds like fate."

"Still, we can't——" Dónall began, but Alais cut him off.

"I've already lost Geoffrey's lands," she said. "That scroll was his final legacy, and if it meant something, if it's as important as he claimed, then this is the last thing I can do for him."

Dónall started to grumble, but Ciarán swelled with hope. "Which means . . . ?" he asked.

She looked determined. "We're going to Spain."

CHAPTER 36
MORTAL SINS

Prior Lucien ushered Father Gauzlin into the small chapel on the east side of the Church of Saint-Etienne. The priest was shaking. His left eye was swollen shut, and his whole face was crosshatched with bloody scratches. Feathers—and worse —stuck to the bloodstains on his robes.

"What happened to *you*?" Lucien asked in a hushed tone.

"We were attacked by crows. And pigeons, hundreds of them," Gauzlin replied with a hint of fear lingering in his voice. "Summoned by Dónall mac Taidg."

Lucien clenched his jaw as they entered the chapel. Dónall was becoming difficult to deal with.

Inside, next to a bishop's miter, a dozen candles glowed on the altar, while only the faintest hint of daylight seeped through the vellum sheets that covered the window slits. Beside the altar stood Adémar, still clad in his episcopal robes. He studied one of the reliquaries of Saint Etienne, cradling it in his hands. The reliquary was a life-size replica of the saint's arm, with a forearm shaped like the sleeve of a bishop's robe, and coin-size stones pressed into the gold encasement, complete with a gleaming silver hand, slightly open at the palm, with two fingers upraised. Adémar did not look up as they entered.

"They say this contains the bones of Saint Etienne's entire right arm—and his hand, too," Adémar said, shaking the reliquary so the bones rattled inside. "I find it odd that your people revere these dead clerics like little gods."

Lucien stepped from the shadows of the tiny nave toward the chancel, and Gauzlin followed nervously behind him. "Every church needs some saint's bones, my lord," Lucien replied. "They draw in pilgrims and their donations."

"But it is more than that," Adémar said, still examining the golden arm. "So many think these relics carry some form of power. Just a touch of this saint's silver hand, and one's pox could be cured. If only I could kiss its golden sleeve, then my gout would be gone. It's ridiculous." He stepped closer to them, running his hand across the reliquary's silver fingertips. "So where are the girl and the Irishmen?"

"They escaped, my lord," Gauzlin stuttered. "Dónall mac Taidg summoned a storm of pecking, screaming, shitting birds."

Lucien's heart drummed in his chest. He fixed his eyes on Adémar, who chuckled and looked wistfully toward the chapel's ceiling. "They are no threat to our plans," Adémar said. "And they have no idea how much danger they are in."

Gauzlin gave a relieved sigh.

"But I cannot abide failure!" Adémar went on, his eyes igniting with feral rage. In a flash, his arm whipped forward, thrusting the reliquary of Saint Etienne like a sword, straight through Gauzlin's gaping mouth. The priest's jawbone snapped, and the silver fingers of Saint Etienne protruded through the back of his neck. The golden forearm jutted from the priest's mouth as if he had tried to swallow the reliquary whole.

Lucien watched in horror as Gauzlin staggered for a moment, scratching at the sliver fingers protruding from his neck, while his face turned a horrid shade of purple. Then he dropped to the stone floor with a loud thud.

Adémar looked up at the ceiling as if Gauzlin's lifeless body were not even there. "All of our plans are falling into place, Lucien. Duke William will do as I suggested, especially with that hog of a prior whispering my admonitions into his ear day and night. And then we shall have *two* armies—and, best of all, a war. Death and carnage. A legion of souls loosed into the ethers."

"Yes, my lord," Lucien replied, trying to calm his jittery nerves.

"And when it's all done, who knows?" Adémar asked "Maybe these good Christians will even make me their pope. Imagine what I could do in that seat of power!"

"The world would be yours."

"Indeed," Adémar said, looking Lucien in the eyes. "But first we must taste victory in this prime conflict."

"We have read the stars," Lucien offered. "It shall happen on the fifth of March, when Mars crosses between Scorpio and Sagittarius."

"And on that day," Adémar said, "victory will be ours."

Adémar took his miter from the altar. He looked one last time at Gauzlin's body, lying on the floor with the reliquary of Saint Etienne protruding from his mouth.

"Failure is an unforgivable sin," Adémar said coldly. He nodded at Lucien. "You would be wise to remember that, Prior. I leave the priest, and what remains of this pathetic saint, to you."

PART FOUR

He reveals deep and hidden things; he knows what is in the darkness, and light dwells with him.

—Daniel 2:22

CHAPTER 37
THE VOYAGE SOUTH

T he merchant ship's prow cut through the sea, spraying brine over the hull and up onto the deck. Ciarán leaned against the railing and looked out to the coastline of narrow beaches and rolling hills draped in a collage of dark foliage and wild grass. As they neared the Basque waters north of Spain, he realized this was the last he would see of Aquitaine. But despite the land's beauty, Ciarán found himself longing for Ireland's moss-covered cliffs and misty green hills—an emerald land touched by the hand of God.

Yet Ireland seemed but a dream now. At times since they left Bordeaux, Ciarán had felt like Odysseus, blown farther and farther from home by the whims of the gods. He reminded himself that Odysseus eventually found his way back to Ithaca, but then, Ciarán and Dónall were not even seeking the way home. Their quest had become far more like Jason's for the Golden Fleece—a mythical treasure guarded by a dragon, no less. Ciarán wondered whether the fleece shared some connection with Enoch's device, as if Jason and his tale were yet another reflection of the universal myth, stemming from the same Atlantean source.

Ciarán glanced to the southern horizon, where no ship followed.

271

Ever since Isaac's family had smuggled Alais and the two Irish monks out of Poitiers in a cart full of merchant's wares on the morning after Christmas, Ciarán felt certain they had escaped Bishop Adémar and Prior Lucien, but he remained wary of storms. Even the hint of a darkening sky or the distant rumble of thunder caused his nerves to tense, for the demons manifested themselves as storm clouds, and although he had seen no sign of them since the amphitheater in Poitiers, he doubted very much that they had returned to whatever dark hell spawned them.

Since leaving Poitiers, Ciarán, Dónall, and Alais had traveled under the protection of one of Isaac's many nephews. Josua was a slender man with a sun-baked complexion and a talent for guile, which had proved useful in evading the guards at the Poitiers gate. Isaac joined them in Bordeaux a week into the New Year—998 by the Christian calendar, although Isaac reminded them it was still the year 4758 by the Jews' reckoning, and the year 388 to the Moors, to whose lands they were traveling. According to Isaac, Bishop Adémar had left Poitiers, but not before convincing Duke William to ready for war in the spring, against the viscount of Limoges. Why Adémar sought to turn William against the allies of Fulk the Black remained a mystery, but Ciarán felt certain the bishop's motives were anything but pure.

In the days that followed, Josua had introduced them to his business partner, Évrard de Barsac, a Christian merchant and captain of the ship that now bore them toward Moorish Spain. Évrard had the round belly of a man who ate well and regularly, and a seafarer's oily hair, thick with the smell of brine, which hung over his broad forehead above a protuberant nose and jutting jaw. His twelve-man crew seemed wary about Alais, for a woman at sea was held to be bad luck. But Évrard was smitten with the raven-haired noblewoman, and loyal enough to Josua to allow her aboard. While gruff with his crew, Évrard was cheerful toward the Irish monks and eager to hear stories of the Emerald Isle, which to him was little more than a mythical land at the edge of the world.

At night, the captain revealed his fondness for Spanish wine, and his robust laugh grew heartier with each cup. While Évrard drank his fill, he left the sailing to his curly-haired first mate, Eli, who was Josua's nineteen-year-old son. Ciarán found Eli to be a studious young man intent on mastering the mariner's trade, while his father managed the inventory bound for Córdoba and handled the duties of principal negotiator and tradesman. Aboard the ship, Christians and Jews worked in harmony. "One day," Évrard had said after a mouthful of wine, "the merchants will own Europe. Whether Christian or Jew is the least of it. Money is money, I always say."

The merchant ship, which Évrard leased to Josua for a cut of his profits, was a sheer marvel to Ciarán. A potbellied craft built of thick timber, it had a hold for the Jews' cargo, and a deckhouse protected from the elements. It had a tall mast and broad sail with sturdy rigging, and nary an oar—testament that in other parts of the world there lived shipbuilders with far greater talents than the Irish with their ox-hide curachs.

At night, the captain offered his deckhouse to Isaac and his new companions. Alais slept beside Ciarán, where he could feel the warmth of her body and breathe in the honey smell of her hair. On their first night at sea, her closeness aroused him, but he calmed the unbidden urges by focusing on the sounds of the sea.

During the day, Ciarán found reasons to stay near her by having her teach him the Aquitaine tongue, and if Dónall thought they were growing too close, he didn't say. Instead, he spent much of his time with Isaac, poring over the symbols in Maugis' book. Isaac firmly believed that the Fae characters contained Hebrew letters as their root, which made Ciarán wonder whether a language as ancient as Hebrew had been derived from a far older tongue, one that dated to the time of creation—or even before, if such a thing were possible.

At the ship's rail, Ciarán glanced at Dónall and Isaac, who sat toward the bow with the Book of Maugis open between them. On the open page, Ciarán spied the picture of the wheel cross, with Dónall pointing out the four symbols that reminded Ciarán of the four treasures of the Tuatha Dé Danann: the sword for air, staff for fire, stone for earth, and cup for water. Beside Dónall, Isaac's eyes gleamed as if he had discovered a hidden treasure. Dónall gestured passionately, and Ciarán found it remarkable how fondly Dónall had taken to the rabbi. Perhaps it was their common love for knowledge, or maybe their shared proclivity for laughter, for as scholarly as the rabbi could appear at times, he had a ready sense of humor.

Alais sat aft with Eli, leaning against the deckhouse, where the two had spread out large sheets of parchment. She waved for Ciarán to join them. On the parchment were drawings of lands and seas, similar to the ones Merchant mac Fadden used on their journey to the mainland, but these were far more elaborate in design. "Eli says they show every kingdom in the world," Alais said, "but I thought you'd like the drawings." She was right. Illuminations decorated the charts: tentacled sea monsters and serpents with many humps, giant toothy fish and spewing whales, and a compass pointing north, embellished with an elaborately drawn rose. Each sea was marked by a ship with wind-filled sails.

Ciarán sat down beside them, studying the drawings. "They're masterful," he breathed.

Eli smiled. "We bought them in Córdoba."

Alais placed her hand on Ciarán's arm. "Show me Ireland."

He found it for her and then showed her the Isle of Britain, with the Scott lands in the north. Eli pointed out Iceland, near the top of the world, and the lands of the Northmen. The map depicted France across the Celtic Sea, along with Bavaria and Saxony, moving east to the Hungarian lands and the home of the wild Magyar horsemen, and south to the Black Sea and the Byzantine capital of Constantinople. South of Europe was the mysterious African continent, land of the Berbers and Egyptians, and across the narrow strait of the Mediterranean Sea, where stood the Pillars of Hercules, was the Iberian Peninsula, with the city of Córdoba marked by a star in the heart of the Moorish lands.

Alais traced a slender finger around the outer edge of the ocean. "What's past here?"

"The edge of the world," Eli said. "You'd plunge into the abyss."

"Actually," Ciarán remarked, "Dónall thinks the world is round."

"*Round?*" she asked as if uncertain she had heard aright.

"Seriously," Ciarán said, "that's what some of the scholars at Reims believe." Of course, the theory belonged to the notorious Gerbert of Aurillac, and given the source, Ciarán left some room for doubt. "The Irish claim there's another land out there, far to the west: Tír na nÓg, the Land of Eternal Youth. It's where the Tuatha Dé Danann, the Fae folk of my homeland, sailed after they left Ireland's shores. They say it's the most beautiful place in all the world."

"Like a Garden of Eden?" she asked.

"Maybe so."

"Do you think it's real?"

"Maybe someday I'll sail there and find out."

Alais rolled her eyes, though the smile never left her face.

The sun was beginning to set and soon would cast a rosy glow over the western horizon. Overhead, three terns glided toward the shore. Évrard soon called the crew to supper, and everyone gathered near the mast. Ciarán sat against the railing, next to Alais and much of the crew, while Dónall, Isaac, and Évrard sat on benches. The meal consisted of stale bread and fresh codfish, hauled up by the crew earlier this morning. Ciarán relished the fresh fish, knowing that if the fishing turned bad in the days ahead, they would soon be surviving on the salted leftovers.

Évrard passed around a skin of Spanish wine. After taking a sip, Dónall asked him about events in the Moorish lands.

Évrard drained his cup of wine in one long gulp. "All you need to know about what happens in Córdoba," he said, "is that nothing happens unless Al-Mansor wills it."

"Who's he?" Ciarán asked.

"His title is hajib," Évrard replied, "but he controls the caliph like a puppeteer making a doll step to his tune."

Alais raised a curious brow. "How did he come to do that?"

Josua explained. "It was the classic case of 'be careful what you wish for.' You see, when the previous caliph died, the caliphate passed to his minor son, and naturally, the boy's uncle and the palace eunuchs plotted to kill him, hoping to usurp the throne. But the caliph's old vizier stepped in. He needed to eliminate the uncle, so he found a man untroubled by such messy jobs: Ibn Abi Amir, the leader of the city guard—the man who would become known as Al-Mansor. So Al-Mansor murdered the uncle, but then he slowly eliminated all his rivals one by one, including the general of the army, and finally the poor vizier himself. Now Al-Mansor proclaims himself the noble king of all the Moors."

"Of course," Évrard said, "it helped that while he was conspiring to eliminate his rivals, Al-Mansor had the support of Al-Hakkam's queen, whom he was rutting every night for good measure. And the general's daughter, too, who ended up becoming one of his four wives! Can you imagine, four wives? And a royal mistress on top of that! I have enough troubles with just the one."

The crew erupted in laughter. Alais' cheeks grew flushed, and Josua shook his head and smiled, obviously accustomed to his partner's crude sense of humor.

"Al-Mansor," Josua explained, "retains his power through Al-Hakkam's son, the current caliph, whom he sequesters in the palace and keeps distracted with every form of carnal pleasure."

"He's a devout hedonist," Évrard said, working on his second cup of wine. "But then again, he has a thousand concubines in his harem, so can you blame him? Of course, you monks would know nothing of such things, eh?"

Ciarán glanced at Alais, whose jaw hung open in disbelief. "*Seriously?*" she whispered.

Ciarán held out his palms. "How would I know?"

Isaac said, "I have heard many Christian monks refer to Al-Mansor as your Antichrist. After all, men like Prior Bernard and Canon Frézoul believe he rules a city whose people worship a prophet called Mahomet. But if Al-Mansor is your Antichrist, I tell you, it is the Christian kings of Spain who created him."

Évrard shrugged. "A year or two after Al-Hakkam's death, the Christians sent an army to the walls of Córdoba. But Al-Mansor and his own army fought back and chased them all the way to Saragossa, so the people of Córdoba came to adore him. But he didn't stop at Saragossa. He declared a jihad, a holy war against all the Christians of Spain."

"And so went fifty years of peace between the Christians and the Moors." Isaac sighed.

"He became known as the Illustrious Victor," Josua added, "Savior of Córdoba and Defender of Islam. Every spring he rides from Córdoba on his black stallion with his great army to campaign against the Christian kings, plunder their cities, and add their riches to his vast treasury. Twice he attacked León and pillaged it ruthlessly. Barcelona was next. Other cities surrendered by the time his army arrived. After every campaign, he returned the victor."

"But León and Barcelona weren't the worst," Évrard said in disgust. "Last July, he ravaged Santiago de Compostela and the tomb of blessed Saint James—the apostle, no less. He razed the whole town, even taking the great iron bells that rang from Saint James's Church. Those beautiful bells. And you know what he did with them? He turned them into lamps for one of his mosques. Lamps!"

"I'm beginning to understand the whole 'Antichrist' thing," Dónall quipped.

"And we're going to his city?" Ciarán asked warily.

Évrard winked back. "Al-Mansor won't give a rat's turd about you two or our pretty lass. Half his own army is Christian malcontents from León and Castile. He doesn't care. It's the kings he hates, but it's no matter. He keeps Córdoba safe and orderly, which is good for business. And that's what matters, I always say."

"Besides," Isaac said, smiling, "wait until you see her. Córdoba will make you forget about the hajib who rules her."

"Not to mention the beautiful women, eh?" Évrard said, slapping his knee. "Like flowers waiting for bees like us to dip into their nectar!" The crew burst out in laughter. Alais blushed again. Évrard took another swig of wine. Then Eli ran up and tugged at his sleeve.

"Captain," Eli said nervously, "there are storm clouds abaft."

Évrard's eyes narrowed. "The weather should be clear."

"They came in fast," Eli explained.

Ciarán looked to the stern. Amid the growing dusk, black clouds boiled, rapidly filling the sky well before the horizon.

"I swear," Eli stammered, "those clouds are following us."

Dónall's face turned ashen. His gaze reflected Ciarán's thoughts.

"What?" Alais said, catching the look that passed between them.

"Get in the deckhouse," Ciarán told her.

"But what's happening?"

Ciarán jumped to his feet, ignoring her question, as Dónall hurried aft and stared into the face of the gathering storm.

At the forefront of the clouds, three great thunderheads billowed. As Dónall muttered a curse under his breath, a wave of raw fear washed through Ciarán's gut.

For here at the edge of the Basque Sea, the demons had found them.

CHAPTER 38

EYE OF THE STORM

"Full sail!" Évrard cried. "We'll outrun it!" Crewmen hurried to the riggings. Eli darted toward the rudder.

"No!" Dónall shouted. "If you value your mast, reduce your sail. You'll not outrun this storm."

Ciarán rushed to Eli's side, where the young Jew held the tiller in a panicked grip. The storm surged forward, crossing leagues of water in mere heartbeats. The three storm heads, swelling and growing ever darker, billowed into snakelike shapes, dipping and soaring and pulling the force of the tempest behind them.

"What is that?" Alais cried.

Ciarán grabbed her shoulders. "Trust me, and get in the deckhouse."

Lightning flashed within the clouds, and a chill wind swept over the ship, whipping the lines and battering the sail. Waves crashed against the hull, making the ship lurch violently. Crewmen fought to keep their feet. Ciarán grabbed for the rail, struggling to stay upright, and reached out for Alais. He caught her hand as frigid water washed ankle-high across the deck.

"Go!" Ciarán told her. Her eyes opened wide at the oncoming

storm, but she scrambled for the deckhouse. Amid battering waves, the ship pitched again, the planks of the hull creaking.

Ciarán glanced at Dónall. No longer ashen, his face was that of the man who had unleashed destruction against the Franks at Derry and the Angevins at Selles. "Captain," Dónall commanded, "help your first mate with the tiller. The rest of you get in the deckhouse or the cargo hold!"

"We'll need the crew to keep her on course!" Évrard bellowed back through the roar of the wind.

Dónall grabbed Évrard by his tunic. "This is not a natural storm."

"What do you mean?" Évrard demanded.

Isaac tugged at his arm. "Do as he says, my friend, and pray to your Christian god." Isaac looked Dónall in the eyes. "But I am staying with you."

Another wave lapped over the railing. Around them, the wind crescendoed to a deafening howl. Évrard grasped the tiller as his men reduced the sail and battened the hatch to the deckhouse.

The ship rode on the edge of the storm. Dónall steeled his gaze and unsheathed the sword hidden under his habit. "Listen for my command," he told Ciarán.

Dónall crossed the deck in a deliberate pattern, tracing a shape with the tip of his blade, chanting a hymn in the graceful Fae tongue. Ciarán recognized the pattern at once. A flicker of Saint Elmo's fire followed the tip of Dónall's sword like ink from a quill, stretching from bow to stern and starboard to port, until Dónall had traced a seven-pointed star, encircled by the frame of the potbellied ship, faintly glowing with wisps of blue fire.

Eli's hands shook with fear. "What is he doing?"

"He has a plan," Ciarán said, praying under his breath that it would work.

The wind shrieked savagely as the clouds loomed over the ship's stern, billowing thousands of feet high, like a giant gaping mouth threatening to swallow the ship whole.

"Dónall!" Isaac cried. Rigging snapped, and Eli let out a terrified scream.

"Now, Ciarán!" Dónall yelled. "Show them your talisman!"

Ciarán nodded warily and pulled the talisman from his habit. A hint of blue fire flashed across the silver disk. Dónall raised the face of his own talisman into the mouth of the storm.

"Megaera!" he cried, "By the power of the Fae! The angels, your masters! You and your sisters will not harm this ship!"

The massive storm moaned before the cloud crashed down onto the vessel, and in that moment, Ciarán expected the mast to snap. He could not hear his own screams amid the storm's fierce wailing. Then suddenly, dense fog engulfed them, followed by driving rain. But as the raindrops hit the deck, they sizzled into steam. The symbol across the ship's deck flared, and the fog began to burn away. Évrard and his crew looked on, awestruck, at the curtain of rain surrounding the ship, none of it reaching the deck. Without warning, walls of water exploded skyward from the sea, drawn toward the boiling storm in three churning spouts that roared with the same fury as the cyclone at Selles-sur-Cher. The three water-spouts, terrifying in their height and breadth, whipped toward the ship.

Then Dónall began to laugh.

Blue flames flicked over the talisman in Ciarán's hand, and the waterspouts writhed away like snakes fleeing a grass fire. The ship rocked with the waves, but the mast held, and despite the chaos raging around it, the vessel stood becalmed in the eye of the storm.

"Megaera!" Dónall cried. "I defeated you before; I've done so again! Tell your masters, we will not be deterred!"

A piercing wail erupted from the storm. The rain around them ceased, and the waterspouts collapsed into the churning sea while thunder exploded above. And as quickly as the winds blew in, they died. The sea grew calm, and the storm billowed backward, as if some inexorable force were sucking it toward the horizon, and vanished from sight.

A smile crept across the astounded captain's face, and Isaac and Eli raised their arms triumphantly. Only Ciarán and Dónall looked at each other warily. For in the core of that thunderclap before the storm dissipated, they both had heard it, a haunting promise shrieked in unison by a trio of voices: *"Revenge."*

CHAPTER 39

THE BRIDE OF ANDALUSIA

lais cowered in the deckhouse with the panicked crew. A violent gust had torn open one of the wooden hatches, giving her a glimpse of the black cloud crashing down upon the ship, consuming the deck in swirling darkness. She feared that the raging winds would rip the deckhouse apart. Her heart pounded with terror beyond the merely physical, for she sensed in that black cloud a presence that was cold and evil and not of this world.

The ship pitched, followed by a roar of water, as if the sea itself were rising into the sky. But then she heard Dónall crying out to the storm, challenging the very winds. And to her utter astonishment, the sea grew calm, and the storm *retreated!* Whether this was sorcery or some other magic that the Church condemned, she could not say, yet three times now it had saved her life—this time, she knew in her bones, from something wholly unnatural.

She ventured out onto the deck, where the water was steaming away like raindrops off hot paving stones. Dónall and Ciarán looked on triumphantly in their wringing-wet robes. The mast had not snapped, and the sail looked unharmed. Évrard hugged Eli, and Alais smiled with relief. Only Isaac appeared troubled.

"Dónall," he said, "you have not been candid with us. You owe us an explanation."

Dónall insisted on waiting until the crew calmed down, for they were giddy with joy. They gathered around Eli, who could not stop chattering about how Dónall had turned away the storm. A few of the sailors crossed themselves or knelt, muttering prayers.

Évrard and Josua demanded the same answers as Isaac. But what the monks finally told them shook Alais to her soul. "The storm was the work of demons," Dónall said bluntly, "summoned by sorcerers who wear the robes of the monks of Saint-Bastian's."

Alais shuddered. Could it be true? Beside her, Évrard and Josua had turned pale, though Isaac's expression remained unchanged.

"I, too, sensed the perversion in the air," Isaac said. "The Song of Moses warns of demons. In Hebrew, they are called *mazzikin* and *ruhin*—bringers of storms. Do you think they seek the Urim?"

"They want to keep us from finding it," Dónall said grimly.

Puzzled, Alais glanced at each of them. "What is the Urim?"

"A gemstone," Ciarán explained. "But you've heard us call it by another name, I think: 'Enoch's device.'"

"The thing mentioned in my husband's scroll? But . . . why should they want to stop you from finding it?"

They told her about the prophecy. "It was discovered by a king of long-lost Atlantis," Dónall began. "A prophecy embedded in the twelve constellations of the zodiac." She had heard about Atlantis in the songs of the jongleurs who performed in the palace when she was child, but she knew little of the constellations that so fascinated the astrologers. Then Dónall's expression turned gravely serious. "The prophecy speaks of the apocalypse—a conflict waged every thousand years to determine whether the end times will follow."

Alais ran her fingers nervously through her hair. *The Four Horsemen of the apocalypse now rode these lands,* Prior Ragno had said. A chill ran through her veins.

"But the prophecy tells how to prevent the end times," Ciarán added. "To survive the first conflict, a champion of men must wield a weapon against the enemy. That weapon is Enoch's device."

His words struck like lightning. She remembered what the

284

monks had said on Christmas Day, about a champion's bloodline, the line of Charlemagne. But surely they did not think *she* was this champion. For while some infinitesimal fraction of Charlemagne's blood may course through her veins, she was no hero—she felt as certain of that as of her own name.

Isaac remained silent during the monks' explanation. Finally, he spoke. "Astrology is no secret to our mystics," he said. "When you first mentioned this prophecy, I did not think much of it. So many Christians obsess about the end of the world. But now, with the emergence of these *ruhin* . . ."

"Even worse," Ciarán said, "we're running out of time."

"What do you mean?" Isaac asked.

"One of our murdered friends, Brother Remi, believed that the first conflict will come when Mars passes between Scorpio and Sagittarius, on the fifth of March, just seven weeks from now."

Isaac sighed. "This is much to ponder. I would like to see the reference to this prophecy in Maugis' book." Ciarán glanced at Dónall, who nodded. Évrard and Josua slumped against the ship's railing. Their faces betrayed what Alais felt: overwhelm. She rubbed her fingers over her eyes. Had Geoffrey believed in this prophecy? Was this why he and his ancestors had protected the scroll?

Soon, they retired to the deckhouse. She lay next to Ciarán but tossed fitfully. Her thoughts drifted across a field of wheat, to a vision of a woman in white. The woman's face was beautiful, ageless. Alais recalled her haunting command.

Choose.

And Alais had chosen. She chose Geoffrey—and, with him, the secret that set her on this voyage. As she drifted off to sleep, she wondered, had the woman in white had been the hand of fate, reaching out to her?

THE NEXT MORNING, Isaac emerged from the deckhouse looking pale and shaken. Dónall glanced at Ciarán, clearly concerned.

"He's still troubled by what happened," Dónall said under his breath.

"Wouldn't you be?" Ciarán replied. "Especially after what we told them."

"You are both right," Isaac interjected. "But there is more. I had another dream."

New concern gathered in Dónall's brow. "Like the one about the dragon and the Urim?"

"The dream felt equally as real," Isaac said, "but this one did not concern the Urim. Instead, I saw Goliath, standing on the battlefield in all his fearsome glory. He was dressed like a Greek warrior and led an army of pale-skinned giants." The rabbi closed his eyes as he spoke, as if reliving the dream in his mind. "The army marched from great ships with many oars, across a desert plain. I could feel the air, as if I stood there among them. It was not hot like the deserts of the east, but very cold. And then my vision whipped over the barren land, as if I were but a feather blowing in the harsh wind. Across the desert, I saw a woman, beautiful and dressed in white, looking like an angel. Behind her, billowing up in the distance, was a black cloud, like those that pursued our ship last night but far larger and in the form of a great beast with broad wings and a long, craning neck. It was the spirit of the Dragon. I could feel it, like death itself, drawing closer until the blackness enveloped all my sight. And I awoke, shaking with dread." Isaac opened his eyes. "What does it mean?"

"You dreamt of the Nephilim," Dónall said. "Perhaps it's a connection to the demons that attacked us. The Book of Enoch claims that demons are the spirits of slain Nephilim."

"Goliath was a Nephilim," Isaac said with a sigh. "Scripture makes clear that many of the giants survived the Deluge. But the message of the dream . . . I agree, it must confirm that the demons who attacked us—these Nephilim spirits—serve the Dragon."

Dónall's eyes narrowed. "The book of Revelation states that after a thousand years, when the Dragon is freed from his prison, he will gather the nations of Gog and Magog for battle. Some believe that Gog and Magog were kings among the giants."

Isaac shook his head. "This is deeply troubling."

"I know," Dónall said. "But I can protect us from the demons." He tapped the talisman around his neck. "And having a few more of these around wouldn't hurt."

"You can *make* these?" Isaac asked.

"It'll take some time, but we may as well get started."

Ciarán had turned to go with them when he saw Alais standing at the threshold to the deckhouse. Seeing the troubled look on her face, he realized that she had overhead everything.

"I've seen a woman in white as well," Alais said.

"You had a dream?" Ciarán asked.

"No. I *saw* her. This was no dream, though it felt like one. It happened years ago, in a field of wheat. She was like an angel standing on the wind. It was she who told me of my choice, she who brought me to Selles-sur-Cher."

Ciarán saw the sincerity in her gray eyes. "If you had never been in Selles, you would never have learned your husband's secret . . ."

"I know," Alais said. "It's as if she set me on this path."

Ciarán could not imagine how her story was connected to Isaac's dream, yet somehow, it must be.

Alais smiled at him. "Let's eat something," she said, "even if it's only stale bread."

DÓNALL SPENT the rest of the day and much of the next crafting seven talismans from silver coins donated by Josua. He gave the first three to Isaac, Josua, and Eli. Confident that the addition of a Hebrew symbol would not weaken their power, he had etched a Star of David in the center of the heptagram that dominated each. The remaining four talismans he gave to Alais, Évrard, and two members of his crew, who were so shaken after the sudden storm that, every night, they redrew the heptagram Dónall had traced across the deck. The talismans and the heptagram seemed to calm the superstitious crew, who had been terrified by the storm yet strangely accepting of its supernatural origins, perhaps because the sea had always held deep mysteries.

Although the seas remained calm in the days that followed, the storm clouds frequently gathered on the horizon, trailing the ship to the Moorish lands, and Évrard and his crew never doubted that the demons were following them. Ciarán sensed this as well, though somehow, Dónall's magic was keeping the demons at bay. Dónall believed it was the collective power of the Fae words embedded in each silver disk, fueled by the life-bearing essence of the human soul so long as the talisman made contact with its wearers, that was warding off the demons. But he suspected that if the talisman were removed from the wearer's body, its power would fail. Perhaps that was what the demons were waiting for: a careless moment when the talisman might be removed. But he could do little beyond sharing his theory with everyone who wore them.

AFTER CROSSING THE BASQUE SEA, they rounded Iberia and sailed along the coast of Andalusia for more than a week before reaching the river that wound its way through the land of the Moors. Évrard and his crew navigated the waterway, which the Moors called Guad al-Quivir, or "Great River." By the second day of February, the crew spied Córdoba, rising above the river's north bank.

Even from a distance, the city seemed a sprawling marvel of human construction. Its stone walls rose over a sea of sand-colored buildings shaded by date palms. Behind the wall, atop a hill, stood a gigantic structure whose grand spire towered above the city of the Moors like an ornate spear.

"Unbelievable," Ciarán breathed.

Spanning the river ahead of them was the grandest bridge he had ever seen. A chain of stone archways supported it, each archway tall enough for a small boat to pass beneath, though not a ship the size of Évrard's cog. At the river's south bank, scattered buildings emerged from the palms, as if a whole other city existed across the river, and atop the most prominent hill, leagues beyond the urban sprawl, stood a palace with gleaming white walls and a golden dome glistening in the sunlight.

Alais looked on, wide-eyed. "That's all one city?"

"I told you she was amazing," Isaac smiled. "They call her the Bride of Andalusia, whose necklace is strung with the pearls of learning."

Dónall leaned over the rail, agog. "Not even Rome . . . !"

"Not even Poitiers and Paris combined!" Ciarán said. "And throw in Rouen, too!" Indeed, nothing in all Ireland, nor anything he had seen in France, approached Córdoba's grandeur. The Moors must surely be the most skilled builders in all the world—maybe the most skilled who ever lived.

"How many people live here?" Alais wondered aloud.

"Ten times more than in any city in France," Évrard said, smiling. "Which, of course, makes for *very* good business."

ÉVRARD GUIDED his ship past fortified water mills to a crowded harbor east of the bridge, where the crew tossed ropes to a gathering of half-clothed men, who pulled the ship to the docks. Eli spoke to these men, whose skin had been bronzed by the sun, in a throaty foreign tongue—Arabic, Ciarán presumed. After the ship was unloaded of its cargo of wine barrels from Bordeaux, Josua led the two wide-eyed Irishmen from the docks up a flight of stairs to the bridge, where they entered the city through a towering archway that, he explained, was one of the city's seven gates.

Beyond the gateway, Moors bustled through the streets. They were an exotic mix of people, some with skin that gleamed black as ebony, others of a deep bronze hue, and many others of a rich olive color. The men wore robes of striped cloth, or else shirts with flowing sleeves, baggy trousers, and soft boots. Many wore head cloths, while others wore round hats of wrapped silk, which Isaac called turbans. The women dressed in shimmering silks or full-length robes. Many wore veils covering their faces beneath eyes lined with kohl, or head scarves that concealed everything except their eyes, while others wore no veil or scarf and let their berib-boned black hair spill down their backs. Many women wore jewelry in their ears, and silver bangles adorning their arms. Others wore anklets of silver above slippers with upswept toes. Ciarán found many of the 'women stunningly beautiful—Évrard had not exagger-ated when he boasted of the city's feminine treasures.

Ciarán looked in awe at the graceful iron posts and hanging glass lanterns that lined the streets, which were free of mud and dung and paved with brick. But most of all, he noticed the air. "What's that smell?" he asked.

Isaac laughed. "A lack of refuse."

"How can that be?"

"It's carried beneath the streets in something called a *sewer*. It has always amazed me that you Christians never got around to it."

They soon found themselves passing the magnificent spired structure they had seen from the river. It was the most splendid building Ciarán had ever seen. Palm trees fanned out above its crenellated surrounding walls, whose horseshoe-shaped archways stood on slender pillars inlaid with mosaics of red and gold. A montage of interlacing ribbons and geometric shapes wove their way over every remaining detail of marble and stone. The central structure, with a conical roof rising high above the outer wall, was flanked with turrets and a slender minaret with three tiers of pillared balconies.

"Whose palace is this?" Alais asked.

Isaac smiled. "No, not a palace. It is the Great Mosque—a Muslim church."

Ciarán glanced at Dónall, who was clearly awestruck at the sight. It was hard to imagine a cathedral anywhere in Europe approaching such grandeur.

They continued past the Great Mosque, up a main street, passing narrow side streets and plazas filled with merchants' tents. They turned down several smaller streets—enough to give Ciarán the impression that he was in some type of maze—until they reached a neighborhood of whitewashed houses, which Isaac said was the city's Jewish quarter. It was nothing like the cramped Jewry of Poitiers. These houses were large and sided in stucco, with flowering vines spilling from boxes beneath each windowsill. The air smelled of bluebells and lilacs, and gardens and courtyards could be seen behind many of the homes.

Looking around him, Dónall said, "Your people seem quite welcome here."

"We pay a tax called a *jiyza*," Josua explained. "Upon payment, the Moors are bound by their laws to protect us."

"But it is because of the Moors' tolerance," Isaac added. "To the Moors, both Christian and Jew are considered 'people of the Book,' because, like the Moors, they trace the origins of their faith back to Abraham. Traditionally, we are respected here."

Ciarán thought about Prior Bernard and Canon Frézoul—small wonder the Jews had such an affinity for the Moorish lands.

No sooner had they arrived than a group of bearded men hurried to welcome them. Isaac introduced the monks to his cousin Abir ben Hillel. He resembled the rabbi, though taller and fleshier and with a beard less flecked with white. Abir's three sons, like Isaac's two nephews, ran the Córdoban side of the family's mercantile business. The sons had gracious wives, who offered the travelers a meal of tangy white cheese, flat bread, and grapes. The wives also offered the travelers warm baths and, more astoundingly, the Jews' own bedrooms. Ciarán and Dónall, who were used to sleeping on floors and pallets, tried strenuously to decline, but their hosts insisted.

After the meal, Isaac spoke with his cousin and then shared their conversation with Ciarán and Dónall. The rabbi's eyes were sparkling. "Abir knows someone who could get us into the bowels of the great library—a poet named Khalil al-Pârsâ. He is a Persian who has influence with the caliph, who controls the library."

"Perfect!" Dónall said, beaming. "So this poet performs for the caliph?"

"Not quite," Isaac said. "For the caliph's mother. He was her lover."

Ciarán's eyes grew wide. "The same woman who was mistress to Al-Mansor? Is the man *mad*?"

"My cousin tells me this poet is accustomed to taking risks," Isaac said.

A wry smile had spread across Dónall's lips. "Then he sounds like just the man for the job."

"Abir has promised to send for him," Isaac replied.

"Well done," Dónall said. "But while we're waiting, I'd like to see this great library."

"Then follow me," Isaac said, "for the Bride of Andalusia awaits us."

Ciarán glanced at Alais. "I want to go, too," she said.

Eli bounded toward them. "I can show you around," he said eagerly.

Alais flashed the young Jew a fond smile. Ciarán felt a momentary pang, though it faded quickly, for he had grown fond of the curly-haired first mate and knew that any affection Eli had for Alais was harmless. Besides, Ciarán reminded himself, he was still a monk, and a monk had no room for jealous thoughts of a woman—even though that was proving more difficult than he had ever imagined.

Under a late-afternoon sun, the five of them set out from the Jewish quarter. Ciarán glanced around for any sign of the storm clouds that had followed them up the river, but saw none. Perhaps the demons still lingered at the horizon but had not followed the monks into Córdoba. Ciarán pulled the silver talisman from the neck of his habit. The sun glinted off its surface.

"Tuck that back in," Eli murmured. "The Moors forbid Christians and Jews from displaying symbols of their religion."

Ciarán did as Eli bade him, and glanced at a passing Moor to make sure he hadn't noticed. "Thanks," Ciarán said, grateful now that Eli had tagged along.

From the Jewish quarter, they headed back in the direction of the Great Mosque and soon found themselves in a marketplace. The market occupied a large plaza and spilled over onto several adjoining streets. Striped merchant tents cramped the center in a chaotic labyrinth of narrow aisles, while the shops of artisans and craftsmen surrounded the plaza's perimeter. There were silversmiths and coppersmiths, ivory carvers and glassblowers, tanners, carpet weavers, and sellers of colorful trinkets of every sort. The smells of sizzling meats, spiced stews, and warm bread mixed with those of animals, sweat, and sweet perfumes and frankincense. The merchants' tents harbored an array of strange creatures: birds of green, red, and blue, several of which could speak Arabic words, and one that even cawed out insults in Latin; snakes that danced rhythmically to their handlers' flutes and oboes; and, most marvelous of all, hairy childlike beasts, some of which wore skull-caps and tiny vests, looking like miniature versions of their merchant owners.

Amazed, Ciarán and Alais watched the hairy creatures. "What are they?" Ciarán asked.

"They're called monkeys," Eli said, smiling at the foreigners' amusement. "They bring them over from Africa, and they are said to run wild on the Pillars of Hercules."

"They're so humanlike," Alais noticed aloud.

"They make lots of noise," Eli said. "And some bite."

"I think they're adorable," she said, watching a monkey take payment for a vendor of silk scarves.

Dónall and Isaac walked over from the tent of a physician peddling treatments for a long list of maladies.

"Ah, Lad!" Dónall said in an exuberant tone. "Imagine, the practice of medicine—real, Arabic medicine—available to anyone! And not administered by some grimy-handed leeching monk, but the doctor was a woman! And a Jew, no less! Never in all my years have I seen such enlightened practices!"

Emerging from the bazaar into the maze of narrow streets, they zigzagged along the streets and alleyways until they found them-selves in another plaza, dominated by an enormous building that must have been a fortress or palace built on the remains of some earlier structure. Columns of Greek and Roman design supported its many parapets, while the outer walls—like the Great Mosque, made of marble—displayed Moorish archways and geometric mosaics. Towering above the outer wall was a central edifice with a domed roof and scores of windows and balconies on every side, each framed by graceful archways. Only the nearby mosque exceeded its grandeur.

"Here it is," Isaac announced, "the great library of Córdoba."

Ciarán's jaw went slack. "That's a *library?*"

Isaac smiled broadly. "There is more knowledge within her walls than in all France."

"And I thought the library at Fleury was big," Dónall murmured.

"What's going on?" Alais asked, noting a large crowd gathering around the library's steps. From the crowd, a crier yelled in Arabic. Voices responded, yet Ciarán could not tell whether they were shouts of anger or unity, or both. Men and women descended the library steps to stand at the edge of the crowd. Others gathered on balconies.

"This does not look good," Isaac said.

"Maybe we should go," Eli offered.

A tendril of smoke rose from the center of the crowd, and Ciarán hurried toward it.

"Careful, lad," Dónall said, trying to keep pace.

The smoke thickened, and some men shouted angrily while others cried out in protest. Near the center of the crowd, four bearded, black-robed men, turbaned and stern-faced, surrounded a raging bonfire. The oldest of them, a severe-looking man with a white beard, shook something in the air. Then, with a vehement cry, he cast it into the flames.

Ciarán felt a sinking in the pit of his stomach. The object was a book. *The entire pyre was made of books!*

The crowd roared, and the parchment crackled as it burned. One of the black-robed men threw another tome into the flames, and as the cries of the crowd grew more violent, the older man read bitterly from one of the tomes.

"Why?" Ciarán asked.

Dónall grabbed Ciarán by the shoulder, pulling him back.

"But . . . who would burn books?" Ciarán asked, still stunned.

The fire claimed another book, then another, cast by the dour black-robed men, to the cheers of the impassioned mob.

"We must leave now," Isaac implored.

Ciarán backed away, but his gaze remained on the pyre. All that knowledge, all that glorious work by authors, copyists, and illuminators—precious gifts of civilization, *gone.*

~

THE BLACK-ROBED MEN, according to Isaac, were called imams, clerics of the Muslim faith. Yet the rabbi had no explanation for their barbarism outside the library. "The imams have never acted in such a way," he said. "Al-Hakkam devoted his life to those books. His library was a shining beacon in the darkness of Europe. The imams never opposed his wishes."

"Then why would they burn precious books?" Dónall asked as they entered Abir's home.

"Because the imams have become fanatics," replied a bronze-skinned man sitting with Abir at his table. The stranger, who spoke fluent Latin, peered at them through keen eyes set in a comely face with a well-groomed beard. "They interpret Islam through a viewpoint of intolerance and hatred. So if you've come here seeking the treasures of Al-Hakkam's library, I fear you are too late."

Ciarán gave Dónall a concerned look.

"Forgive him," Abir said gruffly. "Despite his famously eloquent tongue, he often speaks bluntly. Meet Khalil al-Pârsâ."

Khalil wore a blousy silk shirt and black pantaloons striped with gold, and a finely crafted curved scabbard and sword hung from the sash at his waist. He tipped a cup in greeting toward the monks and took a long drink, then plucked an olive from a small bowl.

"Why was this allowed to happen?" Isaac asked.

"There was a time in Córdoba when books were more prized than jewels, or even the caress of a beautiful woman," Khalil said. "Yet now the fanatics fear that books spread heresy. It is the intellectuals, who do not bow to the their extreme views, that they truly fear. Al-Mansor allows this, because he needs the imams to maintain his power. But I promise you, their ways shall be the downfall of great Córdoba."

Dónall bit his lip pensively. "Do the imams know where the rarest books are held?"

Khalil shrugged. "Al-Mansor has legions of spies. But can I say for certain? No."

"Then there's still hope," Ciarán said.

Khalil took another sip from his cup. "Why don't you tell me what you are looking for?"

"We're not certain," Ciarán replied. Dónall gave him a hard look, but he went on. "In France, we found a copy of a lost book of scripture, which had been referenced in a work by one of the paladins of Charlemagne. The book mentioned a great and glorious device . . ."

Ciarán's words trailed off as Khalil's expression, so confident a moment before, melted into astonishment. "Charlemagne?"

Khalil set his cup on the table and rose from his chair.

"This thing you are looking for—by chance, is it known as Enoch's device?"

CHAPTER 40

FIERABRAS

Seeing the astounded faces all around him, Khalil explained, "It is referenced in a poem by Faris al-Basir. You may know him as Fierabras."

Ciarán had never heard the name. He glanced at Dónall, who studied the poet intently.

"One of Charlemagne's paladins," Dónall said.

"Fierabras was a Moor who converted to Christianity in the service of your famous emperor," Khalil replied. "He was a warrior poet—very much my inspiration despite his religious conversion. He typically wrote of the beauty of women or the passion of battle, lamentations for fallen friends, and the deeds of great men. But he penned one curious poem about this device you mentioned, belonging to Enoch. I have never understood what it meant, but I always wondered."

"What did it say?" Ciarán asked.

"It has only three lines." Khalil recited from memory:

In Virgo's seed of Charlemagne's line,
and Enoch's device where the answer lies,
in the whisper of breath, or all hope dies.

Ciarán and Dónall stared at each other. "Those lines come from Maugis' book," Ciarán said.

"Of course!" Dónall said, as if struck with a revelation. "Maugis would have shared the secret with his peers."

Khalil's eyes narrowed. "Maugis d'Aygremont, another of Charlemagne's paladins?"

Dónall nodded. "Maugis had a theory, just like the riddle in your poem. It speaks to the purpose of Enoch's device."

"But what *is* this thing?" Khalil asked.

Dónall raised an eyebrow. "The answer to that question, hopefully, lies within your caliph's great library." He let the statement linger. "Can you get us in?"

Khalil turned and plucked another olive from the bowl. "This is a perilous time to go hunting for rare books."

"We will need access to the secret collection," Isaac told him.

Taking the carafe, Khalil refilled his cup and drained it before speaking again. "You are convinced that Al-Hakkam's library contains the answer to the riddle of Fierabras's poem?"

"If any library in Europe does," Isaac replied, "it is this one."

"So," Abir asked, "will you help them?"

Khalil tapped an index finger to his bearded chin, and a shrewd smile spread across his face. "I owe you many favors, my friend, and I must admit that I have longed to know the meaning of that poem. In the morning, I will go to the palace and see if the sultana can get me the access your cousin desires." Khalil paused, eyeing Ciarán. "But I shall take him with me. She fancies young men—the sight of this northern boy may please her."

Alais flashed Khalil a bitter look, and Ciarán felt his face go warm.

"Maybe this one, too," Khalil said, looking Eli up and down.

Eli's eyes grew wide, though Isaac was beaming. "Good," he insisted. "By all means, take the boys. They must be good for something besides eating and taking up space!"

So it was decided. Khalil made arrangements with Ciarán and Eli to leave in the morning for the palace, where they would seek an audience with Subh, the sultana of Córdoba. Khalil thanked Abir for the food and drink and bade his friends farewell.

After he had left, Dónall said to Ciarán, "You think this is fate again, don't you?"

"Either that or good Irish luck," Ciarán replied.

THE NEXT MORNING, Khalil al-Pârsâ rode up to Abir's house on a gray stallion, leading two black geldings behind him. Wisps of white cirrus streaked an otherwise blue morning sky, and already the air was pleasantly warm. Ciarán glanced at Eli. "No sign of the demons," Eli said.

Ciarán nodded warily. "Let's pray it stays that way."

"Look at you two," Khalil said from astride his mount. He wore a white silk turban with a long gray feather clasped by a jeweled pin. His curved sword hung at his side. "You are like two eager pups. But how do you know I'm not leading you into the lions' den?"

Ciarán grinned. "I'd tiptoe through a lions' den to get into that library."

"This device is that important to you?" Khalil said, raising a brow.

"You could say that—our lives may depend on it."

The Persian eyed them shrewdly. "Then we best get going, he said," gesturing toward the two Arab geldings.

THE PALACE of Medinat al-Zahra stood several leagues outside the city, at the base of a mountain that Khalil called the Hill of the Bride. Once they left the city gates, Khalil, Ciarán, and Eli found themselves alone on the road. "How is it," Khalil asked, "that two Irish monks and a rabbi are looking for an object described by one of Charlemagne's paladins nearly two hundred years ago?"

"Isaac says the Jewish mystics have searched for it for centuries,"

Ciarán explained. "But there are other men looking for it now—rivals of Dónall."

"How desperate are these rivals to find it?" Khalil asked.

"Desperate enough to have killed for it."

Khalil frowned. "So that is why your lives may depend on finding it?"

"In a way," Ciarán replied, unsure whether to trust the Persian with theories about the prophecy. He glanced at the curved sword that hung at Khalil's side. "Why do you wear that?"

"I have my enemies, too. And, I've found that artistry with a sword, just like artistry with a pen, is good for the soul—and for keeping it united with the body."

For a while they rode in silence. As they passed a hillside lined with shrubs of lavender, Ciarán asked Khalil how he came to know the sultana of Córdoba. "Through my art," Khalil replied. "As I earned a reputation as a poet, rulers throughout Al-Andalus would invite me to perform for them. In time, they brought me before Al-Mansor. He sponsored competitions among poets, in which two men would challenge one another to see whose verse was more elegant and whose wit more biting. For a time, these were wonderful affairs that made men like me quite wealthy. But they also introduced me to the more influential *women* in Córdoba. And that is how I met Subh."

"Is it true they call her Aurora?" Eli interjected.

Khalil nodded. "Because she is as beautiful as the dawn. She was a Basque, a Christian at the time, who became a slave to Al-Hakkam and soon became his favorite. Of course, Al-Hakkam's true interests lay with boys, shall we say, so in the bedchamber he had her dress as a boy and called her Ja'far."

Eli snickered, and Ciarán's eyes grew wide. "Really?"

"To Al-Hakkam, she was like a songbird, a treasure to be displayed. But she gave him a son, who is now our caliph, and, in doing so, became the most powerful woman in Córdoba."

"What is she like?" Eli asked.

"Very much like a tigress: beautiful to behold, but deadly when provoked."

Concern gathered in Ciarán's brow as he recalled Khalil's comment about the lion's den. "Is she the only way we can get access to the great library?"

"Only Talid, the caliph's librarian, has access to the places you wish to go," Khalil explained. "And Subh is one of the few with access to Talid."

"Who are the others?" Ciarán asked.

"The caliph, of course, but he is a recluse. I do not know if Al-Mansor has access, but if so, I suspect that the secret collection you seek has already burned in the streets."

Ciarán sensed bitterness in Khalil's voice. "You disdain Al-Mansor."

"The feeling is mutual, I assure you."

"Did he dislike one of your poems?"

Khalil shrugged. "Let's just say I was unwilling to flatter him as much as one of my opponents, so the Illustrious Victor sent me to one of his prisons."

"For *losing a contest?*" Ciarán asked.

Khalil smiled. "Better than losing my head."

Ciarán's eyes widened. "He would do that?"

Khalil nodded. "He is especially fond of doing that to Christians."

As they rode, Ciarán mused that the last thing he wanted to do was cross the king of the Moors.

"Look," Khalil announced after some time. "We are nearly there."

From their new vantage point, Medinat al-Zahra looked more like a city than like a palace. It consisted of a number of structures built across three ascending terraces, each surrounded by high turret walls. On the first terrace, a minaret rose skyward amid a structure resembling a smaller version of the Great Mosque. Palms and cypresses hung over the crenellated walls, climbing each tier to the top, where a many-pillared edifice stood crowned with a golden dome that blazed like a jewel in the sun.

"Amazing," Ciarán said, shaking his head.

"I've only seen her from the river," Eli added. "Never would I have imagined . . ."

"How many people live there?" Ciarán asked.

"About thirty thousand," Khalil replied.

He could hardly believe his ears. "All serving the caliph?"

"There are thousands of slaves, attendants, and guards, as well as the caliph's harem."

"Évrard says he has a thousand concubines," Eli said.

Khalil raised a brow. "Try *six* thousand."

Ciarán's jaw dropped.

"Under our law, a man can have only four wives. But he can have relations with all the female slaves he possesses. His is a rather large harem."

Ciarán could not shake this thought as they approached the palace gates. There, Khalil spoke in Arabic to the guards, bearded men who wore turbans of rich fabric, hauberks of polished mail, and curved swords slung from their leather belts. After taking Khalil's blade, the guards summoned a man named Najah, who held the title "keeper of the wardrobe." A tall, bare-chested man with a sash of fine purple cloth draped over his left shoulder answered the summons. His chest and arms were clean-shaven, as were his head and face. Through kohl-lined eyes, he regarded them with a severe expression.

Najah addressed Khalil in Arabic, speaking in a sharp tone, while Khalil replied in a gentler manner. Their exchange lasted longer than Ciarán expected, and the longer it went, the more concerned he grew that they might never gain admission to the palace.

Eli leaned toward Ciarán and whispered in Latin, "Khalil is talking his way inside."

"Who is this man?" Ciarán whispered back.

"One of the palace eunuchs," Eli replied. "You know, they're missing some things below the belt, but their treacheries are legendary."

"What do they do here?" Ciarán asked.

Najah glared at them crossly. "We are servants of the caliph," he responded in perfect Latin, "and guardians of his harem."

Ciarán exchanged a sideways glance with Eli, whose face was glowing.

"Follow me," Najah snapped, "and obey my every command."

Khalil shot Eli and Ciarán a reproachful glance. He was clearly annoyed that they had talked about the eunuch in his presence.

Najah escorted them through horseshoe-shaped archways into corridors as wide as city streets. More bare-chested men, and also veiled women, moved among marble buildings decorated with mosaics of geometric design, and floral motifs of acanthus and vines. After leading them through a bewildering series of turns and archways, the eunuch took them up a wide flight of steps flanked by Romanesque pillars, to another golden archway. From there, they entered the most magnificent garden Ciarán had ever seen. Ornate fountains spouted water into shimmering pools surrounded by flower beds, fruit trees, and palms. Short-cut grass carpeted the entire terrace, and rosemary and jasmine scented the air. And all around this manmade eden, exotic animals roamed: graceful, long-necked beasts that Khalil called *giraffas;* birds of red, green and blue; and small creatures that looked like sleek goats and hopped like rabbits over streams filled with huge yellow and orange fish. Ciarán could scarcely believe his eyes.

"Do they come from around here?" he wondered.

"You truly are from the edge of the world," Khalil said, nudging him along. "They come from Africa."

Najah led them down a stone pathway and up another flight of steps, through the gateway to the palace's topmost terrace. From there, he took them through a more private garden with orange trees, flowering vines of jasmine, and a central fountain that trickled water from the mouths of great stone fishes. At the far end of the garden, another arch framed the entrance to another of the palace's structures. "Wait here," Najah commanded before departing through the archway.

"When we see her, let me do the talking," Khalil said.

Ciarán nodded. After a short time, Najah reemerged. "The sultana will see you now," he told them.

Leaving the eunuch there, Ciarán and Eli followed Khalil through the archway into a dim parlor lit by oil lamps. A divan laden with pillows sat in one corner, and a sprinkling of flower petals dotted the tiled floor, filling the room with the scent of lilacs. Long drapes covered what appeared to be the entrance to a balcony fronted by a half-dozen slender columns, and a curtain of beads hung across the far end of the parlor. In the shadows, the beads parted, and a lithe figure emerged.

Ciarán's breath caught. The sultana's face, still beautiful and only subtly touched by age, was framed by long, shimmering hair the color of spun bronze. Golden earrings like teardrops dangled past her cheeks, and a necklace bearing the shape of a heron rested in the naked valley between her breasts. The outline of her nipples pressed through her silk sheath dress, and Ciarán felt an unexpected warmth stirring in his loins.

"Subh," Khalil said to her, bowing slightly.

"Khalil," she answered in a sensuous voice. She wrapped her slender arms around his neck and brought her lips to his. Ciarán's heartbeat quickened as she added to her first kiss.

"You must visit me more often," she said, brushing Khalil's cheek with her lips. "I am lonely. Ever since I turned my son against him, Al-Mansor has kept us prisoner in the palace."

Khalil looked at her fondly. "I shall be more diligent with my visits."

She strolled toward Ciarán and Eli, her eyes aglow. "Who are your friends?" She patted Eli on the chest. Then her fingers caressed Ciarán's shaven face. "This one's a northerner, too. But he looks like a priest," she said with a frown. "Alas."

"He and his companions have come a long way to see the secrets of Al-Hakkam's library," Khalil explained. "That is why I am here."

Subh pursed her lips. "Al-Mansor will destroy those priceless works, you know. He has caved to the imams."

"Which only increases the urgency of their mission," Khalil

said. "I need you to speak with Talid. Have him let us into the library, to where the rarest books are kept."

Subh glanced wistfully toward the ceiling. "Talid has become distrustful lately. Al-Mansor's spies crawl around the palace like cockroaches, and he's horrified about what the imams would do to those rare books. He loves each of them like the children he could never sire."

"But he trusts *you*," Khalil pressed.

She turned away. "Why should I care about my husband's old books?"

"They were his treasures," Khalil said.

"But what good do they do me now? And why should I further risk the anger of Al-Mansor?"

A sense of unease replaced Ciarán's arousal. "The books hold the secret to a weapon," he said, thinking quickly. "A weapon known to the paladins of Charlemagne—the type of thing a man like Al-Mansor would kill to possess."

Khalil glared at Ciarán, while Subh looked at him as if surprised that he could talk. "Does Al-Mansor know of this?"

"I don't know, Your Highness," Ciarán admitted, "but we could make sure he never learns how to find it."

"You realize," she said sharply, "that to defy the Illustrious Victor is to court death."

Ciarán swallowed hard. "I'll take that risk."

"Then you are either extremely brave or a fool." Her lips curved into a slight frown. "Still, why do I care if Al-Mansor has another weapon? He already has the army, and I've abandoned any more thoughts of overthrowing him. He's too cunning."

"There is always his considerable pride," Khalil interjected. "If we were to find the secret to this weapon in Al-Hakkam's library, a poem of how such a secret slipped away under Al-Mansor's very nose might find its way around Al-Andalus. *Al-Hakkam, the caliph most wise, kept the secret to a weapon the invader Charles prized. But Al-Mansor lost the secret, believing the imams' lies, for it was stolen from the library as books burned upon the pyres. Now, in Jannah, the wise caliph laughs, while the Illustrious Victor cries.* This tale could become quite popular in León and

Barcelona, not to mention the many places in Córdoba where people delight in any misfortune that befalls the king of the Moors."

A wicked smile spread across Subh's lips. "I *may* consider your request," she said, reaching for Khalil's hands. "But first, let us speak privately."

Khalil followed her, disappearing behind the curtain of beads. Ciarán looked at Eli, who had stared dumbstruck at the sultana of Córdoba. They waited in the parlor for what seemed an hour. The whole time, Ciarán worried about the sultana's decision.

When the beaded curtain parted, Khalil emerged alone. His face looked as hard as stone, and Ciarán's heart sank. Then the Persian's smile flashed. "She will get us the access we need. We go there tonight."

Ciarán's spirits soared. "What made her decide?"

Khalil smoothed his beard. "I have certain talents in the art of persuasion."

Ciarán blushed as they left the parlor, only to walk straight into Najah's bare chest. With his powerful arms, the eunuch pushed Ciarán aside. "I see your time is done," Najah snapped.

Khalil's eyes narrowed. Ciarán glanced between the Persian and the eunuch, wondering if he had been outside the entire time.

"Follow me," Najah commanded.

Khalil gave Ciarán a nod, and they followed Najah back through the garden. By the time they strolled past the giraffes and gazelles, Ciarán had forgotten about the eunuch's rough treatment and was instead brimming with anticipation.

For by this evening, they would stand inside the great library of Córdoba.

CHAPTER 41

THE SECRET
COLLECTION

A half hour after sunset, Khalil met Dónall and Ciarán outside Abir's house. His curved sword hung at his side, and his dark cloak fluttered in the chill wind that howled through the Jewish quarter.

"It is odd how that storm swept in so quickly," Khalil remarked.

Isaac looked beyond the rooftops, where the obscured half-moon painted the edge of the storm clouds in an eerie glow. "This is not good," he said to Dónall.

Alais gave Ciarán a worried look. "They must have followed us up the river," he said under his breath. "Let's hope the talismans keep them at bay."

Dónall clung to the strap of his book satchel and glared at the storm. Then he pulled the talisman out from beneath his habit and let it dangle in plain view. "To hell with the Moors' laws!"

Following Dónall's lead, Ciarán pulled his talisman out. So did Alais.

"My thoughts exactly," Isaac said with a nod. His talisman with the Star of David in the center showed just below his beard.

Khalil looked at them with a bemused expression. "Can we go now?"

Ciarán, Dónall, Isaac, and Alais followed Khalil down the winding streets lit by hanging oil lamps, to the plaza of the great library. Ciarán half expected to see angry clouds billowing up behind them, but there was only the wind whistling through the plaza.

At the plaza's entrance, Khalil held up his hand to stop them while a trio of Moorish guards strode past. When they had gone, he drew the hood of his cloak over his head and said, "Follow me."

He led them to a side door under an arched alcove far from the library's main entrance. An unlit lantern hung over the door. Cloaked in the shadows, Khalil knocked three times.

"Are they gone?" a voice asked through the door—surprisingly, in Greek.

"There are no guards," Khalil answered.

"Are you the poet?" the voice asked, this time in Latin.

"It is I," Khalil responded.

The door cracked open, and an old eunuch peered out. His wide eyes and sharply hooked nose made him look like a strange, effeminate owl. Tufts of curly gray hair above his ears only added to the effect. A brass holder with a burning candle trembled slightly in his right hand.

"Only an educated man speaks both Greek and Latin," the eunuch said with a certain air of pomposity. "It has been a long time, Khalil al-Pârsâ. Come in—quickly."

They entered into a musty corridor. The eunuch closed the door behind them. In the candlelight, his eyes shifted nervously. "The imams have spies everywhere," he said. "They would like nothing more than to see what is in the chamber you seek."

"We were careful not to be followed," Khalil assured him.

The old eunuch exhaled, trying to calm his nerves. "The sultana said you are scholars from the north. I am Talid, royal librarian to the caliph. Normally, I would not do this, but the sultana can be persuasive."

Talid led them up a flight of stairs to a broad hall lit by hanging crystal lamps. Mosaics of marble and gleaming black stone adorned the walls, and on each side of the hall were rooms with sandalwood bookshelves, reading tables, and more hanging lamps.

"Can you *believe* this?" Ciarán whispered to Dónall. "There must be more books in one room than in all Derry!"

"A great many more," Dónall replied.

They followed Talid down the hall, past more rooms, some of them scriptoriums with long rows of desks and arcades of windows nearly two stories tall.

"How many scribes work here?" Ciarán asked.

"At least twelve score," Talid replied. "We have separate rooms for copyists, binders, illuminators, and translators."

"I don't smell any vellum," Ciarán observed, noticing only the fragrance of sandalwood.

"Of course not. We use paper."

"Paper?"

"I suppose they don't have it in your infidel homeland," Talid said. "It's made from wood instead of calfskin. It's cleaner and far smoother to write on. And it makes our calves much happier than in your part of the world."

"Do you have to scrape it?"

"Of course not," Talid replied, rolling his eyes toward the ceiling. "What a primitive waste of time."

Dónall stared at the library in wonder. "Never in all my years . . ."

"I told you," Isaac reminded him with a smile.

Their footsteps echoed down the hall as Talid took them through an archway near the end, which led to a dark, zigzagging corridor that ended abruptly at a large bronze door. Alais gasped, grabbing Ciarán's hand, when the flickering candlelight reflected against the face of a roaring lion.

"It's only a relief set into the door," Khalil whispered.

"The door has no handle," Dónall said.

"Quite unnecessary." Talid reached his left hand up into the lion's gaping maw until it disappeared. If the lion were real, Ciarán imagined, it would surely have bitten the hand clean off. But then he heard a faint click, and with a grunt, the librarian pushed open the heavy door.

"Clever," Dónall said.

Past the doorway, Talid led them up a steep, curving stairwell, and Ciarán supposed they were ascending one of the library's towers. At the top of the stairs, after a long climb, the candlelight revealed an archway of ebony and gold framing another door. Talid placed a burnished key into the lock and pulled the door open.

A scent of antiquity flooded the stairwell. "We are here," Talid said, smiling.

He lit the first of three hanging lanterns. Suddenly the hexagonal chamber blazed to life. "Behold!" he proclaimed. "The Chamber of Enlightenment!"

Ciarán gasped. Twenty feet above, the domed ceiling glittered with gold and jewels set into ebony tiles to look like a clear night sky, depicting the constellations in their proper configuration. At the dome's center were seven jewels of various sizes, arranged as planets around a sunlike mosaic of red and gold.

Talid lit the remaining two lanterns, which hung above a small reading table, making the dome's jewels shine brighter. Small wooden drawers lined three of the chamber's five walls. Against the fourth wall stood a gigantic bookshelf, as tall as the ceiling and crammed with hundreds of tomes bound in wood or leather, many of them shimmering with jewels set into their spines. The entire shelf was secured by twin cagelike doors of burnished bronze, with bars cast in a hexagonal pattern similar to that of the tiled floor. Two ladders, which seemed attached somehow to the walls and had tiny wheels at their bases, allowed one to reach the higher works.

"The wisdom of the ages surrounds you," Talid declared.

Dónall stood in mute wonder.

"I never could have imagined such a place!" Ciarán told Alais.

"Nor I," she whispered.

"So," Talid said, "tell me what is it you seek."

Dónall and Ciarán looked to Isaac. "We are looking for records from the time of Cyrus the Great," Isaac said.

Talid sighed. "Can you be more specific? Al-Hakkam was very

fond of Cyrus. For decades, he sent envoys to Baghdad, Damascus, and Alexandria to procure from their libraries the rarest of works: scrolls transcribed from the Persians' clay cylinders, and original artifacts lifted from the ruins of ancient Babylon, some even dating back to the time of Assyria or even Sumeria. In this room alone, there may be scores of such works."

"These would concern the capture of Babylon," Isaac explained. "Specifically, the fate of treasures of the Jewish Temple taken to Babylon from Jerusalem."

"That's not much to work with," Talid sniffed, "but I'll try to make do." He reached for a leather-bound tome set in its own narrow shelf among the walls of drawers. From around his neck, attached to a golden chain, he took a smooth glass disk slightly smaller than his palm. He opened the tome and began reading through the glass.

"What is that?" Dónall asked.

"A lens," Talid replied, "invented by the great Abbas ibn Firnas. It makes the words easier on these old eyes."

"Moorish science," Dónall remarked. "Fascinating!"

The page Talid read from did not contain words at all, but line upon line of symbols.

"Those symbols are astrological!" Ciarán said.

"Observant, eh?" Talid said, looking up from the page. "This is the catalog of every work collected in the Chamber of Enlightenment. It is priceless, though dangerous in the hands of men like the imams. So I had it written in a cipher based on the signs of the zodiac. Each symbol corresponds to a letter. Of course, there are scores upon scores of possible combinations, so to read it you need a key to match the symbols to the right letters. Without it, you'd be hopelessly lost. It's my most brilliant security measure, I must say."

"How do you know what the key is?" Ciarán asked.

"Ah, for that you'd have to know who invented this particular cipher, and then know where to find his particular key. I am fond of the cipher of Faris al-Basir, but there are others."

Ciarán turned to Khalil. "Fierabras," he whispered, and Khalil nodded, as if he, too, wondered whether it was a coincidence, or something more.

Meanwhile, Talid ran a bony finger down each page, puckering his lips as he read in silence. After a dozen or so pages, he looked up again. "There is nothing listed about the treasures of the Jewish Temple in Jerusalem, although there are several scintillating works on the famous Hanging Gardens."

"That would not be it, I am afraid," Isaac said.

Dónall looked to Isaac. "Where would the Babylonians have taken the Ark?"

"An ark?" Talid asked, taking the glass from his eye.

"The Ark of the Covenant," Dónall explained. "The Jews' most sacred treasure."

Khalil stared at them incredulously. "*That* is what you are looking for in the hope of finding Enoch's device?"

"Not exactly," Isaac said. "But it is the only lead we have. As for where the Babylonians might have taken the Ark, let us start with Nebuchadnezzar. He was a conqueror, and the capture of Jerusalem would have been a significant event. To him, the treasures of the temple may have been trophies of war, to be put on public display or kept in his personal treasury."

Talid searched the lists with his index finger. "There is a record from the siege of the palace of Nabondus, the last of the Babylonian kings. It refers to the treasury and an earlier list, from one Nebuzaradan."

Isaac brightened. "That may be it! Nebuzaradan was Nebuchadnezzar's captain of the guard—the very man who pillaged Jerusalem."

"By Patrick's beard!" Dónall breathed.

As Talid pulled a brass ring with scores of tiny keys from under his robe, Ciarán's anticipation mounted. The old man's gnarled fingers jingled through the keys until he found the one he wanted. Then, walking over to one of the walls of drawers, he inserted the key into a tiny slot, pulled open the drawer, and lifted out a heavily stained papyrus scroll. Carefully, he unfurled it. The scroll was written in a foreign script.

"It's in Persian," Khalil said. "May I?"

"Better you than I, my friend," Isaac said, smiling.

Khalil took the scroll from Talid and read for some time. "It's an inventory from the Persians' seizure of Nabondus's palace. And it does mention a list, prepared by Nebuzaradan, of what was taken from the temple of the Hebrew god in Jerusalem. The author transcribed this list from the Chaldean tongue."

"What is on it?" Isaac asked eagerly.

"Pillars of bronze, shovels, basins, ladles, and the vessels of bronze used in the temple's service," Khalil said. "Also, fire pans, pots, lamp stands, incense dishes, bowls for libations, and the bronze oxen that supported the basin of the sea. But it says nothing of your golden ark."

Isaac rubbed his fingers over his eyes. "That is it, then?"

"There is nothing more," Khalil said.

Dónall grimaced. "Maybe Jeremiah did hide the Ark . . . So now what?"

Ciarán shook his head. "What if Nebuchadnezzar was scared of it? After all, the Ark contained the power of the Hebrew god. He might not have wanted it in the palace."

"Then where would it be?" Dónall pressed.

"If I may?" Khalil said. "Suppose the Babylonians believed their gods were more powerful. Might they have charged their own gods to look after such a treasure?"

"The Babylonian temples, maybe?" Isaac said. "Are there records?"

"Perhaps." Talid set the lens to his eye and began scanning more pages in the catalog. "There is a document, written by a Persian scribe, about the Etemenanki."

"What's that?" Ciarán asked.

"The ziggurat of Marduk," Talid said as he began to climb one of the ladders. He stopped at a point about half way up the wall. "The largest of the temples, set in the center of Babylon, beyond the famous Ishtar Gate. Herodotus once described it as eight square towers, with one erected atop the other. At the summit of the topmost tower was a great temple, whose only resident was a Babylonian girl—whichever one the god Marduk had chosen." He unlocked another drawer and removed a thick papyrus scroll.

"It is long." Khalil remarked.

"The Etemenanki was one of the most significant structures in the world," Talid said. "It stood nearly three hundred feet tall. Some scholars believe it was the fabled Tower of Babel."

As Talid descended the ladder, Ciarán could only imagine how old that temple must have been. Talid handed the scroll to Khalil, who began reading. After some time, he looked up. "Here," he said, "the scribe talks about a chamber they discovered beneath the lowest tier of the ziggurat. He read it aloud, translating the Persian into Latin:

At last we came upon the oft-rumored chamber where Nebuchadnezzar, in his madness, hid the most sacred treasures of the Hebrew god, for these were things the king feared. The chamber's entrance was marred with symbols of the Chaldean gods. Past it, on a stone slab, we found a budding almond rod, a serpent made of bronze and shattered into pieces, and the signet ring of the Judean kings.

Khalil shook his head. "There is no mention of your Ark."

But the monks and the rabbi glanced at one another with shared recognition in their eyes. "A signet ring," Ciarán said. "It could be the Seal of King Solomon!"

"Is there more?" Isaac asked.

Khalil gave them a puzzled look and then read more of the text.

And so the magi were summoned, but when they arrived in the chamber, the ring was gone, leaving only the large gemstone that had been in the ring's center. The magi took this gemstone, for they recognized it and were unafraid of the power of the Hebrew god. And they vowed to keep the stone until the time of the prophecy of Zoroaster.

"My God!" Dónall murmured. "A magian connection."

"But what about the Ark?" Ciarán asked.

"That is no matter," Isaac insisted. "As in my dream, the Urim

314

must have been removed, along with the rod of Aaron, and kept with the brazen serpent of Moses, which was broken by King Hezekiah. Who knows when that happened? Yet if these magi found the Urim, where would they have taken it?"

"And what about this prophecy of Zoroaster?" Ciarán added.

"Tell them, Khalil," Dónall urged.

Khalil's eyes narrowed as if he was trying to figure out where Dónall was going. "The magi," he said hesitantly, "were the priestly caste of the Persian Empire, deeply devoted to astrology. As you know, there are four elements, each represented by three zodiacal signs. The magi tracked the conjunctions of Jupiter and Saturn through these elemental signs, looking toward a time called the Great Conjunction, after the four elemental conjunctions had passed and the cycle had come full circle, every one thousand years, at the dawn of the new millennium.

"Zoroaster was the greatest sage and seer among the magi. He prophesied that in the next three millennia, at the time of the Great Conjunction, a world savior would come to continue the battle between Ohrmazd, the god of good, and Ahriman, the god of evil. Thus, the magi looked to the time of these world saviors, each a messiah born to a virgin mother."

"And to find him," Dónall said, "they followed a star. And I'm certain they would have taken the device."

"But who are they?" Alais asked.

"Why, my dear," Dónall replied, "you know of them as the Three Wise Men."

CHAPTER 42

THE SEQUENCE

"There is one problem," Isaac said. "I am no expert on your Christian gospels, but I recall no mention of a jewel or a stone, and no reference to the Urim."

Dónall shook his head. "There must be a connection. To the magi, the birth of Christ would have appeared as the fulfillment of Zoroaster's prophecy. Surely they would have entrusted Enoch's device to one they believed to be a messiah." He turned to Khalil. "What do you know about the magi and sacred stones?"

"Next to nothing," Khalil said. "The magi focused on the primordial elements of water and fire. One of their symbols was a chalice of flame."

"Wait," Ciarán said. "What was this chalice made of?"

"Gold, of course," Khalil replied.

"The Three Gifts," Ciarán said, thinking quickly. "The Wise Men brought gifts of frankincense, myrrh, and gold. What if that gold had been shaped into an object—into, say, a chalice?"

Dónall looked stunned. "The cup of Christ?"

"But the Urim is a *stone*," Isaac insisted.

Ciarán ran his fingers through his hair. They must be missing something. Then suddenly, he looked to Talid. "Does your catalog reference a Book of Enoch?"

Talid raised a curious brow. "It should." He began flipping through the catalog, his lips pursed. "Right here," he said, looking up from his lens.

"Brilliant, lad!" Dónall said, his eyes aglow.

Ciarán could hardly wait as Talid climbed the tallest ladder to retrieve an age-worn scroll from one of the drawers. Climbing back down, he carefully unfurled the cracked and brittle papyrus.

Ciarán looked at the brownish script. "It's not in Greek—I can't read it."

"That one's more than a thousand years old," Talid said, "so it's in Aramaic."

Isaac looked hopelessly to Khalil, who just shook his head.

"Fortunately for you," Talid continued, "I can read eight languages, one of which happens to be ancient Aramaic."

Ciarán gestured toward the scroll. "Look toward the middle, for a passage that reads, 'And there I saw a great and glorious device at the ends of the whole earth.'"

Khalil's eyes narrowed with recognition. "The reference to Enoch's device?"

"Yes," Dónall said.

Ciarán waited anxiously while Talid read in silence. "I've found it," he finally said. "'A great and glorious device.'"

"Good," Ciarán said. "Before that reference should be a series of verses where the archangels show Enoch the world. Look for the part where they take him to a mountain and reveal the secrets of the heavens."

Talid's finger ran up the scroll. "Here it is."

"Read it aloud."

And the angels carried me to the summit of a mountain, which reached to heaven. And I beheld the light and the mysteries of the stars and the thunder in the deepest depths, and I saw among the heavens a fiery bow and arrow . . .

"There!" Ciarán exclaimed. "We must have overlooked it at Saint-Bastian's, but the bow and arrow is a symbol for Sagittarius, the prophecy's sign for Enoch's device!" He could scarcely contain his eagerness. The next verse would be critical. "What does Enoch see next?"

"'*And to the west I saw a river of fire,*'" Talid read. "'*To the south I beheld the great mountains. To the east I saw the rivers of the earth and the deep of the sea. And to the north I saw the storehouse of the winds.*'"

Ciarán's mind was racing. *The four elements: fire, earth, water, wind.* In the symbolism of the Fae, the sequence became clear: *Staff . . . stone . . . cup . . . sword!*

Dónall's jaw dropped. Talid, meanwhile, turned ashen. Eyes wide, he looked past Ciarán. Behind him, Alais gasped, and Khalil reached for his sword.

Ciarán whirled around. In the chamber's threshold stood the eunuch Najah, gripping a curved sword. Beside him were more than a dozen Moorish warriors, with blades drawn. A black-robed imam looked on, shouting commands in Arabic.

Talid fell to his knees, his face twisted in agony.

Najah lunged, the tip of his blade aimed at Khalil's neck, as a Moor grabbed Khalil's sword arm, forcing his blade back into its scabbard. Dónall yelled at two Moors who were wrestling him back against the wall. His shouts echoed through the chamber, mixing with the imam's cries. A burly warrior grabbed Ciarán by the shoulder, while three others brandished their scimitars at Alais and Isaac.

On his knees, Talid cradled the Book of Enoch, pleading, but the imam ripped the ancient scroll from his grasp. The scroll tore in half, and a handful of papyrus wafted to the floor.

Talid's face twisted in agony, and he let out a horrid, bloodcurdling cry.

~

THE MOORS LED their prisoners into the plaza. A heavy mist soaked the air. Overhead, black clouds loomed, shrouding the library's turrets and the minaret of the Great Mosque.

The warriors numbered at least twenty, all with spears or swords and all answering to the severe-looking imam, whom Ciarán recognized as one of the leaders of the book-burning two days ago. Alais clung to Ciarán's hand, and he could see the fear in her eyes. Khalil knew better than to resist their captors, as did Isaac, who trudged alongside Dónall, defeated. Next to them, two of the warriors dragged the hysterically sobbing Talid.

Over the river, lightning flashed, and nearer by, a gust of wind rocked the oil lamps that surrounded the plaza. In that wind, Ciarán heard the faint whisper of voices.

The Moors, led by Najah and the imam, escorted their prisoners from the plaza, glancing nervously at the brewing storm.

"Where are they taking us?" Alais whispered.

"To the Court of Al-Mansor," Khalil said quietly. "When we get there, let me speak."

Ciarán barely nodded, wondering whether Khalil heard the whispers in the wind or realized that a smoky fog was following them down every narrow street, gliding over the rooftops and through the winding alleys.

The air was growing colder. Alais shivered, and Ciarán realized that she, too, heard the whispers. Dónall and Isaac glanced at the creeping fog with a look of dread in their eyes.

Before long, they arrived at a small fortress. Its domed turrets were barely visible beneath the dark mist that fell from clouds so low, they seemed about to swallow the building. Wind battered the banners that hung over the grand entryway.

In the wind, the voices were laughing.

The Moors escorted their captives through towering double doors, into a large hall dimly lit by bronze lamps suspended from the ceiling two stories above. Lining the hall were arcades of tall, narrow windows lined with intricate mosaics of colored glass, now darkened by the brooding clouds outside. On a dais at the far end of the hall, more warriors stood behind a thronelike chair flanked by glowing braziers.

A roar echoed through the hall. At the foot of the dais lay two great cats: one, a panther as black as the night; and the second, a tiger as pale as ivory, purring loudly. Each wore a golden collar attached to chains held by the burly warriors behind them.

Footfalls sounded against the tiled floor as Najah led the prisoners toward the man on the throne. He had a warrior's physique and wore golden armlets, and black robes adorned with jeweled medallions. He regarded them through cunning eyes set in a cruel, handsome, gray-bearded face. An aura of power surrounded this man, who could be none other than Ibn Abi Amir, known to all as Al-Mansor.

Alais shuddered, and Ciarán squeezed her hand in reassurance that he did not feel.

Their captors stopped them five yards from the dais. Al-Mansor began speaking in a confident tone, while Isaac whispered a translation.

"Khalil al-Pârsâ," Al-Mansor said with a dry smile. "The great poet has finally returned to my court. Your talents were once so promising. You were a painter with words, who could best my finest laureates. And now, look what has become of you. I thought your imprisonment would have cured you of your disrespect for my authority. Yet tonight you are found cavorting with foreign spies."

Ciarán looked to Dónall. *Spies?* Dónall slowly shook his head, then winced as a flash of lightning lit the room, and thunder shook the windows lining the hall.

Al-Mansor cast a fleeting glance to the storm, then leveled his gaze again at Khalil. "Najah told me of your visit to the sultana."

"Your own spy," Khalil observed.

"Surely, you did not expect me to leave unwatched a woman as calculating as Subh?" Al-Mansor looked to his eunuch. "Najah, of what did they speak?"

"Of a weapon, my king," Najah replied.

"This weapon," Al-Mansor said icily, "is it for the kings of Spain? Did not the names León and Barcelona roll off your tongue in Subh's parlor? Is that whom these infidels serve? Do the Spanish kings think they can use this weapon to defeat me?"

The anger beneath Al-Mansor's voice made Ciarán's blood run

cold. Then another thunderclap shook the windows. Behind the glass panes, black fog surged.

Khalil answered in a tone that was confident almost to the point of nonchalance. "My colleagues do not serve the kings of Spain," he said. "They are scholars from the Irish isle, and the weapon they spoke of was nothing more than a fanciful myth, a ruse to get us inside the Chamber of Enlightenment, where they sought to find some rare texts. So you see, we have broken no laws."

Al-Mansor slammed a fist into the armrest of his throne. "Lies! You were found in a chamber of forbidden works offensive to Islam!"

Outside, the thunder growled.

"The documents sought were merely historical," Khalil argued. "That is no crime."

Al-Mansor's eyes narrowed, surveying his captives. "*You* may or may not have committed a crime, Khalil, but *they* have. Those amulets around their necks—we have laws against displaying the symbols of infidel religions."

Najah grasped the talisman hanging between Alais' breasts. She looked desperately to Ciarán.

"A cross," the eunuch spat.

Outside the windows, the air was pitch black. The panes shuddered at each thunderclap, and at the foot of the dais, the great cats stirred.

A narrow smile formed on Al-Mansor's lips. "Bring those symbols to me."

Najah took the talisman from Alais' neck. She clenched Ciarán's hand. The eunuch removed Ciarán's talisman, then Isaac's. The rabbi closed his eyes, muttering a Hebrew prayer.

Around them, the windows shook violently.

"You don't want to do this," Dónall told the eunuch in Latin.

Najah answered with a queer look. Then he ripped the final talisman from Dónall's neck.

Glass began to crack, and then the windows exploded with a deafening sound. Glass shards sliced through the air as dense black fog poured through the breach.

Najah and the other Moors turned away in horror, and Al-Mansor shielded his face. With a roar, the great cats leaped to their feet as three snakelike clouds writhed toward the dais.

Dónall turned to his companions. "For the love of God, run!"

CHAPTER 43

REVENGE

Dónall did not look back, even as a choked scream erupted behind him, followed by fierce roaring. The Moors, paralyzed with terror at the demons' attack, ignored their fleeing captives. In the confusion, Khalil reclaimed his sword from the warrior who had dropped it when the windows exploded, and Dónall slung the book satchel over his shoulder. Amid the Moors' cries, he saw Ciarán pulling Alais by the hand. She looked back toward Al-Mansor's hall in horror while Isaac did his best to urge her forward. From the rabbi's eyes, Dónall knew that they shared the same thought: there was very little time.

Outside, the thinning black clouds unveiled the light of the half-moon. Wind whipped from the hall into the plaza, rocking the lamps on their poles.

"Get to the ship!" Ciarán cried.

"During a *storm*?" Khalil asked.

"Do as he says," Dónall shouted. "There's protection there!"

Behind them, a collective cry rose from the hall—not a cry of terror, but one of zealous fury. Like a battle cry.

Dónall's heart raced. He blew on his crystal, uttering the Fae word, and swept it into his line of sight. Through the crystal's glow,

323

he saw Najah rallying the others in the hall strewn with shattered glass. The shadowy form of the Gorgon's hair wreathed the eunuch's head, confirming Dónall's worst fears. The demon's fire burned red within the eunuch's eyes. *Twice you failed to kill us with storms*, Dónall thought, *so now you'll try to do it with swords.*

"We'll never make it to the docks!" Dónall yelled. In the moonlight, he could see the minaret of the Great Mosque towering over the rooftops. "Flee to the mosque instead!"

Khalil glanced at the Moorish swordsmen pouring from the hall. "Are you *mad?*"

"We need hallowed ground!"

Isaac nudged Khalil in the direction of the mosque. "Listen to him, my Muslim friend—those are demons that pursue us."

Khalil looked back in disbelief.

"Go," Isaac prodded.

Reluctantly, Khalil followed, but Dónall could not tell whether the Persian remained skeptical or was merely realizing the magnitude of the evil they faced.

Ciarán and Alais streaked toward the Great Mosque, with Dónall and Isaac doing their best to keep pace, as angry cries in Arabic echoed behind them.

The streets emptied into the plaza of the Great Mosque. In the shadow of the minaret, Ciarán and Alais ducked through the open gateway. The others followed. A garden of cypresses and palms filled the courtyard, flanked by porticoes. Moonlight shimmered on the surface of a long basin amid the soft chirring of crickets, and fog clung to the wet ground, giving the courtyard an eerie beauty. Ciarán and Alais headed for the entrance to the mosque, though Dónall wondered if that was necessary. The last time, the demons could not even cross the threshold of Saint-Hilaire-le-Grand.

Khalil scanned the courtyard for Moorish swordsmen. All was quiet, almost peaceful, and what clouds remained in the night sky gave way to a tapestry of stars behind the tranquil foreground of palms. Then Khalil grabbed Dónall's sleeve and pointed toward a second gateway. "Look," he whispered.

Two large creatures stalked into the garden. The beasts strode on all fours, one white and striped, the other black as night, their feline tails swaying back and forth. Dónall felt a sinking in the pit of his stomach. A low, deep growl drowned out the crickets. In the crystal's light, red eyes glowed in the faces of the great cats, and serpentine shadows wreathed their heads. "By Patrick's beard," Dónall muttered breathlessly, "this is a mosque—how . . . ?"

The white tiger roared, displaying great yellowed canines longer than a man's fingers. The cats were but forty yards away.

"Hurry—in here!" Isaac called out from beneath one of the porticoes at the doorway to the minaret.

Across the garden, Alais screamed, and Ciarán pulled her toward the mosque. In a flash, the panther darted after them.

Khalil pushed Dónall toward the minaret. In the garden, the tiger bounded toward them. Dónall dived into the doorway. The tiger raced down the portico, its powerful muscles rippling beneath the striped white fur.

"Close the door!" Khalil cried.

Inside the darkened minaret, Dónall could hear the tiger's breath as he swung the door shut. A simple iron bolt provided the only latch. Khalil slid it across the breach, just before the door shuddered from the great beast's weight. An angry roar reverberated through the wood, and the door shook again under another impact.

Dónall had already started up the winding stairs. "I saw them in your light," Isaac said, following him, huffing for breath. "You said hallowed ground would protect us."

"Their spirits are encased in mortal shells; that's the only explanation I can think of," Dónall said, and bounded up the stairs. "Perhaps, in those bodies, they can go wherever mortals can." He had to see what was happening in the courtyard. Below, the door shook again as the tiger raked the wood with its claws.

"This was a dramatically bad idea," Khalil said as they reached the top, where the moonlight shone on a large, ornate carpet covering the floor beneath the minaret's dome. Dónall strode through a pillared archway onto a circular balcony and leaned over the parapet. Ciarán and Alais were nowhere in sight, and warriors were pouring into the garden. Najah ran toward the portico. They would soon break down the door, Dónall realized.

Khalil unsheathed his sword, and Isaac looked at him as if he had gone mad. "You plan to kill a tiger with *that?*"

"Tell me a better idea," Khalil insisted. "You led us here; now we're trapped."

Dónall glanced down to the garden's floor, some seven stories below. From the stairwell, another thunderous impact rocked the minaret's door, and this time he heard wood crack. The crystal's light had begun to fade as a fierce crash resounded up the stairwell, followed by a triumphant roar. Dónall cursed, thinking, *it can't end now.*

Seeing Khalil standing ready with his sword, Dónall remembered his own leaf-shaped blade. And as he reached for it, an idea struck—a desperate, foolish idea. He prayed it would work.

Exhaling, he relaxed his mind, focusing on the air around him, and uttered a Fae verse. Then he raised his sword, and a rush of wind blasted up the tower. "Grab the carpet!" he ordered. "Bring it to the edge, and hold on for your lives."

"You want to leap from the tower?" Khalil yelled. "Are you *insane?*"

"The wind will hold us!" Dónall insisted, trying to concentrate on his summoning.

Inside the minaret, Isaac pulled the edge of the carpet off the floor. "I trust him," he told Khalil.

A fierce growl echoed up the stairwell. Shaking his head, Khalil grabbed the carpet's other edge and helped Isaac drag it onto the balcony. The wind howled, whipping the carpet's tasseled fringe. Dónall grabbed hold. "Run toward the parapet—and jump."

"You are certain this will work?" Khalil pressed.

Another roar, closer now, reverberated through the minaret.

"Let's hope," Dónall said. "Now, jump!"

They leaped, hurling themselves off the parapet with the carpet beneath them.

And then they fell.

Drawing on all his strength, Dónall summoned more wind, and

as they neared the topmost branches of the cypresses, a powerful gust slowed, then stopped, their descent. The carpet rippled and rolled, kept aloft on the rushing wind as if riding a wave. Dónall held on tight with his left hand, while directing the wind with his sword. Terrified, Khalil clung to the carpet, his hair blowing behind him in the crisp night air. In the garden below, the Moors looked up in awe.

"We're flying!" Isaac exclaimed.

The fluttering carpet soared over the courtyard and crossed the Great Mosque's crenellated wall. Beneath them, Córdoba sparkled with a thousand lamplights. The carpet glided over rooftops, rising for an instant. But then the carpet buckled. Dónall fought to control the wind. They began to dive. Dónall felt his power slipping.

"We're going to crash!" Khalil cried.

Dónall's eyes grew wide. "Hold on!"

The carpet banked sharply, narrowly missing a clay-tiled roof. They gained speed, careening forward, straight for a cluster of stuccoed buildings. Dónall frantically swung his sword, and with a burst of wind, the carpet veered away from the sharp corner of one of the structures. Isaac, who had turned deathly pale, pointed ahead. "Aim for that bazaar!"

Ahead, the buildings surrounded a plaza filled with scores of striped tents. The carpet dropped sharply, and Dónall flung back his blade, hoping to summon the last vestiges of wind to slow their fall. And with a loud rending of cloth and snapping of poles, the carpet dived into the cluster of tents, ripping tethers from their stakes.

Tent cloth enveloped the three riders as they collided with the ground. Pain shuddered down Dónall's spine, and he feared that he had broken something, but he found he could still wiggle his fingers and toes. Beside him, Khalil groaned.

As Dónall's head cleared and his pounding heart began to slow, he looked around him, but everything was dark. Then he realized they were buried under a tent canopy. "Isaac," he muttered.

"Never again," the rabbi moaned.

After a long moment, Khalil sat up and struggled to pull away the layers of tent cloth that covered them. He tugged at the cloth, folding it aside. "How large was this tent?"

A loud rip answered his question, followed by the tip of a curved sword. Between Dónall and Khalil, the blade sliced through the tent. Hands emerged in the breach, tearing the severed cloth.

Dónall muttered an oath. Standing over them, with a sword arched above his head, was the broad-chested eunuch, Najah. His mouth twisted into a wicked grin, and hate blazed in his eyes.

Dónall uttered a fearsome word: "Megaera."

CIARÁN AND ALAIS darted through the entrance to the Great Mosque, only to find themselves within a forest of slender columns supporting horseshoe-shaped archways of alternating red brick and white stone. It was like no place of worship that Ciarán had ever seen. Each archway sat atop another, identical in pattern and shape, so that it appeared as if hundreds of archways filled the chamber, which was so vast, the other side disappeared in the dim light of the oil lamps that hung from the vaultlike ceiling. At first glance, the myriad of archways and columns seemed like a maze, but soon he discerned that the archways were arranged in aisles from one end of the mosque to the other.

"Are you sure about this?" Alais asked.

"They shouldn't have been able to enter the mosque," he whispered, wondering where they could go from here. Everywhere he looked, row upon row of archways stood on columns of marble, granite, and onyx. He started down one of the aisles, moving toward the back of the mosque. Their sandals echoed against the mosaic-tiled floor.

An instant later, Alais gripped his arm so hard, her nails bit into his flesh. In the glimmer of moonlight, a dark feline form emerged at the mosque entrance. Then a great black paw reached across the threshold.

Alais gasped, and a chill washed over Ciarán as the panther's deep growl echoed through the mosque. Unsure whether it had seen them yet, he grabbed Alais and tried to hide in the shadows between the archways.

"Over there," Alais whispered, pointing toward the north end of the mosque, where a series of wrought-iron gates enclosed the northernmost aisle. A gateway stood open just ten aisles away.

"Let's go," Ciarán said under his breath. "And run!"

They bolted toward the gate, and with a roar, the great cat bounded through archways, skidding around the columns and quickly closing the gap. But Ciarán and Alais were much closer to the gate. Ciarán grabbed the iron bars as Alais jumped through, and he followed, slamming the gate shut. The panther lunged, fire in its eyes. On the other side of the gate, a small key jutted from the only lock. Ciarán reached for the key and turned it. He could feel the panther's hot breath as he wrenched the key from the lock and pulled back his arm. Biting pain shot up his arm, and he jerked back, fearing that the panther had hold of him. The sleeve of his habit was ripped to shreds, and blood soaked his arm, but it was free. The panther thudded against the gate, clawing and thrashing, roaring in its fury.

"Ciarán!" Alais cried, seeing his arm.

Clinging to the wound with his other hand, he watched the blood seep through his fingers. He peered down the aisle, gritting his teeth. Moonlight spilled through an archway at the far end. It must lead back into the garden. Grimacing in pain, he said, "That way."

As they hurried down the aisle, the panther tracked them, its eyes never leaving theirs. It growled and hissed but could do nothing against the iron barrier.

Ciarán's arm throbbed. When they reached the archway that led back into the garden, the panther gave a final hiss and darted back into the shadows of the mosque.

Outside, the Moorish swordsmen paid them no attention. Some chattered frantically, while others looked up transfixed, pointing at the sky.

Just yards away, another gateway in the curtain wall opened back into the city. "Thank God!" Ciarán whispered. "We have to get to the ship—it's our only chance."

Alais nodded, still panting, and off they ran.

～

AMID A SEA OF STRIPED TENTS, Najah brought down his sword. He aimed the blade's sharp edge for Dónall's head, but it met the scabbard Khalil thrust into its path. The eunuch's sword cleaved into the scabbard's leather until it hit the steel of the Persian's own blade. Najah struck again, his face contorted in rage, and the blow nearly drove the scabbard into Khalil's chest. Dónall twisted away as, behind Najah, a dozen warriors watched, some apparently intrigued by the spectacle of single combat. Others looked on warily, as if fearful of whatever magic had lofted the carpet into the bazaar. Isaac scurried to Dónall's side. Najah kept hacking away at Khalil, who defended with his scabbard held in both hands.

Another blow threatened to drive Khalil to the ground, but Najah's curved blade caught on the scabbard's brass fittings. Khalil jerked the hilt, and his blade slid free from the scabbard.

Najah swung with reckless ferocity. Khalil jumped to his feet and sliced low at his attacker, but the eunuch parried and then struck again with inhuman fury. Khalil's sword saved his life, but the force of the strike knocked him off balance.

Dónall's pulse began to race. Though Khalil was skilled, he looked weary from the crash, and he faced an opponent fueled by a supernatural evil. Hammering blows struck again and again at his blade, the clang of steel ringing through the bazaar. Then Khalil's knees began to buckle.

Dónall had to do something. Raising his blade, he cried, "Megaera! It is not him you want, but me, Dónall mac Taidg, who have defeated you and your sisters twice since you were summoned from hell!"

The eunuch hissed at Dónall, and in the moment of distraction, Khalil swept a backhanded stroke across his belly. Najah's mouth fell open in horror as his bowels spilled like a nest of writhing snakes to the ground. The fire in the eunuch's eyes flickered as he slumped to his knees. Khalil swung again, his blade cleaving through the eunuch's throat, just below the chin.

Then chaos erupted.

A fierce gale exploded through the plaza, whipping the fallen tent canopy and tearing lines from their stakes. Dónall and Isaac shielded their eyes as the tempest howled around them like a banshee, funneling toward the scattering Moors. One of them, a large, bearded warrior with a barrel chest and wearing a bow slung over his shoulder, clutched at his head, as if trying to claw out his own eyes. He let loose an anguished cry.

"She's possessing another," Dónall said, grabbing Khalil by the sleeve. "Now, go!"

They fled down an alley. Khalil seemed to know every narrow outlet and street in this part of the city. With the Moor's screams fading behind them, Khalil stopped to catch his breath.

"That name—Megaera, was it?" Khalil said between gasps.

Dónall held his hands on his knees, also trying to calm his breathing. "Yes. It's the name of the demon that possessed him."

Khalil looked up. "It is also a name from mythology—one of three Furies of ancient Greece."

"Say that again?"

"The Furies," Khalil replied. "Vengeful spirits of the gods: Megaera, Alecto, and Tisiphone."

Dónall stared at Khalil as the realization sank in. There was truth behind the old myths, so why couldn't the Furies be demons—the souls of fallen Nephilim?

Isaac scratched his head. "Then if you know all their names . . ."

"By Patrick's beard . . ." Dónall's mind was racing. "Of course!" He shrugged the book satchel off his shoulder and pulled out the Book of Maugis d'Aygremont. Flipping through the pages, he settled on the nearly blank page with the scrawled words *The warding and binding of demons.* He removed the crystal from his habit and summoned his soul light. Amid the white glow, the words began to roll clearly down the page. And so did the solution. He cursed himself for not realizing it sooner. For when he challenged Megaera in the battle over Ciarán's mind, he had learned her true name, the one precious secret she could never afford to reveal.

"Find the ship, and wait for me," he told them, stowing the book.

"Where are you going?" Khalil asked.

"Trust me," Dónall said. "I have a plan."

ALAIS CLUNG to Ciarán's good hand. His other was slick with blood. They emerged from one of the cramped alleyways onto a main avenue lined by oil lamps swaying with the wind. She feared she heard the panther behind her, purring as it stalked its prey, but when she glanced back she saw only the few Córdobans who walked along the avenue this evening: merchants in turbans leaving their shops, a Berber soldier walking with a woman, two urchins begging for handouts. Ahead loomed one of the city's massive gates, standing open. Alais wondered for an instant whether they ever closed it, but right now she didn't care. All she wanted to do was find the docks and Évrard's ship.

Their run had slowed to a hurried walk as they fought to catch their breath. Somewhere, she knew, a gang of warriors also pursued them, and she feared them nearly as much as the great cats. The air held the faint smell of fish and water weeds—the river was close.

Ciarán grimaced. His right arm dangled at his side. Four Moorish guards were posted at the gate, but two were dozing, slouched against the sandstone wall, while their companions passed the time in idle conversation. Alais and Ciarán neared the portal as, behind them, a chorus of startled cries rang out. The Córdobans scattered as the panther leaped into the avenue with a threatening roar.

"Through the gate!" Ciarán urged. Alais prayed that it led to the docks. They ran, and the guardsmen awoke, but only to gape at the panther bolting toward them. As they reached the arched opening of the massive gateway, Ciarán swore, and Alais' heart sank. For the gateway led to the vast Roman bridge that spanned the river. The other side was hundreds of yards away, obscured by the fog rising from the water.

She glanced over her shoulder to see the panther bounding down the street. To her horror, the white tiger trailed not two lengths behind it.

"There's two of them!" she said frantically as she and Ciarán hurried onto the bridge. To the east, not far down the riverbank, the lights from the dock shone like a beacon. Only a few ships were docked there, Évrard's among them. A frightened yell came from the guards at the gate as the paws of the great cats padded against the paved street.

Ciarán looked at her with a glimmer of hope. "Can you swim?"

"Yes," she said, recalling the days when she and Adeline would play in the Clain.

"Then, we'll jump!"

She looked down at the river, more than twenty feet below. The panther roared as the great cats leaped through the gateway.

Ciarán lifted her onto the bridge's broad parapet. "Now!"

She jumped first, arms flailing as she fell. Then she plunged into the chilling water. She sank for an instant, then kicked to the surface. Already, the current was carrying her downriver. Ten yards away, Ciarán splashed into the water. Above him on the bridge, the great cats climbed onto the parapet.

Ciarán began to swim. Looking back past him, Alais gasped as the creatures leaped into the night air.

"Swim!" he yelled.

Alais swam furiously as the cats splashed into the river. The current drifted her toward the ships. Wide-eyed, she looked back at the slick, wet shape, like a giant otter, of the panther pursuing her. It moved faster than she could have imagined.

She kicked and stroked through the water, but the creature was gaining. A cry echoed from one of the ships. She heard men clamoring from the decks. Her arms began to ache, and she feared she might not make it.

"Over here!" a voice cried.

Through the splashing water, she saw Eli, clinging to a loop of rope lowered from the ship. He hung just above the water, offering an outstretched hand.

She grabbed and missed as the pursuing panther behind her grew nearer. She extended her arm again, and this time her fingertips caught Eli's. He grabbed her wrist, pulling her close.

As Eli drew her in, a terrible roar erupted, and the panther thrashed violently. Something dangling from her rescuer's neck glinted in the moonlight. *Eli's talisman—it can't get near it,* she realized. With a hiss, the panther turned away and dived beneath the surface.

Alais scanned the river. "Where's Ciarán!" she cried.

Eli gave her a hopeless look. "It pulled him under. It's too late . . . He's gone."

CHAPTER 44
SHOWDOWN

The water turned red with Ciarán's blood. The tiger had swum faster than he could have imagined, and to his horror, it dived beneath the surface. Dagger-sharp claws raked his legs, snagging his habit and pulling him under.

His lungs burned. Then a primal instinct seized him: to fight, to live. He tore off his cowl, and it drifted through the water, into the path of the great hooked claws.

The beast flailed, shredding the cowl as Ciarán rent the ties of his habit. He wriggled out of the habit and kicked it into the tiger's path. The habit wafted underwater like a giant jellyfish, enveloping the tiger's head. Furious, the beast thrashed wildly in the dark water.

Ciarán kicked toward the surface, struggling to propel himself farther from the possessed animal. That his legs still functioned meant his wounds were perhaps less severe than he had thought, though pain still lanced through his limbs as he swam for the dock.

The pilings emerged from the river's surface just strokes away. He had lost sight of Alais but prayed she was safe. He glanced back; the tiger was nowhere in sight. Grabbing one of the wooden pilings, he embraced it and worked his way up. Splinters gouged his arms and the insides of his thighs, which were already bleeding from the mauling he had taken, but at last he pulled himself onto the dock, gasping for breath. His soaked undertunic, dark with his blood, clung to him.

He fought the urge to lie there and surrender to the pain and fatigue. His wounds throbbed, and he knew that they must be bound or his life would drain away as his mind faded into delirium. He clung to thoughts of Alais and Dónall and the mystery that consumed them. The device. The apocalypse. And the unthinkable consequences if he let sleep take him now.

Grimacing, Ciarán rose to his feet. Lanterns glowed, appearing as opaque halos of light in the eerie fog that cloaked the docks. From one of the ships, voices called out. Évrard's men. *Nearly there.* He limped down the wooden dock toward the vessel. As he approached, two figures hurried down the pier from the direction of the city. Ciarán wiped the water from his eyes as Isaac and Khalil ran toward him. Khalil's sword was blooded.

"On to the ship!" Isaac shouted.

At the entrance to the pier, a cry in Arabic rose up. A score of warriors emerged, led by a huge bearded Moor clutching a recurved bow. From Ciarán's left came a fierce roar. Dripping wet, the tiger padded down the dock, with the panther following in its wake.

Ciarán's pulse quickened. Khalil and Isaac backed toward him, just twenty yards from the great cats. Then a cry sounded from the direction of the ship.

"Ciarán!"

Turning, he saw Alais rush down the gangplank from Évrard's ship. Eli bolted after her.

"Go back!" Ciarán yelled.

At the pier's entrance, the large Moor drew back his bow, and Ciarán heard the whir of an arrow.

As he watched, Alais fell headlong toward the pier. He dived toward her. She caught herself with her hands, tears streaming from her eyes. He reached for her outstretched hands as another arrow whizzed overhead. *Please, God, let her live!* He felt for the arrow shaft that must have pierced her flesh. Her fingers tightened around his.

As Ciarán clung to Alais, the tiger bounded toward them. Khalil advanced to face it, sword in hand.

Then an Irish cry challenged the tiger's roar.

"By Saints Patrick and Columcille, hear me!" Dónall stormed down the dock south of Évrard's ship. His left arm cradled the open Book of Maugis d'Aygremont, and in his right hand, one of the kettle-shaped Moorish oil lamps glinted in the moonlight.

As the tiger turned toward him, Fae words rolled off Dónall's tongue—a verse of an ancient song. The Moor, who had nocked another arrow from his quiver, stopped halfway through the pull of his bowstring. Both great cats froze in mid stride.

"Megaera! Alecto! Tisiphone!" Dónall shouted in Latin. "By the power of the Fae and the angels, your masters in heaven, be bound!"

Dónall uttered a final word in the Fae tongue, and blue flames rose around the large Moor and the great cats. A ghastly wail erupted as the air whipped into a howling gale. From the three possessed hosts, the blue fire streaked toward the oil lamp, and in its glow, the reflections of three hideous women screamed in agony as the lamp sucked the fire into itself until it was gone. The huge Moor's eyes rolled upward in his head, his knees buckled, and he collapsed on his bow. The great cats slunk back on the dock as the rest of the Moors looked on in dread. Dónall mac Taidg stood triumphant in the dying wind. In his hand, the lamp lid clattered against the brass vessel, as if the spirits inside fought to be free.

Ciarán wrapped his arms around Alais. "Where are you hurt?" he asked. She shook her head, her mouth twisted with grief. Then he noticed Eli, slumped behind her with two arrows in his chest. Blood seeped from between his fingers clutching the wounds.

"He pushed me aside," she said, her lips trembling.

Isaac rushed to the young man, whose eyes stared blankly down the pier. From the ship, Josua cried out, "My son!"

Tears stung Ciarán's eyes. Then he felt Dónall tugging his shoulder.

"Get up lad! They're coming!"

Ciarán looked up to see a dozen warriors racing down the pier toward him, swords drawn.

"Hurry!" Dónall yelled.

Aboard the ship, Évrard's crew were already in action, drawing in the mooring ropes, preparing to let the current pull the ship away from the wharf. Isaac and Josua pulled Eli aboard, and Alais climbed the gangplank, still clutching Ciarán's hand. He tried to follow her, but his vision grew blurry. Then his legs buckled, and he fell face-first onto the deck.

CHAPTER 45
THE URIM'S FATE

Ciarán opened his eyes. He stood in a glen of clover, with green hills rising on either side. A bone-chilling mist hung in the air. Was this home?

Through the mist, a group of men approached. All save one wore gray habits. The man in the group's center had short-cropped hair the color of orange autumn leaves. *Niall?*

Ciarán blinked. Seven men stood before him, all of them his friends. On the far right stood Senach, his wiry frame leaning on a staff. But instead of his shepherd's crook, it was a tall, black staff topped with a golden ankh. In the center of the ankh's loop, a bright gem shone.

"Why are you here?" Senach asked.

Beside him, the twins, Áed and Ailil, watched dispassionately, their habits shredded and muddy. Next to them stood Eli. The curly-haired Jew looked wide-eyed, his chest still slick with blood. In his outstretched palms, he cupped a glittering gemstone. "Take care of her," Eli said.

On the right stood Murchad, his habit torn and stained where the Frankish blade had impaled him. Next to him, Fintan held a golden chalice as if presenting it for communion. A familiar gemstone gleamed in the chalice's thick stem.

From the center of the group, Niall stepped forward. A crescent-shaped scar arced across his chest, and his left hand rested on the pommel of a broadsword in a thick leather scabbard. Embedded into the pommel beneath his palm shone another gem. He shook his head, his jaw clenched. "We didn't die for nothing."

Then anger flashed in his eyes. "So bloody wake up!"

"Wake up Ciarán," a voice pleaded.

He opened his eyes to see Alais staring back at him. She breathed a relieved sigh and kissed his cheek. The touch of her lips warmed his face.

He was sitting on the deck of Évrard's ship, leaning up against the mast, beneath a star-filled sky. Alais knelt beside him, next to Dónall, who smiled faintly. With a jolt, Ciarán remembered his dream. "I know what happened to Enoch's device," he said weakly.

"Me, too, lad," Dónall replied. "Sit tight and we'll tell everyone."

Dónall left, and here was Khalil, with a bottle of one of Évrard's tawny wines.

"Drink this," he said.

Ciarán did. The wine warmed his throat and chest. He glanced at his arms and legs, now wrapped in bandages. He looked around, and Córdoba was nowhere in sight. "You stayed with us?"

"I killed one of Al-Mansor's men," Khalil replied. "Where else was I to go? Besides, I want to know what happened to Enoch's device."

Ciarán gave a grateful nod. "How long was I out?"

"Two hours, perhaps."

"What happened to the demons?"

"After we left Córdoba, Dónall had the lamp wrapped in sack-cloth and bound it seven times with an iron chain. Then he and

Isaac uttered prayers to God and the angels and cast the lamp into the river, where I saw it disappear beneath the water."

"And Eli?"

Alais' eyes were red from crying. "In the deckhouse," she said. "There was nothing they could do to save him."

Ciarán dropped his head into his hands, wondering if his experience in the glen was more than a dream. Had he stood at the threshold of death's door—a threshold that Eli had crossed forever?

A moment later, Dónall returned with the grief-stricken rabbi. "Now that we're together," Isaac said, "let us pray my family's sacrifice was not in vain. Tell me what happed to the Urim."

"The Book of Enoch gave us the answer," Dónall explained. "The fiery bow and arrow that Enoch sees from the summit was an unmistakable reference to Sagittarius, the prophecy's symbol for Enoch's device. What Enoch saw next was a river of fire, great mountains, the sea, and the storehouse of the winds—each a symbol of the four primal elements: fire, earth, water, and air. But it is also a sequence. Since ancient times, the four elements have been embodied by four fundamental objects: a staff for fire, a stone for earth, a cup for water, and a sword for air. That's when I understood: in each millennium, the device had taken a different form."

Ciarán nodded feebly. His discovery in the Chamber of Enlightenment and his vision in the glen confirmed this.

"In the first millennium," Dónall continued, "the time of Arcanus and Atlantis, the device was a staff, albeit with a jewel embedded in a headpiece shaped as an ankh. By the second millennium, in the time of King David and King Solomon, the device existed in its purist form: as a stone, the symbol of earth. By the next millennium, during its possession by the Zoroastrian magi, it was a golden chalice, taken by the Wise Men, where it likely became known as the Holy Chalice, the cup of Christ."

"But as I said before," Isaac interrupted, "the Urim is a gemstone, not a cup."

"True," Ciarán said. "But what if the gemstone was embedded in the cup's stem? I've seen a chalice thus adorned before."

"Perhaps," the rabbi admitted. "And now?"

"The sequence is complete," Dónall replied. "In this millennium, the Urim is in a sword."

Khalil sipped from the bottle of wine. "Do you have any idea how many swords there are in this world?"

"This is no ordinary sword," Dónall said. "Yet first, we must start with the Holy Chalice, which leads us to the legend of Saint Joseph of Arimathea. Joseph was a Christian who gave his own tomb for the Savior's body after the crucifixion. When he fled the Romans, Joseph took the Holy Chalice and traveled north to the British Isle long before it became Saxon England. In the few historical accounts that exist, the chalice fades into mystery, but there is an oral account among the Celts that Joseph took the chalice to an isle in a lake—an isle called Avalon, and a home of the Fae."

"So we're back to your Fae," Isaac said. "But what of this sword?"

"I'm getting there," Dónall replied. "While there are many tales of cups and cauldrons among the Fae of Avalon, there is only one legendary sword. To the Irish, it was called *Caladbolg*; to the Welsh, *Caledfwlch*. But to the Romanized Britons, it was known as *Excalibur*."

A BREEZE WAFTED off the river, fluttering the sail. Alais took Ciarán's hand.

Dónall went on. "The sword was given by the Fae to Merlin of Britain, a druid of the late fifth century but a powerful ally of the Fae, according to the Book of Maugis. Merlin gave this sword to a Celtic warlord named Arthur, who, for a time, united the kings of Britain against the Saxons. But upon his death, the sword was cast back into the lake, where it remained with the Fae of Avalon."

"The sword and the stone," Ciarán mused.

Dónall nodded. "In legend, it was the sword that was embedded in a stone. But as we know, the truth is sometimes obscured by the legend surrounding it."

"So the Urim may now be embedded in this sword?" Isaac asked. "But where is this Avalon?"

"In the Otherworld," Dónall said with a sigh, "the realm of the Fae. Whether it's possible to find our way there, I don't know. But it's far away, in England. We'll never get there before the prime conflict."

A wave of apprehension churned in Ciarán's gut. Surely they couldn't have failed already. "Why would Maugis send us on a wild-goose chase?" he pressed. "Enoch's device is critical to the prophecy, yet Maugis would have us stumble around looking for some mythical isle lost in the mists of Britain? We must be missing something."

"Does Maugis have any connection to the British Isle?" Khalil asked.

Dónall rubbed his forehead as if he were sifting through the vast trove of knowledge stored in his brain. A moment later, he brightened. "Turpin's diary contained a brief account of Roland and several of the paladins traveling to Britain to find Merlin's tomb."

Ciarán's mind stirred, quickened by Dónall's revelation. "Does Maugis ever mention a sword?"

"He had a sword called *Flamberge*," Dónall replied.

"The name would translate as 'flame blade,'" Khalil added.

"Of course!" Ciarán said. "Get the book."

Dónall shook his head. "There's no mention of the sword in the book."

"It wouldn't be the first time the monks of Reims overlooked something." Ciarán took the Book of Maugis from Dónall and flipped through the pages to the massive hieroglyph of the prophecy. He scanned the outer ring of zodiac symbols and the larger of the heptagrams. Between the heptagram's seven points he found them: seven more astrological symbols. Isaac and Khalil now stood flanking Ciarán, studying them.

"Fierabras," Khalil said.

"The cipher," Ciarán answered. "Can you read the symbols between the points of the heptagram?"

"I know the cipher," Khalil replied, "but the symbols are arranged in a circle. Where to begin?"

"The one nearest Virgo," Ciarán said.

Khalil pointed to each of the symbols, in the order Ciarán directed.

"The first is the sun," he said, "then Mars and Jupiter, Saturn, the moon, and Venus. It ends with Mercury. Now, the letter for the sun is "R." Mars is "O," Jupiter is "S," Saturn is "F", the moon becomes "L," and Venus is the letter "E." Mercury is "U."

"R-O-S-F-L-E-U . . ."Ciarán had gone through them all. Full circle, the sun added another "R." *"Rosefleur!"*

"By Patrick's beard, that's it!" Dónall said.

Isaac looked perplexed. "It's what?"

"It's the home of Orionde," Ciarán explained. "The Fae who tutored Maugis d'Aygremont. He and his companions must have retrieved the sword from Merlin's tomb. The location of the device was hidden in the book all along!" He turned to Dónall. "What did Maugis say about Rosefleur?"

Dónall replied, "*In the heart of Aquitaine lies the gateway to Rosefleur, the house of Orionde, the woman in white, savior of queens.*"

344

Alais' eyes went wide. "The woman in white," she repeated. "The savior of queens . . . *Queen Radegonde.* I've seen this woman before."

Dónall stared at her. "Where?"

"In the Val d'Anglin," she said. "Near a place called Brosse."

"Holy Mother . . ." Ciarán's blood ran cold. To his horror, it all made sense now. "They know."

Isaac's eyes narrowed. "Who?"

"Adémar and Lucien," Ciarán explained. "That's why they wanted the book, because the hieroglyph contained the location of Enoch's device. And we let Lucien see it back at Saint-Bastian's."

Dónall gave a long sigh.

"What is it?" Khalil asked.

Ciarán's heart sank. "Our rival, the bishop, implored Duke William of Aquitaine to take his army to Brosse as the winter snows thaw. We can get there in time, but we'll be heading straight into a war."

PART FIVE

The first angel blew his trumpet, and there came hail and fire, mixed with blood, and they were hurled to the earth . . .

—Revelation 8:7

CHAPTER 46

BLOOD AND SOULS

Tendrils of fog hovered around the castle of Montrésor, clinging to the stone walls like the webs of some monstrous spider. The fog wafted across the rocky spur on which the castle stood, and filled the narrow valley carved by the Indrois River.

From the battlements of the rugged keep, Lucien peered into the torch-lit courtyard crammed with horse lancers and spearmen. The force numbered a full three thousand men at arms, all hungry for battle yet ignorant of the sacrifice that many of them would soon make.

Beside Lucien, Adémar of Blois surveyed the army with grim satisfaction.

"Will they be enough, my lord?" Lucien asked.

"Yes," Adémar replied. "And we shall have my legion as well."

Lucien gulped. The thought of Adémar's legion both excited and terrified him.

Behind them, the tower door swung open. Fulk the Black, clad in a mail hauberk, stepped out onto the battlement. His thick black beard hid his relative youth, and Lucien reminded himself that the count had inherited his title before his seventeenth birthday. Only ten years had passed since his brutally successful reign began. Fulk appeared to be in one of his darker moods.

"Are you certain about this, Adémar?" Fulk asked. "William's army is large, yet you want me to give you six-hundred of my men. I may need them."

Adémar's eyes narrowed. "Are they not worth your absolution? Need I remind you, my lord, that the debt of your sins is *substantial?*"

Fulk winced, and a familiar fear showed in his eyes. At that moment, Lucien knew that Adémar had won, for despite Fulk's legendary cruelty, he remained terrified of hell. Lucien, on the other hand, had grown far more accepting of such a fate, for they would all be consigned to the lake of fire unless the Dragon's forces prevailed.

Adémar drew Fulk into a one-armed embrace. "With this single act, my lord, the debt of your sins can be wiped away. For your men shall do the work of God, reclaiming the most sacred relic in all Christendom: the Holy Chalice of Christ! With it, I shall go to Rome and become pope. And you shall become king of all France."

"And in time?" The count's rapacious personality quickly reasserted itself.

"Why, emperor, I should think. Reuniting Charlemagne's glorious empire under a single banner."

"Yes!" And there was the crafty smile that Lucien had come to expect. "Adémar, I swear by the souls of God that you shall have your men."

Fulk looked out over the courtyard. Drawing his broadsword, he thrust it above his head. "Warriors of Anjou!" his voice boomed, and a hush fell over the crowd. "William of Aquitaine brings his army to Brosse, believing that this time he will taste the victory we have long denied him. He rides with his army, thinking he will find only Guy of Limoges. But instead, *he will find us!*"

A roar erupted from the warriors below. Spears rose, and swords clattered on shields in a great din.

"Angevins!" Fulk yelled. "To war!"

The battle cry resonated through the courtyard. Looking out over his new army, Adémar gave a cold smile.

Lucien felt reassured, for their sorcery would have the potent fuel it required: blood and souls.

CHAPTER 47

THE VALLEY IN THE SHADOW OF DEATH

F ive riders galloped toward Brosse, thundering across roads and meadows muddied by the cold rains that drenched Aquitaine in the first days of March.

Rain soaked the cloak and tunic that Ciarán had worn since losing his habit in Cordoba's Guad al-Quivir. He no longer resembled a monk, for his tonsure had long since grown out, and now his rain-slick hair fell nearly to his shoulders. He rode a piebald colt beside Alais' chestnut mare. Khalil, whose raven-black steed was fastest of the five, led the way, while Dónall, on a roan gelding, and Isaac, on a dapple gray, followed.

Évrard had provided the horses when they reached the seaport of La Rochelle, where they bade farewell to the captain and Josua, still stricken with grief over Eli's death. In the days that passed, Ciarán's sadness over Eli's death had given way to anger, which only drove him to ride harder.

They raced through rugged hill country, with thick woods broken by green pastures, passing farms and villages depleted of food and firewood by Duke William's four thousand spearmen and mounted lancers. They had set off a week ago in the bleak wake of William's army, and by dusk on the third day of March, they

352

reached a tiny village called Bélâbre, where they sheltered at a dilapidated priory dedicated to some obscure saint.

That night, gathered around a crude table in the priory's guesthouse, they supped on stale bread and watered-down wine in the dim glow of a single rushlight. Ciarán was so excited, he could hardly eat.

"How much farther is Brosse," he asked.

"We should be there before nightfall tomorrow," Alais said.

"That's the eve of the prime conflict—not much time to find the gateway to Rosefleur."

Alais sighed. "I never saw a gateway or a tower there."

Isaac set down his hard crust of bread. "Then what will we do?"

"Rosefleur lies in the Otherworld," Dónall said. "There should be some sign of the gateway. In legend, they come in many forms: rings of standing stones, ancient burial mounds, mist-shrouded lakes."

Khalil lowered his cup. "Tell us about this Otherworld."

"To the Celts," Dónall said, "it is the land of the Fae, though it goes by other names. The Northmen call it Álfheimr, and the ancient Greeks called it Elysium, a secret world on the edge of our own. My old friend Thomas described it best. Imagine an oak, he said, where the fullness of its leaves and branches are the world we live in. Its trunk is the center of the earth, and its roots bore into the underworld. But there are the shadowy places in between the leaves and branches. Those places are the Otherworld."

"It sounds like the land of the Jinn," Khalil offered. "In Persian tales, it is a dangerous place, which men should avoid."

"We don't have a choice," Ciarán said.

"I still do not understand how we will ever find such a place," Isaac remarked.

"I wouldn't worry," Khalil said. "This is all Kismet—*fate*. How else do you explain how a poet inspired by Fierabras encountered two monks—in the land of the Moors no less—with a book by Maugis d'Aygremont? You needed the cipher of one to solve the riddle of the other. *Kismet*—that's why we will find it."

"Thomas was the believer in fate," Dónall said.

"Let's hope he was right," Ciarán replied.

Dónall's expression grew dark. "If he is, then by tomorrow we'll stand at the brink of the apocalypse. And may God help us all."

~

THE NEXT DAY, they rode hard, and by twilight, they arrived at a part of the valley where the Anglin River was flanked by wildly overgrown hills damp with rain. The view from this vantage point was chilling. Smoke from hundreds of campfires rose above the valley's tallest hill, above the fortified walls of Castle Brosse.

"My God," Dónall murmured. The fortress capped the rugged hill, which bordered the river and was ringed by streams or moats carved into the hillside's rocky terraces. A winding path, broken by the streams, climbed the hill to the fortress gate and a sheer wall of stone, capped by battlements. Within that wall, at the far end of the fortress, another earthen mound supported an ominous-looking timber keep surrounded by a palisade of standing logs sharpened to spearlike points. In the dim twilight, ravens circled overhead, diving occasionally toward the battlements to feast on things dangling from the walls.

Beside Dónall, Ciarán tried to imagine how such a fortress could ever be taken. For Castle Brosse loomed over the Val d'Anglin like the shadow of death. And within that shadow, between the river-bank and a vast forest that spread east to the valley's edge, sprawled the sea of tents and campfires of William of Aquitaine's army.

Dónall pointed to a small cluster of tents set behind the main encampment. Women tended campfires, and a few monks and nuns in black habits moved about.

"Those women followed their men here," Alais said. "And the monks and nuns are here to care for the wounded."

Dónall studied one of the larger tents near the monks. "An infirmary's my guess. No one will pay much attention to us back there." He drew his cowl over his head. "Let's go."

In the larger encampment, grim-faced horsemen tended their destriers, and spearmen and lancers sat by campfires sharpening their weapons. Some looked as young as fourteen—barely men at all despite their iron helms and mail hauberks. Many bore round shields covered in leather and painted with colorful images of birds or beasts—the devices of the lords who led these men. Similar shields were propped up beside the tents.

Two men trotted their horses around the perimeter of the camp. They wore white cloaks over polished armor, and falcon plumes in their helms.

"Raymond and Dalmas," Alais whispered.

She hid her face behind the hem of her cloak and walked with her eyes down. Ciarán drew his own hood over his head, and they hurried out of Raymond's sight.

As they walked, the smell of horses soon gave way to a far worse stench. Not far ahead were rows of freshly dug graves numbering in the dozens. The stench wafted from the cluster of tents that made up the infirmary. Monks holding cloths over their mouths ducked in and out through the openings. Around open fires, bleak-faced women mended tunics and stirred bubbling pots.

"We should be safe here for the night," Dónall said as they reached the women's camp. "Talk to some of the women," he told Alais. "See if you can find us shelter." She nodded and headed toward a cluster of women, none of whom looked older than sixteen.

Khalil wandered off in search of news about the siege. Meanwhile, Ciarán, Dónall, and Isaac wandered toward the encampment's eastern edge, where a deep forest began just a few hundred yards away.

Nearing the camp's perimeter, Dónall stopped and gazed out at the forest. It stretched as far as the eye could see, dominating the entire eastern side of the valley. It had a feel about it—a certain primeval aura. Perhaps it was the combined effect of the gnarled oaks with their twisting branches and moss-covered trunks, the beeches choked with thorny vines, and the thick carpet of leaves that disappeared within the shadows of the ancient oaks. It was the type of forest that even the most seasoned Irish hunter would be wary venturing into—a place perhaps haunted by leprechauns and goblins and wicked woodland spirits, and surely the home of wolves and wild boars with tusks that could disembowel a man with one fell swipe. Few woodsmen had disturbed the place, for only a scattering of tree stumps marked the forest's edge, which meant the men of Brosse feared these woods enough to take their timber elsewhere.

A breeze soughed through the ancient treetops, and Dónall began to smile. Isaac gave the two Irish monks an uneasy glance.

Ciarán placed a hand on the rabbi's shoulder. "You were worried about finding the gateway," he said. "I'd bet anything it's somewhere in those woods."

KHALIL RETURNED GRIM FACED. "We do not want to stay here long," he said.

They huddled beside a campfire, supping on bowls of porridge that Alais had procured from a group of nuns who hailed from the abbey of Sainte-Croix. The nuns had also found them a tent, abandoned four days ago by a group of women whose men had died in battle. And these men were not the only ones to die, Khalil reported, for William's siege had not gone as planned.

"They did not foresee the treacherousness of that hill," Khalil said. "The duke sent men with a ram to batter down the gate, but they never gained their footing, and were slaughtered by defenders on the wall, who rained arrows and stones and boiling oil upon them. The duke lost forty men in that first attempt—their bodies now hang from the walls, feeding the ravens.

"Next he tried to mine into the hillside and sap the walls to collapse them. But the hill is solid rock, so his miners went nowhere. Meanwhile, the viscount of Limoges sends skirmishers from the fortress. They kill only a few of the duke's men at a time, but they are slowly filling those graves." Khalil nodded toward the mounds of earth near the infirmary. "Were that not bad enough, a sickness has spread within the camp. Men's bowels run like water. They are succumbing to dehydration and filling the infirmary's beds and not a few of the graves. Hence this fine stench."

"What does William plan to do?" Alais asked, looking pale.

"There is a cleric here who apparently whispers in the duke's ear," Khalil said, "assuring him that God will reward him with victory. So he plans to stay here and starve the defenders out. His men have burned every farm and field to the south and east, but some fear that the fortress could hold six months' worth of food. The duke also has a siege engine like one of the old Roman catapults. They have tried slinging stones at the curtain wall, but I understand it did little good. So instead, they lob the carcasses of dead horses and cattle, hoping to spread disease within the fortress. Or they catapult bales of burning hay to set fire to the defenders' grain stores. But to prevent that, all they need inside the fortress is a good well and some buckets. The duke has dispatched men to build two more of these siege engines, but who knows when they will be ready? So for now he bides his time, like Agamemnon waiting forever outside the walls of Troy."

"This cleric who whispers in the duke's ear," Dónall said, "did you see him?"

Khalil took another sip of watery porridge and grimaced. "He wears the black habit of a Christian monk and is as fat as a hog ready for slaughter."

"Ah," Dónall quipped. "That would be the good Prior Bernard."

"Have you seen a cleric in bishop's robes?" Ciarán asked. Beside him, Alais stiffened.

Khalil thought for a moment. "No," he finally said.

"William shouldn't have come here," Alais muttered.

"No," Ciarán replied. "You can be sure Adémar of Blois goaded him into it."

"So you think it's a trap?" she asked.

Ciarán glanced at the sky, where a sliver of a moon had emerged over the hills. Just below the horizon and soon to shine over Brosse, Scorpio and Sagittarius waited.

"I don't know," he told her, "but I don't like the timing of it one bit."

AFTER SUPPER, they tried to sleep. From the main encampment came the songs of men drinking wine to numb their pain and summon the courage needed for battle. Embers in the campfire crackled, and in the forest, a lone wolf howled. Alais nestled against Ciarán. He found himself yearning for her, yet he knew that even if he abandoned his vows and forsook the life of an Irish monk, he and Alais could never be together like a common man and wife. For their fate seemed headed along a different path.

In time, Ciarán's eyes grew heavy and his restless mind surrendered to uneasy dreams. He didn't know how long he slept, but he woke suddenly when the men outside started screaming.

CHAPTER 48

WAR AND BLOODSHED

O utside the tent, wolflike howls mixed with the screams of men. Ciarán scrambled to his knees, his mind racing. Alais grabbed his shoulder. "What's happening?"

Khalil gripped the hilt of his scimitar. "Another skirmish," he said, bolting from the tent. Ciarán hurried after him into the foul-smelling air. Above him, stars shone in the night sky.

The clamor came from the western edge of the encampment, near the riverbank, where glowing flames engulfed two of the tents. A band of warriors, howling like wolves, hurled firebrands into tents and engaged the loose muster of spearmen who hurried to protect the camp. Panicked horses whinnied. Spearmen rushed into the fray, raising their shields and rallying the camp as their comrades, surprised by the initial attack, lay wounded and moaning on the ground wet with dew.

From the surrounding tents scurried women and monks, crying out at the sight of the conflict scarcely forty yards away. Another firebrand streaked through the sky, and several monks crossed themselves, muttering prayers. Alais hurried next to Ciarán, followed by Dónall and Isaac. The rabbi bore the befuddled look of a man woken from a deep sleep.

"They came up the riverbank," Ciarán told Dónall.

Ahead, the skirmishers hurled axes and spears into the growing wave of William's spearmen. One of William's white-cloaked lords charged toward the black-garbed raiders, who cast their remaining firebrands before making a fast retreat down the riverbank. Breaking ranks, the spearmen pursued them. In the main encampment, men tore down the burning tents, trying to stop the spread of the flames.

"Look!" Alais cried.

Atop the hill, the battlements of Castle Brosse suddenly ignited.

"Holy mother," Ciarán said under his breath.

Rows of torches bathed the fortress in a hellish glow, illuminating the warriors assembled on the walls, and the corpses of William's dead dangling in a ghoulish fringe below. The warriors beat their swords against shields in a thunderous din. Then a crease of light appeared down the center of the castle's gate, and a great roar resounded from the walls. The gates opened, unveiling an army of warriors who shook torches and shields, howling like beasts. They mocked the spearmen, who pursued the skirmishers fleeing toward the castle.

"This is bad," Isaac said.

Khalil nodded. "They are welcoming an attack."

The drumming from the castle grew louder. Stone-faced, Dónall seemed lost in his own thoughts until, behind them, one of the women gave a panicked scream.

Ciarán whirled to his right as a firebrand streaked overhead to land on a nearby tent, setting it ablaze. From the riverbank charged a half-dozen men, shrieking like madmen, their dark cloaks stuck with leaves and mud, their bearded faces contorted with drunken rage. The women scattered, and monks hurried toward the infirmary as two flaming brands fell on its main tent. The cloth ignited, and panicked cries rose from within.

"Into the forest!" Dónall cried, gripping his leaf-shaped blade.

Ciarán took Alais' arm, but she stood frozen. One of the skirmishers charged toward her, eyes burning with carnal fire, and waving a sword above his head. In three strides, he was on them.

Ciarán pushed Alais behind him and stood between her and the attacker's blade, raising his arms as if he could somehow ward off the blow.

"Ciarán!" Alais screamed.

Instinctively he closed his eyes, and for an instant he felt as if he were back in Derry, about to join his fallen brethren. But his attacker's howling cry suddenly became a choking gasp, for Khalil had reached the attacker first. A fount of blood jetted out from the man's throat, darkening his beard as he dropped his blade and tried in vain to stanch the flow. Khalil nodded to Ciarán, who nodded back, still stunned. Alais tugged urgently at his arm as the remaining attackers beheld their fallen comrade. Their eyes filled with hate, and on they came.

Ciarán felt the sizzle in the air, and the sudden wind whipping the hem of his cloak an instant before the ghostly blue flames wreathed the treetops at the river's edge. The skirmishers did not realize what was happening until it was on them. A ferocious gust tore the flaming tents from their stakes and sent a curtain of fire onto the charging men. Their dark cloaks exploded into flame, and their lupine howling soon turned to horrified screams.

Dónall stood defiantly against them, making a circle with his leaf-shape blade, and the wind whipped the flames up into an inferno.

Behind them, men were shouting. Ciarán spun around. At the edge of the main camp, a group of spearmen looked on. Duke William, wearing a hastily donned hauberk, was among them. By his side, Lord Raymond tried to pull the duke toward the front of the camp, but William just stood there, staring aghast at the raging fire. In the glow of the flames, his handsome face looked pale and frightened, like that of a lost child stunned by the chaos all around him.

"William!" Alais screamed. "Pull your men back! It's a trap!"

"Alais?" William gasped, but did not move.

"My lord," Ciarán yelled, "listen to her. More is afoot than you suppose!"

A corpulent man in a black habit pushed his way through the

crowd of spearmen. It was Prior Bernard, wearing a crazed look. "The witch!" he bellowed. "Ignore her lies, my lord! You must fight. God favors the victor!"

Dónall tugged Alais back and grabbed Ciarán by his cloak. "Let's go," he said, glancing to the sky. "We're out of time."

Ciarán looked up. In the blackness glittered the constellations of Scorpio and Sagittarius, and between them blazed a reddish star. For Mars ruled the night.

SMOKE from the burning tents wafted through the camp like an acrid fog. Ciarán glanced back at the main encampment, where William's spearmen mustered in the broad field between the encampment and the fortress. From the battlements of Castle Brosse, swords drummed on shields, and the taunting howls grew to a fierce roar.

Ciarán grabbed a still-burning firebrand and followed Khalil, who held another. Dónall led the way to the forest's edge, Isaac struggling to match his stride.

Ahead, the treetops at the forest's edge reached out over the grassy field like the grasping claws of some wild beast, while the arcing limbs of the massive oaks formed shadowy corridors into the forest's hidden depths. Dónall chose the nearest opening: a wide seam between two oaks whose trunks were covered in a web of twisting brambles. The wind whistled faintly through the gaps between the beeches and oaks, as if the forest itself were breathing.

Khalil stepped first into the seam. His torch illuminated a chaotic maze of tree trunks and brambles and a deep carpet of dead leaves. Toadstools and mushrooms of every shape and size sprouted from the huge gnarled roots, and overhead, moss hung like cobwebs from the branches, obscuring any glimpse of the night sky and making the place seem more cavern than woodland. From the forest's depths, leaves rustled as something beat a hasty retreat from the torch's glow.

Dónall glanced warily at Khalil and then followed him into the forest. Isaac went next. Behind him, Alais hesitated.

"It'll be all right," Ciarán said, although the feeling in the pit of his stomach suggested otherwise.

He took her hand and slipped sideways between the massive roots bracketing the seam. Breathing in the thick smell of damp earth and dead leaves, he was reminded of Derry's grove, but there was something far more ancient and primeval in these woods.

Dónall and Khalil led them, stepping over moss-cloaked roots and wending their way ever deeper through the gnarled pathways between the trees. The crunch of leaves beneath their feet made it difficult to tell what else moved in the forest, though things certainly did. An owl's low "*Who? Who?*" above them made Ciarán jump, putting his nerves further on edge. Looking for any sign of wolf or boar, he saw only the shadows that shifted and danced with every movement of his torch, though he felt as if hundreds of eyes peered out at him from the gloom. He tried to shake the feeling, telling himself it was just the way the flickering torchlight moved over the vine-covered trunks, but then a twig would snap or a branch would rustle in the darkness, and his anxious imagination was off and running again. Beside him, Alais gasped and squeezed his arm at every strange sound and whisper of the breeze that stirred the moss dripping from the branches in their path.

The deeper they traveled into the forest, the more Ciarán began to wonder whether they would ever find their way out. He could still hear the drumming of swords on shields on the battlements of Castle Brosse, but the sound grew fainter with every new turn through the maze of trees. Sometimes it all felt like too much—that he and his ragtag band of visionaries were laughably unequal to the task before them.

~

SOON THE FAINT light of dawn began to penetrate the treetops. In the distance, a war horn sounded. Alais looked to Ciarán and Khalil for answers.

"The battle has begun," Khalil told her.

Her eyes welled with tears. "Then William stayed to fight."

Ahead of them, Dónall had stopped. "Look," he said. Beyond the next line of trees, a curtain of mist obscured everything. "See how the mist doesn't seep past those trees? It just hangs there, like a barrier. Nothing natural about it. If I'm not mistaken, that's our gateway."

"*This?*" Khalil asked skeptically. He passed his hand through the gray shroud. "It's just a fog bank," he said. Then he stepped through a gap between two trees.

"No!" Dónall shouted, grabbing Khalil by the arm and yanking him back. "Don't be a fool!"

Khalil flashed an angry stare, but Dónall pointed to the base of the trees just beyond the misty verge. "Do you want to end up like *them?*"

Amid the mist, what looked at first like moss-covered tree stumps or fallen limbs now appeared as skeletons, hunched over and clinging desperately to the trees and massive roots. Green moss covered every inch of bone, and freckled orange toadstools sprouted between the fingers and toes. The skeletons lay everywhere beyond the misty border, their hollow eyes and gaping mouths a grim, silent testament to their fate.

Khalil recoiled, and Ciarán realized that it was the first time he had seen fear in the Persian's eyes.

"Turpin said the gateways to the Otherworld can be disastrous for men who do not know the proper way to enter them," Dónall said. "You might have wandered through the mist forever, lost until you met the same fate."

Ciarán glanced at the moss-laden bones and shook his head. "What *is* the right way to enter?"

Dónall frowned and rubbed his beard. "Turpin never was too clear on that point. Thomas and I always figured we'd solve that problem when we came to it."

"And now we have," Khalil said, having regained his composure. "Do you have any bright ideas?"

"Not yet," Dónall grumbled.

"What about the light?" Isaac said. "Is that not how you discovered the secrets of Maugis' book, which set you on this path? It would seem that the light should show us the right path through the mist." He held out his hand. "May I?"

Ciarán knew that Isaac was keen on Dónall's crystal, for the old rabbi had mastered many of Maugis' secrets during their voyage from Spain, perhaps through his knowledge of Jewish mysticism.

Dónall looked back at the mist, then handed Isaac the crystal. "Let's hope you're right."

Isaac cupped the crystal in his hands, closing his eyes, then blew softly on it and murmured the Fae incantation: "*Eoh.*"

White light blazed from his palms. Holding the crystal, he extended his right hand into the barrier, and the mist parted before him, forming a clear path through the trees.

"Patrick's beard!" Dónall whispered. "Lead the way, my friend."

Isaac stepped onto the path, and as he moved his hand, the breach in the mist shifted slightly, though staying true toward a gap between the trees. The mist now formed a wall on each side of the path, faintly obscuring the moss-covered bones that blended in with the tree trunks and sprawling roots.

Isaac led the way, followed by Dónall and then Khalil, his right hand resting on the pommel of his sword, while Ciarán and Alais took up the rear. As they moved in single file, Alais glanced fearfully at the bones so near her feet.

As they walked, Ciarán glanced behind him. With each step, the pathway they had traversed the moment before filled in with mist and was gone. As Isaac moved, so did the path, winding through the ever-twisting maze of trees. In the beginning, the only sound on the path was the soft crunch of forest duff beneath their feet, but as they traveled deeper into the mist a new sound emerged. At first, it was a faint beating, and Ciarán wondered whether they had turned back toward the valley and were once more hearing the drumming from the walls of Castle Brosse. But this sound was different— sudden and without any discernible rhythm. As they ventured farther, the sound grew louder, like random muffled thunderclaps.

"I see a clearing up ahead," Isaac said.

In the faint light that spilled through the trees, the gray mist faded to a reddish haze as it neared the ground. At the edge of the trees, the air grew bitterly cold. Then another low, booming explosion shook the ground. Isaac stopped dead in his tracks, and the light in his palm dimmed. Dónall reached for the sword sheathed beneath his habit. Khalil glanced back at Ciarán, and seeing the Persian's look of alarm, Ciarán rushed forward to see what was happening. When he arrived at Dónall's side, his jaw fell slack.

"Holy Mother of God," he muttered, struggling to comprehend all that he beheld.

For at the forest's edge, they gazed upon an alien land: a vast plain of reddish clay, smoothed by the wind and strewn with narrow fissures so that the ground appeared made of geometric plates. The rock features reminded him of the Giant's Causeway back in Northern Ireland, only perfectly flat and somehow strangely grim. In the center of the plain stood a spire that seemed hewn of a single piece of reddish stone. Rising more than two hundred feet, it was carved with what appeared to be windows and balconies, suggesting it was the work of some craftsman instead of a natural phenomenon. But the strangeness of the landscape was not the cause of Ciarán's alarm. For behind the spire billowed a broad column of smoke, forming a swirling vortex over the plain, and around the spire amassed a besieging army conjured from the darkest Enochian myth.

Hundreds of mail-clad Franks with shields and spears made up most of this army, but more than three score were gigantic warriors a full head taller than the Franks and thickly muscled, with skin the color of bleached bone. Their heads were shaven, although a few had beards, and all wore armor from some ancient time, with iron breastplates, and carried spears as long as a ship's oar.

"Nephilim," Isaac said softly. "As in my dream."

"They must dwell now in the Otherworld," Dónall said. "Gog and Magog."

Ciarán gazed in horrified awe at the pale giants halfway across the plain—and at the massive beasts beside them. For amid the besieging army were five enormous wheeled carts, pulled by long-horned aurochs larger than any bull. The carts carried great iron beasts, barrel-shaped, with stout necks ending in dragonlike heads with gaping maws. Smoke rose from their mouths and nostrils, lacing the air with the stench of brimstone.

Suddenly, one of the beasts belched a stream of fire, accompanied by a thunderous roar. Ciarán covered his ears as the fiery vomit blasted against the side of the spire, shattering rock into fragments and leaving a smoking divot in its side. A myriad of similar wounds pocked the spire in other places.

"The tower," Ciarán said. "They will destroy Rosefleur."

Khalil stared hopelessly into the reddish plain. "They have already destroyed its defenders."

Eighty yards ahead, the carcasses of white and gray chargers lay in heaps—so many dead, it seemed a small cavalry had met its end. And the riders, too, for near the horses sprawled crumpled bodies clad in silvery mail. Tendrils of smoke wafted up from the fallen riders, who numbered a score or more. In their midst, spears jutted from the bodies of hundreds of men, their round shields laying beside them. Other men, still living, traipsed through the field, stabbing any horse or silver-clad rider who showed signs of life.

"Is there anyone left?" Ciarán asked, beginning to comprehend what had happened.

Isaac was shaking as he peered through the crystal. "Many of those are not normal men," he said grimly. "They are possessed. I can see the demon forms clinging to their flesh. Dozens more of them, *ruhin*, rule the sky, circling within those clouds. This is very bad, and whatever is happening behind that tower is worse. That smoke is red like fire, gathering in the sky above as if it is feeding the *ruhin*."

"Those riders . . ." Alais pointed but twenty yards from where they stood, where one of the mail-clad figures sprawled dead on the red plain. Where its armor was not streaked with blood, it shone like polished silver. It was mail, not of chain but of scales, like silver feathers that fit snug against the rider's lithe form. Beneath its plumed helm, the flesh of the rider's female face was in a state of rapid decay. Particles wafted like dusty smoke from the rider's skull, revealing the origins of the wispy strands rising from the field.

"Are they the Fae?" Alais managed to ask.

Dónall shook his head sadly. "They *were*." He ran a hand nervously across his face. "It's everything Remi and Thomas feared, everything the prophecy had warned of. We're too late."

"But the device?" Ciarán asked, alarmed by the despair in Dónall's voice.

"You'll never get inside that tower," Khalil muttered.

Behind them, something moved in the forest. Khalil snapped alert and drew his curved blade.

A spear shaft appeared through the thick growth, and Khalil readied to meet this new threat. Brushing past the low-hanging tree branches, a figure emerged, and Ciarán wondered for an instant whether he gazed upon one of the Tuatha Dé Danann or, perhaps, a Valkyrie of Norse myth. For the slender figure, clad in a tight-fitting hauberk of scaled mail stained red with blood, had long copper tresses and a face as beautiful and pure as any he could imagine. As she opened her lips to speak, her eyes were wide and pleading.

"Who among you is the champion?"

CHAPTER 49

THIS IS OUR PURGATORY

Ciarán had not expected to hear those words. In the red plain beyond the trees, the iron beasts unleashed another booming roar, belching their fire at the walls of Rosefleur and filling the air with brimstone.

The warrior woman eyed them carefully. She held a hand over her abdomen, where blood seeped from a gash in her mail.

"You're hurt," Ciarán said.

"It is no matter now," she said. "I must know: who among you is the champion?"

Dónall stepped forward, his despair from a moment ago having given way to awe. He gestured toward Alais, barely taking his eyes off the woman standing before them. "She is the one descended from Charlemagne."

Ciarán turned to Alais and said, "You don't have to do this."

She looked into his eyes and nodded, then turned to the woman in mail. "It's true."

"If you are the champion," the woman said, "then you must come with me."

Alais nodded solemnly. "I'm going with her," Ciarán insisted.

The woman flashed him a curious look. "The choice is yours, but we must hurry, for there is little time."

"First," Khalil demanded, having lowered his blade, "who are you? And where are we?"

"I am Una of the Fae," she said, "and this is our purgatory, the realm where we have lived since before the Deluge, when we were forbidden to return to our true home."

Isaac, who had been listening in rapt silence, found his voice at last and said, "What is happening?"

"Before dawn," she said, "the Nephilim sailed up the river Lethe with their engines of war to lay siege to Rosefleur. They are led by a Nephilim prince of the Dragon's line, who gathered his own army of Franks from your world. From beyond the forest wall, he led this second army through the misty gate and then poisoned them with the breath of the demons who rule the sky overhead. Human sorcerers aid the ultimate purpose of this attack. For the Dragon's bonds are weakening, and they seek to draw him from his prison to this realm."

Dónall's expression turned grim. "What sorcerers?"

"Men willing to sacrifice their souls for answers to mysteries they were never meant to know. They have made a death pit behind the tower, and there they feed its magic with sacrifices of blood. That smoke," Una said, tilting her spear toward the billowing column behind the spire, "rises from the underworld. Soon the Dragon shall come, and nothing here can stand against him."

Ciarán felt queasy. "What about Enoch's device?"

"That is why we must ride," Una said. "To save it."

Overhead, the smoke swirled over Rosefleur and threatened to blot out the faint sunlight that penetrated through the blackening sky. She glanced at Dónall and the leaf-shaped blade in his hand. "You can use the power?"

"Yes," he replied.

"Can you slow their sorcery?" she asked.

Resolve settled in Dónall's brow. "Lucien was a brother of mine at Reims, and those sorcerers are his men. We're due for a reckoning."

Isaac placed a hand on Dónall's arm. "You will not go alone, my friend." Dónall smiled faintly. Then Isaac turned to Khalil and said, "We could use your sword."

Khalil drew a deep breath and nodded to Dónall. "I will follow your lead." He looked to Una. "But how will we ever cross that plain?"

"Travel along the forest's edge. The Nephilim and their men will not be watching you. And we can provide ample distraction."

Una whistled a long, melodic note. From the forest came a loud rustling of foliage as two pale mares emerged from the trees. Both were well-muscled chargers, each with a saddle and bridle. Una mounted the first charger.

"You two," she told Ciarán and Alais, "ride close, and do not stray."

Ciarán swung up into the second mare's saddle, then helped Alais up behind him. As soon as they had mounted, Una turned toward Dónall, Isaac, and Khalil.

"You fight today to save your world. Go now, and Godspeed."

Dónall nodded grimly as Una raised her spear and kicked her charger's flanks. Ciarán gave his horse rein, and the powerful animal bolted after her. He felt the exhilaration of the charge, only to realize a moment later that he had not given a parting glance to Dónall or the others. Yet by then it was too late, for Una was riding like the wind across the red plain, and an army of the apocalypse stood before them.

FIVE HUNDRED YARDS across the plain loomed Rosefleur. Ciarán's charger darted through the carnage of men and horses and the decaying bodies of Una's fallen sisters, whose remains wafted up into the air like windblown dust. For an instant, he wondered what had happened to these women, for their wounds on the battlefield looked no different from those on the hundreds of Franks who also lay dead and bleeding on the plain, yet the flesh and bone of these warrior maidens was decomposing so fast that soon only their scaled silver armor would remain. He had no time to ponder this thought, however, for the mail-clad spearmen ahead had seen them, and more than a score of Franks rallied for an attack, raising their spears and painted shields and howling crazed battle cries.

Una hurled her spear at one of the black-bearded men, hitting him dead center. The impact knocked him ten yards back, leaving him impaled along with the scores of dead littering the plain. The other men rushed at her like a pack of wild dogs. She whipped a long sword from her scabbard and sounded her own battle cry: a shrill, unearthly sound that chilled Ciarán's blood and cut through even the booming of the iron beasts . . . and that heralded a slaughter.

The head of the first man to meet her blade tumbled through the air, hitting the dusty plain while his body rode on for another dozen paces before pitching sideways from the saddle. With merciless precision, Una cut a swath through the raving Franks, cleaving through mail and bone and flesh. Others fell under her charger's hooves, and soon only a few remained on the fringe of what had been a wedge of attackers.

Ciarán spurred his mount into the breach Una had formed. Behind him, Alais clung on tightly as the surviving Franks charged. Wild eyed, they foamed at the mouth and cursed in some unknown tongue. But the charger was too fast and too strong for them, and it burst through the ragged wall of men, trampling the first warrior in its path. In another heartbeat, it was again behind Una, racing toward Rosefleur.

More Franks poured across the red plain, but on foot they moved too slowly to reach the swift chargers. Ciarán's nerves tensed, however, at the sight of what they now approached. It was a gap, little more than fifty yards wide, between two of the iron beasts and their gigantic carts with massive wheels. The beasts did not move but, rather, kept their gaping iron maws pointed at Rosefleur, and as his mount drew him closer, Ciarán suspected that they were not beasts at all, but monstrous siege engines of some Byzantine design, spewing Greek fire. Yet the iron beasts were not the problem. For in the gap, the Nephilim massed.

There were ten of them, each at least seven feet tall and garbed in an ancient style of armor, with iron breastplates, broad shields, and helms with cross-like openings for the eyes and mouth, like the images of Ares or Hector that Ciarán had seen decorating the pages of Greek tomes. The Nephilim moved with colossal strides, and what flesh showed beneath their armor was as white as bone. They gripped massive war clubs—all but one, who held a sword long enough to cleave a horse in two. The gap was wide enough, but the speed at which the charger moved caused Ciarán to sit low in the saddle and hug the horse's sides with his calves. On the back of his neck, he felt Alais' breath.

"Follow to my left," Una called over her shoulder. Then suddenly, she broke left, heading toward the iron beast. Ciarán's charger veered to follow her. The Nephilim amassed in the center of the gap, but Una raced for the edge.

The nearest giant moved swiftly to block her path, but Una raised her sword, unleashing another shrill battle cry, and charged. The giant's blood arced through the air as her sword lopped off its arm. Ciarán never slowed his mount, though his jaw fell in horror as the sword-wielding giant closed on Una and chopped her mare to the ground. She leaped from its saddle, swinging at her nearest attacker and hewing halfway through its neck.

Ciarán rode on. The iron beast boomed behind him, and his ears throbbed in pain. A fiery blast arced overhead, raining a shower of burning embers from the sky. An ember seared his arm, and Alais brushed another from her shoulder. An instant later, some eighty feet above them, the walls of Rosefleur shuddered, spilling rubble from the smoking divot in the cylindrical wall.

Then, behind them, Una screamed.

Alais gasped, and Ciarán glanced over his shoulder. The six remaining giants surrounded where Una had stood, hammering downward with their clubs. Ciarán felt a pang of grief for the brave woman warrior, then looked ahead to a new horror, for the charger was galloping straight toward the walls of Rosefleur. In the urgency of their ride, Ciarán had never thought to look for a gate, trusting that Una knew where to find it. Yet now the mare was running headlong toward a face of sheer red stone. He jerked on the reins, and the charger slowed, but the Nephilim had broken from their kill and now came rushing toward him.

Alais tugged hard on his shoulder. "Look!" she cried, pointing to the walls. Where the wall had seemed solid an instant before, the outlines of a portal began to define themselves. A seam appeared and slowly parted. Ciarán kicked his mount. The Nephilim were but twenty yards away as the mare charged toward the widening breach. The giants raced toward them, but with a leap, the mare crossed the threshold.

In that instant, a blinding light engulfed them, as if the mare had leaped straight into the sun. Ciarán dropped the reins to shield his eyes. Then, with a loud slam, the gateway closed behind them.

FOR A MOMENT, Ciarán thought that perhaps he had been struck blind. But then the brilliance began to fade, and he perceived the outline of a figure slowly coming into view. As the light continued to wane, the figure's shape grew clearer. It was a woman, taller than most men, yet slender. A white cloak draped her shoulder, falling onto a mail shirt that seemed sewn of silvery feathers and clung to her lithe torso. The woman gazed at them with piercing eyes in a sculpted face framed by flowing hair the color of platinum.

Alais stared in awe at the woman. "Orionde?"

"Yes, child," the woman said. "You remember me?"

Alais stammered, "In the field of wheat . . ."

Ciarán touched Alais' hand. Could this be the same woman in white Isaac had seen in his dream? Surely it must be. Yet, if this was indeed Orionde, the Fae who instructed Maugis d'Aygremont, she was more than two hundred years old—and even older still, for the Fae were timeless, like the angels themselves.

Orionde was not alone. A half-dozen Fae, all warrior maidens dressed as Una had been, stood behind her in a vast torch-lit hall encircled by towering archways of reddish stone. Behind the Fae, in the spaces beyond the archways, were horses, all of them pale like

Ciarán's charger. Piles of rubble dotted the floor beneath gaps where portions of the ceiling, thirty feet above, had collapsed into the hall.

Ciarán regarded the Fae with awe, before realizing that he still sat astride the charger. Quickly, he eased Alais down from the mare's back and then dismounted from the saddle. He started to bow, when another thunderous boom came, and more reddish debris spilled from the ceiling to the floor.

Orionde looked to Ciarán and said, "We must hurry. These walls will not hold much longer. The moment of the prime conflict is nearly upon us. You must come with me and take Enoch's device. It will be safe only in your world."

"But I am not the champion," he said. "I'm not of Charlemagne's blood."

"There is no bloodline," Orionde replied. "That has long been an error in human understanding. Rather, the mystery of Enoch's device is revealed only to those who have deciphered its inherent truth and ancient purpose—those who can see the beckoning light. The champion is the one who answers that call."

Ciarán stood stunned. For an instant, he struggled to grasp this reality, but then it settled within him like the stillness of a deep lake. Whether Kismet or fate, events had guided him to this point, and, strangely, he felt ready.

"Then it's not me?" Alais asked in a relieved tone.

"You have made your choice and have yet another role to play," Orionde said. "But not now." She gestured to Ciarán. "Follow me."

He looked at Alais, relieved that she was free of this burden and the danger that he knew would come with it. She put a hand on his shoulder. "Be brave," she whispered. "And be careful." He touched her fingers and then turned to follow Orionde.

The archway she had entered led to a stairway of reddish stone that ascended the curve of the tower. They climbed nearly fifty feet past candle lamps set into narrow sconces along the wall, until they reached an iron-bound door. Orionde pushed it open to reveal a chamber, round like the tower and lit with more candle lamps. The candlelight gleamed off coats of silver mail draped on racks along the room's perimeter, and behind these hung shields, flanked by spears like the one Una had held. The shields were polished to a mirror finish that reflected the candlelight, which blazed through the armory, for that was what this place must be. Orionde moved swiftly toward a tall archway across the chamber, where the stairwell resumed its spiral ascent up the tower.

"Did you know this attack was coming?" Ciarán asked Orionde as he tried to keep pace with her long strides.

"We assumed the Nephilim would eventually learn where Maugis had hidden the device, but I had hoped you would arrive here first."

"But if you wanted us to come, why didn't you help us get here?"

She paused for a moment and looked back at him. "I did what I could. But in the end, you had to find your own path. It was the only way you would be ready."

"For what?" Ciarán pressed.

"To fulfill your purpose," she said as she marched up the stairwell. "The prophecy in the stars is told through twelve signs in three groups, with each group representing a stage in the life cycle of the prophecy. We are at the birth of this cycle, the time of the prime conflict, when the champion of men must unite with the device—the weapon—and prevail in the initial battle with a champion of the Dragon's line. Beyond the prime conflict, a great journey lies ahead, like the stage of life after birth. But first, you and the weapon must survive this present battle, or all will be lost."

Everything she had said, Ciarán realized, was what Remi had theorized. *And now it was happening.* As this understanding sank in, a deafening boom split the air, and the stairwell shook like the deck of a ship in a storm.

"We must hurry!" Orionde demanded. Her pace quickened, and Ciarán found himself struggling to keep up. Every forty steps, the staircase reached a landing with an iron-bound door set into the interior wall, before continuing up Rosefleur. Ciarán counted five doors as he did his best to keep up with Orionde. His legs began to ache, and his heart drummed in his chest. The higher they climbed, the more debris littered the stairwell, and cracks ran down the walls like spidery veins. Ciarán glanced warily at the cracks and then noticed that the stairwell ended about twenty feet up ahead, blocked by one more iron-bound door.

Just then, another boom shook the walls, and Ciarán stumbled forward, catching himself just before his head could smash against the stone steps. As the quaking subsided, a smoky haze began to seep from under the door ahead, and the stench of brimstone flooded the stairwell. Then a ghastly sound resonated from beyond the door, like a legion of banshees squealing in triumph.

Orionde looked grave. "The Nephilim engines have breached the tower's walls," she said. "The demons have found their way through."

"Demons . . . ?" Ciarán's heart sunk. Behind her, the door began to shake, as if something were trying to batter it down.

"We counted more than a hundred circling above the tower."

"What will we do?" he asked, alarmed.

Orionde shook her head gently. "I'm afraid the prophecy comes with a few rules. And one of them is that only the champion can take Enoch's device."

Ciarán's mouth fell open, while the door at the top of the stairwell clattered as if it would burst from its hinges.

Orionde glanced at the door, then back at Ciarán. "Which means," she said, "that you must fight your way through them —alone."

CHAPTER 50
SANCTUM SANCTORUM

"How will we stop them?" Isaac asked.

Dónall grimaced. "I'm working on it," he said.

They stood at the base of a broad oak festooned with moss and ringed by toadstools, while overhead a canopy of tangled branches blocked out the sky. A curtain of cold mist surrounded the forest's edge, stopping abruptly where it met the barren red plain. Isaac peeked out of the foliage and looked across the plain to the east, where giant warriors gathered around one of the iron war beasts that spewed fire at the walls of Rosefleur.

"Look at them," Isaac said in awe. "Hebrew scholars believe the Israelites killed all the Nephilim that survived the Great Flood—including Goliath, who was among the last. But clearly they were wrong."

Dónall rubbed his chin. "Some of them had to survive. It explains the Formorian giants of Irish myth, and the frost giants of the Norse. And if Enoch was right, the Nephilim have angelic blood, so perhaps they're immortal or live extra-long lives, but for centuries they've hidden in the shadows of the Otherworld."

"And now they serve the Dragon."

"Just as John of Patmos wrote in the book of Revelation,"

Dónall said. "When the Dragon is released from his prison, he shall gather the armies of Gog and Magog for battle. It's all coming true." Dónall looked up the trunk of the tall oak beside them. He could no longer see Khalil, who was lost in the leafy branches. "Have you reached the top?"

"Yes," Khalil called down.

"What can you see?" Isaac asked.

"It does not look good," Khalil said. "Across this plain is a river, where I count five ships lined with oars, and five barges, which they must have used to transport those iron beasts. Between the river and the tower is a huge pit, about four hundred yards from here. It glows as if some great fire burns deep inside it, and that is the source of the smoke that gathers in the sky. Around the pit are black-robed men, twenty or more. But with them are at least three of these pale giants, and one of them looks like a priest performing some type of ritual. There is also a large cattle pen filled with scores of men—Franks, like those on this battlefield. Yet I am afraid that these men are in no shape to fight, for they are being slaughtered one by one and cast into the pit."

Isaac's eyes narrowed. "Human sacrifice, then."

Dónall shook his head. *My God, Lucien, is this what you've become?* He called back up to Khalil. "Have they posted sentries around the pit?"

"None that I can see," Khalil replied. "They seem intent on this ritual."

"How far is the pit from the forest's edge?" Dónall asked.

"No more than forty yards, at best."

"Good, then they won't see us coming." Dónall waited until Khalil climbed down the tree, and then explained his plan. Then, turning toward the smoke billowing from the underworld, he said, "It's time to end this."

ATOP THE NARROW stairwell inside Rosefleur, the iron-bound door shook violently on its hinges, and black smoke seeped under the crack between the door and the stone floor. Ciarán stared slack-jawed at the door, knowing what was behind it. *More than a hundred demons,* Orionde had said.

"How am I supposed to fight my way through them?" he asked her.

"Beyond this door is a circular hall," she said. "In the center of the hall is our sanctum sanctorum, sealed with another door. You will recognize it. Beyond that door is Enoch's device. When you see it, remember the form it takes in this millennium, and seize it. As for the demons, there are many of them, but they are incorporeal, so their greatest weapon is possession."

A shuddering chill ran down Ciarán's spine as he recalled the terror in the amphitheater outside Poitiers. "What can I possibly do to prevent that?"

"Steel your thoughts," she told him sternly. "Focus your mind on something dear to you—an emotion so deep it will become an iron wall against the demons' attack."

Ciarán thought of Alais, but then a new fear invaded his mind. *If I fail, what happens to her?* He could not think of her, he decided; the thought felt too fragile. He thought harder and, after a few moments, focused his mind on Derry. On Niall, Murchad and Fintan, and Bran and the twins. On the brothers who fought so bravely to save Dónall and Ciarán from Bishop Adémar.

From behind the door came the sound of whispers in some dark, alien tongue. The smoke seeping beneath the door began to fill the stairwell. "All this smoke . . . how will I see?"

"That I can help you with," she said. "Are you ready?"

"Yes," he replied.

"Then, go!" Orionde jerked open the door. Beyond it rose a hissing, whispering wall of black smoke, which began to flood the stairwell. Ciarán drew in a breath as the whispers coalesced into a frightening squeal that sent a shiver of panic up his spine. He could see nothing through the thick smoke, but then he heard Orionde utter a familiar word: "*Eoh!*"

From her outstretched hands sprang beams of bluish light that flickered through the chamber before them like an inferno of Saint

Elmo's fire. In the light, the smoke became an opaque gray haze, but it was the other things caught in her light that made Ciarán gasp: scores upon scores of demons, stacked one upon the other, climbing, groping, and clawing their way toward Ciarán like a horde of insects pouring from their nest. Their collective mass filled the chamber beyond, from the stone floor to an arched ceiling a dozen feet above. With eyes smoldering like hot coals, their faces contorted in ghastly screams. Some had hair that writhed like Gorgons' manes, while others were hairless, with skin stretched over gaunt skeletal forms, and all of them reaching toward Ciarán with spidery fingers and ragged nails. Ciarán stood frozen at the sight. In the doorway, the nearest demon, a childlike imp with a hateful gaze, raked a clawed hand across Ciarán's face. Ciarán winced, anticipating the biting pain from its jagged claws, but the phantom hand passed right through him, leaving a bone-tingling chill but no physical wound.

"They cannot harm the flesh," Orionde insisted. "Guard your mind, and force your way through them!"

Ciarán nodded. Then, focusing all his thoughts on his fallen friends, he stepped into the bedlam.

The horde of demons came at him. Incorporeal nails scratched at the edges of his brain, and the smell of smoke and brimstone overwhelmed him as the maniacal howling rose in a deafening crescendo. Though the demons clawed relentlessly at his mind, the more he focused his thoughts on the memories of his brethren, the less he felt their presence. Ciarán took another step and pushed past the demons as if they did not exist. To his surprise, the only resistance was a buffeting wind that blasted through the circular chamber, between the doorway and a wall, a dozen feet away, that curved parallel to the outer wall. Both the outer and inner walls flickered with blue flames from Orionde's light, but the wind carried smoke, and for an instant Ciarán feared he may run out of breath. In that momentary panic, he felt the demons surge into his thoughts. So he pushed back the fear and concentrated on Derry's grove and the bravery his friends had shown there.

He fought his way through the wind, searching for the door to the sanctum sanctorum, when he felt something sting his arm. Glancing down, he saw blood on the sleeve of his tunic. Then something bit into his leg. It was not the demons' claws, he realized, but debris. Ahead, he could see a man-size hole in the tower's outer wall. Smoke and wind poured through the hole, and all around it were demons, spinning their arms and whipping the wind into a frenzy that flung bits of shattered stone through the air. Ciarán shielded his head as another piece glanced painfully off his forearm. Most of the debris was small, but it hit him like a swarm of hornets, and soon blood was welling from many tiny wounds. Then he saw the door.

It stood in the inner wall, just ten feet away, and though wailing demons blocked the way, he could see through their ghostly forms to a symbol on the portal: an eye beneath a curved brow, glowing with Saint Elmo's fire. Like the ankh, it was a symbol in Coptic texts: the Eye of Horus. Wondering how these symbols related to the Fae, Ciarán pressed his way toward the door, doing his best to ignore the stinging pain.

Then, without warning, the direction of the wind changed, the sudden new blast knocking him sideways. The wind pushed him toward the breach in the outer wall while, all around him, the scores of demons looked on, their burning eyes and gaping mouths wide with bloodthirsty glee. His feet skidded on the rubble as he staggered backwards, only just catching himself at the ragged edge of the breach. His left arm flailed in the open air, and for an instant he glimpsed the battlefield some fifteen stories below. His left leg dangled outside the breach, but his right hand clung to the edge of the gaping hole, and he struggled to pull himself back inside the tower.

He tried bracing his right leg inside the broken wall, but he still hung precariously halfway out of the breach, unable to buck the buffeting wind that threatened to suck him outside to his death.

The demons surged toward him like a wave. Cascading over his dangling body, they pulled and wrenched at his limbs with their phantom claws as a loud cheer rose from the besieging army below. Then one of the iron beasts let loose with another thunderous roar.

The projectile whizzed over Ciarán's head and struck the outer wall, several yards above the breach where he hung, but the shuddering impact sent him sprawling forward onto the stone floor. He tried to ignore the shooting pain in his shoulder, for he realized he was back in the tower—and just eight feet from the door.

The demons' wind screamed above him, so that if he stood up, it would blow him back into the breach. So Ciarán began to crawl. The smoke, caught up in the wind, stayed inches above the floor, and he sucked in enough clean air to keep moving forward. The demons crawled over him, hissing and howling and prying at the wall he had erected around his mind. But he pressed on, keeping his thoughts on Derry and his gaze on the Eye of Horus.

Reaching the door, he lunged against it, only to have it fly open into the room beyond and send him stumbling to the floor. Behind him, the wind sucked the door shut again. Exhausted, Ciarán took a long breath and closed his eyes. When he opened them, he found himself staring at a stone tile embedded in the floor. An ankh had been carved into the tile, and surrounding it were more tiles with more symbols, as if Remi had recreated his madman's shrine, but this time with the precision of a master artist. Many of the symbols were Fae sigils, like those in Maugis' book, while some were astrological signs, and others were distinctly Hebrew in shape. Still others appeared to be Egyptian hieroglyphics. Yet it was the source of the amber light in the center of the chamber that captured Ciarán's attention. For in the middle of the sanctum sanctorum stood a round pedestal, and floating above it was the source of the glow: an object that made him gasp in awe.

Enoch's words repeated in his mind: *"For at the end of the whole earth, I saw a great and glorious device."*

At the object's center was a brilliant gemstone the size of a large denier. This was the source of the glow, yet the object around the stone was in constant flux. One moment, it was a chalice of gleaming gold, with the gemstone embedded in its stem; then the bowl collapsed and the base elongated, its color shimmering as gold became steel. At one end of the lengthening blade, a hilt and a cross-shaped guard appeared, the gemstone embedded in the pommel. Then the sword grew longer still, its steel darkening into a black staff. What was the sword's hilt morphed and shimmered into a golden ankh, with the gemstone glittering in its center. And then everything around the gem—the ankh and staff—was sucked into it until nothing was left but the stone, glowing in the air above the pedestal. A moment later, the bowl of the chalice sprouted from the top of the gem, and a base grew beneath it, shimmering until it solidified into gold, holding its shape for a moment until the shape changed again, repeating the cycle.

From cup . . . to sword . . . to staff . . . to stone.

Ciarán watched, fascinated, until he realized that set in the floor surrounding the pedestal was a ring of twelve tiles, each bearing a symbol of the zodiac. Four of the tiles glowed more brightly than the rest: *Virgo, Libra, Scorpio, and Sagittarius—the symbols of the prime conflict.*

Ciarán knew what must be done, and he recalled clearly Orionde's words: *"When you see Enoch's device, remember the form it takes in this millennium, and seize it."* Outside, another boom echoed, and the chamber's walls quaked with the impact. *We're running out of time,* he reminded himself.

He approached the pedestal and waited through the transformations, from staff to stone, to chalice, until the blade of the sword grew from the cup's base, and the hilt was fully formed. Then, wrapping his fingers around it, he drew it from its place above the pedestal.

The sword felt heavy in his hand, but its form held. He stared at the diamond-bright gem embedded in the pommel. A flickering light danced across its facets for an instant before fading to a dull-gray opacity, blending with the iron of the hilt.

He glanced back toward the door, wondering for an instant why the demons had not poured, gibbering and howling, into the chamber. The answer came quickly. Orionde had called this place "sanctum sanctorum"—*holy of holies. Hallowed ground.* But as soon as he stepped out of the chamber, he would be back among them, and dangerously close to the gaping breach in the outer wall.

He looked again at Enoch's device, this fabled object that,

according to Isaac, contained the stone etched with the one true name of God. Other than the gemstone in its pommel, it had no elaborate metalwork or adornments—just a dark leather grip, a sturdy guard, and a long, double-edged blade of gleaming steel. Ciarán swung, and the blade whooshed through the air. It felt well balanced in his grip. It was time. He drew a long breath and let it out, then pulled open the door and stared into the mass of demons.

Their squeals had hushed into a buzz of anxious whispers. At the sight of the weapon, the eyes of the nearest demons sprang wide. Ciarán turned at the hip, swinging the sword straight through them. The first demon it struck exploded into crimson flames, as did three more, leaving not even a smoking remnant of their existence. Feeling a surge of hope, Ciarán arced the sword upward. The blade passed through demons as if through thin air, and the five demons in its path flared red and were gone. The demonic horde broke into a terrified wail. Then, with a loud sucking sound, those still living turned and fled through the breach, taking the wind and black smoke with them until nothing remained in the chamber except Orionde, standing at the doorway to the stairwell, a faint smile on her lips.

"Now," she said, "you are ready."

Ciarán and Orionde hurried down the stairway, through the lingering haze of smoke. As they passed the fourth doorway on the way down, another crashing impact rocked the tower, and a shower of rubble collapsed onto the stairs behind them.

"We have little time," Orionde said. "You must take the weapon from the Otherworld before the Dragon arrives. I can lead you to the nearest gateway, at the forest's edge, but first we must fight our way clear of Rosefleur. Among my sisterhood, only seven remain, but we are formidable. Yet once you have crossed the gateway, you still will not be safe. The Nephilim prince can pass through the gateway, too, and in the valley beyond the forest, a war rages. For the count of Anjou has laid a trap for the duke of

Aquitaine, and now the air of that valley is thick with the souls of the dead."

"Can't the other Nephilim follow us through the gateway?" Ciarán asked.

"No," she said. "Long ago, the druids of Gaul sealed the gateways to the Otherworld so the Nephilim could not pass through. Only a powerful summoning, like that of the sorcerers who serve the Dragon, could weaken this seal and bring the Nephilim prince to your world. That same sorcery allowed the prince to pass freely through the gate, just as you and your companions have done."

As they passed the last door and descended through the archway that led to the armory, the thought of this powerful Nephilim prince began to unnerve Ciarán. He struggled once again to keep pace with Orionde's long strides, until she stopped at a rack draped with a knee-length hauberk of polished mail, and a leather baldric hung with a scabbard.

"These belonged to Maugis d'Aygremont," she told him. "Wear them." She took the baldric and hauberk off the rack, as well as a thick wool jacket worn beneath the mail. "The warriors call it a gambeson," she said. "It will cushion the shock from a weapon's blow."

Ciarán looked into her ice blue eyes. "You trained Maugis and sent him to claim Enoch's device from Merlin's tomb in Britain."

Orionde nodded. "Along with Turpin and Roland and the warrior-maiden Bradamante. The knowledge of Enoch's device and the prophecy were the most precious secrets of the paladins of Charlemagne." She handed Ciarán the armor. "Now, wear this and walk in their ways."

Sobered by Orionde's words, Ciarán looked at the mail, then at the sword clutched in his hand, and realized the place he now took in the chain of history—and the grave challenge that lay ahead. His thoughts ran back to Niall and his long-bladed knife, then to Murchad and Bran, Áed, Alil, and Fintan. And the battle cry that inspired their courage: "*Columcille!*" It was true, he realized. Monks weren't natural warriors, but the warrior's spirit lived in every drop of Irish blood, and in desperate times it could be summoned. So Ciarán donned his hauberk and readied for battle.

On the tower's ground floor, the barnlike hall had become a staging area for war. A Fae woman with hair like spun gold had dressed Alais in an oversize tunic of silver mail unlike any she had ever seen before entering this Otherworld. There were no chain links, but scales with the textured patterns of a swan's feather, bound together with tiny silver rings. The other Fae had donned similar hauberks, along with helms adorned with eagle plumes, and bore long spears that jutted like deadly thorns above the cavalry. Even their horses, which stood in ranks in the form of a wedge, wore armor with the same feathery texture.

Alais tucked Geoffrey's pendant beneath the neck of her mail tunic, which seemed far lighter than she had expected. But looking down at herself draped in this strange armor, her eyes welled with emotion. The woman in white, this Orionde of the Fae, had found her in the field of wheat by the Anglin River, not far from here. Had this been why? To guide her to Geoffrey, his secret, and this quest? But Orionde had told her to choose, and Geoffrey had given her a choice. She had kept her free will, yet here she was.

You have yet another role to play, Orionde had told her.

Amid the booms of the Nephilim siege engines, and the lethal debris cascading from the ceiling with each shuddering impact, she found the mystery of Orionde's words almost frightening. *Oh, Thadeus,* she prayed, *if only you were here to make sense of this.*

Wiping a tear from her eye, Alais glimpsed movement coming down the stairway. As the figure came into view, she blinked in astonishment. For it was Ciarán, though in his hauberk of polished mail, riding boots, and baldric blazoned with Celtic designs, he looked more like one of William's lords. And in his right hand was a long, double-edged sword.

Orionde followed him, and as they reached the bottom steps, the walls shook with another violent crash. Alais winced at the loud crack that resonated from the ceiling, showering the floor with rock shards and mortar dust.

Ciarán looked awestruck when he saw her standing beside their pale charger. "You look like one of them," he said.

"And you . . ." Her eyes fell to the pommel of his sword. "Is that . . . ?"

"Yes," he said, holding it out to her, hilt first. She brushed a finger over the gemstone in its pommel and gasped as fire blazed from the jewel's depths and rippled across the diamondlike surface. The opaque gray shone white for an instant, then faded again as her touch left it.

"It's beautiful," she said.

"Orionde says we must take it back to the Val d'Anglin."

"That's what they're preparing for," she realized aloud.

He counted the horses, eight in all. "We'll ride together," he told her.

Orionde strode past them. She wore a silver helm plumed with a broad white feather. At her hip hung a sword belt with a sheathed blade. Mounting the destrier mare tethered beside theirs, she said, "Don't unsheathe the weapon until we have broken past their ranks, or the Nephilim prince will sense its presence. Are you ready?"

He sheathed the sword. "As much as I'll ever be." And he swung up into the saddle and helped Alais up behind him.

Orionde called to her warriors in a beautiful foreign tongue, and the Fae raised their spears and bellowed a cheer that echoed through the hall. Alais, with her arms around Ciarán, felt his muscles tense beneath his mail. The gate opened, to the drumming of shields and the howling of madmen. At the head of the column of riders, one of the warrior-maidens sounded a horn, cutting through the cries of the hundred spearmen awaiting them on the red plain. And the Fae set their spears and joined in a fierce battle cry.

Alais wrapped her arms tightly around Ciarán's waist and whispered a prayer to Saint Radegonde. Then the Sisters of Orionde charged.

CHAPTER 51

THE DEATH PIT

ehind Rosefleur, the death pit glowed a fiery red. A column of smoke wafted from its depths and gathered overhead in a swirling black vortex humming with the whispers of demons. The air stank of brimstone and ash, and the smoke mingled with the clouds, blocking out the sunlight and leaving only the pit's hellish glow. Through powerful sorcery, the pit had been cracked from the earth according to ancient ritual, in a span sixty-nine feet long and forty-six feet wide. Around it, twenty-three black-robed monks chanted in the Nephilim tongue, feeding their power to the ritual. From the chasm, a deep growl echoed, and hearing it, Lucien of Saint-Denis grinned a wicked smile.

His hands were slick with blood, and his dagger dripped red from the last victim he had slaughtered. A hundred of Fulk's men had been sacrificed to the pit—unwitting victims all, whose murdered souls fueled the sorcery of the Nephilim high priest. The giant stood naked, his chalk-white flesh painted with runes, chanting the incantation that would break the Dragon's bonds and free him from his prison. With each sacrifice and each unleashed soul, the high priest's power grew and the Dragon's bonds weakened. Lucien's anticipation teetered on the verge of ecstasy. *The Dragon*

389

would be his savior. For Lucien knew that he was now anathema. The ritual murder of a hundred innocent men had sealed his fate with the enemy of God.

Lucien called for another victim.

Behind him, one of a pair of giants drew a prisoner from the crude cage that held the hundred or so who remained. The giant, a heavily muscled Nephilim, carried the naked prisoner to the edge of the pit. He was an Angevin, no older than seventeen judging by the thin, wispy beard on his chin. The boy did not resist, for Lucien had sedated him and the others with a brew of mandrake root. Instead, he sat on his knees, staring vacantly into the death pit. The wind whipped, blowing the cowl from Lucien's head as he readied himself for the kill. At first, the cold-blooded murder had sickened him, but after a few, the sickness had settled and, in time, blossomed into bloodlust, for each killing drew the Dragon closer to this world.

Lucien grabbed the boy's hair and jerked his head back, exposing his neck. Placing the dagger at the boy's throat, he uttered a prayer in the Nephilim tongue.

Then, over the high priest's chanting, came a man's scream. To Lucien's surprise, it had not come from his victim.

Across the pit, a sorcerer fell, arms and legs flailing, into the abyss. The man next to him turned in horror, and then he, too, toppled over the edge, blood streaming from a wound in his side.

Lucien's jaw dropped. For where two of his sorcerers had stood was a dark-skinned man with a curved Moorish blade. He whirled like a demon from Lucien's nightmares, slicing into another of the oblivious sorcerers lost in their ritual song. The black-robed man fell screaming into the pit.

But now something beyond the death pit held Lucien's gaze, for the treetops were strangely wreathed in blue flame. The surrounding air sizzled, and then, with a great sucking moan, the wind sped toward the cage, swirling violently and drawing red earth into its midst, building into a cyclone.

The sorcerers surrounding the pit ceased their chanting and gasped in horror. Lucien whisked his dagger across the boy's throat and pushed him into the pit, and in the same moment another sorcerer fell as the brown-skinned swordsman continued his murderous rampage. Lucien grabbed his blackened staff and felt the power surge up his arm as he darted from the pit's edge, his mind focused on a single thought: *Dónall mac Taidg must die!*

AT THE FOREST'S EDGE, Dónall spun his leaf-shaped blade through the air, reciting poetic Fae words to feed the cyclone's fury. Their plan had worked perfectly. Khalil had dispatched the sorcerers who posed the nearest threat, while Isaac focused the light of his crystal onto Dónall, combining their energies and strengthening their collective power.

The howling wind eclipsed the chanting of the sorcerers and the Nephilim priest who towered over the pit, weaving patterns in the air. His hands glowed with a ghostly blue fire, leaving momentary streaks in the air in the shape of perverse symbols. The giant appeared ancient. His beard, streaked with white, hung past his groin, his long hair spilled like a wild mane over his shoulders, and his muscles bunched and knotted like the gnarled roots of an ancient tree.

Dónall focused on the prisoners, for their sacrifice empowered this ritual. He whipped his sword in the direction of the cage, and the cyclone lurched, sucking the poles from the ground and shredding ropes. He concentrated to keep the tempest away from the men, who staggered from the breach as if in a fog. The two hulking Nephilim who guarded the cage backed away in retreat, shielding their eyes from the debris torn up by the cyclone, and the sorcerers at the pit's edge were scrambling. Dónall pointed his sword at the two closest to the cyclone, and though they tried to scatter, the cyclone struck, sucking them into its ravenous maw. The whirling vortex, devouring earth and rocks from the chasm's edge, flung three more black-robed forms screaming into the pit.

Dónall's hope soared as he stepped out into the red plain. The closer he put himself to the cyclone, the greater his control over it. He strode toward the pit.

Khalil continued the attack, leaving one of the sorcerers moaning on the ground, trying to hold in his spilling guts. The curved blade plunged through another's chest, and as Khalil pulled it free, the man tumbled into the pit. Isaac followed Dónall onto the plain, focusing the light, which bathed Dónall in a hazy white glow.

As the cyclone sucked in smoke from the pit and chewed up the surrounding earth, the bearded giant stopped weaving its fell symbols in the air. It stood seven feet tall, but Dónall's cyclone was many times its size.

Dónall thrust his leaf-shaped blade outward, and the cyclone swelled and then struck, meeting the giant's outstretched hand. Blue fire flared from the giant's palm; then, suddenly, the cyclone exploded. The power that encircled Dónall's blade drained from his hands, and the funnel cloud began to dissipate, spraying smoke and earth across the pit. Particles of debris rained down on Dónall and Isaac. The vortex was gone, as if it had never existed. Across the pit, the giant laughed.

"What happened?" Isaac cried.

Dónall's legs buckled. He felt drained, as if whatever dissipated the cyclone had sapped his own energy as well.

"At six hundred years old," said a familiar voice, "the Nephilim high priest is far more adept at the Fae arts than you."

Dónall turned to his left. Ten paces away stood Lucien. Two feet of flame blazed from the tip of the staff in his hand.

"I should have killed you with the others, old friend," Lucien snarled. "But this is just as well." Winding back his arm, he hurled the staff, like a lance, toward Isaac and Dónall.

As the staff hit the earth, its tip erupted in a ball of fire, knocking Dónall backward with the explosion. Burning pain enveloped his face and arms, and he collided hard with the ground, his habit smoking from the heat.

He struggled to move, but his limbs lacked the strength. He was at the brink of the pit and could feel its heat and smell the suffocating stench of brimstone. Hearing a deep growl from the pit's depths, Dónall slowly turned his head. Ten feet away lay Isaac, smoke wafting from his robes, his beard singed to his chin, his skin blistered. He moaned faintly. To his left, Dónall heard Khalil groan.

Sandals crunched over the charred ground. Lucien looked down at them. "You cannot stop it, Dónall. This time, the drama shall have a different ending. Can't you hear the Dragon's growl?"

Dónall winced. His chest ached with every breath. His right arm fell over the pit's edge, into the hot air of the void below. From the depths of the pit, the growling rumbled again, growing louder with each breath.

"Yes," Lucien said. "The Dragon shall come, and you shall provide the final sacrifice that brings him here." As he spoke, the ground shook with faint tremors. Behind Lucien loomed another figure: that of the long-bearded giant. Its mouth opened in a tooth-less grin. Sigils and runes covered its bone white flesh.

Dónall glanced away and caught Isaac in his gaze. The rabbi dug his fingers into the earth, and white light glowed from the crystal beneath his palm.

Should I? Isaac mouthed.

And at once, Dónall knew. Isaac had recalled their lessons well. *With a crystal, a man could split the earth.* Summoning what strength remained to him, Dónall nodded to Isaac. *Do it.*

Isaac thrust his palm harder against the ground. The tremor began faintly but quickly intensified until the earth beneath them shook violently.

For an instant, Dónall's thoughts returned to Reims, to a time with Thomas on the wooded hilltops outside the city, and the murder that followed, when everything changed so horribly.

Feeling the rage invigorate his limbs, Dónall lunged and grabbed the hem of Lucien's robes. Lucien flailed as his sandals slipped on the quaking earth and Dónall wrenched him to the ground.

Around them, the earth cracked. Dónall pressed his face against Lucien's and stared into his terrified eyes. "This is for all of them," he growled. "For Nicolas, and Remi, and Thomas and Martha!"

At the death pit's edge, the ground gave way, and chunks of earth crumbled into the chasm. The earth beneath the giant's legs collapsed, and losing its balance, it toppled forward into the pit like a hewn tree. The earth beneath Dónall's shoulder began to sag. And then he fell, clinging to Lucien's robes, caught within a landslide of clay and rock, as Isaac plunged with them into the heat and smoke and ash.

Lucien unleashed a horrific scream, the wild cry of a damned soul.

Dónall closed his eyes and made the sign of the cross. And surrendered to the abyss.

CHAPTER 52

THE PRIME CONFLICT

The Fae cavalry crashed into the Franks like the tip of a giant spear. Horses, spears, and shields clashed with a thunderous sound. Beneath the darkening sky where smoke from the death pit swirled over Rosefleur, Fae riders drove their spears into the first wave of Franks.

Ciarán's heart pounded beneath his mail. As the first line of Franks buckled, Fae swords rang from their scabbards. The raving Franks fought wildly, which only quickened their deaths as the Fae attacked with preternatural strength and speed, cleaving through the Frankish spearmen, severing heads and limbs.

Alais clung to Ciarán, who rode behind Orionde in the center of the Fae's deadly wedge. The Franks howled like beasts as their comrades fell silent under the Fae blades. Blood flew through the air, and spears glanced off Fae armor and off their horses' barding. The wild men put up only a feeble resistance, but then came the Nephilim behind them. Wielding spears ten feet long, the giants stabbed over the ranks of men and into the oncoming riders. Beside Ciarán, one of the spears impaled both rider and horse. To his right, one of the Nephilim thrust its spear, impaling a Fae rider and lifting her from her mount. Without its rider to defend it, the charger became easy prey for the spearmen's wild thrusts. A Frank charged, his spear leveled at Alais. Ciarán began to draw the blade from its scabbard, but in a heartbeat one of the Fae intercepted the Frank, shearing his helmed head from his shoulders.

In front of him, Orionde repeated her command: "Keep the weapon sheathed!"

The Nephilim formed a wall behind the Frankish spearmen, and the riders crashed into it like a wave against a sheer cliff. Horses toppled, impaled on the massive spears. Fae leaped toward the giants, slicing through iron breastplates. In front of Orionde, the lead rider raised her sword to parry a spear thrust from one of the seven-foot giants. The spear glanced against the blade and slid into the Fae's gut. Orionde whipped her sword from its scabbard and spurred her mount into a thickly muscled giant whose chalky face was a twisted mask of fury. The two collided, and Orionde cut a gash through the giant's ribs. He recoiled, clutching at the gushing wound. The giant had been the last of the enemy ranks standing in the way; the plain beyond was now clear.

"Now!" Orionde cried, and charged the gap in the Nephilim ranks.

Ciarán kicked his charger's flanks, and it surged ahead in Orionde's wake as the battle raged on around them. The surviving Fae fought on, screaming their shrill battle cry.

Behind Ciarán, Alais screamed. Her arms, wrapped around his waist only moments ago, were losing their grip. Turning his head, Ciarán understood, for one of the Franks had grabbed Alais' right leg and was being pulled alongside their mount. Two more Franks clung to the first, forming like a human chain, using their collective weight to drag her from the horse. The Franks glared up at her, wild-eyed, their faces consumed with madness.

"Ciarán!" Alais screamed.

Without a second thought, Ciarán pulled the sword from its scabbard and swung downward, severing the Frank's forearm. Wailing, the man fell away, and the three Franks tumbled over each other on the red plain. Alais hugged Ciarán tightly. "Thank you," she gasped. He smiled back, realizing that she was safe—and that they had broken free of the enemy lines.

Ahead, Orionde sped over the wind-swept plain, through the carnage of the earlier battle, heading for the forest's edge, her white cloak streaming behind her. Ciarán urged his mare forward, praying it could keep pace. Then the earth beneath the horse's hooves quaked. Hearing Alais gasp, he glanced back over his shoulder to see massive chunks of Rosefleur crash down into the plain with a deafening sound, throwing a cloud of reddish dust and debris over the men and Nephilim and Fae on the battlefield. As tons of stone from the great spire toppled to the earth, the cloud of debris exploded outward. At the edge of that billowing cloud fed by Rosefleur's cascading remnants rode three figures. Fear clenched Ciarán's gut, for their pursuers were Nephilim.

Ciarán looked at the unsheathed sword in his hand and, realizing his mistake, sheathed it quickly. But the damage was done.

The pursuing Nephilim rode aurochs, the great bull-like beasts that pulled the massive siege engines. Two of the riders carried massive spiked clubs, but the lead rider held a lance.

Orionde glanced back. "You should not have used the weapon," she said. "The Nephilim prince knows you hold Enoch's device, and comes for it now. We must hurry!"

The aurochs, with horns as long and as thick as a man's arm, moved faster than their size suggested, and were closing on the horses. A hundred yards ahead, mist wisped from between the tree branches at the forest's edge.

"Faster!" Alais pleaded.

Ciarán glanced backward to find that the aurochs and their riders had closed half the distance between them. The lead rider's face burned with inhuman rage and black runes decorated his muscled torso, as if Abaddon himself pursued them from the edge of Hell.

Orionde reached the forest first, but Ciarán and Alais were just a mare's tail behind her. They plunged into the wet, murky mist, scraping past branches and brambles. Orionde stretched out her hand, and the mist parted as if blasted away by a sudden gale, revealing a corridor two hundred yards long, blanketed with fallen leaves. It formed a straight path down a tunnel of overarching branches stretching from the shadowy oaks.

"Through there!" Orionde cried out. "It is the gateway to the valley!"

They raced down the tunnel, approaching the opaque curtain of mist at its end. Behind them, Ciarán could hear the aurochs' great cloven hooves thundering over the forest floor. In a few heartbeats, Orionde was but thirty yards from the end, with Ciarán and Alais just behind.

Alais' fingers dug into Ciarán's side. "Oh, God," she cried. "Ciarán, jump!"

Looking back, he saw the Nephilim prince draw back his lance. Ciarán wrapped his arm around Alais and leaped the instant before the lance hurtled through the air, hitting the mare. The beast lost its legs and tumbled onto the leaf-covered ground.

Ciarán and Alais crashed to the earth, their momentum driving them forward until they rolled to a stop. The lance had caught the mare in the rump and traveled straight through its belly. The panicked beast, still aware, slid toward the gateway along with its fallen riders.

Cool mist brushed across Ciarán's face. By the time he stopped rolling, he found himself on the grassy field of the Val d'Anglin. Alais lay beside him, struggling to catch her breath.

Across the battlefield, Angevin horsemen pursued clusters of William's spearmen. The bodies of warriors and horses littered the grass. The corpse of a slain spearman, one of the younger boys Ciarán had seen upon their arrival at the camp, lay not ten paces away. Spears and weapons lost in the battle lay scattered across the nearby grass.

Behind Alais, where the wall of oaks towered at the forest's edge, something moved in the shroud of mist. A figure stepped out of the murk. At first, its shadowy form looked eight feet tall, yet as the giant neared the threshold to the Val d'Anglin, it diminished to human proportions, though still taller than most men.

Alais let out a horrified gasp as Adémar of Blois stepped through the misty veil.

The bishop's chest was bare and still painted with runes, and his feral visage shone with the same rage that Ciarán had seen on the face of the Nephilim prince. Sorcery had allowed the Nephilim prince to pass freely from the Otherworld, just as Orionde had warned. With a chill, Ciarán realized what she had meant, and suddenly the bishop and his perverse motives all made sense.

Adémar picked up a weapon from the ground—a flanged mace large enough to be wielded with two hands, although Adémar hefted it with one, as if its weight were nothing.

Aching and rattled from the fall, Ciarán lifted himself off the ground. He grabbed the hilt of the sword and whisked it from its scabbard.

"So the champion of men is the heretics' son?" Adémar smirked. "For all the centuries I have waited, I expected to face a great warrior like Charlemagne, not some whelp from an island of drunken Celts."

Before Ciarán could reply, Adémar struck, and Ciarán just managed to jerk his blade into the mace's path. As pain reverberated down his arms, Adémar whipped the mace around and hammered Ciarán's hip, knocking him to the ground. The mail hauberk might have saved him from a sword cut, but it offered little protection against the mace's bludgeoning blows. Ciarán scrambled, relieved that he could still walk but worried that his hip bone might be cracked. Adémar drove the mace downward, but Ciarán rolled, and the head of the mace smashed into the earth.

"Prepare to die," Adémar hissed, "just like your friend Niall."

In a surge of anger, Ciarán thrust the sword toward Adémar's legs. Adémar heaved his weapon up from the ground, and the blade clanged against the mace's iron shaft.

"Your ancestors have failed you, boy," Adémar growled. "The truths of Arcanus were forgotten, their very existence shrouded by ignorance and piety. Your mentor's discovery came too late!"

On his feet now, Ciarán staggered backward, panting, the sword growing heavier in his hand. He swung again, and the tip of the blade grazed Adémar's chest, drawing a thin thread of blood. With a roar, Adémar struck a fierce upward blow, which glanced off the mail of Ciarán's chest and into his chin. He toppled backward, arms windmilling, and the sword slipped from his grasp.

Ciarán crashed to the ground, blood gurgling in his throat, and slowly raised his throbbing head. Looming over him, Adémar hefted his mace.

"And so it ends," he said.

ALAIS WATCHED, tears streaming down her cheeks.

Ciarán lay prone, blood spilling from his lips as he fought to lift his head. And there, standing over him, was the man who had raped her. On Adémar's naked back, an old wound ran between his shoulder blades—the spot where her dagger had struck. She glanced over at the slain spearman and saw something lying beside him in the grass.

Fire filled her veins. Grabbing the spear, Alais rushed at Adémar, sinking the spear tip into the old wound.

Adémar howled in pain and rage and flailed, ripping the spear shaft from her hand. Then he grasped at the spear and pulled it from his back.

Alais glared at him in defiant rage. "I won't watch you kill him, you god-cursed monster!"

Adémar swung his free hand, catching her in the chest. The air rushed from her lungs, and she felt herself falling, fighting to draw another breath.

"ALAIS!" Ciarán cried. The shock of what she had done jolted him to his feet as his anger swelled.

"Nephilim!" he cried, picking up the sword and swinging at Adémar's flank. Adémar spun and parried with the mace, then landed a fist to the base of Ciarán's jaw, knocking him onto the wet grass. Ciarán's eyes fell to the sword.

"It's powerless, you know," Adémar mocked. "Nothing more than a myth."

Ciarán glanced between his attacker and the weapon with its gray gemstone. Adémar's words reminded him of something Dónall often said: *"There's truth behind those old myths—just like the ones Maugis scrawled in his book!"* The realization crashed over Ciarán like a wave. Recalling the last of Maugis' riddles, he looked at the gemstone embedded in the sword's pommel.

In Enoch's device the answer lies,
In the whisper of breath, or all hope dies.

Ciarán pressed his lips to the pommel and blew on the gemstone, whispering the Fae word: *"Eoh."*

From the opaque jewel erupted the blazing light of a hundred torches. Power surged up Ciarán's arm to his chest, into his lungs, and through his veins.

He rose to his feet and raised the blade, now wreathed in white flames. *Excalibur, Caladbolg, Flamberge*—so many names it had borne through time.

Adémar paused, and for the first time, Ciarán saw fear in his eyes.

Ciarán lunged, swinging the sword in a downward arc. "For Niall!" he cried.

Adémar hefted his mace to deflect to blow, but the sword cleaved through its shaft and into Adémar's unprotected flesh. In the gash, fire blazed up.

Adémar let rip a ghastly scream as the sword sliced into his chest, shearing through the rib cage. He sucked in a rattling breath as Ciarán tore the weapon free from his chest, and then his balance failed him and he crashed onto the grassy field, blood spilling from his mortal wound.

Lying on the grass, Adémar's body flared with white fire, as if all the heat that had blazed into the wound now suddenly released itself, erupting in a flash so hot that Ciarán staggered backward and covered his eyes with his mailed sleeve. Then, with another flash, the heat dispersed as quickly as it erupted, leaving nothing of Adémar but ashy remnants that wafted like dust on the faint breeze.

The Nephilim prince of the Dragon's line, Adémar of Blois in this world, was no more. And in Ciarán's hand, the weapon blazed.

~

THUNDER ROLLED across a sky dark with clouds. In the valley, groups of Angevin horsemen roamed across the field of dead and wounded warriors.

Ciarán searched for Alais and found her on the ground, struggling to regain her breath. He dropped the sword and fell to his knees.

Her storm-gray eyes opened faintly; then she threw her arms around him, crying, "You're alive!"

"He's gone," Ciarán said, unable to contain his joy at finding her unhurt.

Alais closed her eyes and pressed her lips against the small corner of his mouth that wasn't cut and bleeding. A spark of heat surged from her lips to his, filling him with warmth and hope, like the first rays of sun on a gray winter morn. He tasted the salt of her tears and let it linger on his tongue, feeling content never to move from this place, until he heard a moan from the mists at the forest's edge.

There lay Orionde, between the bodies of two slain Nephilim. Blood spattered her white cloak—Nephilim blood, to be sure, but her own life ebbed from a gaping rent down the front of her feathery mail.

"Orionde!" Alais gasped. She rushed to the edge of the misty shroud, but the Fae raised her hand. "Do not enter, child, for I doubt I am strong enough to reopen the gate."

"But you're hurt," Ciarán pleaded.

Orionde's eyes were barely open. "The journey begins and ends with sacrifice," she said. "This is the way it has always been."

"Is it over?" he asked her.

The Fae shook her head. "Now the prophecy's focus turns to the journey ahead."

"But . . . how will I know where to go?"

"Trust in everything you have learned," Orionde said, her voice weakening, "and in time, you shall find your way." As her words trailed off, the mist grew thick, like a dense, pale smoke filling the gaps between the trees, until she and the fallen Nephilim faded from view.

Ciarán lifted the sword from the ground. A flash of white fire still burned within the gem in the pommel. Lightning flashed overhead with a loud crack, and a raindrop brushed his cheek. A second drop splashed onto his hand. Ciarán looked where the drop had fallen, and his eyes grew wide.

For the rain was as red as blood.

"What's happening?" Alais asked fearfully.

As the rain began a steady fall, staining the grass, Ciarán watched it in awe, recalling the scripture clearly. "*The first angel blew his trumpet,*" he recited, "*and there came hail and fire, mixed with blood, and they were hurled to the earth.*"

The color drained from Alais' face. "Did we fail?"

Ciarán shook his head. "No," he said. "I think it's meant to be this way. The cycle has begun, but we've won the first battle. And we still have time to end it."

Brushing the red rain from her eyes, Alais reached for Ciarán's hand, and together they walked into the open field, watching the rain form crimson pools across the uneven ground. Ciarán wondered about Dónall, and Isaac and Khalil. What Una had asked of them was madness. The Dragon had not come, but had that victory cost them their lives?

The red rain poured down as if the sky wept blood for Orionde and all those who had fallen today, both in this world and in the Other. Then the pounding of hooves to Ciarán's right snapped him alert. Five horsemen rode furiously toward them, one of them bearing the blue banner of Anjou. Another, larger than the rest, wore a familiar black beard, now slick with red rain, and the bloodstained armor of an Angevin noble. Fulk the Black waved his sword, while a crazed look burned in his eyes.

Ciarán stepped defiantly between her and the horsemen, ready to do whatever he must to protect her. He held the sword above his head, and white fire flared from the stone in the pommel, gleaming upward to the tip of the blade. Heat surged through his limbs, and an Irish cry rang from his throat:

"Columcille!"

Fulk stared in horror, and his lips opened in a terrified scream, as if Ciarán, brandishing a blazing sword in the bloody rain, were the Angel of Death, conjured from the Apocalypse of John and made flesh.

Fulk wheeled his mount, unable to look at the apparition that challenged him. His panicked riders also turned and fled, and as the five riders retreated toward Castle Brosse, Ciarán's heart began to calm.

Alais embraced him again, and they strode unmolested across the battlefield, heading west. In the distance, a crimson banner flew from a cluster of retreating men. "That's William's banner," Ciarán observed.

"Then he lives," Alais said with a grateful sigh.

As the red rain continued to fall around them, another figure approached on foot from the forest. Ciarán wiped the rain from his eyes, and his heart warmed at the sight of Khalil's exhausted face. The grim look on the Persian's face said it all: Dónall and Isaac were dead—two more lives given for the cause.

Ciarán strode toward Khalil, and the two embraced. "I figured you were dead," Ciarán said.

Khalil shook his head and gave a faint smile. "Thank Allah that I am a hard man to kill."

Alais kissed his cheek. "Thank God indeed."

Khalil told them of Dónall and Isaac's heroic final act. The Dragon never did rise from the death pit, and Lucien and all his sorcerers were dead—Khalil had seen to that before the surviving Fae arrived and opened a gateway allowing him to leave the Other-world. Ciarán choked up at the loss of the man who had been a father to him since childhood. But the tale of Dónall's bravery made him proud. He found himself grateful that he had not betrayed Dónall's faith, and confident that Dónall's courage would live within him until his own dying day.

"Where do we go now?" Khalil asked.

"We'll find our way," Ciarán said, "just as Dónall would have done. But you don't have to go. The rest of your life is free."

Khalil clapped Ciarán's shoulder. "Like Fierabras and Maugis, we are brothers now. You have my word—and my sword."

Grateful tears welled in Ciarán's eyes. He slid the weapon into its scabbard and nodded to his brother in arms, then took Alais' hand and pulled her by his side.

"I know this," he said as the red rain fell. "Whether it's fate or the choices we've made, together we have hope."

HISTORICAL NOTE

O bviously, this novel is a blend of history and myth, but there may be "truth behind those old myths," as Dónall would say.

One event that is both history and myth is the rain of blood around the year 1000 in Aquitaine and elsewhere in France. Reports exist from the early eleventh century of a blood rain that "fell upon the clothes of many men, and so stained them with gore that they shuddered at the sight of their own garments and tore them off." Fulbert of Chartres wrote that account in a letter to King Robert of France, after the worried king received a report from Duke William V about a rain of blood that fell in Aquitaine. Scientists today believe that historical reports of blood rain may have been due to dust containing iron oxide, or the presence of microorganisms in the rainwater, but back in the Middle Ages many perceived this event as a sign of the end times. The blood rain joins numerous other portents identified around the year 1000, including reports of meteors over England and Germany, earthquakes in Saxony, and an eruption of Mount Vesuvius, all which fueled millennial fears in Christian Europe. The extent of these fears that the world would end one thousand years after either the birth of Christ or his crucifixion is still debated by historians, but such fears undoubtedly were inflamed by the words of Revelation 20:7: "When the thousand years are ended, Satan will be released from his prison . . ." For its part, the late tenth century provided enough war, famine, and plague to make even the most reasonable people wonder whether the Four Horsemen of the apocalypse were indeed charging across Europe, or whether the armies of Gog and Magog, in the guise of the Vikings, Magyars, and Moors, had been sent by the devil to wage war against Christendom. Historical accounts of these apocalyptic fears became the backdrop for *Enoch's Device*, although the blood rain comes several years early because it's convenient to the story.

The novel features a number of real historical events and characters, yet a certain degree of artistic license figures in their presentation. Around the year 998, Duke William V of Aquitaine, later known as William the Great, led an army against the castle of Brosse, held by Guy of Limoges, an ally of Count Fulk the Black of Anjou. While there is no evidence that Fulk participated in the battle, it did end badly for William, whose forces were tricked into besieging the castle and then soundly defeated in the open field. William would go on to earn a reputation for piety within the Roman Church, but only after he and his own ally, King Robert of France, suffered a number of military defeats against forces aligned with the aptly named Fulk the Black. Known for his ferocious temper and extreme cruelty, Fulk was a man untroubled by violence or murder, willing to ravage the lands of any who opposed his will. Yet Fulk also had an enduring fear of hell, which led him to perform numerous acts of penance throughout his life. Still, his fears of the afterlife did not prevent him from having his wife, Elisabeth de Vendome, burned at the stake—in her wedding dress, no less— in December 999, after suspecting her of adultery. Fulk the Black seemed like the perfect ally for Adémar of Blois, who is an entirely fictional character. In fact, Blois did not become a bishopric until 1697, but it seemed a better idea to move this up seven centuries and create my own bishop rather than besmirch the name of some real French bishop who lived a thousand years ago.

If France in 998 was plagued by a weak king and warring magnates, the southern realm of Al-Andalus was ruled by a single man with an iron fist. Muhammad Ibn Abi Amir, known to the world as Al-Mansor, was the self-proclaimed "noble king" of the Moors. He rose to power after the death of the great caliph Al-Hakkam II, by murdering his rivals, including the vizier of Córdoba and the general of the Moorish army. Al-Mansor accomplished this coup with the aid of his lover, Subh, Al-Hakkam's beautiful and most favored wife, all the while keeping Al-Hakkam's son, the new caliph, sequestered in the palace city of Medinat al-Zahra. During Al-Mansor's reign, Córdoba was the most spectacular city in Western Europe—a shining jewel of learning, tolerance, and pros-perity, many times larger and far more sophisticated than any other city west of Constantinople. As proof, the great library of Al-Hakkam alone contained hundreds of thousands of books at a time when the largest library in France might hold fewer than four or five thousand volumes. The infamous burning of books depicted in the novel was ordered by Al-Mansor to appease some of the more fundamentalist imams and suppress dissent by free-thinking schol-ars. Many historians consider this the most terrible act of Al-Mansor's reign.

Of the two books featured most prominently in the novel, one is completely real, the other based entirely on legend. The Book of Enoch is an ancient Jewish text, which indeed elaborates on the cryptic verse from Genesis 6:4: "The Nephilim were on the earth in those days—and also afterwards—when the sons of God went into the daughters of men." While scholars disagree about when the book was actually written (with some putting it at ca. 300 B.C.), the book is cited in the New Testament Letter of Jude and the First Letter of Peter, and copies of it were found among the Dead Sea Scrolls. The book was clearly known to first-century Jews and Chris-tians but was considered apocryphal by St. Augustine, among others, and disappeared for more than a thousand years. By the tenth century, the Book of Enoch would have been considered a lost work of scripture, only to be rediscovered centuries later, in 1773, by the Scottish explorer James Bruce during his travels in Abyssinia (Ethiopia).

The Book of Maugis d'Aygremont finds its origins in the legends surrounding Charlemagne. Maugis is considered one of Charlemagne's twelve paladins, or peers, although there is no evidence from the eighth or ninth centuries that he actually existed. The first reference to Maugis appears to come from French *chansons de geste* in the late twelfth century. Maugis becomes a prominent character in Renaissance epics about the paladins of Charlemagne, in which he is depicted as both a belted knight and a magician known for using a book of spells. This inspired the Book of Maugis featured in the novel. It is portrayed as containing the secrets of the Fae based on another medieval legend associated with Maugis: his tutelage in the magical arts at the hands of Orionde le Fae, who supposedly lived in the tower of Rosefleur with a sisterhood of faeries.

If a copy of the Book of Maugis were to be kept anywhere in Europe, the Cathedral School of Reims would have been a likely hiding place. By the late tenth century, Reims had become the intellectual center of Western Christendom—an oasis for scholars amid the violence of medieval Europe. The scholars of Reims treasured the classic works of Aristotle, Cicero, and Virgil, while others, such as the monks of Cluny, deemed these pre-Christian works poisonous and corrupting. The school's most famous member was Gerbert of Aurillac, an ambitious monk who had studied in Barcelona and brought knowledge of Arabic medicine, mathematics, and astronomy to Reims. Gerbert was ahead of his time, believing that the earth was round, creating both an armillary sphere and an abacus, and using sighting tubes to observe the stars. He is precisely the type of man Dónall and Thomas would have been drawn to while studying at Reims.

As Gerbert's fame grew, rumors spread that he was a sorcerer who had sold his soul to the devil. Some even had him associating with a brotherhood of evil magicians, including fellow monks, while others told of a secret book of spells that held all Gerbert's magical knowledge. These rumors would follow Gerbert throughout his life, but they did not impede his ambition or success as he became a counselor to French and German kings and rose up the clerical ranks from monk to abbot, to bishop, to pope. As Pope Sylvester II, Gerbert celebrated mass on New Year's Eve of 999, when thousands gathered in Rome at the basilica of Saint Peter, weeping, praying, and wondering whether the end times would arrive at the stroke of midnight. So, it would seem, Gerbert of Aurillac still has a role to play in this drama, as Ciarán mac Tomás, Alais of Poitiers, and Khalil al-Pârsâ race to fulfill the Arcanian Prophecy.

THE JOURNEY CONTINUES in *The Key to the Abyss...*

BOOKS BY JOSEPH FINLEY

The Dragon-Myth Cycle

Enoch's Device

The Key to the Abyss

Dragon-Myth Prequels

Hela's Bane

The Fae Dealings

Other Tales

Mava's Echo: A Short Story of Celtic Myth and Magic

ABOUT THE AUTHOR

Joseph Finley is a writer of historical fantasy fiction. Following a tour as an officer in the U.S. Navy Judge Advocate General's Corps, he returned to Atlanta where he lives with his wife, daughter, and two mischievous rescue dogs. A lifelong love of medieval history, vintage fantasy, and historical mysteries helped inspire his writing, along with a penchant for European travel. Joseph is a member of the Science Fiction and Fantasy Writers of America, and posts frequently about historical and fantasy fiction on his blog. He can be found most nights enjoying a hearty glass of wine, and in the wee hours of most mornings surrounded by history books and plugging away on his next story.

To receive a **free novella**, as well as emails with updates on Joseph's next novel and special offers, join his Reader List by signing up **here** or at his website, below:

www.authorjosephfinley.com

Lastly, if you enjoyed this book, please consider leaving a review (even if it's only a line or two) at Amazon or Goodreads. Word-of-mouth is essential to an author's success, so your input is greatly appreciated!

facebook.com/AuthorJosephFinley

twitter.com/joseph_finley

instagram.com/josephfinley

Printed in Great Britain
by Amazon

16228463R00243